SEARCH
the
DARK

Inspector Ian Rutledge novels by Charles Todd

Wings of Fire
A Test of Wills

SEARCH
the
DARK

Charles Todd

THOMAS
DUNNE
BOOKS

St. Martin's Press New York

THOMAS DUNNE BOOKS.
An imprint of St. Martin's Press.

SEARCH THE DARK. Copyright © 1999 by Charles Todd. All rights reserved. Printed in the United States of America. No part of this book may be used or reproduced in any manner whatsoever without written permission except in the case of brief quotations embodied in critical articles or reviews. For information address St. Martin's Press, 175 Fifth Avenue, New York, N.Y. 10010.

Design by Nancy Resnick

Library of Congress Cataloging-in-Publication Data

Todd, Charles.
   Search the dark / Charles Todd.
      p.   cm.
   ISBN 0-312-20000-5
   I. Title
   PS3570.037S42   1999
   813'.54—dc21   99-13786
                                 CIP

First Edition: May 1999

10 9 8 7 6 5 4 3 2 1

For J.
For all those places on the map
and all the memories that went with them.

SEARCH
the
DARK

1

$\mathscr{T}$he murder appeared to be a crime of passion, the killer having left a trail of evidence behind him that even a blind man might have followed.

It was the identity of the victim, not the murderer, that brought Scotland Yard into the case.

No one knew who she was. Or, more correctly perhaps, what name she might have used since 1916. And what had become of the man and the two children who had been with her at the railway station? Were they a figment of the killer's overheated imagination? Or were their bodies yet to be discovered?

The police in Dorset were quite happy to turn the search over to the Yard. And the Yard was very happy indeed to oblige, in the person of Inspector Ian Rutledge.

It began simply enough, with the London train pulling into the station at the small Dorset town of Singleton Magna. The stop there was always brief. Half a dozen passengers got off, and another handful generally got on, heading south to the coast. A few boxes and sacks were offloaded with efficiency, and the train rolled out almost before the acrid smoke of its arrival had blown away.

Today, late August and quite hot for the season, there was a man standing by the lowered window in the second-class car, trying to find a bit of air. His shirt clung to his back under the shabby suit, and his dark hair lay damply across his forehead. His face was worn, dejection sunk deep in the lines about his mouth and in the circles under tired eyes. He was young, but youth was gone.

Leaning out, he watched the portly stationmaster helping a pale, drooping woman to the gate, the thin thread of her complaining voice just reaching him. ". . . such hardship," she was saying.

What did she know about hardship? he thought wearily. She had traveled first class, and the leather dressing case clutched in her left hand had cost more than most men earned in a month. If they were lucky enough to have a job.

There had been no work in London. But he'd heard there was a builder hiring down Lyme Regis way. The train was a luxury Bert Mowbray couldn't afford. Still, jobs didn't wait, and you sometimes had to make the extra effort. He refused to think what he would do if he'd guessed wrong and there was nothing at the end of his journey but a grim shake of the head and *"No work. Sorry."*

His gaze idly followed a porter awkwardly trundling his cart full of luggage across the platform, followed by a pair of elderly women. The cars were already jammed with families on their way to the seaside, but room was found for two more. Then his eye was suddenly caught by another woman outside one of the cars farther down the train, kneeling to comfort a little girl who was crying. A boy much younger, not more than two, clung to the trouser leg of the man bending protectively over them, speaking to the woman and then to the little girl.

Mowbray stared at the woman, his body tight with shock and dismay. *It couldn't be Mary—*

"My God!" he breathed, "Oh, my *God!*"

Turning from the window, he lunged for the door, almost knocking the wide-brimmed hat from the head of a startled farmer's wife who couldn't get out of his way fast enough. He tripped over her basket, losing precious seconds as he fought for his balance. Her companion stood up, younger and stouter, and demanded to know what he thought he was doing, her red, angry face thrust into his. The train jerked under his feet, and he realized it was moving. Pulling *out—*

"No! No—*wait!*" he screamed, but it was too late, the train had

2

picked up momentum and was already out of the small station, a few houses flashing by before the town was swallowed up by distance and fields.

He was nearly incoherent with frustration and the intensity of his need. He yelled for the conductor, demanding that the train be stopped—*now*!

The conductor, a phlegmatic man who had dealt with drunken soldiers and whoring seamen during the war years, said soothingly, "Overslept your stop, did you? Never mind, there's another just down the road a bit."

But he had to restrain Mowbray before they reached the next station—the man seemed half out of his mind and was trying to fling himself off the train. Two burly coal stokers on their way to Weymouth helped the conductor wrestle him into a seat while a prim-mouthed spinster wearing a moth-eaten fox around her shoulders, never mind the heat, threatened to collapse into strong hysterics.

Mowbray had gone from wild swearing and threats to helpless, angry tears by the time the train lurched into the next town. He and his shabby case were heaved off without ceremony, and he was left standing on the station platform, disoriented and distraught.

Without a word to the staring stationmaster, he handed in his ticket for Lyme Regis and set off at a smart pace down the nearest road in the direction of Singleton Magna.

But the woman and children and man were gone when he got to the town. And no one could tell him where to find them. He went to the only hotel, a small stone edifice called, with more imagination than accuracy, the Swan, demanding to know if a family of four had come in by the noon train. He stopped at the small shops that sold food and the two tearooms nearest the station, describing the woman first, then the children and the man. He badly frightened one clerk with his furious insistence that *you must have seen them! You must!*

He tracked down the carriage that served as the town taxi and angrily called the driver a liar for claiming he hadn't set eyes on the woman or the man, much less the children.

"They're not here, mate," the middle-aged driver declared shortly, jerking a thumb toward the back. "See for yourself. No-

3

body like that came out of the station today while I was waiting. If you was to meet them here, it's your misfortune, not mine. May be that you got your dates wrong."

"But they can't have vanished!" Mowbray cried. "I've got to find them. The bitch—*the bitch!*—they're *my* children, she's *my wife!* It isn't right—I tell you, if she's tricked me, I'll kill her, I swear I will! Tell me where she's got to, or I'll throttle you as well!"

"You and who else?" the man demanded, jaw squared and face flushed with an anger that matched Mowbray's.

All afternoon he haunted Singleton Magna, and a constable had to caution him twice about his conduct. But the fires of anger slowly burned down to a silent, white-hot determination that left him grim faced and ominously quiet. That evening he called at every house on the fringes of the town, asking about the woman. And the children. Had they come along this road? Had anyone seen them? Did anyone know where they'd come from, or where they were going?

But the town shook its collective head and shut its collective doors in the face of this persistent, shabby stranger with frantic eyes.

Mowbray spent the night under a tree near the station, waiting for the next day's noon train. He never thought of food, and he didn't sleep. What was driving him was so fierce that nothing else mattered to him.

He stayed in Singleton Magna all that day as well, walking the streets like a damned soul that had lost its way back to hell and didn't know where to turn next. People avoided him. And this time he avoided people, his eyes scanning for one figure in a rose print dress with a strand of pearls and hair the color of dark honey. By the dinner hour he had gone. Hardly anyone noticed.

When a farmer discovered a woman's body that evening, the blood from her wounds had soaked deeply into the soil at the edge of his cornfield, like some ancient harvest sacrifice. He sent for the police, and the police, with admirable haste, took one look at her there on the ground and ordered a warrant for the arrest of the man who had been searching for her. Although there was no identification on the body, they were fairly sure she wasn't a local woman. And the way her face had been battered, there had been a hot,

4

desperate anger behind the blows. The missing wife, then, had been found. All that was left was to see that her murderer was brought to justice.

Late that same evening Mowbray was run to earth, roughly awakened from an exhausted sleep under the same tree outside the railway station. In a daze, not understanding what was happening to him or why, he allowed himself to be led off to the small jail without protest.

Afterward, the inspector in charge, congratulating himself on the swift solution of this crime practically on his doorstep, boasted to the shaken farmer on the other side of his tidy desk, "It was all in a day's work. Just as it should be. Murder done, murderer brought in. Can't stop crime altogether, but you can stop the criminals. That's my brief."

"I thought he was the one hunting all over town for his lost family?"

"So he was. Silly bugger! All but advertising what he was going to do when he found them."

"But where are they, then? The husband and the children? They aren't somewhere in my fields, are they? I won't have your men tramping about in my corn, do you hear, not when it's all but ready for the cutting! My wife will have a stroke, she's that upset already! The doctor's been and gone twice."

Inspector Hildebrand sobered. He much preferred expanding on his success to any discussion of his failure. "We don't know where they are. Yet. I've got my men searching now along the roadside. More than likely he's done for the lot, but so far he's sitting in his cell like a damned statue, as if he's not hearing a word we say to him. But we'll find them, never fear. And they'll be dead as well, mark my words. Probably saved the woman for last, she got away from him, and he had to chase her. Just a matter of time, that's all. We'll find them in the end."

He didn't. In the end, it was Scotland Yard and Inspector Rutledge who had to sort through the tangled threads of deception and twisted allegiances. By that time it was far too late for Hildebrand to retreat from his entrenched position.

2

Ian Rutledge drove through the countryside with Hamish restive and moody in the back of his mind. Around them in the car the warm air carried the heavy smell of new-mown hay.

The scent of phosgene . . .

Will any of us ever be free of that memory? Rutledge asked himself. Of the silent destroyer that had rolled across the battlefields of the Front in clouds of gas? One learned quickly enough to tell them apart—mustard or phosgene or CNS. But familiarity had made them more terrifying, not less—knowing what they could do.

"It's no' the gas I can't forget," Hamish said roughly, "but the haying. August 'Fourteen. I did na' know there was an archduke getting himself killed somewhere in some place I'd no' heard of. The hay . . . and Fiona dusty with it on the wain, and the horses dark with sweat. God, it was fair, that August, and the MacDonalds swearing like wild men because they couldna' keep up wi' one MacLeod . . ."

"Yes, you told me that, the night—" Rutledge began aloud, and then quickly stopped. Corporal Hamish MacLeod had talked to him about the August haying the night he'd died. In France. Odd that memory turned on something as simple as the smell of new-mown hay!

And yet he was accustomed to answering the voice in his head out of old habit. The Somme. A bloodbath for months, the toll climbing astronomically, and men so tired that their minds simply shut down. Assault after futile assault, and the German line still held.

Set against such appalling losses, one more casualty was insignificant. Yet in the midst of such horror, the death of a young Scottish corporal had incised itself on Rutledge's soul.

The man hadn't been killed by enemy fire. He had been shot by a firing squad for refusing a direct order in battle, and it was Rutledge's pistol, in the shell-riven darkness before dawn, that had delivered the coup de grâce.

The act had been military necessity. Not cowardice, but exhaustion—and the sheer bloody senselessness of throwing lives away—had broken him. Hamish MacLeod had refused to lead his men into certain death.

Military necessity. For the sake of every soldier watching, an example had to be made. For the sake of thousands of men readying for the next assault an example had to be made. You had to know, facing death, that you could depend on the man next to you, as he depended on you.

Rutledge could still feel the late summer heat. Hear the din of artillery, the rattle of machine-gun fire, the cries of wounded men. Smell the fear and the rotting corpses. He could still see the defeated look in his corporal's eyes, the acceptance that it was a relief to die rather than lead his men back into the black hail of German fire.

And all for nothing!

The artillery shell found its mark an instant later, buried living and dead, officers and men, in heavy, stinking mud. Killing most of them outright and leaving the wounded to suffocate before the search dogs could find them many hours later. And ironically, the next shell sprayed shrapnel into the machine-gun position they had failed to take all that long night.

Rutledge had barely survived. Deaf and blind, badly stunned, he lay under the corpse of one of his men in a tiny pocket of air. It had sufficed. He hadn't known until someone told him at the aid station that it was Hamish's blood soaking his coat, Hamish's flesh clotting his face and hair, the smell of Hamish's torn body haunting him all the rest of that day as he lay dazed. Severely claustrophobic from a living grave, severely shell-shocked, bruised and disoriented, he was allowed a few hours' rest and was then sent back to the front. And Hamish went with him. A living reality in his mind. A voice with its soft Scottish burr. A personality as strong in death as it had been in life.

Rutledge never spoke of it. He fought it alone, silently, as certain as the breath in his body that it was only a matter of time before death—or madness—put an end to it. *That* expectation kept him sane.

And so he had brought Hamish home again, not as a ghost to be exorcised but as a deep-seated presence in the shocked and numbed recesses of his brain where only sleep could shut it out.

He'd shared his thoughts with a dead man for so long it was easier to respond than risk the tap of a ghostly hand on his shoulder to attract his attention or see a white, empty face at the edge of his vision, demanding to be heard. That hadn't happened—yet—but Hamish was so real to him that Rutledge lived in mortal dread of turning too quickly one day or glancing over his shoulder at the wrong instant and catching a glimpse of the shadowy figure that must surely be there, just behind him. Within touching distance. Close enough for its breath to ruffle his hair or brush his cheek.

"There was a picnic, that August," Rutledge said, desperate to change the drift of thought. "Up the Thames, beneath a stand of beeches so heavy the sun came through the leaves in purple shadows—"

And *that* particular memory led to Jean . . . she was as dead to him as Hamish. This very week he'd seen her engagement announced in the *Times*. To a man who'd served in a diplomatic posting in South America through most of the war. Away from guns and carnage and nightmares.

"He's in line for a position in Ottawa," Frances had said when she called round to offer what comfort there was to give. His sister knew everyone there was to know—few bits of gossip failed to find their way to her. "Away from all this." She waved a languid hand in the air, and he'd known what she meant.

Away from a Britain still wearing the scars of death and pain and the poverty of peace. Away from Rutledge's torment, which had frightened Jean.

"Jean has a knack for ignoring unpleasantness," Frances had

added wryly. "You won't let it bother you, will you? That she found someone else so quickly? It simply means, my dear, that you're well out of it, whether you're aware of it yet or not. Shallow women make damnably dull and demanding wives. Although I must say, even I thought there was more to her. Or was that wishful thinking on my part too? Well, never mind, you'll soon meet someone you can truly care about."

Why was it that the mind was so adept at finding its own punishment? Jean—or Hamish—to fill his thoughts.

A bitter choice, Rutledge acknowledged with a sigh. The woman who had promised to marry him or the man whose life he'd taken. There was no surgery to mend a broken heart nor any to mend a broken mind.

The doctors had shrugged and told Rutledge, "Shell shock makes its own rules. When you're able to sleep better—when the stress of the Great War—of your work—of your memories—fades a little, so will the reality of Hamish MacLeod."

But stress was the nature of war. Stress was the very heart of his work at the Yard. He lived with death and blood and horror every day. It was what he did best, investigating murders. Hardly the most suitable work, perhaps, for a man back from the trenches, but he was trained for no other and didn't have the spare energy to look for any other. And a prospective employer might well dig more deeply into his medical file than the Yard had done, taking him back after the war. Opening a Pandora's box of things best left locked away.

Superintendent Bowles knew more of Rutledge's war years—Rutledge was convinced of it—than anyone else at the Yard. It was there in his eyes, watchful and wary. In the sneer that sometimes passed for a smile. But there had been no overt attack on Rutledge's character. Only the assignments that no one else wanted, for one reason or another. Like the summons taking him now to Dorset.

"Inspector Barton's wife's in the middle of a difficult pregnancy, and Dorset might as well be on the moon, she's that upset about him leaving her. And Trask's no countryman, they'll be sending out search parties for *him*! As for Jack Bingham, he's due for leave in two days." Or so Bowles had claimed.

Not that it mattered; Rutledge was glad to be out of London.

Loneliness had its own compensations, even when it brought Hamish in its wake.

Rutledge found his turning from the trunk road at the next signpost and was soon moving more southwesterly into the heart of Dorset. And with it the scent of hay faded. His mind found its way back from the past and slowly focused on the present.

This was Hardy country. But it was the difference in light that impressed Rutledge more than the author's dark and murky characters. There was a golden-brown tint to the light here that seemed to come from the soil and the leaves of the trees. Not washed pastel like Norfolk, nor rich green like Kent. Nor gray damp like Lancaster. Dorset had been wool trade and stone, cottage industry and small farming towns strung along old roads that the Saxons had laid out long before the Norman conquest. Outlying meadows where cattle quietly grazed.

Rutledge found himself wishing he could ask a painter like Catherine Tarrant if she saw light in the same way, or if it was only his undependable imagination.

He came into the town of Singleton Magna almost before he knew it was there, the abrupt shift from fields to houses almost as sharp as a line drawn in the earth. The railroad's tracks parted company with him and ran on to the station.

Slowing as he motored down the main street, with its shops still doing a brisk business and farm carts pulled up at the curbs, he searched for the local police station.

It was no more than a cubbyhole next to the town's one bank, a small offshoot of the main building that must at one time have been a shop. The front window had been painted white with the letters POLICE in black, and the heavy green door was nicked by time and hard use, its iron handle worn with age. The bank it adjoined was more majestic, with a handsome porch above its door, as if it too had begun life as something else, a merchant's house or a church office.

After finding a place to leave his car and stepping out into the warmth of the afternoon, he saw a tall, stooped man of middle age just coming out of the green door. The man looked at him, frowned, and came over to speak. "Are you Inspector Rutledge, by any chance?"

"Yes, I'm Rutledge."

The man held out a long-fingered hand. "Marcus Johnston. I'm representing that poor devil Mowbray. Nasty business. Nasty. And he's not saying a word, not even to me. God knows what kind of case I can build for him. My advice at the moment is to throw himself on the mercy of the courts."

Rutledge, whose father had followed the law, said only, "I don't know a great deal about the man or his crime, except for the scant information the local people sent up to the Yard. He was searching the town for his wife, I understand? And her body has been found, but not the others he was after."

"That's right. The police have done their best, they've covered the ground hereabouts for miles in every direction. No bodies. No graves. More important, no one inquiring about her. No distraught husband and sobbing children, I mean." He sighed. "Which leads to the conclusion that they're dead. And all Mowbray will say to me is that they were his children, why should he want to kill them?" A woman passed and Johnston tipped his hat to her. She nodded and then eyed Rutledge with curiosity as she walked on.

"I did some checking before I left London. I'm told Mowbray was in France in 1916 when the bombing occurred. He was sent home on compassionate leave to bury his wife and children. They were identified by the constable when they were pulled from the rubble of the building. Mother and two children, dead. Mowbray himself never saw the bodies; he was told it was better to remember them as they were."

"Inspector Hildebrand believes there must have been a mistake of some sort—the constable felt fairly certain the bodies were Mowbray's wife and children, but they could have been another family altogether. The bombing demolished one building, as I understand it, and that brought down those on either side. Fifty or more dead. Easy mistake for the constable to have made—especially at night, fires, injured people everywhere. Absolute horror and chaos." Johnston grimaced. "Bombs and tons of masonry don't leave much to look at, I don't suppose."

"If it had been another family who died in the raid, why hasn't someone come looking for them? Parents? Sisters? Husband home on leave? Seems odd no one did, and discovered the mix-up."

"God knows," Johnston answered tiredly. "My guess is, there was nobody to care about the dead woman—and Mowbray's wife probably took advantage of that to start a new life. Makes sense, especially if she'd grown tired of waiting. Take happiness while you can. No fuss. Easier than a divorce."

In France half a dozen men under Rutledge's command had applied for compassionate leave at one time or another, most of them men whose wives wanted to leave them and had told them so in a letter. One had been furiously angry. . . .

"Private Wilson," Hamish reminded him. "He said he'd have her back or know the reason why. He was brought up on assault charges in Slough and given six months."

Johnston seemed to know what Rutledge was thinking, adding, "Hard on the poor sod who's told his family's dead, but I daresay she never thought about that. Only that he wouldn't come tearing home in a rage." He squared his shoulders with an effort, as if the weight of the world lay on them.

Rutledge studied the long, thin face, lined with something more than age or exhaustion. That was a look he, Rutledge, had seen often enough since he came home from France. And recognized. This man had lost a son in the war and was still grieving hard. The murder of a young woman, someone he didn't know and didn't love, had less reality to him than the death in a foreign country of the only flesh and blood that had mattered to him. Johnston was going through the motions for his client. That was all he could do.

"Thank you for being so frank," Rutledge said, preparing to walk on into the police station.

Johnston seemed to realize how hopeless he himself thought the evidence was. He summoned a smile and added, "Early days yet, of course! Early days!" But there was a hollowness in the words and the smile.

Rutledge watched him move on down the street, then opened the door of the station, finding himself in a scene of turmoil. There were some half a dozen people crammed into a room meant to hold two at best, and the sudden sense of claustrophobia that swept over him was so fierce he drew in his breath with the shock of it.

Someone looked up, a constable, and said sharply, "What is it *you* want?"

"Rutledge, from London," he managed to say, but it came out harshly. Everyone in the room turned to stare at him, making the sense of suffocation worse. He could feel the knob on the door behind him jammed into his back.

"Ah!" the constable replied noncommittally. "Come this way, sir, if you please." He led Rutledge through the anarchy and into a dark, stuffy hall that smelled of cabbage and dust. "That's the leaders of the next search parties," he said over his shoulder. "We've not found the others—the man or the children."

Rutledge didn't answer. They reached a door painted brown, and the constable knocked, then turned the knob.

The room beyond was bright with late sun, and a long pair of windows stood wide, looking out into a small courtyard overgrown with weeds. Although the windows provided little air movement, they gave the sense of openness he badly needed—an escape into light and freedom. Hamish, in the back of his mind, sighed with a relief as great as his own.

"Inspector Rutledge, Inspector Hildebrand. If you'll excuse me, sir . . . ?" The constable left the end of his request dangling in the silence as he retreated, closing the door softly behind him.

Hildebrand looked Rutledge up and down. "They said they were sending an experienced man."

"I was with the Yard before the war," Rutledge replied.

"But away through the better part of it," Hildebrand finished for him. He himself was white-haired, with a youngish face. Rutledge put his age at not more than forty-five. "Ah, well. Sit down, man! Here's what we have. Murder victim presumed to be Mrs. Mary Sandra Mowbray, of London. Matches the general description of the late Mrs. Mowbray, or I should say, *presumed late*. Even Londoners can't die twice, can they? In his wallet Mr. Mowbray had a photograph of her with the children, taken in 1915, just before he was shipped over to France. We've had copies made to circulate. So far nothing's come of it." He tossed a file across the cluttered desk, and Rutledge found himself looking down at a faded photograph of a woman facing the camera and the sun at the same time, squinting a little. She was wearing a floral print dress and a single strand of pearls. Her hair seemed dark blond or a light brown, the way the sun caught it. Her face was oval and pretty, with fine bones and a distinct look of breeding handed down from some remote ancestor. The children by her side were a little clearer. The boy was no more than two, wearing a sailor suit and a hat that had fallen to a rakish angle over one eye. He grinned, squinting, while his hands clutched a ball nearly as large as he was. The little girl, not as childishly plump, had the same fairness as the mother. She could have been a large four or a small five, judging from the shy smile that showed all of her front baby teeth quite clearly. Her hand clutched her mother's skirts, and her head was tilted in a way that promised a sweet nature rather than a rowdy one as she peered up through her lashes with no hint of roguishness.

When Rutledge had scanned the faces, he saw that the file also included official copies from London of a marriage license in the name of Mary Sandra Marsh and Albert Arthur Mowbray, a pair of birth certificates for the children, and the death certificates for all three. Signed in a scrawl by a London doctor. "Severe injuries from falling debris" they all read, and the autopsy had gone on to catalog them.

"Sad business," Hildebrand said after a moment. "Young woman with a husband over in France. Lonely. Probably told the poor devil she took up with that he was dead. Well, it wasn't altogether a lie, was it? So many of them did die. Only not her husband. He lived to come home, didn't he? Must have been one of her worst nightmares, the chance of running into him some day! And as luck would have it, *he* goes from London to the coast in search of work, and there *she* is, standing in the station at Singleton Magna. Plain as day!"

"You think she saw him? Leaning out the train window?" Rutledge asked, reading down the statements of a conductor and several witnesses, one of them a farmer's wife and her sister, the other two stokers returning to their ship.

"Stands to reason, I'd say. Explains why the four of 'em left town in such haste. Not a glimpse of them anywhere! One or two possible sightings of her at the station, probably before Mowbray spied her. After that, she was covering her tracks for dear life. I asked around myself, didn't leave that to my men."

"Very proper," Rutledge said absently, rereading one of the statements. "Still, we have only Mowbray's word that this *was* his wife and family."

"As to that, I checked with London," Hildebrand said with satisfaction. "There were quite a few casualties the night Mrs. Mowbray's street was bombed. Constable Tedley identified her and the children. They were in the stairwell of the block of flats where she lived. And she didn't show up later to prove him wrong, did she? And no one came round looking for someone who *should* have been alive, did they? Straightforward, as far as London was concerned."

Rutledge nodded and handed the statements back to Hildebrand. Then he asked, "How did Mowbray catch up to her later? Has he told you?"

"Man's in no case to talk. Deep depression, according to the doctor. Just sits there, staring at the floor, face drained of emotion. Stands to reason," he said again, as if he used the expression often. "Wife died twice, didn't she? Once when he was told she'd been killed by the Zeppelins and now by his own hand. Shock. That's what it is. I daresay any of us would feel much the same. Not that it explains or excuses, of course. But you can see how it would happen."

Shock. It was something Rutledge understood very well. In a different voice he asked, "What weapon did he use?"

"Now that's an interesting question. Blunt force to batter her face in, which means anything from a heavy stone to a tool of some sort. We examined the tools Mowbray had with him. Hammers, screwdrivers, a pair of saws, a level, that sort of thing. No blood or hair on any of *them*. Which says to me he got rid of whatever it was. I'd guess it's where he left the other corpses."

"And the wounds? Where were they?"

"In the face, mostly. Repeated blows, eight or ten, the doctor says. But there're marks on her neck too. As if he'd caught up with her, running, and grabbed her by the throat, pulled her down, and then went for the face. That's often what you find where jealousy

15

is the motive—make her so hideous even in death that the rival can't bear to look at her anymore. Doctor says the force used was savage, as if driven by terrible anger or fear."

"And no blood on Mowbray or his clothing?"

"No. But then he could have cleaned himself up, couldn't he? Changed shirts even. There's no way of telling how many he'd brought with him. We found one other work shirt in his satchel, and a white one for Sunday. He might have had more."

Rutledge closed the file. "I'd like to see Mowbray, if I may."

Hildebrand got to his feet. "Much good it'll do you!" he said willingly enough. "Let me fetch the key on the way."

They went along the same dark hallway to the end, where the key was kept in a small cupboard. Then Hildebrand turned to another door just to his left and unlocked it. The iron key made a scraping sound that jangled the nerves. As the door swung open, Hildebrand said, "Someone to see you, Mowbray. Scotland Yard. On your feet, man!"

The man on the cot, lying on top of the gray blanket, slowly swung his feet to the floor and stared up at his visitors. His face was empty, and he made no effort to do more than sit, as if doing even so much had drained him of life and hope.

Rutledge picked up the chair on the far side of the narrow cell and brought it over nearer the cot. The room was wider than it was long, and there was no window. The air was stale, seeming to hover in visible layers around them as he sat down. In the back of his mind Hamish was pointing that out, over and over again. After a moment Rutledge said, "Mr. Mowbray?"

The man shifted his feet a little and nodded.

"Did you kill the woman who was found in the field? The woman dressed in pink?" Rutledge kept his voice low, quiet, no hint of accusation in it, only curiosity.

"She was my wife, I'd never harm her," he said gruffly after a time.

"The cabby has said you threatened to kill her—" Hildebrand began from the doorway, but Rutledge waved him into silence.

"You were angry with her, weren't you? For deceiving you, for putting you through such anguish. When you believed you'd come home and buried her with the children? And then—suddenly—she

16

was alive, and so were they, and the first emotion you felt was anger. A great, fierce anger."

"It was the shock—and the train wouldn't stop—I was beside myself—I said things I didn't mean. I'd never harm her."

"Not even for taking your children and going to live with another man?"

Mowbray sat with his head held by the palms of his hands on either side of his temples. "I'd want to kill *him*," he said huskily, "for getting around her. Making her do it. I'd blame *him*, not her."

"His solicitor's just left," Hildebrand put in again. "Told him what to say. You've heard more from him already than I have! It's—"

But Rutledge ignored him, cutting across the flow of words as if they hadn't been spoken. "Where did you leave the children? Can you take us to them? Let us help them?" He waited for an answer, then added gently, "You'd not want the foxes or dogs to find them first."

Mowbray raised his head, and the pain-filled eyes made Rutledge swear under his breath as he met them. "I don't know," the man said wretchedly. "I don't know where they are. Tricia was always afraid of the dark. I'd not leave her alone out in the dark! But I can't remember—they tell me I killed her, and my Bertie, but *I can't remember*! Night and day—that's all I can see in my mind. The children. It's driving me mad!"

Rutledge got up from his chair. He'd seen men break, God knew he of all people could recognize the signs! There were no answers to be had now from Mowbray. The haunting images he'd seen— or been told he'd seen—had been seared deep into his brain, and separating them from reality would be nearly impossible.

Hamish, in the back of his own mind, was dredging up memories that were also safer concealed in the shadows, and he fought them grimly.

Mowbray was watching him like a beaten dog, and Rutledge turned to go, not trusting his voice, unable to offer any comfort. Mowbray's eyes followed him. Then the two men were out the door, leaving their prisoner to the silence and his conscience. Rutledge said nothing as the key rasped again in the lock and Hildebrand turned to put it back in its cupboard, but he could still feel

17

the sense of suffocation, of hopelessness and horror and fear they'd left behind them.

"You could pity the poor sod—if you hadn't seen what he'd done." Hildebrand was waiting with polite impatience for Rutledge to precede him down the passage to his office.

"Put a suicide watch on him," Rutledge said finally. "I want a constable with him, night and day. Never out of sight for an instant."

"I'm short of men—we're seaching for the others—"

"Do it! If he kills himself before you find those bodies, they may never turn up." Rutledge walked away, leaving Hildebrand fuming behind him, wanting to argue. He didn't care. He'd stayed as long as he could stand it in this dark and grim place.

"I can't work miracles, I tell you!" Hildebrand was saying.

Rutledge, still struggling against the strong presence in his mind as Hamish harshly pointed out that Mowbray didn't have such luxury of choice—could never again hope to walk out into the air and sun—silently reminded the bitter voice that Mowbray was very likely the murderer of children and had chosen his destruction himself. "I'll hold you personally responsible if that man dies," he went on as the inspector caught up to him.

Hildebrand answered through clenched teeth, "That one's not likely to miss the hangman, if I can help it. Right, then! You'll have your watch."

3

Rutledge found a room at the Swan Hotel, on the second floor overlooking the main street. He set his suitcase down by the tall wardrobe and went to open the windows. A gust of hot air seemed to roll in, then with the help of the open door behind him, the stirring draft began to relieve a little of the afternoon's heat.

He stood there by the windows, watching the traffic in the street below. The last of the farm carts had gone, but between the trees at the upper end of the street and the old market cross at the lower end he could count some half a dozen carriages still waiting. Two cars were standing just opposite the hotel, and another one was driving away, the echo of its motor rising from the house fronts as it climbed the hill.

He felt depressed. Hamish, silent for some time now, had nothing to say, leaving Rutledge with the heaviness of his thoughts and the sense of guilt for doing nothing to help Mowbray. Instead he'd made certain that the man lived to be hanged. From one suffocation to another . . .

Mowbray was a tragedy. A man who was not, by nature, a killer. Who may have killed out of surprise and shock and instant, over-whelming fury. Which probably didn't matter very much to the young mother who had just died at his hands! It would very likely be kinder to everyone if Mowbray carried out his own sentence of

19

execution. But the law forbade suicide, and it was the duty of the police to prevent it. And let the poor bastard suffer from the knowledge of what he'd done until His Majesty's hangman legally put him out of his misery.

Sighing with the uselessness of it all, Rutledge turned to unpack. There was a tap at the door and the chambermaid came in bearing a tray. "I thought you'd like some tea, sir. It's too late to have it in the parlor, but there were still cakes and half a dozen sandwiches in the kitchen." She smiled shyly.

"Thank you—" He hesitated, and she supplied the name for him as she set the tray on a table and whisked off the napkin that covered dainty egg and cucumber sandwiches and a plate of iced cakes. There was also what looked like two fresh pasties. Apparently tea at the Swan was hardy fare.

"Peg, if you please, sir."

"Thank you, Peg."

She curtsied, then turned for the door. He stopped her, asking, "Do many of the passengers from the noon train stop here at the hotel?"

"No, sir, not often. Mostly they live around here, in the town or one of the villages with no station. We have more guests on market day. Today, that was. Or when there's an inquest. Sometimes for a funeral, if the deceased was well known." She grimaced. "I saw that man, sir. Mr. Mowbray. When he came to ask if his wife and the children were staying here. Upset he was, nearly snapping my head off when I told him Mr. Snelling—that's the manager—was on the telephone and couldn't come out to speak to him just then."

"Did you see Mowbray's wife and the children?"

"No, sir, they never came here. Constable Jeffries showed me the photograph, but the only children in that day for luncheon were Mr. Staley's, and I've known *them* since they was born! Now Mrs. Hindes said she believed she saw Mrs. Mowbray at the station, when she was there to pick up her niece from London. But Miss Harriet's never comfortable on a train, and Mrs. Hindes was that worried about the girl being sick before they reached home, she never really paid much heed to the other passengers." Peg grinned.

"Miss Harriet is always being sick. It's her revenge for having to stay two weeks with her auntie."

Rutledge smiled, and Peg recollected her place. "If there's nothing else sir?" She left, closing the door softly behind her.

He ate the pasties and two of the cakes, drank his tea while it was hot, then wished he hadn't. Leaving his coat over the back of his chair, he opened the door again for whatever air was stirring and finished unpacking, his mind on the dead woman.

Singleton Magna was not where she lived. Everyone in such a small town, including Hildebrand, would have known her instantly if this had been her home. And she didn't live close by, or by this time someone would have recognized her photograph or the children in it. Or come looking for her.

The question then was, had she and the man with her left the train because they'd seen Bert Mowbray there in one of the cars, staring at them in shocked surprise, and in a panic decided to make a run for it? Or had the family been on its way to a place beyond Singleton Magna? If so, how had they planned to travel that distance after leaving the train?

Could they have been completely oblivious of the man watching them?

Because sometimes you felt eyes on you, when there was some strong emotion behind the stare. Had *she* sensed them, as the guilty often did? And what had she told the man with her? "There's my husband! The one thinks I'm dead!" Or had she told lies? Anything to make him trust her?

Come to that, how much did the man himself know? Enough to make him accept the need for haste and putting distance between themselves and Mowbray? Or was he as much a victim of her scheming as Mowbray himself?

What if, somewhere along the road, the truth had sunk in and he'd decided that running wasn't the answer. And instead chosen to confront the man from this woman's past? Or—decided to leave her to face the consequences of her folly alone.

Interesting conjectures, but only that—conjectures. They'd know when the other bodies were found. . . .

———

Rutledge spent what was left of the afternoon coordinating a widening search. Making telephone calls to towns along the railway in both directions, asking local police for assistance in locating any passengers on Mowbray's train who might have information about the woman and her children. He persuaded police in the busy holiday towns along the coast to do the same, though they were not sanguine about finding any needles in the haystack of people on their doorstep. They had already passed around the circular Hildebrand had sent them. It hadn't brought any response.

He called in more searchers from the nearest towns and outlying villages, telling constables and sergeants and inspectors that any men they could spare would be greatly appreciated. A thinly veiled order, couched in the politest terms. Then he and Hildebrand looked at a rough map of Singleton Magna and its environs, already quartered with lines showing where the search had scoured the landscape. Next Rutledge read reports from earlier parties, all of them ending with the same last line: "Nothing to report."

Hamish, reflecting his tiredness, pointed out that it was useless to go back over the same ground again and again, but Rutledge knew the value of many pairs of eyes. What one had missed, another might see. It was harder to convince Hildebrand of that.

"I can't grasp how a man in his state of mind could be so clever," he said again, tossing his pencil back on the cluttered desk. "It's not likely he knew more about this territory than we do. Stands to reason! And yet we're fair flummoxed! I can't understand how we've missed them."

"I don't know that it's cleverness," Rutledge said thoughtfully. "A small child can be buried in a field. Tucked under a hedge or loose stones by a wall. Stuffed in the hollow of a tree. He might have felt compelled to bury them, whether he remembers it or not. It's the man whose body should have turned up by this time."

"I've climbed up church bell towers," Hildebrand told him defensively, "taken pitchforks to haystacks, walked the railway tracks for five miles in both directions, even looked down wells and run sticks up chimneys."

"Very resourceful of you," Rutledge applauded, sensing ruffled feathers. "What we need now, I think, is to try to follow in his footsteps. It might be helpful to send men back to every person

Mowbray encountered, then use the time they saw him as a map to chart his movements. That could give us a better idea of where he might have gone when no one was looking."

Grudgingly Hildebrand agreed. "If those extra men come in, I'll see to it. I've looked into what gaps I discovered. But I suppose it won't do any harm to go over those two days again."

He stared consideringly at Rutledge. Quiet enough, and competent, he had to give him that. One to check every detail, which was frustrating, knowing how thorough he'd been on his own. Still, that wasn't unreasonable, it was the sort of thing he himself would expect, in Rutledge's shoes. Hadn't arrived demanding an office and a sergeant either, setting himself up as God Almighty, wreaking havoc in another man's patch. But somehow distant, not the sort you'd ask to join you for a pint at the end of the day. And there was an intensity about him, underneath it all. Hildebrand found himself wondering if the Londoner was still recovering from war wounds. That thinness and the tired, haunted eyes . . .

None of which was worrying to the local man in charge. It was more a matter of pride that drove him.

Rutledge didn't appear to be a meddler, but you could never be sure. There'd been rumors about what he'd done in Cornwall. Simple enough case to begin with—and look how that'd been turned inside out! Well, Scotland Yard would learn soon enough that Singleton Magna knew what it was about.

Best course of action, then, was to say yes to everything and quietly do as you thought best. And hope to hell London was kept well occupied sorting out jurisdictional squabbles.

Hamish, without fuss, said, "Watch your back, man!"

Rutledge nodded. But whether in answer to Hildebrand or his own thoughts it was hard to tell.

When a frail thread of cool air ushered in the evening, Rutledge went down to his motorcar and drove out of Singleton Magna on the road that led to the farmer's field where the body of Mrs. Mowbray had been found. The sun slanted low in the west, turning trees and steeples and rooftops to a golden brightness that seemed timeless and serene.

The place was comparatively easy to find—a field of grain that ran gently down a hillside toward the road and then continued for some forty feet across it. Beyond the lower field, a pattern of mixed dark green led on toward a clump of trees along a small stream, and beyond that he could just see the tall church tower of Singleton Magna, apparently not so far away as the crow went, but possibly four miles by the high road.

To the west of where he pulled over and got out of his motorcar, he noticed a Y in the road and a weathered signpost, its arms pointing toward more villages out of sight over the slight rise.

As a place to commit murder, he thought, standing there in the golden light, this was as isolated a spot as any.

And by the same token, as isolated as it was—how had Mowbray and his victim come to meet here? Or had they come here together from some other place?

"Ye'll not be getting answers from yon puir sod in the gaol," Hamish reminded him. "He's a witless man."

Which was a very good point, Rutledge thought.

This case, so obviously clear-cut and so near to being closed, was going to sink or survive in the courtroom on the basis of cold, hard fact. Weapon. Opportunity. Motive. And the how and when and where of the act.

"Aye," Hamish replied, "broken men conjure up sympathy. Unless they're branded cowards . . ."

Rutledge winced and turned his back on the motorcar, looking up at the field. *Why here?* he asked himself. Because she had gotten away from Mowbray, as someone had suggested? And it was here that he'd caught up with her again? Simple happenstance?

All right, then, where had she run *from?*

To search for the children, he told himself, I'll have to work out the direction she'd be likely to come from—and how Mowbray had followed her.

Yet there was nothing in any direction to suggest a sanctuary where a frightened, weary family might have taken refuge.

He tried to picture them, the children crying, spent and thirsty, the mother trying hard to shush them and soothe them at the same time. The man—her husband? her lover?—carrying the little girl, while she held the boy. Four miles—but still not far enough. They would want to get clear of Singleton Magna and the pursuing Furies as quickly as possible, which told him they wouldn't have asked for a ride on a wagon. Nor would they stop at a farmhouse door to ask for a glass of water or an hour to let the children rest. Either way would leave traces of their passage.

It had taken Mowbray two days to catch up with her. . . .

Consider a different point of view. Where had the family *intended* to leave the train? They could have been traveling to the Dorset coast or any town in between. Or beyond, to Devon, even to Cornwall. All right, given that their direction was south, or even southwest, they'd most likely keep to that. However indirectly. Which meant, in theory, that they'd have left Singleton Magna by the same road he'd just traveled. Where, then, had they spent that last night?

Rutledge slung his coat over one shoulder and walked on to the signpost where the road divided.

Two arms pointed southwest. The faded letters read STOKE NEW-TON and LEIGH MINSTER. From there the road might well carry on to the coast. The third arm pointed northwest, to Charlbury.

He went back to the field and climbed the shallow bank—his footsteps lost in a morass of many prints now—and walked toward the spot where the tidy rows of grain ended in a flattened fan. Just before he reached it, he saw the darker stains in the dark earth, barely visible now but clear enough if someone searched for them. Here she'd died, bleeding into the soil, and here she'd been abandoned.

He knelt there in the trampled dust and stared at the earth, trying to reach out to the mind of the woman who had lain here. Hamish stirred restlessly, but Rutledge ignored him.

A terrified woman. Coming face to face with a man bent on vengeance, knowing she was going to die—knowing her children were already dead—or soon would be—

Did she beg? Make promises? Was there anything she had left that Mowbray wanted, besides her life? Or was death an end for her to terror and horror—the doorway into the silence where her children had gone before her?

Had she hidden them and protected them with her own blood? Knowing that once she was dead—and couldn't be made to tell—they'd be safe? Buying time while they reached some kind of safety.

Was that why he'd beaten her face so savagely? Trying to force the truth from her, trying to make her give him what he believed was his, his flesh and blood?

But the ground here was silent. And Rutledge, listening for answers in his own mind, seeking something real and deeply felt that could show him the way, could hear nothing. Whatever had brought this woman to the edge of an abyss, whatever emotions had roiled the air and left grisly traces on the ground were still her secret.

In the end he stood up and shook his head, unable to reach what had happened here. My fault? he wondered, and Hamish said it was.

What about Mowbray's point of view? Take the living man, instead of the dead woman, and delve into *his* feelings.

He'd killed her here—and abandoned her here.

Why? Why not pull the body into the rows of grain, where only the field mice and crows would spot it so soon? Why leave it close to the road, where the farmer, coming to look over his crops, might stumble across it and raise the alarm?

"Because," Hamish answered him, "the man was no' thinking with cold logic. He was distracted and angry and vengeful."

"Yes," Rutledge agreed aloud. "He wanted her dead, he didn't care whether he'd be caught or not. They found him, after all, asleep under a tree."

He looked from this vantage point around the circle of corn and trees and distant church tower, the horizons of this place of death. But he saw nothing to draw his attention. No shed, no barn with its roof falling in, no farmhouse. The clump of trees, then? They were far enough off the road. . . .

Rutledge spent a good quarter of an hour searching among the trees and came up emptyhanded. No sandwich wrappers, no scuffed earth, no suitcases—

Suitcases.

No one had mentioned the family's suitcases. Had these been left on the train? Or had they tried to drag their luggage with them, down the hot and dusty road? It was a point to consider. Another point to consider . . .

He went back to his motorcar, hot and dusty himself, to drive on down the left, southwestern, fork in the road.

It led to two straggling villages, houses lining the road, water meadows at their backs on either side, and farms in the outlying fringes. In each one Rutledge sought the local constable and questioned him. The first one was still enjoying a belated dinner, and the other was in his shirtsleeves gossiping over the garden wall with his neighbor. But they answered him readily enough.

Rutledge learned that Hildebrand, in his thoroughness, had preceded him here, and there appeared to be nothing left for him to discover in either Leigh Minster or Stoke Newton. No strangers have come through here in the past week—both constables assured him of that, and he believed them. They appeared to be steady, careful men who knew their patch well. Nor had an ownerless suitcase turned up in the middle of a field or under some hedge. Apparently neither village had been pulled—wittingly or unwittingly—into the tragedy at Singleton Magna.

Back in his motorcar again, the cooling wind of twilight swirling about his shoulders, Rutledge listened to the voice in the rear seat. It seemed to breathe on him, though he knew very well it was only the soft Dorset air.

"I do na' think he'd have come so far. The man was certain his wife was still in Singleton Magna—he went raving about yon town for two days, searching. People saw him. And he was asleep there when the police came looking for him! But what's no' been answered is, what made him so certain they'd be found *there*? That the townsfolk must have hidden them from him?"

"I don't know," Rutledge said. "In the end, he did find the woman close by. He caught up with her there in the cornfields. And he killed her there and left her there. Unless . . ."

"Aye, *unless*. Unless the man with her got rid of her because she was the one Mowbray wanted. And he and the children got clean away."

Rutledge had been considering that possibility. "If he killed her here in the open and the children saw him do it, how could he persuade them to come away with him after that? It was a bloody crime, she'd have screamed the first time he struck her. They would

27

have cried out in alarm, pulled at his coat, his arms—trying to stop him—then fought to stay by her, because they wouldn't have understood that she was dead. And if she was a liability to him, why did he stop at killing *her*? Why not rid himself of both the children—they weren't his, after all. No, that line of investigation is taking us nowhere."

"But it's the children that'll tell you the rest of the truth. Alive or dead."

"I know," Rutledge said. "And where shall we find them?"

It was nearly dark when he got back to Singleton Magna and left his car behind the inn. In his absence Hildebrand had come to find him and written a message on hotel stationery, its thick, crested paper incongruously scrawled over in heavy black ink.

"London just replied to your request for more information on Mrs. Mowbray. She was from Hereford. No known connection with Dorset. That may mean that the man with her lived or worked or had relatives in this county. I'm looking into that now."

It was one of the telephone calls Rutledge had made that afternoon, asking a canny sergeant he knew in London to look into Mrs. Mowbray for him. Gibson always had his ear to the ground. If anyone could uncover information on the dead woman, it was he. A pity there was no way Gibson could do the same for the man.

And Rutledge didn't hold out much hope that Hildebrand would fare any better, with so little to go on. It might take weeks to trace him—if he belonged in Dorset. Or years, if he came from another part of England.

"If he got clear, they'd hide him, him and the children. Family. Friends. If he asked," Hamish said as Rutledge took the stairs two at a time.

"Very likely," Rutledge answered aloud, before he could stop himself. "Unless they know that Mowbray is safely in jail."

"But the children are no' his," Hamish pointed out. "And the mother's dead. If yon man wanted to keep them—"

"—he'd stay out of sight. He'd have to turn them over to the police if he came forward. Yes, that's an interesting thought, isn't it?"

The children, again . . .

They were beginning to haunt him.

4

Rutledge spent a restless night, his room too warm for comfortable sleeping, and his mind too busy.

The images flitted and dissolved in a kaleidoscope of anguish. Of Mowbray, broken and in despair in his cell—of the bloody body of his wife lying at the edge of a field in plain sight when the farmer went to see to his crop—of children crying for their mother and a man who wasn't their father offering what comfort he could—of a gallows waiting for a prisoner who might not understand why he was being hanged.

And as always, Hamish, attuned to the tumult in his mind, reminded him of his own fallibility, a policeman driven by his own pain attempting to get to the bottom of another man's. A murderer's. Both of them—*murderers*.

"It's love that's at the bottom of this," Rutledge said aloud in the darkness, trying to silence the voice in his head. And then swore because the word conjured up memories of Jean. Jean, in a fashionable blue gown with ecru lace and the flowers he'd given her pinned at her shoulder. Jean laughing as she swung and missed, and the tennis ball went smashing into the backstop. The sun on her face as they walked through Oxford early on a Sunday morning, drinking in the quiet and peace.

But what kind of love? It had so many faces, so many names.

29

Jealousy wove a thread around it, and envy, and fear. People died for love—and killed for it. And yet in itself it was indefinable, it wore whatever passions people brought to it, like a mountebank, with no reality of its own.

Somewhere in the town outside his window he could hear laughter and music. Happy laughter, without restraint or burdens.

Once Jean was married and off to Ottawa, he told himself, he could finally put her out of his mind. As he had nearly put her out of his heart. Olivia Marlowe had taught him more about the quality of love than Jean ever had.

"What will teach me to forget my Fiona?" Hamish said softly. "Do ye never remember her? Do ye never hear her weeping by yon empty grave, while I lie in France with no way to call out to her or offer comfort? What peace can Ian Rutledge find, loving any woman, when there's Hamish MacLeod on his conscience!"

In the darkness Rutledge turned his head away from the insistent voice. It was true. What woman would be willing to share his life with such demons in his mind?

In the morning Rutledge met Hildebrand for breakfast in the Swan's dining room, the bright chintz curtains bellying like sails in the early breeze. The tablecloths were blindingly white. Hildebrand appeared to be suffering from a headache. Several times he massaged his eyes as if they burned, and he growled at the middle-aged woman who waited on their table. She gave him a withering look as she walked away and said, "I knew you as a lad, with your braces broken and your face dirty! Don't come the grump with me!"

Rutledge suppressed a smile.

Hildebrand, ignoring her, said, "I had a hellish conference last night with my chief. He wants those children found. Yesterday wouldn't be soon enough! Makes the entire county look bad, he informs me, bloody maniacs running about slaughtering their families. He says we're to make haste and finish this business, or he'll know the reason why! It might have taken some of the wind out of his sails if you'd been here to placate him."

"I went out to the scene of the murder. I don't know where they could have hidden themselves—or been hidden, near that field. I keep coming back to Singleton Magna. And whether someone in the town is keeping silent—assuming the children and the man are still alive."

Hildebrand stared at him, then pulled one of the flyers out of his pocket and tossed it across to Rutledge's plate, where it landed on the toast he had just spread with marmalade.

Rutledge picked it up, wiped the back with his serviette, and then said, "What's this in aid of?"

"The fact that that flyer was given to every household in the town and all the outlying farms. Somebody—*somebody!*—would have come forward with information. Stands to reason! If not the family, a nosy neighbor, the old biddy across the road, some child wanting to be noticed. Do I have to spell it out for you?"

"No," Rutledge said, reining in his temper. He was looking at the flyer, at the faces. "This should have brought results. I agree. But it hasn't. And I keep asking myself *why* no one has come forward."

"Which tells *me*," the other man responded acerbically, "that they're dead. The man *and* the children. Which is where we've been for some days now—looking for their bodies."

"There can't be all that many hiding places within walking radius of the town. And if Mowbray caught up with his wife by that field along the high road, it narrows our search even more. The western side of Singleton Magna, not the east. Otherwise he'd have had to bring her—or chase her—through the town itself. And that's not on."

"We've looked. There isn't a stone as large as that plate in front of you that we haven't lifted, not a tree we haven't climbed, not a stream we haven't walked through up to our knees. Not a wall, a plot of disturbed ground, a shed, an outhouse, bridges, or any other conceivable place we haven't searched at least three times. And are searching yet again!"

They've vanished, then, Rutledge thought. Like foxfire, the nearer you come, the farther away it appears to be.

Hamish was saying something, but Rutledge ignored him.

"I went on to Leigh Minister and Stoke Newton. You've searched there as well?"

"Yes, on the premise that the train was going south."

"What about the other fork?"

31

"The way to Charlbury? That's another three miles distant. We spoke to the constable there, in the name of thoroughness, but I wasn't surprised when we drew a blank. A long way for a man and a woman to walk, encumbered with children. And Stoke Newton's closer than Charlbury. Stands to reason, if Mrs. Mowbray was looking for sanctuary, she'd have chosen Stoke Newton."

"What if she considered that herself—and chose Charlbury instead, to throw us off the track?"

Hildebrand shrugged. "It's possible. But likely? No. You're hunting for straws, man!"

"Then clear up another puzzle for me. Why was Mowbray so certain he'd find her here in Singleton Magna?"

"I spent most of the night turning that over in my mind. I don't think he *was* certain. Look, she wasn't on the train when he saw her, she was already on the platform, kneeling to speak to the little girl. They'd gotten off the train *before* he saw her—and very likely before she saw *him*. Stands to reason, he'd tell himself, if they got off here, this was where they planned to be. So he hunted for her here—and in the end, he got it right."

Was that how it had happened? It might explain why the suitcases hadn't been found. He mentioned them to Hildebrand, who shook his head.

"I've thought about that too. Mowbray's not the only poor sod out of work. If someone had come across the cases and had need of whatever was inside, what's to prevent him from keeping the lot and his mouth shut at the same time?"

Rutledge felt depression settling in, and Hildebrand didn't seem to find the endless circle of supposition any more joyful. He rubbed his eyes again and turned the subject to the men who had arrived that morning, and where he had sent them to search.

"Meanwhile, I've got my own men asking questions in town. They know what they're after, we should have some answers by late afternoon."

When they'd finished their coffee, Rutledge stood up. "I've one or two matters needing my attention. I should be back by three o'clock."

Hildebrand felt relief wash over him. Out of sight was out from under foot. London's task was diplomacy, where the investigation crossed parish boundaries and sensitive toes might feel trod upon. If that kept Rutledge occupied most of the day, he himself might accomplish a hell of a lot more.

With a brief nod, Hildebrand strode out the door like a man with a heavy schedule ahead of him.

Rutledge stared at the flyer again, deep in thought.

The woman who'd waited on them looked down and saw it. "A sorry business!" she said pityingly. "I blame the war. Disrupting a family, putting ideas into her head. It's the little ones I feel most for, truth to tell. Losing their father, and a mother no better than she ought to be!"

"From all accounts she was a good mother."

"That's as may be! But it's a sorry business, and mark my words, it's her that's to blame!"

"Small as they are, how much would these children remember about Mowbray?" he asked, curious. "He was in France most of their lives. Surely they'd come to accept any replacement as their real father?"

The woman looked up at him, her face scornful. "What makes you think this was the first and only man she'd taken up with?"

It was a very good question!

As she piled dishes on her tray, she added, "My eldest daughter lost her children to the influenza. Too little to live, the doctor told her. I don't think she's slept a night since they died. And here's someone puts her own fancies before her children. Doesn't sound to *me* like a good mother!" She lifted the heavy tray and marched off toward the swinging door that led to the kitchens, her pain evident in her straight, unyielding back.

Too little to live . . .

His war had been broken bodies and the sucking black mud. Unbearable noise—and unbearable silence. Artillery barrages, machine guns, strafing aeroplanes. Horses and men dying, their screams splitting the mind, the sound going on and on long after it had stopped. A war of attrition—meant to kill to the last man. Where one's own survival seemed beyond any prayer.

In England it had been different. For the exhausted people at home, carrying the burden of deprivation, stunned by the long lists of dead and wounded, worn down by helpless waiting and uncertainty, influenza had come as the silent, stealthy scythe of God, striking without warning, killing with the same certainty as wounds in the flesh gone septic but not confining itself to the trenches. It killed young and old, without rhyme or reason, striking down the healthy, sparing the ailing, leaving children without mothers and mothers without—

He stopped halfway to the hall and spun on his heel to look back at the still swinging door to the kitchen.

Too little to live . . .

He stared down at the flyer in his hand. The pale faces of the children stared back at him.

Why hadn't the children changed since 1916? Mowbray had described them as he'd seen them on the train platform as if they'd not altered from this faded photograph. Children who should have aged three years—in size and appearance. Did that mean he hadn't seen them, except in grieving imagination?

No wonder the flyers hadn't brought any results!

"But the woman's dead—*she* was real enough," he told himself.

Missing suitcases. A woman who'd vanished for over twenty-four hours, between hastily leaving the train and her murder. The ages of the missing children. Questions that niggled at the edges of his mind, with no answers.

Unless the poor devil living with his own madness in that jail cell had killed a woman and children he'd never seen before!

Gentle God!

Rutledge took the stairs to his room two at a time, as if trying to outrace the horror he'd evoked. There he picked up his hat, stood thoughtfully in the middle of the floor as he debated the best course of action, then ran lightly down the steps again and out to his car.

On the road west, he could see small groups of men in the distance, searching, covering again ground they'd already tramped over three and four times. Heads bent, sticks poking into undergrowth and among the thick boughs of trees, they moved steadily and carefully across the terrain assigned to them. In the field where the body had been found the grain was alive with them, and there was a fuming, red-faced man sitting his horse at the edge of the corn. The farmer, most likely. Rutledge considered stopping to speak to him and then decided it could wait until the man's temper had subsided. This was his best crop of the season, trampled through no fault of his own. A policeman from London would be no different in his book than one from Singleton Magna.

At the signpost, Rutledge took the northwest road this time, toward Charlbury. He drove slowly, scouting for a likely outbuilding that might offer shelter. But the two dilapidated sheds he did investigate were empty of anything except pigeons, mice, and a swarm of insects rising into the stuffy air from the dust beneath his feet.

Tramping back to his car, he heard the sound of another automobile coming fast along the lane. He stopped to watch it, his coat over one shoulder, his shirtsleeves rolled up on his forearms, wishing he'd thought to bring a Thermos of tea or water with him. His throat felt parched.

The motorcar slowed as it came nearer and then braked as it drew abreast of him. A woman was driving it, and he knew the instant he saw her face that she wasn't English. There was something about the way her dark hair was swept up into a bun, the blue dress she wore with a scarf around the throat. Style. His sister Frances would have recognized it instantly.

She was French—

"Are you in trouble?" she asked, her English lightly and fascinatingly accented. He found himself suddenly at a loss for words.

It wasn't beauty. Not that she wasn't damned attractive. But it was more subtle. Good bones, his sister Frances could have told him. A sensuality that came from within, a curve of the lips, a lift to the eyebrows. The way her clothes set off her coloring, the shades of blue in the scarf like stained glass, vivid and rich, bringing light to the gray eyes that shifted as he watched from clear, still water to dark, unfathomable pools of speculation.

He spoke quickly, and in French. "No, I'm a policeman. Inspector Rutledge from London. I'm taking part in the search for the missing Mowbray children."

She smiled a little, hearing his French, unexpected in a deserted lane in the middle of Dorset, then she caught what he was saying. "Ah. The children. It is very sad, is it not? I hope they will be found alive. But one wonders, as the time goes by. I have no children—" She stopped, then went on wryly, "—it is something one feels, I think, about children, whether one is a parent or not."

The smile, even as brief as it was, had been like sunlight over the sea. What in God's name had brought such a creature as this to England? Rutledge glanced at her hands on the wheel and saw a wedding band. That explained it then. A man . . .

"Yes." He moved slightly, away from her car.

She took that as a signal that the conversation was finished, although he'd meant it in another sense. "Then I shall leave you to your search. I wish you success with it—and living children at the end of it."

The motorcar moved off, and as he watched her drive on, he cursed himself for being a tongue-tied fool. He hadn't even asked her name, or where she lived. And what had brought her here, to this stretch of road connected with a murder investigation. If she knew of any place the police had not thought to search—

"She's a stranger here hersel'," Hamish reminded him. "She'd no' be likely to ken what the police have na' thought of."

Which was true. He couldn't hear her engine in the distance now. She was gone.

Rutledge started his car again and got in.

"And a woman like yon is naught but trouble!" Hamish added for good measure. "Leave her out o' this business."

Rutledge laughed. But he could still see the softness of her skin, warm with the sunny day, and the dark tendril of hair that swept across her cheek like a caress. Why was it that French women had a knack for disturbing a man, whether they were beautiful or not? Whatever it was, most of them were born with it, and he didn't need to understand it to recognize it.

In a ramshackle barn, swaybacked with age and a roof half fallen in, he was startled by a small hawk he'd disturbed. She came sailing down toward him, defending her fledglings, and swooped near enough for him to hear the soft *whish* of her wing feathers on the still air. And then she was back in the beams again, well hidden. He could feel her eyes watching him. Nothing here, only prints of the heavy nailed boots of searchers.

He hadn't expected to find anything. The effort had been made in the name of thoroughness. A policeman needed patience. And hope?

At the outskirts of Charlbury, which straggled in Saxon style along the road like beads on a string, he paused long enough to get his bearings.

It was no more than a village, houses facing each other across the high road and, at the far end, a stone church. There was a long narrow green, with its pond and white geese sailing above their reflections like frigates in the sun, an inn, some half-dozen shops, and on a slope behind an outlying farm, a round building with a thatched roof, gleaming whitely. It looked as if it had been stranded there, with no connection to Charlbury except perhaps fate.

Most of the houses were small, but between the common and the church they were larger and better kept. He thought it likely that the well-to-do farmers lived there. The grandest of the lot, with a slate roof and a sizable wing on its westerly side, was set well back from the street and boasted a fine garden behind a low, gated stone wall. There was little activity in Charlbury, as if people were working in their back gardens or on the farms that spread out around the outskirts. One shopkeeper was washing his windows, and farther along a small boy squatted by a bench, teasing a cat with a string. It played with the end desultorily as if preferring to doze peacefully in the sun. The boy gave up as Rutledge watched, and turned to run toward the pond. As he did, he cannoned into a man coming out of the small bakery, who bent double from the force of impact and swore feelingly at the child. The words carried in the warm air.

They didn't appear to have much effect. The boy was soon throwing sticks at the geese on the pond. A woman coming out of another shop, a basket over her arm, called to him, and he came reluctantly to walk beside her, his shrill voice bouncing off the water as he wanted to know *why*. The town brat, Rutledge thought, amused.

Then he noticed that the man the boy had run into was still leaning against the baker's wall, as if in pain. Finally the man straightened gingerly and moved on. From the blacksmith's shop came a sudden gust of black smoke as the bellows were worked. Somewhere Rutledge could hear cattle lowing.

His first stop was at the small, thatched stone house, marked by a sign, where the Charlbury constable lived. But there was no answer to his knock. Rutledge took out his watch and looked at the time. The man must be making rounds, then.

He drove back to the inn and got out, leaving the motorcar in the yard beside it. The inn was old, stone built, with a tidy thatched roof that overhung the dormers like a thick rug. It was comfortably situated where the street began a gentle curve to the common, and there was a small garden in front, in the middle of which rose a wooden post, covered for half its length by a profusely flowering vine. Hanging above that, incongruously, the sign portrayed a distinguished, graying man in frock coat and Edwardian whiskers, one arm raised as if giving a speech. THE WYATT ARMS was scrolled in gold above his head.

Wyatt? The name was familiar, but Rutledge couldn't place it immediately.

Two farmers were coming out of the bar and held the door for him, nodding in countryman's fashion as he passed. Inside the room was dark paneled oak, and Rutledge nearly stumbled over a chair before his eyes adjusted to the stygian atmosphere. Then he saw another doorway and went down a narrow passage into a room that looked out over a neatly kept garden with several tables set up beneath a striped awning. They were presently filled with women listening to a thin, elderly speaker reading from a sheet of paper.

He stopped.

"The ladies find it more to their liking than the parlor, on fair days," a voice said out of the dimness, and a strong man in a white apron came in after him, gesturing to the garden. "That's the Women's Institute meeting. The ladies take their tea out there often, on a fine afternoon. What can I do for you, sir?"

A graceful but heavyset woman with dark hair and an unusual white streak that ran from her temple to the bun at the nape of her neck interrupted the speaker with a question. The speaker deferred to her, then went on.

Rutledge said, turning away from the windows, "Time for a pint, I think. Will you join me?"

The bar and the snug were empty, and the landlord said affably, "Don't mind if I do. Thank you, sir."

38

Rutledge sat at the heavy wooden bar—as black as the walls and the beams that supported them—on a stool worn shiny by generations of trousers sliding across the wood. The landlord lighted a lamp to one side of the mirror, and it gave a sense of reclamation to the room. The brass appointments gleamed like gold.

"Passing through?" the innkeeper asked as he pulled a pint and set it on the bar in front of Rutledge.

"I'm staying at Singleton Magna," Rutledge said, sidestepping the question. "Yesterday and this morning I've been taking in the countryside."

"Any word on the murders over there?" As if Singleton Magna were across the Channel, somewhere in the neighborhood of Paris, and news was hard to come by. "Sorry business," he added, echoing the words of the woman at the Swan. He pulled a second pint and drank deeply, appreciatively, as if he enjoyed his own wares.

"They've got the man in custody. You probably know that. But no signs of the children still. They—that family, I mean—never came as far as Charlbury?"

"No, we don't run to many visitors here. Not like in the old days. Not since the war, at any rate. I see strangers once or twice a month at best."

"What brought visitors before the war?"

"Some came because of the Wyatts. Old Mr. Wyatt was MP for nearly forty years, and that drew the curious. He cut quite a dashing figure in his youth and was as popular in London as he was here. Mr. Simon was cut from the same cloth. Mr. Wyatt served this constituency his life long, and we all looked up to him in Charlbury, aye, and so did most of Dorset."

The memory clicked. The sign—and the family that had made a name for itself in Parliament for three generations. Like the Churchills and the Pitts, a long tradition of public service and golden oratory.

"He's dead, I think?"

"Aye, in the last year of the war, that was. He wanted to see his son take his seat, and he lived three years longer than anybody thought he might. But to no purpose." A veil came down over the man's eyes, as if the subject was ended.

Rutledge paid it no heed. "His son died in the war?" It was no

39

more than an attempt to keep the innkeeper talking, but something flared behind the veil.

"No, Simon Wyatt came through it with hardly a scratch. But somewhere along the way he lost his taste for politics."

It was a warning not to ignore the message a second time. Rutledge changed the subject. "And once the Westminster connection was gone, Charlbury settled back into tranquility again?"

The innkeeper made a wry face. "Not so's you'd notice," he said reluctantly. He put down his beer and looked out at the garden. "People are queer, you know that? Simon Wyatt's grandfather, now, the one on his mother's side of the family, *he* lost his wife early on. Nothing seemed to count with him after that, he couldn't settle to farming or anything else. Then one fine day he went off to see the world. Sent home boxes of whatever struck his fancy— dead birds and strange-looking statues and other knickknacks he picked up along the way. He was set on making a museum, though who'd come to look at such oddities, I ask you?"

"Not every man's taste," Rutledge agreed. "In London? That might make a difference."

"No, here in Charlbury," the innkeeper said. In the back toward the kitchen a man's voice called, "Mr. Denton?"

He answered over his shoulder. "Aye, I'm coming, man!"

"Shall I carry down the next keg, then?"

"Put it with the others, Sam. I'll sort it out later." He smiled ruefully at Rutledge. "Anything else, sir? The dray brought my beer this morning. If I don't watch, Sam'll be drunk as a lord on whatever he can find that's open. Old fool! But help's hard to find. If there's no work on the farms, the younger ones are off for London or wherever they can find a job. If he wasn't so good with the horses, I'd have been shut of him years ago."

Rutledge drained his glass and thanked Denton, then made his way out into the sunlight again. Sitting on a bench outside the door was the man he'd seen earlier. He was pale, his face beaded with sweat.

"Are you all right?" Rutledge asked. "I saw what happened."

"Bloody brat! His mother can't do anything with him. Needs a man's firm hand. Preferably applied to the seat of his pants!" He cleared his throat and said, "I'm all right. As right as I'll ever be."

Something in the timbre of his voice made Rutledge turn to look at him. "Canadian, by any chance?"

"I lived there for a time. Alberta. Damned beautiful part of the country! Ever been there?"

"Never had the chance," Rutledge answered. "I met a number of Canadians in the war."

The man held out his hand and Rutledge took it. "My name's Shaw. You aren't a Dorset man."

"Rutledge. I'm from London."

"I hate the bloody place. Too crowded, too dirty, too old. A man can't breathe there."

"No," Rutledge said, knowing what Shaw meant. "Do you have family here?" It was the opening he'd waited for, to bring up the subject of the Mowbrays.

"I'm Denton's nephew. He's kept an eye on me since I left hospital. The doctors won't let me go back to Alberta, and I've not made up my mind what to do with myself." Shaw grimaced. He wasn't used to telling strangers his life story. It was a bad habit to get into. . . . "Sorry! I'm not usually this garrulous. It's the fault of that bloody child!"

"I don't mind, if it helps. Anything is better than what they give out in hospital for the pain."

"God, yes!" Shaw got to his feet and took a deep breath. "It never lasts long," he said, although the tension around his eyes hadn't gone away. "Thanks for not making a fuss."

As Rutledge nodded, Shaw opened the door and went inside. As if afraid that staying would lead him into other confessions he didn't want to make.

5

Rutledge turned toward his parked car and then changed his mind, walking back up the street instead. He knocked several times at the constable's door, without an answer.

A woman busily sweeping her walk shaded her eyes and said, "If you're needing Constable Truit, he's out."

"Know where I might find him?"

"Business or trouble?"

Rutledge laughed. "I wanted to ask him how to grow fine marrows."

She grinned, not a bit affronted. "Well, he's not likely to be back before the day's out. There's no Mrs. Truit, you see, and he's got courting on his mind."

Rutledge said with interest, "Makes a habit of not being at home, does he?"

"Makes a habit of being wherever Mrs. Darley's daughter is. In my view, she's leading him a merry dance before choosing Danny Marker. Danny works over to Leigh Minster and comes to Charlbury only at the week's end."

A born gossip . . .

"I wanted to ask Truit about the day that man in Singleton Magna killed his wife. I'd like to know if there were any strangers in Charlbury at that time."

She cocked her head and looked him over. "You aren't from the London papers?"

Rutledge said apologetically, "No."

She sighed. "I thought not. You must be the London policeman, then, the one they was expecting over to Singleton Magna." She waited, pointedly, until he gave her his name. "There was a guest at the Wyatts', that came by car. But no one on foot, no woman with small children, if that's what you're asking. It's a long walk, anyway, for little 'uns. D'ye know what I think?" She didn't give him a chance to answer. He'd have her opinion, wanting it or not. "They're buried in a churchyard. What's a better grave than a fresh one, to hide bodies in!"

"Anyone dead of late in Charlbury?" he asked, amused by the ghoulish relish with which she offered her suggestion.

"No." There was disappointment in the admission. "We've got a maid missing, but no one's likely to want to kill her. She was uppity, and good riddance, Mrs. Bagley says."

"How long has she been missing?"

"Getting on for five, six months," the constable's neighbor admitted reluctantly. "I've got a sheet with the picture of that family on it. Constable Truit, he was handing 'em out. Betty's hair was darker, nothing like the woman they was looking for. Besides, she weren't married, nor had any children. At least, not that we knew of! But pretty enough to want more from life than scrubbing another woman's floors. Gone to London, more than likely. Looking for trouble."

Rutledge thanked her and turned to go.

"If you'd come in another month, you'd've seen the museum open," she said to his back, eager to keep his attention. "There's to be a party then. They're hoping for grand guests down from London, but they won't come. Not now that Mr. Wyatt is dead. What's the point? Unless it's curiosity brings them. But who's likely to want to see pagan statues and dead birds? I ask you!"

He glanced toward the churchyard farther along the road. Someone was standing there, watching, from the shadows of the tall trees. "You never know."

She laughed, a hoarse croak. "No. Not with people, you never do."

43

And with a final whisk of her broom she walked back inside her door. Having had the last word? And garnered enough information from him to regale her neighbor on the other side?

Constable Truit would hear about Rutledge's visit before he turned the knob of his front door.

Hamish said out of a long silence, "If yon constable has his mind on courting, he'll no' see all that happens."

"But that woman will, be sure of it." Rutledge walked slowly along the street, getting a feeling for Charlbury. As in most villages, people went about their own business and left others to mind theirs. Dorset had not held a very large place in English affairs, over most of the country's history, and seemed content to leave it that way.

Beside the church was the tidy rectory, the gardens by its front windows heavy with August bloom, and the path to the door was neatly raked. He stopped, as if admiring the effect.

Yes, the figure he'd seen in the trees was still there. He continued on his way. The church was strikingly Norman, with a truncated tower just roof high that seemed to be wanting the rest of itself, as though the builders had stopped working one day and never returned to finish the job. The apse was firmly rounded and the walls appeared to be thick, for the windows were deeply set. They caught the sunlight with darkness rather than light, as if they hadn't been intended to shed a glory of color across the nave. There was no grace or symmetry here, only a statement of power and might. He thought the builders might have anticipated using it as a fortress one day, for want of a castle nearby.

Peripherally he could observe the man in among the heavy, low-branched trees. Reasonably tall, straight—young. A shadow across his face. And something in his cupped hands—

Rutledge froze. The man held a bird in his fingers.

Turning to him, Rutledge called, "What's the date of the church, do you know?"

"Yes," he replied, coming toward Rutledge and into the light. "Early Norman with some later additions. It was never worth anyone's time to rebuild it in a later style. So it hasn't changed much in six hundred years." The words sounded as they'd been spoken by rote—or the man was so accustomed to the question he needn't give the answer any thought. Then he held up the bird. It was just beginning to struggle in the light clasp. "Flew into one of the church windows and knocked himself silly. Cat would have had him if I hadn't found him first!" He opened his fingers very carefully, and after a moment, the freed bird shook itself and took off toward the nearest tree. He grinned at Rutledge. The very blue eyes were wide and guileless.

Looking into the man's face, Rutledge saw that the odd blankness was explained by the terrible, deep scar that started over the bridge of his nose and ran above one eyebrow around the side of the head. The fair hair had grown back stiffly over the healed wound and stuck out at odd angles.

"In the war, were you?" he asked conversationally.

The man nodded. "Everybody asks that. Do I look like a soldier?" The question was serious, considered.

"Yes," Rutledge answered after a moment. "You stand quite straight."

He smiled, sudden pride in the damaged face. "Yes, I do, don't I?"

Rutledge said, "I must go now. Thank you for the information on the church."

"My father was rector here all my life," the man said as Rutledge turned. "He died of the influenza. I know every nook and cranny of the church. Even some *he* didn't find!"

Rutledge studied the open face, his thoughts going suddenly to the missing children. But there appeared to be no intentional double meaning in the remark, only simply a statement of fact and unassuming self-satisfaction. In this one thing, if nowhere else, he had exceeded his father.

The man's eyes followed him as Rutledge turned back down the street toward the inn. Hamish, as aware of it as he was, muttered uneasily. "He's no' a simpleton," he said. "There's the mind of a child, all the same. I canna' trust it."

"He let the bird go," Rutledge silently reminded Hamish. "No, I don't think he'd harm children. Although he might be persuaded to hide them. . . ."

As he passed the largest house, the one with the wing set back beside it, he heard a woman calling a man's name from somewhere out of sight. And then, more clearly, the response.

45

"No, don't bother me with that. Not now!"

The owner of the voice came around the corner of the house, carrying one end of a ladder and in his rough clothes looking more like a laborer than the man lugging the other end did. But his fair hair and fairer skin, flushed with heat and exertion, weren't a working man's. He shifted the ladder with dexterity and said as he lifted it to the gutters, "No, let me go first! It will save time!" and went smoothly up to the roof with the apparent ease of long practice.

The Wyatt home? Rutledge asked himself. It was the only one he'd seen so far with room enough to house a museum, even a tiny one.

Outside the milliner's shop, a woman came hurrying through the door to hand a small box to a younger woman pushing a pram. The two of them looked up at Rutledge as he passed, then began speaking again in lowered voices. The news of his arrival was already moving quickly along the village grapevine. As interesting gossip always did, it seemed to fly on the very wind.

Then why, in God's name, had there been no gossip about the Mowbray children?

Even Hamish had no answer to give to that.

He retrieved his car from the inn and was halfway out of Charlbury when he saw the constable coming toward him on foot, a sturdy, youngish man with red hair, the stiff collar of his uniform unbuttoned in the heat.

Pulling over to the side of the road, Rutledge waited for him, and the man came up to the motorcar with an arrogance to match his stride.

"Something you're wanting, sir?" he asked, his eyes sweeping over Rutledge in what was close to incivility. Hamish growled under his breath, describing the man and his ancestry in Highland terms.

"Inspector Rutledge, from London. I've been looking for you, Truit," he replied, and the constable's eyes narrowed, but there was no other change in his manner. "I've been scouting the ground between here and Singleton Magna, looking for any information that's still to be found."

"It's not very much," Truit answered. "As far as I can find out, the Mowbray woman never got this far. Nor did we see any sign of the accused, Mr. Mowbray. He wouldn't have come this far either, would he? A long hot walk, not for the likes of small children, and he'd know that. Besides, we haven't had many strangers in Charlbury, not this summer. And I haven't found any connection between Mowbray and any of our local people. I asked at every house, to be certain, though I knew from the start it wasn't very likely."

A policeman seldom finds what he's already convinced can't be found, Rutledge thought.

It was one of the faults of the profession, an ease of making up the mind when the most obvious facts seemed to point in one direction. And sometimes in the general run of crimes, where the facts pointed turned out to be right. But where there was murder, there was often a complexity of personalities and secrets that could take an investigation in any direction—or ten directions at once. If he wasn't prepared to follow the most unlikely possibilities as well as the most likely, a policeman ran the risk of committing an injustice.

"The family might have been offered a ride. On a dray or a cart. In a car."

"As to that, if they were taken up by a vehicle, it won't have been a local one," the constable said pedantically, as if explaining matters to a man of limited intelligence, "which tells me they'd be far beyond Charlbury by now. What would persuade them to stop here, when they could be miles away with a farmer who came from anywhere 'twixt here and the Somerset border?"

"Even so, he didn't have wings! How did he reach Somerset without passing through Charlbury? Or Stoke Newton? This farmer of yours? He couldn't drive his wagon through one of these villages without being seen by someone."

"A number of carts and a wagon came through Charlbury," Truit admitted. "None of them with any passengers! I asked around about that. And no one in my town offered a lift to someone coming from Singleton Magna."

"Then why haven't we found the other bodies?" Rutledge asked, not intending any reflection on the constable's efforts, his mind instead on what the carts and wagon might have carried, and whether three people, two of them children, might have hidden themselves behind or under the cargo. But Truit chose to take the remark as a distinct challenge.

A deep flush spread up the man's face. "That's a matter you'll have to take up with Inspector Hildebrand, sir. It's not my place to answer for him!"

Washing your own hands, are you? Rutledge thought, but said only, "You're right, of course," and left it at that.

But as he drove on, he and Hamish entered into a lengthy discussion of Constable Truit's abilities and how he did his job. Hamish had taken a strong dislike to the constable and made no bones about it.

A chain was no better than its weakest link. And in the chain of villages that blocked the most likely direction the Mowbrays had taken from the railway station at Singleton Magna, the other two constables had been brisk, businesslike, and courteous, men who knew their worth and took pride in exhibiting it.

Rutledge, thinking about it, decided he was coming back to Charlbury. Something at the back of his mind, unformed and more intuitive than rational, was aroused. Even Hamish was aware of it, though he said only, "It's trouble you're stirring up, but you'll no' be satisfied until you've sorted that one out!"

"He's not dependable," Rutledge pointed out. "He tells you whatever he thinks will make less work for him. He's certain there's no connection in Charlbury with the Mowbrays, and he may be right. But what if he's wrong?"

"You no' can walk away from it," Hamish agreed. "Until somebody's found the bairns!"

6

Hildebrand was out to lunch when Rutledge walked down to the police station, and rather than wait in the dark smothering confines of the place, he asked if he could speak to Mowbray instead.

The constable on duty, mindful of the tightrope he walked between this man from London and Inspector Hildebrand, dithered for two whole seconds, thinking it through. But Rutledge knew his man, and with the commanding presence of a former army officer standing in front of him and brooking no nonsense, the constable came down on the side of prudence and offered to take Rutledge back personally.

They found another constable in the cell with Mowbray, a cadaverously thin policeman who looked to be in the last stages of tuberculosis, but his voice was strong and deep as he stood up, speaking politely to Rutledge.

"He doesn't have much to say, sir," the watcher told him. "Just sits and stares. Or cries. That's the worst, just tears rolling down his face and no sound. . . ."

"Go have yourself a smoke," the first constable told him, and he left with a swift stride that spoke volumes. "We can only keep a man here two hours," he went on to Rutledge in an undertone. "I'd have a riot on my hands, else. Not the best of assignments."

"No." Rutledge turned to Mowbray, and said in a firm, quiet voice, "Mr. Mowbray? It's Inspector Rutledge, from London."

The bowed head came up with a jerk, the face tight with fear. "You've found them, then?" he asked, voice a thread of sound. "Are—are they—dead?"

"No. But I'd like to ask you—it's hard searching for someone you've never seen. I'd like you to describe the children for me. As you saw them on the railway platform."

Mowbray shook his head. "No, please—I can't—*I can't!*

"It would help," Rutledge told him gently, "if we knew. If they seemed healthy—lively—or were quiet, shy—"

Mowbray clapped his hands over his ears, swaying with pain and grief. "No—*don't!* Oh, God, don't!"

He was relentless, it had to be done. "They grow fast, children do. Would you say Mary was a good mother? That she'd cared for them properly? Were they well filled out? Or had she neglected them, let them grow thin and pale—"

The bowed head came up again, eyes suddenly fierce behind the tears. "She's a good mother, always was, I'll not hear anything against my Mary!"

"You must have found it easy to recognize *her*—but much harder to be sure of them. The little girl must have gone up like a weed—they do, sometimes—"

But perseverance got Rutledge nowhere. With a gasp Mowbray threw up his hands, as if warding off blows. "I tell you I couldn't harm them—they were alive!—I loved them—I wanted to hold them—*for God's sake, I loved them!*"

Rutledge reached out and touched the stooped shoulder, avoiding the eyes that looked into hell.

Like Hamish's eyes, if he ever turned and found them watching him—

Rutledge spun on his heel and went out of the room, his breathing disordered, his mind in turmoil. The constable came after him, then stopped. "You got him to speak—it's more than I've been able to do!"

"Not that it did any good! Are you coming?"

"I'll have to wait for Hindley to return," he said. "If you don't mind—"

"No, I'll find my own way!" Rutledge walked down the passage, his breath coming roughly in his throat. Outside on the steps of the building, he ran into Hildebrand.

"You look like you've seen your own ghost," he said, staring at Rutledge. "What's happened?"

I'll not go back into that building! Not yet! Rutledge told himself and said aloud, "Nothing has happened. But I want to speak to you where we can't be overheard. Shall we walk down to the railway station?"

Grumbling about the heat, Hildebrand followed him as he strode off. "I've been out in the sun most of the morning," he was saying. "I'll be dead of sunstroke before we find those bodies. And half my men with me!"

"That's what I want to speak to you about. I don't think Mowbray saw either his wife or his children at the railway station—"

"Don't be daft, man!" Hildebrand said harshly, stopping to stare at Rutledge. "Of course he did! That's what started the poor sod's rampage!"

"Listen to me, damn it! I think he believed he saw his wife—or someone who strongly resembled her. And children of the ages he remembered. They reminded him so forcibly of his family that he was thrown into emotional confusion. Just then the train pulled out, which meant he couldn't confront the woman and sort it all out. By the time he'd made his way back to Singleton Magna again, he was convinced he had to be right, that she and the children had somehow survived. But when he couldn't find any trace of them here, the longer he searched the more certain he was that there must be a conspiracy afoot to conceal them. And the angrier and the more determined he became—"

Hildebrand watched him with disbelief. He was in no *mood* for folly—

"The sun's turned *your* wits, man! He knew his wife, he came after her, he killed her, and that's why we're searching high and low for those children—"

"Mowbray may well have killed the woman," Rutledge agreed, holding on to his own temper. "But every time we ask anyone about the missing woman or the missing children, we begin by telling them that we're searching for the Mowbrays. And no one

51

has seen them! If we had another name to put to the woman—the children—even the man—we might hear a different answer."

"The man's name? You're saying that if he believed he married her, and we knew what name she'd taken, we could set things straight by saying 'Here, we're looking for the Duchess of Marlborough, this is her photograph, and these are her children,' and some bored footman might say, 'She's gone to visit her cousin over in Lyme Regis, we don't expect her back for days!' And we find ourselves telling him that she's not in Lyme Regis, she's dead."

Rutledge took a deep breath. "If we knew who was missing, we might have a place to start. Yes. That's what I'm saying. After a fashion."

"But we've known that all along!" Hildebrand retorted, exasperated. "And you're not having me believe that it wasn't Mrs. Mowbray that's dead. I don't believe in coincidence!" His instincts had been right—this one was a meddler!

"It isn't coincidence. It's the mind of a man who sees someone out a train window, thinks he's recognized her, and by the time he's walked all the way back to Singleton Magna, he believes it. And he finds a woman outside of town, on foot and vulnerable, and he kills her, because the only woman he's able to think about by this time is his wife!"

"And what, pray, was the poor woman doing on foot outside of town? And where did *she* come from? And what name shall we give *her*? And why hasn't anyone come looking for her? Answer me that!"

It was hopeless. Rutledge, on the point of bringing up changes in the children's ages, decided it would fall on deaf ears now. Instead he said, "I don't have all the answers. I don't even have most of them. Not yet! But those search parties aren't finding what they're after, and I for one am willing to look in any direction that might clear up this murder."

"We've cleared up the murder, hasn't anyone told you? What's Mowbray doing in my jail, watched day and night by my men, if we haven't? If you can't help me do what has to be done here, for God's sake don't muddy the waters with notions that make about as much sense as—as flying from that rooftop!"

"In my experience—" he began.

"Rubbish!" Hildebrand swung away from Rutledge, then angrily turned back to face him, jaw clenched. He said, "This is my investigation. You've been sent from London to find the children. Or their bodies. To get me whatever I need from another jurisdiction easier and faster. And here I'm the one setting up the search parties, running about in the bloody sunshine while you chase phantoms. Get about your own work, man, and leave the rest of this business to me!"

"Look," Rutledge said, trying a last time, "if you bring Mowbray to court in his present condition, the jury will want to see *proof* that he did what you're claiming he did. They'll want means and motive and a weapon, they'll want to know those children *are* dead, and at his hand, so they can convict a witless man without having it rest heavy on their conscience. His defense will run you in circles, making your life a misery before it's over. They'll put him on the stand and have him swearing he's Jack the Ripper or the Czar of Russia before they've finished with him. And if we're wrong— about any particular—"

"Have you met Mowbray's barrister? Johnston? The man's already in the grave with his son. He'll not fight any evidence we present, he'll be happy enough to see his client sent to an asylum instead of the gallows. And that's supposing he cares one way or another! Once we find the other bodies, no jury in England will let Mowbray off!" Hildebrand strode ten feet and swung around a second time, too angry to let it go. "Do what you were sent to do, man! This isn't Cornwall, you'll not be finding any deep, dark secrets in *my* patch, and you'll not spoil my case."

And he was gone, arms swinging in a barely suppressed need to hit something, anything, if it released the tension in his body. Rutledge watched him, oblivious of the stares of passersby, as Hildebrand crossed the street and disappeared into the Swan.

"I could ha' told you—" Hamish began.

I don't want to hear it!

Rutledge turned and walked on, up the hill toward the common, where the coolness of the trees closed over him.

Mowbray. *Was* he guilty of murdering his wife? And had he killed his children? Or was the body waiting to be claimed in the makeshift morgue a stranger's, with nothing more than coincidence

53

dragging her into another man's madness? And the children—or the man with them? Did they exist, or were they something from the dark reaches of grief, conjured up with the pain of jogged memory?

What was wrong with this murder, what was it that lay beneath the surface, like a corpse beneath the ice, waiting to rise and point an accusing finger when the time came?

Hamish said, "Yon policeman wants his answers tidy, like a birthday box done up in ribbons and silver paper. Never mind what's truly happened. You'd do well to heed him and not meddle. He can make a bad enemy!"

"There's a dead woman to be thought of," Rutledge reminded him. "And that man in the cell." But what could be done for Mowbray now, even if they found a dozen murderers to take his place? The poor devil was broken by his own torment. He looked up at rooks calling from the branches arching high over his head. "I don't think we'll find the children," he added pensively.

"Then where've they got to?" Hamish demanded.

"To safety," he answered, and for the life of him, he couldn't have explained where that notion had come from.

He took his lunch at the Swan, eating in solitary splendor in the dining room. It was nearly two o'clock, and the young woman waiting on him was yawning in a corner, her eyes drowsy as she filled the sugar bowls and then collected the salts and peppers in their turn. She looked enough like Peg, the chambermaid, to be her sister. Rutledge listened to the clink of the silver tops as she worked with them, his own thoughts busy with details.

He had called in at the railway station and persuaded the master to ask down the line whether suitcases had been unclaimed when the train made its last stop.

The telegraph key had clicked swiftly and surely, and then silence. "There's a chance they were found by the conductor, long before the end of the line," the man reminded Rutledge.

"I'd thought of that." But the conductor who had put Mowbray off the train was an experienced man and according to the file had been questioned by Hildebrand himself. He'd have been the first to see the significance of any uncollected luggage that had come to light then or later.

The key began to click in response. The stationmaster listened and then shook his head. "No unclaimed luggage," he said. "Not that day. Nor that week either."

"Then contact any stops in between—"

"All of them?" the man demanded, staring at Rutledge.

"All of them," he agreed. But the second message sent out by the stationmaster brought in the same response. No unclaimed luggage . . .

"They might not've had much baggage with them," the man said, "if 'twere only a day trip. It might help if we knew what we were looking for."

Rutledge shook his head. "I don't know. If anything more comes over the wire, I'm at the Swan. Send word to me there." It was a far-fetched hope.

And so he'd gone for his belated meal, letting the stationmaster do the same. "My wife's waiting my dinner," the man had said, following Rutledge out of the small, cluttered office. "She's ill-humored when I'm late!"

"Tell her it was police business," Rutledge responded, and walked on.

But it was over his meal that answers began to come to him. And he went over them again and again, to be sure he was right.

Whatever else had happened here in Singleton Magna, there *was* a dead woman.

And with that one incontrovertible fact, he must start.

7

Rutledge spent what was left of the day and into the dusk looking for the dead woman.

In Singleton Magna, everyone saw her as Mowbray's wife. The one the man, burning with anger and injustice, had scoured the town to find.

Everyone told Rutledge that. Describing encounters they'd had—or someone they knew had had—with Mowbray. Believing in his anger and his intent to kill. The woman on the other hand was dead. They could tell him nothing about her. It was as if she had no other identity or reality than that of victim.

Even Harriet Mason, the woman who had arrived on the same train for a visit with her aunt, remembered nothing. "I was that sick from the journey, I didn't know or care about anything but getting here to Auntie's," she said pointedly, looking at Rutledge through thin, pale lashes.

Mrs. Hindes, stiff with rheumatism and a strong dislike of being a burden on anyone, said, "The only person besides Harriet I noticed coming out of the station that day was the woman who was met by Mrs. Wyatt. The one in the fetching hat. But of course Harriet was feeling faint and I really didn't have time to pay particular attention to anyone else, though there must have been half a dozen or so passengers arriving." She smiled wryly, her strong face suddenly mischievous. "You must excuse us, Inspector, we are the lame and the halt, I fear."

And she watched with quiet satisfaction as Harriet bristled.

Early the next morning Rutledge left the town to stop at every house near the main road, with no success. From there he drove on to Stoke Newton, the home of three passengers who had arrived on the noon train the day Mrs. Mowbray had been seen on the platform. The farmer, his wife, and their young daughter had been met by a tenant, "fetched home in the wagon," Mrs. Tanner told him jovially in a parlor dominated by a giant aspidistra. To Rutledge it seemed to smother his chair with its broad leaves. "Like so many sides of beef!"

"You didn't see Mrs. Mowbray on the train? Or the children with her?"

"Lord, Inspector, the train was that crowded leaving London! Holidaymakers, mostly, families with children any age between six months and ten years. Full of sauce, they were, but I don't mind, a lively child's a healthy child, I say. I'm sure we was lucky to find a seat!" Mrs. Tanner answered. "No, we've talked it over, amongst ourselves. If Mrs. Mowbray and her young ones was on that train, we took no notice of them—no reason to, one family among so many!"

In the afternoon he found himself in Charlbury again, asking Denton at the pub for the Wyatt house. It was, as he'd thought, near the church.

"Can't miss it. Big, with that wing they added just before the war. That was to be Mr. Wyatt's office, and Mr. Simon's as well, when the time came. Now it's being refurbished to house that museum Mr. Simon's so set on."

Rutledge opened the gate and stepped into a front garden of pink geraniums and warmly scented lavender, with white stock and taller white delphiniums behind them. He climbed the two steps to the small porch, but a maid answered the door before he could ring the bell.

She said in some distress, "If you've come about them shelves that's fallen down, Mr. Wyatt is over in the new wing."

Rutledge followed her pointing finger and took the brick path to the second door of the house, which led into the newest part. Someone shouted, "Come in!" to his knock, and he entered a scene of chaos.

There were boxes strewn about the floor like snowdrifts, and glass-fronted cases filled with the most exotic collection of statuary and weaponry and musical instruments that he'd seen in some time. Eastern, most of them, as far as he could tell. Exotic dancers stood on shelves beside squat gods and animal masks, while daggers and swords were displayed in fans, their points gleaming in the sunlight. Tiered parasols in red, yellow, black, and white were fringed in what appeared to be gold bullion, and there were what looked like parts of doorways or windows, heavy with carved scenes. Garish puppets elbowed each other, some of them three dimensional while others were flat, painted on hide. Below, on another shelf, were fantastic butterflies pinned in tidy rows, like enameled brooches in every color of the rainbow. Nothing in England was that spectacular. Hamish was absorbing the scene with Presbyterian horror, pointing out that these items were pagan and therefore suspect.

Before Rutledge could answer him, a man's voice called, "Well? What are you doing, loitering out there? Come look at this disaster!"

Rutledge went through a doorway to find a man on his knees collecting shells that had tumbled from a tall bookcase, its shelves haphazard and half out of their moorings.

"You're damned lucky they didn't shatter! You swore they'd support—" He was halfway through the sentence when he saw his visitor and realized it wasn't the carpenter he'd sent for. "Who the hell are you?"

It was the fair-skinned man he'd seen yesterday, carrying the front end of a ladder. "Mr. Wyatt? I'm Inspector Rutledge, from Scotland Yard. I've come to speak to you—"

"Not now, man! Can't you see what's happened here? I'm expecting Baldridge or one of his minions, and he's got some explaining to do! I told him a dozen times if I told him once that these shelves had to be well anchored against the weight, or they'd be over before we knew where we were! And I was right."

He got to his feet. Tall, slender, with a face that was both strong and intelligent. There were lines at the corners of his blue eyes that spoke of laughter—belied now by the deep grooves bracketing his mouth. The marks of strain. He surveyed the disaster. "Some of these shells are priceless. They've come from half the islands in the Pacific, and each one was carefully numbered and kept in a box so as not to separate sets. And now look! I suppose I'll have to bring someone down from London to be sure we've got them in the right order again."

"Mr. Wyatt. I only need a minute of your time," Rutledge broke in. "I understand that on thirteen August you or your wife collected a guest from the railway station in Singleton Magna. Is that true?"

"Yes, yes, that was Miss Tarlton, from London. She's my new assistant. Or she will be if I can persuade my wife to let me take her on. Mrs. Wyatt is nothing if not stubborn, and just because—" He stopped, aware that he was talking about his personal affairs with a stranger, and a policeman at that. "Miss Tarlton was recommended by someone whose opinion I trust. Mrs. Wyatt and I hold different opinions on that subject. I hired the young lady, and she's to return at the end of the month to take up her position here." His mouth set sternly, as if he could foresee the battle ahead.

"She returned to London after the interview?"

"Yes, yes. Ah—Baldridge," he said, looking beyond Rutledge. "Come see this mess your workmen have made! I ought to make you return every penny I paid you."

Rutledge turned to see a youngish man in a dark suit standing foursquare in the doorway. "I told you, Mr. Wyatt, to let the bolts dry before you set anything on the shelves!" he was saying.

"Wet plaster, is it! And my fault!" Wyatt snorted scornfully. "I told you to anchor the shelves firmly, and just look at your interpretation of 'firmly'!"

Rutledge said, "Mr. Wyatt—"

Wyatt said, "Go next door and talk to my wife, Aurore. She'll tell you whatever it is you need to know!" And he was already shaking his finger at Baldridge, not waiting to see if Rutledge was pleased with the suggestion or not.

Rutledge left the two men to it and walked back through the first room, wondering if Denton wasn't correct in his assessment of the museum planned for Charlbury. In this out of the way village, who would come to see such exotica?

When he arrived again at the front door, the maid answered the bell and said, "I'm sorry, sir! Mr. Wyatt didn't tell me who to expect. It was the builder in Sherborne he'd been on the telephone shouting at most of the morning, and someone was promised to come."

Rutledge said, "No matter. I'd like to speak to Mrs. Wyatt if I may."

"She's in the back garden, sir. If you'll wait in the parlor, I'll fetch her. What name shall I say, sir?"

"Rutledge. I'll walk out with you, it will save time." He was tired of the Wyatt reluctance to put aside their own business for his.

She looked up at him doubtfully and then led the way through the house and out a tall pair of french doors that overlooked the gardens. He could see someone working in a potting shed at the end of the path and said, "I can find my way from here. Thanks."

The maid stopped, and said, "I think I ought to—"

He looked down at her. "It will be all right. Mr. Wyatt suggested that I talk with his wife, and this is as good a place as any."

That seemed to reassure her, and she left him to continue down the path to the shed. The woman inside, dressed in a gray smock, turned as she heard his footsteps crunching on the graveled path and came out into the dappled sunlight.

They stared at each other in mutual surprise. Rutledge said, "Mrs. Wyatt?"

She inclined her head. "Inspector—Rutledge, is it not?" For an instant she seemed at a loss. "My husband is in the other wing, I think."

"It's you I've come to see."

Her eyes darkened. "You haven't—they haven't found the children."

"No. I'm here in a different capacity today. Asking questions about anyone who got off the train at Singleton Magna at the same time Mrs. Mowbray and her family did. I understand from Mr. Wyatt that you had a guest who also arrived on thirteen August.

Can you tell me about her?" Without thinking, he'd begun speaking to her in French. It had seemed natural. Midway through the last sentence, he realized it and switched to English.

She replied in the same language. "Yes, a Miss Tarlton, from London. She came to be interviewed by my husband concerning the position of his assistant." She answered freely enough, but warily. He could hear the nuances in her voice.

"She arrived at the station and was met?"

"I went to meet her myself. Simon was busy—the museum keeps him quite busy these days." There was, he thought, a faint overtone of irony in the words.

"How long did she stay with you?"

"Only two days."

"You drove her back to the station?"

"I was supposed to drive her, yes. But I was delayed at the farm— I've taken over running it, while Simon is so occupied with the museum. She was already gone when I came back to collect her. I expect he saw to it, in my place. Trains don't wait for cows with colic," she added wryly.

"No, I don't suppose they do," he answered, reminding himself that she was no different from any other witness he might question. And yet he'd met her first with no knowledge of her role—if there was any—in his investigation. It seemed to give her, somehow, an edge. As if she judged him, even as he judged her, because they had begun as equals.

She waited for him to go on. There was a stillness about her that struck him as she stood there, composed and quiet. Even her eyes were still, absorbing him somehow. As if time were not an issue of concern to her. Or possibly to him either. It was a very strong impression and he found it distracting.

Most of the Frenchwomen he'd met spoke with self-possession and a natural sense of self-worth. Vivacity was to them a tool of conversation, half flirtatious, half a mannerism that reflected their view of life. This woman was different. It was something deep inside, a well of stillness that seemed without end. But not, he thought, a well of serenity. . . .

Hamish said, apparently out of context, "She's no' a killer."

She drew off her gardening gloves and pulled the smock over her

61

head. "I've missed my tea, waiting for Simon. Will you have a coffee—or some wine—with me? There's a table under the trees there. I'll just find Edith." She wrinkled her nose. "I've not quite learned to like tea. But I'm trying."

He walked back to the french doors with her. The fragrance of lily of the valley came to him suddenly, and he realized that it was her perfume. It surprised him; the sweetness wasn't what he'd have thought she might have chosen for herself. Something headier—or at least more provocative. And yet today in her plain gray dress with its buttoned belt and square white collar, she was anything but provocative. Quakerish, perhaps.

She called to Edith as she walked through the french doors, leaving him in the garden.

Hamish, unsettled in the back of his mind, reminded him he was a policeman on duty. And to keep his wits about him.

It was a timely reminder. Rutledge walked over to the small table and shook a butterfly off the nearest chair. He wondered what it would think of its gaudy brethren on display in a glass case inside this house. Served them right, for drawing attention to themselves?

Aurore Wyatt came back and took the chair opposite the one he'd moved. "Edith tells me you've already been to the museum. What do you think of it?"

"Unusual," he replied dryly, after some thought.

Her laughter, husky and rich, was unexpected. "How very English of you," she said. "The English are masters of understatement, are they not?" Then she added as if it mattered to her, "It's become Simon's life. I hope it is what he wants to do and not what he feels he ought to do."

"In what sense?"

"The Wyatts have always gone into politics. For generations. It was expected—before the war, you understand—that he would stand for Parliament as well. From childhood he was prepared for nothing else. And by nature it suited him. Handsome, able, a genuinely charming man who commanded respect. He never speaks of it now. Only of this museum, about which he knows so little." There was a wryness in her eyes. "But we are none of us the same after four years of war. And he married me, which was not very wise in a politician. An English wife would have been safer. More—comme il faut?"

He said nothing, but had a sudden mental picture of Aurore Wyatt among the male and female voters of a quiet Dorset constituency. The cat among the pigeons . . . "I understand his other grandfather was an explorer of sorts."

"Yes, in the Pacific and Indian oceans. He left Simon his collections—I think, in the hope that he might display them and make his grandfather as famous as Darwin or Cook. Simon had said nothing of this to me in France. It wasn't until I arrived in England that he seemed to remember anything at all about his grandfather's boxes. They were stored in London, had been for ages. And suddenly he would not hear of anything but this museum." She shrugged in that way that only Frenchwomen have, lifting her shoulders with her head to one side, as if denying any understanding of the matter. "That is why I wonder, sometimes, if he feels an obligation to satisfy one ancestor if not the other. If not Westminster, then this museum. It would be very sad, would it not?"

"What does Simon Wyatt himself want in life?"

"Ah!" Aurore answered ruefully. "If I knew that, I would be a very fortunate woman."

Edith came out with a tray of glasses and a bottle of wine. "The coffee's not done," she said apologetically.

"Wine will do very well, for me," Aurore said, and offered a glass to Rutledge before pouring her own. He accepted, and found the wine very good indeed, dry and perfect for a warm afternoon. She watched him savor it, her eyes observing without judging. "You were in the war, I think?"

"How do you know?"

She tilted her head and thought for a moment before answering him. "You speak French very well. And you know a good wine when you taste it." But he knew that it wasn't what she might have said, if she'd been honest.

"The war was neither wine nor language," he said, more harshly than he intended. "It was a very hard four years. They are finally over."

Somewhere Hamish echoed softly, "Over?"

63

"But not yet forgotten," she said astutely, looking at the man's face and eyes, and reading more there than he was comfortable having her see. "No, I understand. I also have seen too much pain and death. And my husband as well. I thought—there was a time when I thought he might not survive the war. I watched him, and I knew he was expecting to die. Which sometimes means that it *will* happen. Like so many of the young men marching off to war, he didn't understand that he was mortal. He came to the fighting as if it were a game, there on the steps at Eton. And when he discovered it was not like this, it was too late. There was nothing to be done but fight and wait for death to come. And even death failed him. Sometimes I think the survivors feel guilty for having lived, when so many died."

Thinking of Hamish, Rutledge looked away. It was too near for comfort.

She said, putting down her glass, "Is there anything that can be done?"

"No." He wanted to offer her hope, and couldn't. He had none to give. After a moment he realized that Hamish was trying to draw his attention to something—that her digression had led Rutledge away from what had brought him here. Out of purpose? Or because he had listened with some sense, some knowledge of the suffering she was talking about?

"Why do I tell you these things?" she asked, frowning. "I have not spoken of them to anyone, not even the nuns!"

"She's no' a woman to do anything by chance," Hamish reminded him.

He brought the topic of conversation abruptly back to Miss Tarlton's visit. "I'm under the impression that Mr. Wyatt offered Miss Tarlton a position. As assistant. Is that true?"

Aurore Wyatt looked away. Even in profile, the stillness about her was striking, as if her body were attuned to it in blood and bone. Yet there was a strength too, which seemed to mask a great, unspeakable pain. Part of that she had told him about—but not all. Not nearly all. He was sure of it.

"If you are asking if I approved, no. But not because of Miss Tarlton. She seems to be both respectable and capable, with a surprising knowledge of Asia. Her family had served in India for gen-

64

erations, as I understand it. As an assistant she would have been very useful to Simon. It was—my opinion—that Simon himself should have advertised. Instead he left the task to someone else."

"I'm afraid I don't see the problem. If she's competent."

Aurore turned to look at him, her fingers on the rim of her glass, her eyes a darker gray that he remembered. "My husband's assistant will live here, in this house. Take meals with us. Share our lives. That will not be comfortable when I am strongly aware that this person does not approve of me."

He was surprised. "Why? Surely not because you're French? She can't know anything else about you in such a short time."

"Yes, because I am French! I married Simon Wyatt in France, during the war. There are some who think—well, never mind. It is not your affair, you wish to speak of Miss Tarleton, not of me!"

After a moment he said, "They think you took advantage of Mr. Wyatt's loneliness?"

She lifted her glass and drank, then set it down. "You didn't know my husband before he left for France. Nor did I. But I'm told—very often I'm told!—that he was destined to be a famous cabinet member—a great prime minister—or God Himself, for all I know! They believe—his father's friends and associates—that the change in him now is the result of his marriage. And so my doing. They blame me, because it is much easier than understanding why he prefers this ridiculous museum to what he was bred to do!"

"As long as Wyatt doesn't blame you, what difference does it matter what other people think? Or say?"

"How like a man," she said in gentle derision. "You do not live in a woman's world, you don't know the savagery there. It can be worse than the jungle—"

At that moment Simon Wyatt came storming through the french doors and out into the garden. "It's *my* fault, he says! Idiot! I'd like very much to nail him to that wall with one of his own damned bolts!" Coming to the table, he pulled up the third chair. "What's that? Wine! Good God, I hope you offered him gin or a scotch first!"

"Edith will bring you one, if you prefer it," she told her husband. "But I think the inspector was leaving. I'll see him to the door."

Surprised, Rutledge finished his wine and set the glass on the table. "Thank you, Mrs. Wyatt." He stood, offering his hand to Simon. "I hope the museum is a success," he said.

Simon said, moodiness settling in on him like a cloak, "I don't know that it will be. But the important thing is to try. It's all I can do." He shook Rutledge's hand and then Rutledge was following Aurore into the house.

At the front door she said, "I hope we've answered your questions."

"There's one other," he told her reluctantly. "I'd like Miss Tarlton's full name, and her direction if you have it."

"Her first name is Margaret. And she lives somewhere in Chelsea. You'll have to ask Simon for the street and number."

"Thank you," he replied. "Good-bye, Mrs. Wyatt."

She nodded and watched him walk away.

The watching bothered him. It hadn't been simple curiosity, nor the look of a woman intrigued by a new man in her sphere, only uneasiness.

But whether it was uneasiness for herself—or for Simon Wyatt— he couldn't tell.

Margaret Tarlton. Of Chelsea, London.

He had a strong feeling that she wasn't the woman he was searching for.

Rutledge placed a call to London as soon as he reached Singleton Magna. The reply came before he went down to his dinner.

Bowles said peremptorily, "What's this Tarlton woman got to do with the Mowbrays?"

"She was on the same train. She got off at Singleton Magna that day. We want to know what she saw—if anything."

"See to it you're not stepping on any toes, man!"

"I'm care itself."

Satisfied or not, Bowles became crisp and to the point. He said, "We sent a man around to find Miss Tarlton. Her maid says she went down to Singleton Magna last week and afterward was to go on to Sherborne. To the country house of a Thomas Napier. One of the political Napiers, Rutledge! He's in London, but his daughter, Elizabeth Napier, is staying in the house presently. We haven't been able to reach *her*."

"Never mind," Rutledge said. "I'll drive over there myself." He jotted the names in his notebook and closed it. "Any information available on Miss Tarlton or this Miss Napier?"

"Nothing about Miss Tarlton, except that she comes from an Anglo-Indian family that settled in London around the turn of the century, after her father died. Mother's dead as well now. Several aunts and cousins, I'm told. They live in Gloucestershire." There was a pause. And then Bowles went on, "You might be interested in one discovery we've made about Miss Napier. She was engaged to be married to Simon Wyatt, who lives in Charlbury, not far from Singleton Magna. Her father's his godfather, I'm told. In fact, it was Wyatt Miss Tarlton was going to visit, to apply for a position. She used to be Miss Napier's secretary, from 1910 to last year. Lived in the Napiers' London house." The voice stopped again, then added with relish, "Small world, isn't it?"

8

As Bowles hung up, Rutledge took out his watch and considered time and distance. It was still light. He could make it to Sherborne by a reasonable hour. If Margaret Tarlton was there, it would save time to interview her tonight. If he telephoned, she might put him off. Or . . . he refused to consider the alternative, that he might not find her at the Napiers'.

He found he didn't want to go back to the Wyatts' house. If Margaret Tarlton was in Sherborne, he had no other business in Charlbury.

Finding Peg in the kitchen, he persuaded her to put up some sandwiches—"But the meat's left from luncheon, sir!" she'd exclaimed. "And the dinner roast won't be finished for another half hour. Can't you wait for that?"—and set out in a westerly direction for the town of Sherborne.

It was famous for its abbey church, built of golden stone like soft butter, and for the school for boys that had had a reputation for their athletes when he'd been at Oxford. Three former Sherborne scholars had stood between him and a chance at a Blue.

The Napier house was harder to find than he'd expected, set well back from the main road on an unmarked lane that wended its way first this direction and then that, before making up its mind to connect with the gates and the drive up to the house. He could see it ahead, after he'd made the turn.

It was built of the same lovely stone as the abbey and looked to be nearly as old, with oriel windows and pointed arches. The porch was a handsome affair of niches, statues, and a stone balustrade on two sides. He thought this might once have been a small manor belonging to the abbey. Someone had added a wing in the same style, probably a hundred years ago. He could just see the roof of it on the south front. As a gentleman's country house, it was still rather small, but more than made up for that in its architectural quality. Thomas Napier's forebears had possessed both the taste and good sense not to meddle with the fabric. And possibly a thin purse? Often that determined how many changes were made as the family's fortunes rose.

A dark-haired maid in stiff black with an apron so starched it gave the impression it would break before it bent opened the door to him and said, "Yes, sir?" as if he'd taken a wrong turn and had come to ask his way.

"Inspector Rutledge, from Scotland Yard," he said. "I understand a Miss Tarlton is staying here, as a guest of Miss Napier's. Is she in?"

"Miss Tarlton, sir? No, she's not. But I'll ask if Miss Napier's receiving visitors. She's just sat down to her dinner." Her voice was doubtful.

"This won't take long," he said. "There are one or two questions she might be able to answer."

"I'll ask, sir. If you'd care to wait?" She opened the door for him to step into the hall, and he was pleased to see that it was as handsome as the porch, with an elegantly carved fireplace and a high, medieval ceiling. The fine portraits on the walls, placed to catch the eye, were of a succession of men impressively magisterial in bearing, who bore a strong family likeness. Four generations, staring down at him in formidable array.

Rutledge smiled, studying them. He recognized Thomas Napier himself—painted at the age of thirty, at a guess, when he took his seat in Parliament. "A bonny man" was Hamish's verdict. Tall, distinguished, with a short Edwardian beard and dark hair brushed

69

back from a high forehead. The hair had grayed at the temples now, but the firmness of the features hadn't changed at all. Napier was still a striking man. Father, grandfather, and great-grandfather possessed the same strength.

There were no women here. And no sons of Thomas's?

He heard the tap of heels on the stone passageway down which the maid had disappeared, and a slender dark-haired woman came through the door to greet him, her resemblance to the men on the walls very clearly marked. Except that in her the same strong, distinguished features had been softened by femininity. For she was very feminine, in appearance and manner.

"Inspector Rutledge?" she said with a graciousness she must have been far from feeling, for her serviette was still in her left hand and her dinner would be growing cold. "I understand you're seeking Miss Tarlton. May I ask why?" Her voice had a girlish lightness, but she was all of thirty, if he was any judge.

"Miss Tarlton, I'm told, took a train on thirteen August from London to Singleton Magna, where she was met and taken to Charlbury by Mrs. Simon Wyatt. That was the same day, sadly, that a Mrs. Mowbray and her children traveled on the same train. As you may know, we believe Mrs. Mowbray was killed soon after that. We're trying to locate anyone who might remember her or her children or the man believed to be traveling with her. We very much hope that Miss Tarlton can give us information we badly need."

"No, I had heard nothing of this!" she said with a ring of surprise and truth in her voice. "You had better tell me more, I think."

He did, starting from the beginning, when Mowbray had stood in the window of the train, looking out at the woman on the platform. But he stopped with the finding of the body in the field.

She listened intently, without comment, as if he had come to make a report to her father. Her blue eyes were on his, steady and intelligent, reflecting her concern. He was careful in his choice of words, cushioning the purpose of his visit as well as he could, but he quickly realized that Elizabeth Napier's softness covered a very strong mind.

"This Mrs. Mowbray was killed—murdered, you mean?" she

asked, swiftly moving to the heart of the problem. "How dreadful! And they have caught this man? Her husband?"

"We have her husband in custody. It's the children we're still trying to locate. Any help Miss Tarlton might give us will be greatly appreciated."

She frowned. "What do you mean—trying to *locate*?"

"We—aren't sure what's become of them."

Elizabeth Napier shivered. After a moment she said, "I've worked in London with the poor. I've seen men who have lost all hope, who have killed their families rather than watch them starve. But this is different, isn't it? He wasn't trying to spare them."

"We have no reason to believe that's the case," he answered. "But Miss Tarlton might be able to throw some light on the matter."

"Margaret isn't here," she said reluctantly. "I was expecting her a week ago, but apparently she went back to London instead."

"You've spoken with her on the telephone?"

"No, she hasn't called or written. But she was expecting to take up a new position; she may not have had the time. Let me give you her London address—"

"She's not there," he said. "We've spoken with her maid. She says Miss Napier was to come directly here from Charlbury."

"But she *hasn't*—"

Elizabeth Napier stopped, looking at him in alarm, the serviette drawn through her fingers like a handkerchief, over and over again. He couldn't quite read her fear, but it was there. "I don't understand!" she said finally. "Please!"

He took the folded sheet of paper from his notebook and handed it to her. She looked down at the photograph on it, her brows puckered as if she had trouble seeing it. "What's this?" she asked, perplexed by the shift in direction.

"A photograph of Mrs. Mowbray and her children. Does Miss Tarlton bear any resemblance at all to the woman you see there?" Hamish, mindful of the effort Rutledge was making to keep his voice free of any inflections that might lead an answer, began to stir.

"To this woman? No, certainly not!"

Then she hesitated, staring intently at the face. "Well, they're

71

both tall and fair—I suppose that's a similarity—but it isn't strong. It's more in something—I don't know, something about their form, I think. The long bones, the fine hair, the—the delicacy, perhaps?"

"Do you have a photograph of Miss Tarlton?"

"A photograph? Why should—no, of course, there's one in the study. When my father had a house party last spring, she helped me entertain. It was a political weekend, and they're always the worst, the wives are bored to tears or scratching each other's eyes out in the *politest* way whenever the men aren't around. Someone had a camera. If you'll excuse me—"

He could feel the tension in his body now. That odd sixth sense had already leapt ahead, his thoughts tangled with the possibilities opening before him. The warning to let sleeping dogs lie passed through his mind as well.

"Then what about the children?" Hamish was saying, voice low, urgent.

"If it wasn't his wife that Mowbray killed, there won't be any children."

"But there *were* children at the railway station. You have na' forgotten."

"No. But if the Tarlton woman was visiting the Wyatts in Charlbury, she might have been in the right place at the wrong time. Mowbray might have believed he'd found his missing wife." It was the conviction that had brought Rutledge to Sherborne. The need to settle the matter of Margaret Tarlton's whereabouts. Such thin evidence . . .

Miss Napier returned, a silver-framed photograph in her hand. Instead of giving it to Rutledge she walked to the door and opened it, stepping out into the last of the daylight to compare the photograph and the printed flyer Hildebrand had had made up.

After a moment she shook her head, and Rutledge came to take the frame from her, trying to read her expression. He saw only confusion.

He too stood in the light, looking down at several women shown standing by the elegant hearth in the hall, as if posed by someone oblivious to the interplay of relationships among them. There was a stiffness that betrayed their antagonism even while their expressions portrayed polite enjoyment. But second from the left was a young woman with long bones and fair hair, who looked at the camera in much the same way—and yet not the same way—as Mary Sandra Mowbray had done in 1916. An oddly ephemeral thing . . .

Hamish saw the truth as quickly as Rutledge did.

Rutledge told himself, *It isn't real.* This resemblance between the two women. You see it only when you look for it—there's nothing to trigger it unless you're consciously expecting to find it. Or hoping to see it?

"It isn't a likeness. Is it?" Elizabeth Napier asked. "I can't *tell*—"

"It isn't a likeness," he answered finally, "but there's something very—*uncanny*—about the similarity." He had unwittingly used the same word Hamish was repeating in his mind. "At a guess, I'd say that if the two women stood side by side, you wouldn't notice it. There's the voice, of course, and how each carries herself. Her expression—her nature. They're not from the same social background. They've lived quite different lives. These qualities would strike you first."

"I don't follow you—"

He said carefully, looking for flaws himself, "If you saw either woman walking down Bond Street some distance ahead, you might say to yourself, 'I think that's Margaret Tarlton.' If you saw either woman in the slums or along a country road, you might pass her by without a glance, because you wouldn't expect to encounter Miss Tarlton there."

"Except for their clothing. How they were dressed."

"But Mowbray, expecting to find his wife in Singleton Magna, might not know her wardrobe now, in this new life he'd already accused her in his own mind of living. He wouldn't look for differences, he'd look for similarities." Like the color pink . . . if that was a woman's favorite color.

"I begin to see. But go on." Her face had lost some of its color.

"This man survived the war to come back to an empty life. Out of work, no home, no family to support him, nothing safe or familiar. He desperately wants this woman to be his wife, and by the time he does find her, he can't feel anything but anger when she denies everything. He tries to make her stop lying to him—and, in the end, kills her." There were any number of holes in this piece of speculation. He found himself trying not to think about them.

Hamish was asking vehemently how he had overlooked the one salient fact that would negate all his fine theories.

But Rutledge made himself concentrate on Elizabeth Napier's reaction.

"It's still guesswork," he said, forced to honesty. "I can't prove any of it."

She was looking up at his face, dawning horror on hers as she assimilated the images in her mind. "You aren't—you aren't trying to say—that the dead woman in Singleton Magna might possibly be *Margaret Tarlton*! That it explains why she isn't here—or in London. No, I refuse to believe it!"

Yet he could tell that the conviction was growing stronger with every moment. She was an intelligent woman—

Still, she fought against it. Elizabeth stood by Rutledge's side, her hand on his arm, her eyes scanning the two faces, one in an ornate frame, the other a grainy reproduction on cheap paper. Whatever her inner struggle, whatever the deeper emotion that lay behind her fear of the truth, she couldn't ignore the evidence before her.

Then she spoke, with a heaviness that made him ashamed of the necessity of bringing her into this murder. There were tears standing in her eyes, and her fragility touched him deeply. "If it's true— if that poor woman *is* Margaret—then it's all my fault. I sent her there—I thought I was being quite clever. I thought it was incredibly simple and that no one would ever suspect—*how very stupid of me!*" She fiercely blotted her eyes with her serviette, then looked down at it in surprise, as if she'd forgotten her dinner—as if it belonged to a far distant and far different past.

Bracing her shoulders, she said, "It won't do to cry. I'm always the first to say that! *'Don't cry!'* I've told those pathetic women in the slums. *'It doesn't solve anything!'* But it relieves the pain somehow, doesn't it?"

Carefully folding the flyer, she handed it back to Rutledge along with the photograph in its silver frame. "You'll need that, I think. And you'd better come in," she said. "Have you dined? No? That's good, I have need of company just now. We'll eat what we can of dinner. Then I'll change and go with you to Singleton Magna. I want to see this woman—or has she been buried?"

"No, she hasn't been buried. But she isn't—her face was badly beaten. I don't know that you could, er, hope to recognize her."

Her own face went white, and he thought for a moment she might faint. But she said resolutely, "Don't tell me before I've eaten something! Come with me!"

Rutledge followed her back into the hall and down the passage to a room with an arched ceiling and a table down the middle that would comfortably seat twenty or more. At the far end, in isolated splendor, a place had been set for one. She walked to it, picked up the small silver bell by her plate, and rang it sharply. When the maid came to answer her summons, she said, "Another place for the inspector, please. Tell Cook I'll have a fresh bowl of soup as well." She waited until the maid had taken the first course back through the heavy door to the kitchens and then indicated the chair on her right. Rutledge accepted it.

Elizabeth Napier took a deep shuddering breath, closed her eyes for an instant, shutting out what she had, soon, to face, then sipped her wine as if it offered the strength she didn't possess.

"Are you quite *sure* this—this woman—whoever she may turn out to be—was killed by this man, Mowbray? Is that proved beyond a doubt?"

"No. Not beyond any doubt. But he publicly threatened his wife. And then we found the . . . her. There's no one else we have any reason to suspect. At any rate, he's presently under arrest."

"Then," she said, "that relieves my mind—and my conscience."

"In what way?" he asked, looking directly at her. But she was unfolding her serviette and laying it neatly across her lap. He couldn't see—or read—her eyes.

She shook her head.

He said, "If there's information you might have—if the woman in Singleton Magna is Margaret Tarlton, not Mary Mowbray—"

"No," she replied vehemently. "I won't make accusations and turn your policemen loose on an innocent person. That would be morally wrong!"

"Then why did the thought even cross your mind?"

The maid returned with a tray and two plates of a pale-green soup on it, the smell of lamb and white beans wafting to Rutledge, awakening his stomach if not his mind to enthusiasm. The sandwiches had been finished some time ago. She served her mistress and then the guest before filling his glass with wine. With a rustle of those starched skirts, she disappeared again into the kitchen.

"I—Margaret wasn't the kind of woman to have enemies. She worked for her living and knew the importance of being pleasant to everyone. If I had to stand before God in the next five minutes and answer to Him, I'd be hard-pressed to think of anyone who would deliberately want to harm her!" She picked up her spoon and made a pretense of using it.

But Rutledge was good at the same game. "Perhaps not. But what if someone saw a way of getting to you—through Margaret? I offer this, you understand, as an hypothesis."

She lifted her eyes, startled and wary, to his. There was something moving in the blue depths, and he suddenly knew what it was: jealousy.

"This was your suggestion, Inspector, not mine."

And it was the last he could get out of her on the subject.

But he knew whom it was she accused. The name hung between them through the rest of the meal, like a miasma in the air, heavy and fraught with a mixture of strong emotions: Aurore Wyatt.

For the first time since she'd come to greet him in the hall on his arrival, Rutledge couldn't have sworn, with any certainty, whether this woman was telling the truth—or lying.

9

They drove in silence through the night toward Singleton Magna, with Rutledge at the wheel and Elizabeth Napier by his side, wrapped in a light woolen cloak against the chill that had come with darkness. Her small leather case lay in the boot. A wind blew out of the west, and his headlamps picked up scatterings of leaves and dust as they swirled across the road. Shadows loomed black and indeterminate along the way, like watchers in mourning.

From time to time Hamish kept up a steady commentary on the issues in the case and the probability of Rutledge's skills coping with them. But he ignored the voice in his ear and kept his attention on the wheel and the two shafts of brightness that marked his way.

Once a fox's eyes gleamed in the light, and another time they passed a man shuffling drunkenly along the verge, who stopped to stare openmouthed at the motorcar, as if it had arrived from the moon. Villages came and went, the windows of their houses casting golden squares of brightness across the road.

Elizabeth Napier was neither good company nor bad. He could feel the intensity of her concentration, her mind moving from thought to thought as if her own problems outweighed any sense of courtesy or any need for human companionship before she faced the horror that lay ahead of her. He himself hadn't seen the victim. In place her body might have told him a great deal. The coroner had already done what he could, found whatever there was to find. The children had been Rutledge's priority, not the dead woman. Until now.

Then, as the first houses of Singleton Magna came into view, Elizabeth Napier stirred and said, "What was she wearing? This woman?"

He thought for a minute. "Pink. A floral print dress."

She turned to look at him. "Pink? Are you sure? It isn't a color Margaret wears—wore—very often. She likes shades of blue or green."

"Will you mind waiting at the police station while I send for Inspector Hildebrand? It's best if he makes the necessary arrangements." He smiled at her. "The sooner this is finished, the easier it will be for you."

She turned to him in surprise. "I thought you were in charge of this murder investigation?"

"I'm here to keep the peace between jurisdictions," he said without irony, and added, "My priority has been the search for the children. So far I've had other questions on my mind."

"Didn't you care about them?" she asked, curious.

"Yes, of course," he said testily, "but the problem has been where to look. Hildebrand has done everything humanly possible, with no results. I've tried to go in different directions. I've tried to ask myself, if they aren't dead, why haven't we found them? Did someone else see them at the railway station, or are they only part of Mowbray's wretched delusions?"

"Surely not? If he was so very angry, something set him off!"

"Precisely. That's an avenue I'll pursue next."

"And has it been successful?" She was interested, listening. "This rather different approach to police work?"

"I'll know when you tell me who the victim is—or isn't."

It took a constable half an hour to locate Hildebrand and ask him to come down to the police station. Once there he stared at Elizabeth Napier as if she had no business in his office at this hour of the night, and he said as much to Rutledge, his eyes wary and cold.

"Couldn't this wait until the morning? It's been a long day, and I'm tired."

"Miss Napier is Thomas Napier's daughter," Rutledge responded dryly. "I brought her here from Sherborne. It's late, yes, but I felt you should speak with her as soon as possible. Miss Napier, this is Inspector Hildebrand."

Hildebrand looked sharply at her. "Speak to her about what? Get to the point, man! Are you telling me she knows something about those children?"

Rutledge said, "It seems she may be able to identify our victim." He explained, and watched Hildebrand's face change as the man listened.

He didn't answer Rutledge directly but was consideration itself as he turned to Elizabeth Napier. Even in the dark cloak that hung to her knees, she seemed very small and utterly feminine. Lost in this masculine world of violence and dark emotions, where the dusty file cabinets and stacks of papers concealed the secrets and deeds of humanity's least fortunate. Outside the long windows, the shrubs dipped and swayed in the wind, like beggars imploring mercy.

"I'm truly sorry you've been brought into this sordid affair, Miss Napier. And for no reason. Inspector Rutledge hadn't seen fit to confide his intentions to me—or I might have informed him of a decision taken this same afternoon. Mrs. Mowbray was laid to rest shortly before six o'clock. There's no body to show you. The matter is closed."

His eyes slid to Rutledge's face, triumph in them. "In our minds, there was no question of identity—I discussed that issue thoroughly with my superiors and the rector at St. Paul's Church. And Mrs. Mowbray had no family other than her children. There was no reason to postpone the—er—decent interment."

There was a wild fury rising in Rutledge's throat, choking him. He wanted to take Hildebrand by the neck and throttle him.

It had been a deliberate and cold-blooded decision on Hildebrand's part, to make sure that his investigation wouldn't be undermined by what he'd clearly seen as Rutledge's interference.

Satisfied to see the sudden stiffness in Rutledge's face and the anger that surged, barely contained, just behind it, Hildebrand smiled tightly. "I took the liberty as well of consulting your superior in London. He was in full agreement."

Bowles. *Of course* the bloody man would agree!

And the one person who might have verified the identity of the dead woman was standing here, puzzled by an interaction she couldn't quite follow.

Elizabeth looked from one to the other. "She's been buried? But why? I must see her, I've come all this way!" She turned to Rutledge. "You've got to do something, Inspector!"

Hildebrand said, "Miss Napier—"

"No!" she told him firmly. "No, I won't be put off! Will you please tell me where to find a telephone? I must speak to my father, he'll know what I ought to do about this problem—" Her eyes filled with tears, and Hildebrand, who suffered agonies of uncertainty whenever a woman cried, never knowing what to do or say to stem the flood, and inevitably making things worse whatever he did, looked frantically at Rutledge.

This is your doing! his eyes accused.

Rutledge, still fighting against the anger burning inside him, said in a voice he himself hardly recognized, "How did you bury her? In the dress she was wearing when she was killed?"

Hildebrand stared at him as if he had lost his wits. "*Dress?* Good God, no! The rector's wife, Mrs. Drewes, offered to send the undertaker something, and—and the necessary undergarments. What's that to say to anything—"

"Then I'll see her dress," Elizabeth said, looking suddenly very tired and very distressed. "If you please?" The tears sparkled on her lashes, unshed but still threatening to fall, given any excuse. "I must have an end to this!"

Rutledge, angry as he was, heard Hamish admiring such a masterly performance. "Yon lassie's as useful as a regiment," he said, "though you'd no' think it to see the size of her!"

Hildebrand was replying doubtfully, "Miss Napier—are you quite sure that's what you want to do? At this late hour? It's not— there's *blood* over the front of it."

She nodded her head wordlessly. He took her arm as if afraid she might faint on the spot, already promising to ask the doctor to support her through the ordeal. Over her shoulder Hildebrand's eyes warned Rutledge to stay out of it. "You'll be at hotel, then?" he said.

For an instant Rutledge thought that Miss Napier was on the point of objecting, but she caught some nuance of tension in the air between the two men and said only, "Thank you, Inspector Hildebrand."

Rutledge grimly left him to it, still far too angry to trust himself. Instead he crossed to the Swan to wait in the lobby, Hamish already earnestly pointing out the unwisdom of tackling anyone about what had been done behind Rutledge's back.

"The man's no' one to see beyond what's clear in his mind. You must na' threaten his tidy view of yon murder. And he won't thank you or anyone for making him look a fool. If yon lassie from Sherborne tells him she has seen the dead woman's dress before, he will na' pay any heed."

"What is it you want?" Rutledge demanded silently. "Dead children—hidden in a place we may never find? Or their broken bodies brought in, to tighten the noose around Mowbray's neck? I came to find those children, and by God, after my own fashion, I think I have! And it's a conclusion to this investigation that I for one will find one hell of a lot easier to live with!"

"Aye, but Hildebrand's an ambitious man, and if you take away from him the one case that might ha' brought him a promotion, he'll no' forgive you for it. However many children you've spared! He'll no' care, except to see what's been done to him, and your hand heavy in it!"

Which was true. Even in his anger Rutledge recognized it. He made himself stop pacing the floor and silently responded, "It will be worse for him when the Napiers and the Wyatts begin to ask where Margaret Tarlton may have gone. And the search leads in the end to that new grave."

"Aye, but that's to come—and who's to say that it will? Who's to say that Margaret Tarlton is na' in London or any other place that takes her fancy? Who's to say she did na' want this position and went off to think about it? Hildebrand's not likely to blame himsel' if trouble does come home to roost. He'll find a scapegoat. Mark my words!"

"If I back down, and Hildebrand has his way," Rutledge said, "there are still the children's bodies to find. And the black mark

81

will be against me, for that failure. Even though I don't think they're out there."

"It's your reputation in the balance, aye. Your choice of roads. But once you walk down it, there's nae turning back."

Rutledge said nothing, his anger drained away, emptiness left behind. The self-doubt, still so close to the surface—of his skills, his emotions, his wits—seemed to gnaw raggedly at his patience. *"It's your reputation. . . ."*

Very soon afterward a distinctly wobbly Elizabeth Napier reappeared, with a solicitous Hildebrand on one side and a man who turned out to be the local doctor on the other. He was small and thin, with little to say, dragooned into service at Hildebrand's insistence. As soon as he had turned his patient over to Rutledge with a curt nod, he was gone without excuse or farewell.

Hildebrand led them into a small private parlor and then went out to find some brandy. One lamp was lit, and it offered only a funereal lifting of the gloom. Which seemed to match the mood of the room's inhabitants. Rutledge made no effort to turn on another and waited quietly for Elizabeth to speak. She seemed to be having trouble organizing her breathing.

"I lost my dinner," she said after a moment, touching her mouth again with a damp handkerchief. "Made a thorough fool of myself. I thought—I was sure all my long years of service in the slums had inured me to any horror. But all that *blood*!" An involuntary shiver ran through her. "What made it worse was realizing it might have belonged to someone I *knew*. I found myself imagining what her *face* must have looked like—that was the worst part!" She stopped, taking another deep breath, as if she were still fighting nausea. "I don't see how you can harden yourself to this sort of work!" she added after a moment, lifting wry eyes to meet his. "It must be wearing on the spirit."

He said, "Nothing makes it any easier. It helps, sometimes, to remind myself that finding the murderer is my pledge to the victim."

She said, "I don't expect I'll ever read or hear about a murder having been committed without picturing that dress in my mind!"

He gave her another moment or two and then said, "Can you

tell me anything—" He found he didn't want to ask Hildebrand that question.

She said shakily, "Dr. Fairfield took out the box with her clothing in it, and as soon as I saw it, I was sick. But I made myself go back, I asked them to unfold the dress for me." She swallowed hard. "You told me the color was pink!" she went on accusingly. "It's more a lavender rose, and of course I recognized it. Straightaway. The shoes as well. I'd seen Margaret wearing them just last month, when we went to the museum—" Realizing that in her distress she had probably said more than she meant to, she broke off.

He wondered if the purpose of a museum visit had been to refresh Margaret Tarlton's knowledge of the East, before she traveled down to Dorset.

When he said nothing, she went on, "Your Inspector Hildebrand thinks I'm out of my mind, but he's too worried about vexing my father to say it to my face."

"You're quite sure—about the dress and the shoes?"

Her eyes held his. "I can't lie to you. I may be wrong. But I'd be willing to swear, until you show me evidence to the contrary, that the woman wearing that dress must be—must have been Margaret."

"And as far as you know, Miss Tarlton had no connection with the Mowbray family?"

"If she did, I can't imagine where or how she came to meet them."

Hildebrand returned with a small glass of brandy. Elizabeth sipped it carefully, wrinkling her nose in distaste. But it brought a little color back to her face, if only because of its bite.

"I'll see to driving you back to Sherborne, Miss Napier," he was saying. "You've had a nasty shock, and I'm sorry. I hope you'll feel better when you're at home again. I ask your pardon for subjecting you to this ordeal. It wasn't, as I told you before, any of my choosing!"

She nodded, and somehow the chair seemed to envelop her protectively as she leaned back and closed her eyes. After a moment she handed the brandy glass to Rutledge and then stood up tentatively, as if expecting the room to dip and sway. She said to Hildebrand, "Inspector Rutledge put my case in the boot of his car. If you could arrange to have it brought to my room? I think it's best if I stay in Singleton Magna tonight. It's already quite late, isn't it?"

The Swan's manager was delighted to provide a room for Elizabeth Napier, offering to send the bill to her father. She waited patiently while the formalities were completed and then allowed herself to be led to the stairs. As they reached the graceful sweep of marble steps, she touched her temple with her fingertips, as though her head ached. Then she said, "Um—I—don't suppose anyone's called Simon? No, of course not, you still aren't quite ready to believe me, are you, Inspector Hildebrand?" She started up the first flight before he could answer her. Without looking back she added quietly, "Dear Simon, he's known Margaret nearly as long as I have. It would be better for all of us if I *were* wrong. But there's no way to undo what's happened, is there? If it should turn out that I'm right?"

Hildebrand said nothing, trailing her in silence.

Watching her, Rutledge was reminded of something his godfather had told him once about Queen Victoria: *"Small as she was, she moved with majesty."* The same could be said of Elizabeth Napier.

She knew, perfectly, what power was, and how to wield it. Few men could boast the same profound understanding. Rutledge wondered if she'd inherited her skill from Thomas Napier, or if it was natural, as instinctive as the way she held her head, as if there were a diadem balanced in her hair. It gave her, too, a semblance of the height she didn't possess.

"I must telephone my father. He'll want to know what's happened. But not tonight—I couldn't bear to go into it tonight!"

Behind her, Hildebrand grimly shook his head. Stubbornness was his shield. And in the end, it might prove to be enough.

The Swan's manager was fumbling through the keys in his hand to find the one he wanted, oblivious of the currents of emotion around him. In the passage outside her door, he offered Miss Napier everything from a maid to help her unpack to a tray of tea, if she felt so inclined. She accepted the tea with touching gratitude and was bowed into her room as the door was unlocked for her.

Leaving Hildebrand and the manager to see to her comfort, Rutledge went down to his car. Hamish had nothing to say.

By the time he'd delivered the small overnight case to her door, Hildebrand was also preparing to leave, and they walked down the stairs in a silence that was ominous. Rutledge braced himself for the storm that was certain to break as soon as they were out of earshot of the inn's staff.

Hamish reminded him that it wouldn't do to lose his own temper a second time. Rutledge told him shortly to keep out of it.

The storm was apocalyptic. After a cursory glance around the quiet, empty lobby, Hildebrand launched into his grievances in a tight, furious voice that carried no farther than the man opposite him. Among other things he wanted to know why Rutledge had seen fit to go to Sherborne on his own—and why the bloody hell the Napier name had been dragged into this sordid business without Hildebrand's permission. "I don't know where you learned of this Tarlton woman, or why you thought she was in any way involved, but I can tell you now Miss Napier is mistaken! My God, she was too shocked to know what she was saying!" he ended. "And when her father learns what's happened, do you know who will be to blame for this—this exercise in *futility*? *My* people! We'll be damned lucky if none of us is sacked! Thomas Napier, for God's sake! He makes or breaks far more important men than either of us, any day of the week!"

"Do you realize it will take an order from the Home Office to have that body exhumed?" Rutledge demanded harshly as soon as Hildebrand had paused for breath. "And now that there's doubt—"

"Whose doubt? Yours and whatever confusion you've sown in that young woman's mind? I hardly call that a positive identification, damn you!"

"It might explain," Rutledge retorted, "why we haven't found the children. Because there are no children to be found."

"They're out there! Somewhere! And when I find them—mark me, I *shall* find them, with or without your help!—I'll see to it that you're ruined! Whatever you were before the bloody war, you aren't half that man now. And it's time you realized it!"

He turned on his heel and left. In his wake Hamish was asking

"How was it Mowbray found her—yon Tarlton lass? How did *she* come to be walking on the road to Singleton Magna—the Wyatts would no' send her to the station on *foot!*"

Rutledge had considered that himself. On the long dark drive from Sherborne. During the shorter wait in the Swan's lobby. No answers had come to him. Not yet . . .

It had all gone wrong. He told himself that if his skills had slipped so far, he was better off out of Scotland Yard. That if he had seen what *he* wanted to see, and not the truth . . .

"Just because yon fine Miss Tarlton is na' in London and did na' arrive in Sherborne as expected does na' mean she's dead! What if she's gone to Gloucestershire, to tell her family she was moving to Dorset?" Hamish reminded him again and again. The words echoed in his head.

"Without troubling to telephone Miss Napier? Who recommended her for the position in the first place? I don't think it's very likely."

Rutledge could feel the dull ache behind his eyes, the sense of isolation and depression settling in. Fighting it, he walked out into the windy night, looked up at the stars pricking brightly through the darkness.

Damn Hildebrand!

Let it go, he told himself. He'll know soon enough if you're right. And London will hear soon enough if you turn out to be wrong. Sufficient unto the day . . .

Turning, he walked a short distance up the street, realized it was the way to the churchyard, and stopped. He had enough ghosts of his own, without invoking the murder victim's! Coming back to the inn, he looked up in time to see the curtains being drawn in the window of the top-floor room that Elizabeth Napier had taken.

She had brought her case with her because she expected to spend the night in Singleton Magna. What Rutledge hadn't known—but she must have considered from the start—was that she might wish to stay longer than just overnight. He'd overheard her quietly speaking to the inn's manager as she wrote her name in the register, asking if the room might be available for several days rather than just one night.

Whether she had really been sure that the dress and shoes belonged to the dead woman, only Elizabeth Napier could say with any truth.

But she was already looking ahead to anything useful that might grow out of her identification. Inside that fragile shell was a will as strong as steel. What Elizabeth Napier wanted, she was well accustomed to having, of that he had no doubt.

And he thought he knew her target. Aurore Wyatt's husband.

He'd have been willing to wager his life on that certainty.

10

In the early morning, before the town had begun to stir, Rutledge set out again for Charlbury, his mind occupied with how and what he wanted to say. And to whom. Clouds filled the sky, promising rain, and the heat had broken.

He arrived at the Wyatt home while the family was still at breakfast. The maid left him standing in the parlor, and he looked around him at the room. The furnishings were beautifully made and well polished, handed proudly from generation to generation. They were for the most part Georgian, though two of the tables had skirts to the floor and phalanxes of photographs in frames, in the Victorian style of never is too much too much. There was a large portrait over the fireplace, a man dressed in early Victorian black, looking much like a slim and intelligent Prince Albert. At a guess, this was the first Wyatt elected to Parliament. Hinted at in the dark background behind him were the soaring pinnacles of Westminster, as if he'd been painted standing on the bridge at midnight. The inference was both subtle and powerful.

Aurore herself came out to greet Rutledge, a questioning look on her face. Before he could speak to her, she asked if he'd care to join them for a cup of coffee. "Simon is just finishing his breakfast. He'll be happy to see you again."

Rutledge had his doubts about that. "Thank you, no. I wanted to ask you—what was Margaret Tarlton wearing the day she left for London?"

Aurore's face was a polite mask, as if another woman's apparel was something she seldom gave thought to. Rutledge would have wagered she could have described everything Margaret Tarlton had brought with her. He could count on one hand the number of women he'd met who were oblivious to other women's appearance and clothing.

She said, considering his question, "I spent most of the morning at the farm, as I told you when you were here before. I didn't return home in time to drive Miss Tarlton to Singleton Magna. She was wearing blue at breakfast, I remember that. It was very nice with her eyes, and there was a pleat of white in the skirt, to one side, like so." She demonstrated, pleating the soft cream skirt she herself was wearing. He could see what she meant. "But she went up to pack as I was leaving, and to change. She said it had been terribly warm on the train coming down, she thought she might prefer something lighter for the journey. I didn't see her after that. You might ask Edith. Our maid."

To pack. Where was this woman's suitcase? With her in Gloucestershire or buried somewhere in Dorset? Lost suitcases—lost children . . .

"How did she travel to Singleton Magna, if you had taken the only car?"

"I don't know. I assumed that Simon would make another arrangement for her. He had several workmen here, and there's the motorcar at the inn, belonging to Mr. Denton. Simon has borrowed it before. It wasn't impossible to find someone to take her so short a way."

"How many motorcars are there in Charlbury?"

"Simon's of course, which I seem to drive more often than he does these days. And we have a little carriage we use sometimes. That of the innkeeper. And the rector had one; his widow uses it now."

"No one else?"

"No," she said, then added dryly, "but the horse is not dead in the countryside, you know. There are far more carriages and carts and wagons than there are motorcars in a ten-mile radius. Even Dr.

Fairfield who comes to the village drives a buggy. That very fierce little man from Singleton Magna, with the face that looks as if he's bitten into a very sour lemon. If transportation was a problem, anyone in Charlbury would have been glad to take her. If only to please Simon. Why do you ask these things? They have nothing to do with the day that Margaret arrived."

She has a very clear memory for detail, Rutledge thought. What Margaret Tarlton might have seen, arriving on the same train as Bert Mowbray, had been his excuse when he had asked for her London direction.

"We don't know where Miss Tarlton went from Singleton Magna. She hasn't returned to her flat in London, and she failed to arrive at the Napier country home in Sherborne. They were expecting her there."

Her gray eyes changed as he watched. Anger—or was it resignation?—stirred in their depths. "Ah. Why does that not surprise me?"

"Did you believe Miss Tarlton was sent here as a spy in your midst?" he asked bluntly. She had nearly admitted as much before. It hadn't mattered then. . . .

"But of course! Why did Elizabeth Napier all at once have no further need of her services? Why, after nearly eight years with the Napiers, was Margaret prepared to come here?"

"It's the nature of women, sometimes, to look for a change. I don't know that Elizabeth Napier has been an easy mistress. Or Margaret Tarlton may prefer work that reminds her of growing up in India."

"But that's exactly the point, Inspector. The nature of women," she said. "Margaret is nearly twenty-nine years old. The age when a woman is reminded that if she's to marry, it must be soon. How many eligible young men would you say there are here in Charlbury?"

He caught himself wondering how old Elizabeth Napier was, and as if she'd read his mind, Aurore said, "Elizabeth was to marry Simon in 1914. But he asked her to wait, until the war was over. And when he came home from France, there was an unexpected impediment—his French wife. She has wasted five years. She will be thirty next month." The devastating honesty of the French.

Smothering a rueful grin, he said, "The point is, we appear to have lost Miss Tarlton. Possibly between Charlbury and Singleton Magna. It's my task to find her, I'm afraid."

"Then I cannot help you. She went upstairs to pack, and I went to the farm to see to the livestock. As I have already told you."

There was nothing else he could say, except, "I've kept you from your breakfast long enough. I'd like to speak to your husband before I go."

But Simon had already finished his meal and gone across to the museum, and it was there that Rutledge finally caught up with him. Looking up from the small sandalwood figure in his hands, Simon said, "I thought your business was with my wife? Look at this. Shiva dancing. Exquisite, isn't it? Even if I don't have the faintest idea who Shiva might be! I'll leave such erudition to my assistant."

"That's what brought me here, actually. Your assistant. I need to ask you who drove Miss Tarlton back to Singleton Magna, to meet her train."

"I thought Aurore had. Why? Does it matter?" He replaced the carving on its shelf and stood back to see if it was dwarfed by the figures on either side. He picked up one of its neighbors, the fanciful figure of a large bird in flight.

"Yes," Rutledge said, beginning to lose his temper. "Put that thing down and pay attention to me, man! There's a woman lying dead in a pauper's grave at Singleton Magna. I want to know if it could be Margaret Tarlton. And if it is, I want to find out who put her there."

"In a grave? That's nonsense!" He frowned. "Why should you think it's Miss Tarlton?"

"Mr. Wyatt, we can't seem to find Margaret Tarlton. She isn't in London, and she isn't in Sherborne, at the Napiers'. She was last reported to be here, in your house, on the point of leaving for her train. Nor have we located the Mowbray children, and that's the crux of our problem. It raises questions about the identity of the murdered woman. There's just a chance—an outside chance—that the body Hildebrand found in that field near Singleton Magna wasn't the Mowbray woman after all. If that's the case, we're going to have to start all over again. And I intend to start here!"

Simon shook his head. "Margaret Tarlton took the afternoon train back to London. She's most certainly not a murder victim!"

"Then, damn it, where is she now? And how did she get from Charlbury to Singleton Magna?"

"I've told you—I was busy in here, and it was already arranged for Aurore to drive her."

Rutledge swore under his breath. He knew that Simon Wyatt wasn't a stupid man. And yet he didn't seem to hear what was said to him, or register the gist of it. "Are you telling me that your wife is a liar?"

He suddenly had Simon Wyatt's full attention, clearly focused. "Aurore never tells lies," he said curtly. "If she says she didn't drive Margaret to the station, she didn't."

"Then who did? That's what I've come to discover."

The museum's outer door opened and a woman walked in, calling Simon's name. Rutledge, who could see the outer door from where he stood, recognized her at once. She'd been in the garden behind the inn, at the Women's Institute meeting. That white streak in her hair was distinctive.

"Hallo, Simon—" She stopped. "Oh, do forgive me, I didn't know you had a visitor! I was sure this young man was calling on Aurore. I'll come back later, shall I? Nothing important—"

"Inspector Rutledge, Mrs. Joanna Daulton. She's the cement that holds Charlbury together. Her late husband, Andrew, was our rector. He hasn't been replaced yet, and Mrs. Daulton has taken on his work as well as her own for nearly two years now. I don't know what we'd do without her." He smiled at her with more affection and awareness than he'd ever demonstrated when speaking of his wife.

Mrs. Daulton didn't pretend to modesty. She said only, "Well, someone has to do it, while the bishops make up their tedious little minds! How do you do, Inspector? Mrs. Prescott, who lives next door to Constable Truit, has already met you, I think. I've been looking forward to that pleasure as well." She held out her hand and he took it in his. A woman accustomed to social responsibilities and the burden of church duties that fell to her lot as the rector's wife, she was clearly comfortable in any situation.

"Thank you. It must have been your son that I saw the other day. By the church. He told me his father had been rector here."

Something moved in her face, a sadness that was beyond even her ability to deny. "Indeed? Henry was severely wounded in the last year of the war. But he's making wonderful progress; we're all quite pleased."

Was it a polite social response, the "I'm quite well, thank you" that can mean anything from blatant good health to one foot in the grave? Because if Rutledge was any judge, Henry Daulton's brain was permanently damaged. But then he was no judge of how far Daulton had come.

"I'm glad to hear it," he responded with equal politeness, then added, "Did you see Miss Tarlton during her stay in Charlbury? In particular on the last day of her visit?"

"No, I'm afraid I didn't—to speak to, I mean. As I was coming away from the Hamptons', she was at the gate in front of this house, standing there as if waiting for someone. Later Henry told me she'd rung the bell at the rectory, searching for me to ask if I might drive her in to catch her train. But before he could fetch me from the garden, she called out that Mrs. Wyatt had come after all, and she would go with her."

"What was she wearing? When you saw her at the gate here?"

"Oh—I remember thinking how wonderfully cool she looked, on such a warm day. A floral pattern, quite pretty. Mauve or pink or lavender, I'm not exactly sure. It was the overall effect I noticed, and the hat."

"Hat?" He remembered that Mrs. Hindes had mentioned a fetching hat. . . .

"Yes, a straw, with an upswept brim on the left side. Many women can't wear hats like that—I'm one of them! Aurore—Mrs. Wyatt—could, of course, and certainly Miss Tarlton does them justice. It's the height, I'm sure."

She herself was wearing a very conservative hat, in a medium shade of blue. It had an air of efficiency about it rather than style. She was a very efficient woman, Rutledge thought. In a courtroom she would make an unflappable witness, her words well ordered and to the point.

93

But if that indeed was Margaret Tarlton murdered in a field, where was her hat? Suitcases, hats, children . . .

"I'd like to ask your son if she was wearing her hat when she came to your door."

"May I ask why all this interest in Miss Tarlton's apparel?" She looked from Simon to Rutledge. "Is anything wrong?"

Besides being efficient, she was clearly no fool.

"Just a matter of routine. We're interested in everyone who arrived in Singleton Magna on the train last week."

"Ah, yes, that poor man who killed his family. I sometimes think the war has driven all of us into madness!"

Rutledge turned to Simon Wyatt. "You still haven't answered my last question."

Simon took a moment to remember. "No. Because I don't know how to answer it. I told you, I thought Aurore was going to take care of it. You'd better speak with Edith, I suppose. The maid. I'll see if I can find her for you. Mrs. Daulton? I'm sorry—"

"No, no. Come to see me when you have time, Simon, there's no hurry!"

Rutledge held the door for Mrs. Daulton and walked with her as far as the gate.

"What's this all about?" she asked him. "You were questioning Simon as if he'd done something wrong. I've known him since he was a child; I won't see him treated like a miscreant without knowing why!"

"It's just a matter of checking information, Mrs. Daulton—"

Joanna Daulton stopped and looked up at him, seeing more than he expected she might. "Young man, I'm not simpleminded, and I won't be spoken to as if I were. If there's anything that connects Margaret Tarlton to this wretched Mowbray affair, I suggest you ask *her* about it. Simon still has a great deal of work to do before this museum is set to open, it's all he thinks about. And if you want my advice, it's best to let him get on with it! The war nearly destroyed him, and I've never been so grateful as I am to that ridiculous grandfather of his for putting the notion of a museum in his head. It's brought Simon back from the edge of despair. Never mind whether it's a roaring success or not, it has stood between

Simon and self-destruction. I won't let you upset that balance, do you hear me?"

"We can't find Margaret Tarlton. We've looked in London where she lives and in Sherborne, where she was expected next but never arrived."

Joanna Daulton stared at him, and for the first time since she had walked into the museum he watched her grapple with something that was outside her usual experience as community leader. She seemed uncertain how to take him. "You can't find her? In the sense that you don't know just where she may have gone—or in the sense that she's missing?"

"That's our dilemma, actually. We aren't sure."

"Well, Aurore—Mrs. Wyatt—drove her to the station. I should think that's clear enough. Which means to me that Miss Tarlton left Dorset on the train. I should think London is a better place to start searching than Singleton Magna. I was always under the impression that the police knew their business!"

Rutledge said nothing. Hamish, hearing the exchange, said, "She reminds me of Fiona's aunt, Elspeth MacDonald. No man in his right mind crossed her!"

She opened the gate. "Do heed me, Inspector. Walk carefully where Simon's concerned. Don't upset him if there's no need for it!"

Rutledge watched her walk firmly up the street. Had she purposely—or inadvertently—sacrificed Aurore Wyatt to distract him from Simon? On the whole, he'd guess that it was on purpose. Mrs. Daulton's first duty was to the boy she'd watched grow up, not to his foreign-born wife. On the other hand, he told himself, she might feel that Aurore was far better able to protect herself than Simon was.

Edith was nervously waiting for him in the parlor, standing stiffly by the hearth as if the portrait at her back gave her moral support.

"I'm not here to badger you," he told her gently. "It's just a matter of what Miss Tarlton was wearing when she left here last week, on her way to London. Do you remember?"

Surprised at the simplicity of the question, Edith smiled. "Oh, yes, sir! It was a pretty dress, quite summery to my way of thinking! Rose and lavender, with a slim skirt and a belt of the same cloth. And a straw hat that had ribbons of the same colors around the crown. But that wasn't half as fine as what she was wearing when she arrived!" She stopped, her blue eyes alarmed. She had overstepped her bounds—

Rutledge said, "Yes, I'd like to know about that as well."

"It was this silvery gray silk, and it shimmered like cool water when she moved, and she had the most *wonderful* hat to match, the silk ruched down the brim, and a low crown. The only touch of color was this thin crimson ribbon tied in a bow and set to one side. I'd never seen anything quite so—so stylish!"

Had Margaret Tarlton come prepared to outshine the French bride?

"What luggage did she have with her?"

"The one piece, sir."

"Who drove her to the station in Singleton Magna?"

"Mrs. Wyatt was set to do it, but she was late, and Miss Tarlton was afraid she'd miss her train. So she asked if there was anyone else who might take her, if Mrs. Wyatt didn't come in time. But she must have, because I said I'd run down to the Wyatt Arms to ask Mr. Denton for the loan of his car and his nephew, Mr. Shaw, for Miss Tarlton, but he said his nephew was over to Stoke Newton with it, and when I came back, Miss Tarlton had gone."

"You think Mrs. Wyatt carried her into Singleton Magna, then?"

"I don't know, sir," Edith told him honestly. "But Mrs. Wyatt isn't one to forget what she's promised to do."

As Rutledge was leaving, Aurore came around the corner of the house, a basket of deadheaded flowers over her arm. She saw him and said, "Inspector?"

He turned to wait for her. Shielding her eyes against the cloudy brightness of the morning, she looked up at him. "I wish you to tell me what's happening. All these questions about Margaret. It makes me uneasy!"

There was a trowel in her gloved hands and a smudge of damp earth on one cheek. He found himself staring at it. "I don't know myself why I'm asking them," he said, surprising himself. "Every

96

time I think I'm a step closer to the truth, the concepts of what's truth and what's wishful thinking seem to merge, and there's only a muddle where there had appeared to be answers."

Because if Margaret Tarlton was wearing gray silk on the morning she arrived, how could Bert Mowbray have searched everywhere for a woman wearing pink?

Aurore reached out and touched his arm. "You will know what to do," she said. "However difficult it is. You have courage, you see. It's there, in the lines of your face. Suffering has taught you that."

He found himself wanting desperately to tell her about Hamish— and Jean. The words seemed to hover on the edge of his tongue, ready to spill over, wanting understanding—absolution—and afterward, peace.

Stunned by his unexpected and overwhelming reaction to her sympathy, he stood there, at a loss.

Hamish was warning him over and over to leave—*now! While you still have some measure of self-control.*

He thought for one dazed instant that the warm hand on his arm was lifting to touch his face. And he knew, helplessly, that it would be his undoing.

But she stepped back, that deep sense of stillness wrapping her again in her own untouchability.

Without saying good-bye, he turned and walked through the gate. He didn't remember turning the crank or starting the motorcar. He didn't remember driving out of Charlbury. It wasn't until he reached the crossroads that some measure of self-command overcame the turmoil in his mind.

Aurore Wyatt was a suspect in a murder investigation.

And she had been conscious of the effect she'd had on him. . . .

11

Rutledge sat in his car at the crossroads trying to shut out Hamish's voice. "Loneliness leads a man into folly," he was pointing out. "It's *loneliness* at the bottom of it. And she saw that, man, she's no' above using it. The notice of Jean's engagement's left ye vulnerable to such wiles—"

"It was natural—she's a damned attractive woman."

"Aye, and she's got a husband. Besides which, she's French."

Rutledge shook his head. As if being French explained a woman like Aurore. And yet, somehow it did. She knew more about men than was good for them. She saw deeper inside them. But her power was very different from Elizabeth Napier's.

He'd have to remember that.

He sighed and let in the clutch.

He tried to shift the subject in his mind as well, to distract Hamish from coming too close to the truth. And to distract himself from the feel of Aurore's hand resting so lightly on his arm.

What was he going to do about this problem before him? Was the dead woman Margaret Tarlton? Or Mary Sandra Mowbray?

"Aye," Hamish reminded him, "it's a proper puzzle, and if you canna' get to the bottom of it, no one else will!"

Still—did it truly matter, if Bert Mowbray had been the one who killed her, what her name actually was? Murder was murder. The identity of the victim was secondary. It didn't change anything. Death was quite final, and a man would be hanged as surely for murdering a nameless tramp as he would be for killing a peer of the realm. The only difference was in the public attention the trial would receive.

And yet Rutledge knew that to him it mattered.

A victim had no one in the law to speak for him or her. The police were bent on finding the guilty party. The courts were set up to determine guilt, and if guilt was proved, to offer sanctioned retribution for the crime committed. Prison or the gallows. Society was then satisfied by the restoration of order. *Civilized* order, where personal revenge and vendettas were foregone in the name of law.

Was that any consolation to the victim? Did it make up for the missed years of living?

When he himself had stood in the trenches, facing imminent death and seeing it reach out for him in a multitude of disguises, the concept of dying gloriously for King and Country had taken on a different image, a certainty of life ending in a shock of pain and sheer terror, with nothing left of the man he was or might be. Only a bloody ruin to be tumbled into a hasty grave if he was found—if not, lying where he'd fallen, obscenely rotting on the battlefield where even the crows dare not come for him. And in those months when he'd wanted to die, to bring the suffering to an end, he had thought longingly of what might have been . . . if there had been no war. Yes, he knew, better than most, what the dead have lost.

And where was Margaret Tarlton, if she wasn't lying in that grave?

It always came back to the children. Find them—or not—and he would have his answer. But you couldn't wish children dead, to solve a mystery.

Rutledge said aloud, "We've come full circle."

"Aye," Hamish said in resignation.

As he strode into the Swan, the young woman behind the desk called, "Inspector? Inspector Rutledge!"

He turned, and she went on, "A Superintendent Bowles in London has been trying to reach you. The message was, please contact him as soon as possible. He left his number for you—" She held out a sheet of paper.

He hesitated, not sure he was ready to speak to London. The young woman said helpfully, "You'll find the telephone in the cloakroom, just there."

It took ten minutes to put the call through and fifteen more for someone to locate Bowles. In the end, when Bowles finally called him back, Rutledge had prepared himself for a catechism.

Instead Bowles said loudly, as if compensating for the distance between Scotland Yard and Dorset, "Is that you, Rutledge? I'd like to know why Thomas Napier descended on me this morning, concerned about his daughter! What in God's name have you done to the woman!"

"I brought her from Sherborne to Singleton Magna last night. Hildebrand showed Miss Napier the clothing the victim was wearing when she was found. According to Miss Napier, the apparel belonged to Margaret Tarlton."

"Good God, haven't you found *her*? I thought she was in Sherborne."

"She never arrived there. I've located witnesses who place her in Charlbury, on the point of leaving to catch her train. I was just about to ask the stationmaster if he remembered her. Neither Simon Wyatt nor his wife seems to know who drove her to Singleton Magna."

There was an audible sigh at the other end of the line. "First the Napiers, and now the Wyatts. I told you not to tread on any toes!"

"I haven't." So far. He could foresee the possibility of it. . . .

"What's the Mowbray woman doing in Miss Tarlton's clothing, anyway?"

"It's quite possible the dead woman *is* Miss Tarlton."

"Well, get to the bottom of it, man! I don't see what the problem is! And Hildebrand's complaining that you're never around when he needs you, and I'm told the children still haven't been found. That was *your* responsibility! There may be no expectation of finding them alive now—but find them we shall! Do you hear me? What's taking so damned long?"

"The victim has been buried. With your permission, I'm told. If we don't locate Miss Tarlton, we have a dilemma."

There was silence at the other end of the line. "Are you saying you want that corpse exhumed?"

"It may be necessary—"

"No! I'll send someone to Gloucestershire, on the off chance the Tarlton woman's gone there. If she has, we'd look a fool, wouldn't we? There isn't a man in the picture, is there? Someone in London she may not want the Napiers to know about? I'll have Worthington ask her family about that, while he's in Gloucestershire. If she's not with them."

"I don't think London is at the bottom of this business."

"You aren't paid to think, you're there to find answers! And for God's sake, placate that Napier woman before her father comes down on the lot of us! Don't annoy the Wyatts either, do you hear me?"

There was a distinct sound of the receiver at the other end being slammed into its cradle.

Rutledge felt like doing much the same.

He found Peg, the chambermaid, and asked her to take a message to Miss Napier's room.

"Miss Napier left not ten minutes ago, sir. Someone brought a motorcar over from Sherborne, and she's being driven to Charlbury."

He swore, silently, as Peg curtsied and went on her way.

"Aye, you should ha' seen it coming!" Hamish said, commiserating. "But yon Frenchwoman addled your wits. You've no' been thinking straight all the morning, and see where it's got you! A tongue-lashing by auld Bowels, and that headstrong lassie slipping off to Charlbury the instant your back's turned, intent on meddling in this business."

"Making mischief isn't at the bottom of it. Elizabeth Napier still wants Simon Wyatt. The question is, to what lengths is she willing to go, if she thinks there's even an outside chance of getting him?"

"I've a feeling," Hamish warned, "that you'd best be on your way to Charlbury, to find out."

But Rutledge first went to the station to ask the master about Margaret Tarlton, describing her and the clothing she'd worn.

The man shook his head. "I don't remember a woman fitting that description taking the London train. There were three men from Singleton Magna going up that day, and two women who bought tickets to Kingston Lacey. I know them both by name. That was the passenger tally, according to my records."

"She may have taken the train south, rather than to London."

"I doubt it. Not that many people do, from here. I'd recall that. I'd recall her as well."

Rutledge thanked him, then walked back to the inn for his car. He might well need that exhumation order if Worthington came up empty-handed. . . .

Marcus Johnston, Mowbray's lawyer, was coming down the street toward him as Rutledge drove out of the Swan's yard. Just as he was about to make the turn for Charlbury, Johnston hailed him. "Any news? I've been trying to find Hildebrand to ask. But he's out in the field again, which tells me not to be sanguine." He came up to the car and put a hand on the lowered window.

"No. How is your client?"

Johnston took a deep breath, as if bracing himself to think about Mowbray. "Poorly. He forgets to eat, can't close his eyes more than five minutes, which says he's not sleeping. Distracted by whatever wretched scenes he's seeing over and over in his head. When I try to discuss his defense with him, he looks at me as if I'm not there. Damned odd feeling, I can tell you! According to one of the constables, you persuaded him to speak. I'm surprised."

"I was asking him about his children. He wanted to stop me, and the only way he could do that was to cry out."

"I should have been there!"

"With four or five people crowded into that wretched cell, he'd have been suffocated! I wasn't after a confession, I only wanted to know how much the children had grown. Since that 1916 photograph was taken. The flyer hasn't helped; I thought perhaps we could do something more."

Johnston shook his head. "I'm beginning to believe he's hidden them too well. It's unlikely, to my way of thinking, for a stranger in this town to find any place the local people don't know about.

And yet—" He let it go. "I went to the services for Mrs. Mowbray. I felt someone ought to be there besides the police and the undertaker. I don't like funerals. This one was worst than most. The rector didn't know what to say about the poor woman—whether she'd lived a blameless life or was no better than a whore. Which left him platitudes, most of them more apt for a sermon than a burial. No one wanted to mention the circumstances that had brought her there. Murder, I mean. I hadn't thought to bring flowers, and the ground looked appallingly bare and lonely when they'd filled in the earth. I suppose I ought to see to a simple marker—Mowbray certainly doesn't have the resources for it. I don't think he truly undertands that she's dead."

"And you were satisfied in your own mind that you knew the victim's identity? That it was Mary Sandra Mowbray?"

"Yes, of course!" Johnston said, surprised. "In a town this size, if anyone goes missing, there's gossip—and everyone hears about it. I daresay Hildebrand could have told you the instant he set eyes on her that the victim didn't belong here! A man like that knows the possibilties and can discount most of them on the spot, I should think."

"Even though her face was so badly beaten?"

"He's a good policeman. Thorough, dogged. And Mowbray made no secret of his intentions. The first order of business naturally would have been to bring him in and lock him up. Even I find it hard to deny the man's guilt; I can only hope to show mitigating circumstances. And even that's a damned narrow tightrope." He rubbed the bridge of his nose. "Anyway, if the woman had been someone else, it would surely have come to light by this time."

"What if a reliable witness informed you that the dress the victim was wearing belonged to another woman, not to Mrs. Mowbray?"

Johnston smiled, the tiredness in his face reflected in his eyes. "As Mowbray's barrister, I'd be delighted to hear it. As a realist, I'd ask myself why anyone would choose to lie about it." He took out his watch and opened it. "Good God, look at the time! I've another client waiting, I must go."

He walked away, and Rutledge looked after him, his face thoughtful.

The day was gray, humid. Farmers were out in their fields, a sense of urgency about them as they worked, as if they could smell the rain coming.

Charlbury, looking drab in the dull light, seemed unchanged, and yet there was something electric in the air as Rutledge drove down the street. He wasn't sure if that was his imagination or real.

There was another motorcar in the inn's side yard this morning, a stocky man in a dark uniform desultorily polishing the bonnet.

Instead of stopping there, Rutledge went directly to Constable Truit's house, getting out to knock at the door. That sense of pending catastrophe seemed to hold him in its grip as he waited for an answer. *It wasn't his imagination, it was something in the mood of the place.*

For the most part the streets were empty, and the gardens too. Doors were shut. He wondered how many pairs of eyes watched him from behind starched curtains. He could feel their stares, intent and waiting.

"They know," Hamish warned him. "They've already been told."

The second summons brought not the constable but his neighbor, Mrs. Prescott. He had seen the twitch of white lace curtains as she had looked him over before deciding what to do. Curiosity, he thought, had won over prudence.

"He's not to home," she said, standing in her door and leaning out to speak to him. "You won't find him here."

"Where is he?" Rutledge asked. By God, if the man had gone courting again—!

"His turn to lead a search party." She moved down onto the front step, and said earnestly, "Is it true then? Is that Miss Tarlton missing and given up for dead? I'd not like to think of two deaths so close to home in so short a time!"

"Where did you hear about Miss Tarlton?" Rutledge asked, though he knew full well.

"Miss Napier. She came to find the constable herself. And she was that upset to learn he'd already gone out. 'But it can't wait— it's been a week, that's enough time wasted!' she said. I could see her hands trembling, and her face was white, she looked about to cry. I brought her inside for a cup of tea, for she didn't want Mr. Wyatt to see her that way. Took a quarter of an hour to settle her down, poor soul."

Two masters at work, he thought. Mrs. Prescott intent on pulling the truth out of an apparently distraught woman, while Miss Napier was carefully sowing the seeds she wanted to bear fruit.

"Did she tell you what was wrong? Why she needed Constable Truit?"

"Oh, yes," Mrs. Prescott said, casting a glance up and down the quiet street. "She said her secretary, that was visiting the Wyatts, had disappeared. She wanted to know if I could tell her anything that might help. But I couldn't," Mrs. Prescott said, with simple honesty. "I never saw Miss Tarlton leave. Miss Napier, she asked me to make inquiries in Charlbury. Among my friends. To see if they had any word. And that's what I did." She paused, her eyes worried. "All Charlbury knew who she was—the Tarlton woman. She'd come to apply for that position at the Wyatt museum. They was in need of an assistant for Mr. Simon. A pretty young woman. Such lovely hair. I saw her when I carried a jar of my plum preserves along to Mrs. Wyatt. Why should anyone want to harm *her*?" It wasn't a question he could answer. Yet. She added philosophically, "Well, it gives busy tongues something new to wag about. We've nearly talked to death Mr. Simon's choice of wife and still nobody knows quite what to make of *her*."

He was furiously angry with Elizabeth Napier for giving the story her own peculiar twist. No association with Mowbray or his wife—no link with the body found outside of Singleton Magna. It was as if the two crimes—if there had indeed been a second murder—had been unconnected. As if there were still Miss Tarlton's dead body to find, well hidden in someone's bushes or back garden.

Small wonder the village had withdrawn behind closed doors!

Another search, this time turning Charlbury upside down. Delving into secrets that no one wanted to see exposed. Because there were always secrets—whether they had had any impact on the crime in question or not.

And Hamish had been right. Elizabeth Napier had adroitly outmaneuvered him, by coming here and starting her own rumors. By worrying her father and sending him directly to Bowles to complain of the police.

Hamish interjected, "Helplessness is a weapon that's hard to fight."

And Rutledge had no taste for playing the bully.

All right then, he'd see if he could undo some of the damage!

He said to Mrs. Prescott, "We don't know that anyone had a reason for wishing to harm Miss Tarlton. But Miss Napier is understandably concerned that her secretary can't be found, and she's taken it upon herself to initiate a search."

Mrs. Prescott sniffed. "What you're telling me, then, is just what she said you would. It looks bad for the police when there's two mysterious goings-on in one week! First that poor woman in Singleton Magna is killed, with her children. And now Miss Tarlton can't be found. Miss Napier says that that Inspector Hildebrand has all but told her she's making mountains out of molehills. But she won't give up. Not her. And I know Miss Napier from before the war, when she came to Dorset regular. She's not one to run about like a chicken with its head off! If she's alarmed, there's something to be alarmed about!"

Rutledge said, "There's no sign of foul play. For all we know, Miss Tarlton may well be visiting her family in Gloucestershire!"

"She's not," Mrs. Prescott said with conviction. "Miss Napier, she called them last night, and they haven't seen Miss Tarlton since she was down in July for her cousin's birthday!"

"Retreat while there's a way open," Hamish warned him. "She'll no' believe you, whatever you have to say."

Rutledge for once took his advice. After thanking Mrs. Prescott, he drove back to the inn, to leave the motorcar there.

The chauffeur of the other car looked up quickly as Rutledge came to a halt, as if expecting to see someone else. Thomas Napier, perhaps? He nodded politely once he realized that Rutledge was no one he knew and went back to his task of brushing out the interior. It looked spotless.

"Is that Miss Napier's motorcar?" Rutledge asked, getting out. It was a simple way to open a conversation. And the car was, he'd noticed, very like the Wyatts'.

106

"Her father's, yes, sir," the man replied warily. He was sturdy, in his midtwenties, and there were burns across his face and the backs of his hands. Rutledge had seen such wounds before, on airmen sent down in flames.

"Where will I find her?"

"My instructions were to wait for Miss Napier here. That's all I know."

Rutledge turned to look up the road toward the Wyatt house.

"I don't know what there is about this town," the driver said unexpectedly, coming to stand behind him. "It's—unfriendly. I wouldn't want to live here!"

"What's your name?" Rutledge asked over his shoulder.

"Benson, sir."

"I understand Miss Napier came here often in the past. Did you drive her?"

"No, that must have been Taylor. He's retired now. I was hired some six months back to replace him."

"Knew Margaret Tarlton, did you?" He caught himself using the past tense but let it go. He turned. If Benson noticed the slip, he gave no sign.

Instead he studied the man before him. "Who's asking?"

Rutledge told him. Benson nodded. "You must have been the policeman who came for Miss Napier last night! Yes, I know Miss Tarlton—I've driven her around most of London, on occasional business for Mr. Napier or his daughter. Always tries to be punctual and says she's sorry if she keeps me waiting."

"She was expected in Sherborne?"

"On the evening train. Miss Napier wanted the car most of that day and said she'd go along to the station herself to fetch Miss Tarlton. But she wasn't on the train."

"What did Miss Napier have to say to that?"

"She said something must have detained Miss Tarlton, and she'd want me to go back on the next day. But Miss Tarlton wasn't on that train either."

"Which day was it that Miss Napier met the train? And where did she go beforehand? Do you know?"

"Over a week ago, sir. Thirteen August it was, sir. I don't know where she went beforehand. It's often to Sherborne, when I'm not asked to drive her. But that's not to say it *was* Sherborne. Miss Napier just told me I'd have the day and the evening free."

Hamish stirred with sharpened interest.

It was on 13 August, in the late afternoon, that the murdered woman's body had been found outside Singleton Magna.

Rutledge said, "Does Thomas Napier ask you to—er—keep an eye on his daughter? He's a prominent man, and she seems to do some sort of charity work in the London slums. He must feel some concern about that."

"No, sir. He's never seemed to have a particular concern in that direction. It's Miss Tarlton he's always wanting to know about."

12

Rutledge walked up the road to the Wyatt house. Hamish, still mulling over Benson's last remark, demanded, "Why did you no' ask him what he meant?"

"Because Elizabeth Napier might question him, if she saw us there talking together. I'd rather bring up her father to her, not the chauffeur. Bowles might have been on to more than he realized, when he asked about a London connection—"

He saw Mrs. Daulton and her son, Henry, coming toward him. Mrs. Daulton paused to speak to him as he touched his hat, and said in her usual no-nonsense way, "You find the cat firmly ensconced among the pigeons, Inspector."

Was she using the term metaphorically? Or was she being careful not to say in plain terms what Henry might hear and repeat?

He nodded to Henry, who responded in kind.

"You're a policeman," he said, as if glad to have this straight. "I thought you liked old churches."

"As a matter of fact, I do," Rutledge answered truthfully. He'd always had an interest in architecture, thanks to his godfather. David Trevor probably knew more about any given British building than the men who had originally put it up. Stone and brick and wood were profession, passion, and pastime to him.

Mrs. Daulton was saying, "Miss Napier seems to believe something's happened to Miss Tarlton. She's quite worried, in fact. She came to see me before she went to speak to Simon. To collect herself before they met, I expect. I thought there might have been more to your questions than you told us earlier!"

"I don't know myself what my interest is in Miss Tarlton," he replied. "At first it was as a witness. That was true enough. Now she could be involved, in one way or another."

"You're right, young women of her class don't vanish into thin air. But I refuse to believe that there's a murderer loose who might slaughter all of us in our beds—three parishioners have already come to see me this morning with such a story. Apparently *they* had it from Mrs. Prescott."

"I don't think Charlbury is in grave danger," he agreed.

"Then you feel that that poor man in Singleton Magna's jail may have killed Margaret Tarlton—that he may have mistaken her for his wife."

"It's possible," he replied. She was an intelligent woman, one who was plain and uncompromising in her view of life.

"Then it's time I set matters straight. As my late husband would say, the sooner you scotch a snake, the better." She suddenly smiled, transforming her face, giving it an attractiveness and youthfulness that surprised him. "I do not, of course, refer to Miss Napier as the snake." The smile faded as she looked down the empty street behind him. "Still, you can see for yourself what suspicion and fear can do in a small place like this. Everyone is staying indoors."

Henry said, "The last time it was the influenza. Like a plague. Frightened everybody. I'd read about the plague at school." He frowned, then said, "I think I remember Miss Napier. From before the war."

"Of course you do," Mrs. Daulton said calmly. "You and Simon, Miss Napier and Marian were friends." To Rutledge she added, "Marian was my daughter. She died in childhood."

"She died of lockjaw," Henry put in. "It wasn't very pleasant."

In the brief silence that followed, Rutledge seized his opportunity. He said to Henry, keeping his voice on a conversational level, "Do you remember Miss Tarlton coming to the rectory last week? I expect she was looking for someone to take her to Singleton Magna."

110

Henry nodded. "She wanted to know if I could drive her. Or failing that, my mother. She said she didn't want to go in Denton's car."

With Shaw? Interesting! "How was she dressed? Do you recall?"

He smiled. "I don't know much about women's clothes, Inspector. It was summery, like flowers. I do remember her straw hat, though. I didn't much like it. Her hair was pretty enough without it." His eyes were clear, untroubled.

"And after that?"

"She went away. I think she was quite angry."

"Do you know why?"

"She said something about a train. She was afraid she might miss it."

Mrs. Daulton was gazing at her son with rapt attention, hanging on his words as if he were delivering the profoundest of answers, making her enormously proud of him. Rutledge found himself thinking, This man's tragedy isn't his, he doesn't know what he's lost. It's his mother's. His wounds are the death knell to any ambitions for him, and she can't accept it. She'll push her son as long as she can. She's another civilian casualty, like Marcus Johnston. . . .

She turned back to him. "Inspector, if you should want to speak with me at any time, leave a message at the rectory. I always check the little basket by the door." With a nod, she walked on. Henry followed.

Hamish said, "She's a strong woman. I think it did na' come naturally to her. It's there in her eyes. Long years of pain. Did you take note of it?"

"Yes, I saw it." But Rutledge's eyes were on the Wyatt house. He could just pick out the shape of someone in an upstairs room, looking out. He would have sworn it was Aurore.

When Rutledge stepped through the garden gate, he could hear voices from the museum, Simon's deeper tones, and then, as counterpoint, Elizabeth Napier's lighter responses.

He turned that way but glanced up at the window on the first floor. Yes. Aurore was standing there looking out, her face still, her body like a statue in its unyielding stance. And yet behind the stillness was not rigidity, nor was it tranquility. There was only an air of waiting. . . .

He knocked at the door of the museum, although it was open to the muggy air. Surely not, Rutledge told himself, very good for the hide puppets or the small, fragile wings of butterflies.

"Come in!" Simon called impatiently.

Rutledge stepped inside and found Wyatt with his guest in the second room. Elizabeth was holding a lovely sandalwood carving in her hand, this one of a god with an elephant's head, human foot lifted as in a dance, one arm raised.

"—Ganesh," she was saying. "I remember Margaret mentioned him as one of her favorite Hindu figures. And much nicer, I must say, than that ugly one with all the arms! Shiva, I think? The destroyer. Yes, that matches, doesn't it? You find yourself picturing death when you look into his face!"

"Rutledge," Simon acknowledged, over her head. "Have you any news?"

"No," Rutledge answered. "I've come to see what news Miss Napier has to tell me." He turned to her, waiting with polite interest.

She blushed, the rich color rising into her cheeks and giving her eyes a brightness. "You're absolutely right! I should have waited for you to come back to the Swan. But after I'd called Gloucestershire, I thought—I felt I had to tell Simon before that awful man Hildebrand took it into his head to come here, with no regard for anyone's feelings!" There was honest contrition in her face as she swung around to him. "I'm not accustomed to the way the police work. If I've done anything wrong, I sincerely beg your pardon, Inspector!"

Simon said, "You've not done anything wrong, Elizabeth. Don't let them harass you with their nonsense!" He added to Rutledge, "I can't understand why you didn't tell me your suspicions earlier! All that rubbish about what Margaret was wearing! Look, you don't think that maniac Mowbray got to her somehow?"

"How could he? She wasn't walking—she was, as far as I can determine, driven from Charlbury directly to the station at Single-ton Magna. If she had come across Mowbray on the road and he'd attempted to stop the motorcar, she should have been safe enough.

Whoever was driving the car would most certainly have gone straight to Hildebrand afterward, even if Miss Tarlton left on the train. And no such person has come forward."

Simon said, "It was Aurore who drove her. I don't know why she won't come out and admit to it! I asked her myself, as soon as Elizabeth told me what she thought might have happened."

Rutledge felt a wave of disgust. He knew how Simon, with his oddly abrupt, unfeeling manner toward his wife, must have confronted her, making her feel she had been directly accused. . . . *Why have you been lying about this? I'd think it would be better to come straight out with the truth—everyone knows it was you who drove Margaret. . . ."*

"Perhaps she didn't take Miss Tarlton to the station after all," Rutledge replied in her defense, before he could stop himself. His task was to determine guilt, not innocence. But he refused to watch possible innocence trampled.

There was a brief silence.

"I suppose someone else might have driven her," Simon agreed reluctantly. "There are other motorcars in Charlbury. But Aurore promised me she'd see to it. And it isn't like Aurore to lie. I don't understand this, any of it!"

Yet he had told Rutledge earlier that Aurore never lied. . . .

"I think it's too early to go on witch hunts," Elizabeth put in, her voice appealing for reassurance. "Margaret's missing. It—it doesn't actually mean she's—dead. I don't know where she might have gone. Do you?"

"Perhaps your father might know her whereabouts," Rutledge countered, not allowing himself to fall into the neat trap she'd set— expecting him to bring up the dress she'd identified the night before.

There was darker color in Elizabeth Napier's face this time, then it drained away as quickly as it had come. "I asked him myself this morning. He thought she was with me. He was understandably upset that she'd been missing a week and no one had realized it. He likes Margaret, I think everyone does. She's one of the most dependable people I know. That's why her position was so important."

"Then why did she choose to apply for the position here?" Rutledge asked. "Just because some of the things in this room remind her of India? I'd say at a guess that many of them come from other places in the East. Java. Burma. Perhaps Ceylon or even Siam."

"It's much the same culture," Simon impatiently pointed out. "Buddhism. Hinduism. The same *roots*. Margaret told me that herself. What are you doing to find her? Do you have men out looking? Has anyone spoken to the stationmaster in Singleton Magna?"

"I went to see him this morning," Rutledge answered. "And men are searching the same ground two and three times, looking for the Mowbray children. If she's out there, one of the teams will find her. Somehow I don't think they will." His glance moved on to Elizabeth. Let her tell the rest of that story, if she felt so inclined— that the body had already been properly buried. "Now if you'll excuse me, I'd like to find Mrs. Wyatt. Is she at home this morning?"

"Yes, yes, just go around to the house," Simon told him. "And I want a report, Rutledge. What's being done, how you're handling this situation. I still have connections in London. I'll use them if I have to."

"There won't be any need for that," Rutledge said. "The police are quite good at what they do. It's a question of time. That's all. Miss Napier."

He turned and left, irritated by the implied threat.

Aurore must have seen him coming back toward the house from the museum because she was there at the main door as he came up to knock.

"It isn't a very fine morning, Inspector. And so I will not wish you one. Is there any news?"

"I'm afraid not. I'd like very much to talk to you," he said. "But not in the house or the garden. Will you walk with me? As far as the church, perhaps?"

She smiled wryly. "While all those faces are pressed against their windows, wondering if you will arrest me on the way back? Yes, I know what is being said! I can feel it. Charlbury is both titillated and scandalized by this affair. What is that novel one of your famous authors has written about the French Revolution? Where the old women sit by the guillotine and knit as the heads of aristocrats fall into baskets? Except here it is not knitting, I think. It is the face that is just behind the lace of the curtain, each breath stirring it with anticipation!"

"I saw you standing behind a curtain. As I came up the walk," he said.

She smiled. "So I was! Allow me to find my sweater, Inspector!"

She was back in only a moment, as if she'd had it close to hand. They walked out of the house and turned through the gate toward the churchyard.

"I apologize for such stupid bitterness!" she told him, as if there had been no interruption to their conversation. "It is not like me. But Elizabeth Napier is a woman one cannot defend herself against. She uses innuendo like a sword. But then I must remember that I have robbed her of the man she wanted to marry. It is the most unforgivable thing one woman can do to another."

"I think she's worried about Margaret Tarlton."

"Is she?" Aurore turned her head and looked at his profile. "I am glad to hear it. I thought she was worried for Simon."

He smiled down at her. "Touché. A little of both. With Elizabeth Napier, as I am fast learning, there are no absolutes."

She laughed, a deep, brief chuckle.

"You are an extraordinary man," she said. "Are you married?"

"No." It was uncompromising. She read more into it than he intended.

"No," she repeated softly. "It explains much. Now—you wished to speak to me?" She pulled her sweater a little more closely about her, as if as a shield.

"Everyone seems to believe—although so far I've not found one of them who actually saw you!—that it was you who drove Margaret to the station. And therefore, in their view, you're the person who should know whether she got there safely or not. I spoke to the stationmaster. He claims she didn't take either train from Singleton Magna on the day she left Charlbury."

"But I have told you. I was with a heifer that was sick. Whatever Simon may say, we can't afford to lose livestock—Simon is pouring every penny he possesses into this museum. There was not a great deal of money to start with. His inheritance from his father was quite small. And it is this farm that will pay for our food, our car, our clothes. Not his grandfather's treasures."

115

She matched him stride for stride, comfortably walking beside him. And he was a tall man. They had nearly reached the churchyard.

She said, stopping him with her hand outstretched as if wanting to touch him, then deciding against it, "Do you think I am lying to you, Inspector?"

He had never felt his soul stripped so bare by the eyes of another person. It was as if she searched into depths he himself had never plumbed.

"I don't know. But I shall make it my business to find out." He studied her face in his turn, then asked, "Did you drive Margaret to Singleton Magna, quarrel with her, and put her out along the way? Where Mowbray then came across her, walking? No one would blame you for that, you couldn't have known. This might explain to us how Mowbray got to her. And bring an end to all these questions."

She bit her lip. "I would be morally responsible. But you are playing fair with both of us, are you not? To ask? Very well, I will make a pact with you." Her eyes smiled suddenly, with the humor of it. "A pact with the devil, if you like."

"I can't make promises—"

"This one is not a promise. It is a pact. There is a difference. Even I know that difference, in English." She searched his face again and then said quietly, "If you come to the conclusion after your investigations that I have lied about where I was when Margaret Tarlton left Charlbury, if you believe that there is any possibility of my guilt in any harm that may have come to her, then you will face *me* and say such things. Directly. You will not speak first to Simon— nor to Elizabeth Napier, nor to that policeman in Singleton Magna. Do you agree?"

"Are you telling me—"

"No, I am not telling you I have killed Margaret Tarlton. Of course not! But suspicion is a very ugly thing, Inspector, and it destroys both the innocent and the guilty. Sometimes there is no way, afterward, to make right the damage that has been done. If I am to be accused of any crime, I prefer to have it said to my face, not whispered behind my back. Can you understand this? It is not so cruel."

"You're trying to protect someone, is that it? Simon?"

Her mouth turned down wryly. "I am protecting myself, I think. I don't know. But yes, Simon too—this museum must open in one month. It is not the best publicity, do you think, to have it said that the owner's wife is a murderess? People will come out of morbid curiosity, and I could not bear that. I do not think our marriage could survive that. And so I look for a solution of sorts."

"I don't know," he said, trying to make sense of her words, "what you are asking of me—"

She shrugged, that very Gallic gesture that could mean so many things. "Call it intuition, if you like. Or a sense I cannot explain. But I shall tell you this. Where Elizabeth Napier is concerned, there is no question of right or wrong in this matter. She is looking for simple justice. That is for herself, not for Margaret. And justice is sometimes blind. So—I make my pact with you. And try to spare my husband pain, if I can."

Holding out her hand as a man might do, she waited for Rutledge to take it. But deep in his mind Hamish was already coming to another conclusion.

"She's afraid," he said softly, "because there is something she knows and canna' tell. Hildebrand would no' stand for this nonsense—"

Was it that, Rutledge wondered, or the fact that she was sure she could reach him—and so was using him to protect herself by putting on him the onus of betraying her? Using him as Elizabeth Napier was using Simon Wyatt?

"Aye. A woman does na' think the way a man does," Hamish told him.

But Rutledge had made up his mind.

He took the hand she held out and shook it briefly. "Agreed," he said.

And watched the play of expressions across her face. Surprise. A certain wariness. Relief. At the last, a flare of fear.

As if she realized, suddenly and far too late, that perhaps she had misjudged him. . . .

Rutledge walked back to the gate with Aurore Wyatt without speaking. She had slipped into a silence all her own, as if she had

117

forgotten the man beside her. Her face was withdrawn, her eyes shuttered behind the long lashes.

They could hear Elizabeth Napier's voice, and Simon's. Not the words so much as the comfortable rise and fall of a conversation between two people who had much in common. Long years of understanding, respect—love . . .

Aurore said, tilting her head to listen, "I knew when Margaret Tarlton came here to apply for the position of assistant that one way or another, she would bring that woman back into our lives. I was right. Only I didn't see the way of it. Just that it would happen."

"He married you. That's what matters." As Jean would never marry him. It was finished. But then, as Hamish was busy reminding him, Rutledge himself had been the last to let go in that relationship. Why should Elizabeth Napier be any different? If the war years had changed him so much, taking Jean from him, they had also cost Elizabeth Napier Simon Wyatt. Simon too had changed. . . .

"Yes, he married me. But I ask myself sometimes, was it the war? Was he sorry for me and what had happened to me? Was it loneliness, or a man's need for a woman? Or was it truly love? I thought I knew. Then. Now I am not as certain as I once was." She put her hand on the gate, ready to open it and go inside. "Please. Find that woman. Find her soon. For Simon's sake!"

And she left him standing there, watching her graceful stride as she went up the walk, ignoring the voices that seemed to ignore her so completely.

13

There was one other stop Rutledge wished to make in Charlbury. The inn. It was the pulse of village life, oftentimes the place where gossip and conjecture made their first rounds. The question was, would Denton tell him what was being said, or as the outsider would he be shut out of knowledge any villager might be given for the asking?

Nodding to Benson, who was still polishing the boot as if he had nothing better to fill his time, Rutledge stepped into the Wyatt Arms. He saw that Denton's nephew, Shaw, was sitting at a table alone, an empty pint glass in front of him, idly tracing one finger through the rings left by other pints. He looked up, recognized Rutledge, and said, "Why in God's name couldn't you have told me that Margaret Tarlton was missing! Damn it, I had to hear it from that Prescott bitch!" The words were slurred, but behind them was deep anger.

"I didn't know, when I was here yesterday, that she *was* missing."

"Then you're a damned poor policeman! God, it's been over a *week*!"

"How did you come to know her?" Rutledge pulled out the empty chair across from him and looked around. There was no one else in the shadows of the small room, but he could hear voices from the bar, down the passage.

"Not from Charlbury, if that's what you're asking."

"Then where? London?"

"That's right," he answered grudgingly, as if the alcohol in him wanted to talk and the reticence of the man tried to hold on to silence. "I was on a troop train, on my way to the coast. She was one of those women offering hot tea and sandwiches as we came through. I didn't even know her name! Just that she had the loveliest face I'd ever seen." He frowned. "I took it to Egypt with me. I thought, if I die, at least I've seen her—touched her hand. And if I live, I'll find her. Call it a promise to myself. . . ." A bargain with fate.

Rutledge looked away. How well he knew what bargains might be made with fate. To keep a man alive one day longer, one battle longer . . .

"Or come between a man and wanting to die," Hamish reminded him.

"Two years later I was back in London. Sooner than I'd expected. Shipped like a sausage, strapped to a stretcher, out of my head most of the time. A fever, no one, least of all the doctors, could decide what it was or how best to treat it. They sent me home to die. But I was one of the lucky ones, it burned itself out. The first day they let me stand on my feet, all I could think of was getting back to that railway station, finding her somehow. A fool's dream, that!"

"She must have spoken to a hundred men on each train. It's not very likely she'd remember one of them in particular."

"No, you've got it wrong! There was a benefit performance at one of the theaters, and I didn't want to go, but a friend wouldn't take no for an answer—and there she was, sitting in one of the boxes across from me! I couldn't tell you, if my life was on the line, what the program was about. There was a woman singing, Italian arias or something. I thought she'd never finish! At the interval I managed to speak to Margaret. It took some doing to separate her from her party, but I wasn't about to lose her a second time!" There was an echo of triumph in his voice and a lift to his shoulders, as if the memory were still alive in his mind.

Rutledge waited. Silence was sometimes more effective than a question.

"I'd talked to her that day about Canada—how it was out there. I don't know why—it seemed to catch her imagination, and I was afraid she'd move on to the next window if I stopped. I told her about the place where a group of us were planting apple orchards on the slopes facing south and how we'd built the long irrigation lines, wooden troughs, but they worked. How the high peaks were heavy with snow, even into May. Whatever came into my head, to keep that look on her face! The first thing she said to me at the theater was 'Hallo, you're the man who lives with grizzly bears and elk!' "

He stopped, frowned at his empty glass. "I've lost count," he said. "I've muddled the rings too. Can't depend on 'em anymore." Looking up, he said, "You aren't drinking. Why not?"

"I'm on duty," Rutledge reminded him. "What happened after the theater?"

"I escorted her everywhere she'd let me. Riding one day, tennis another, dinner—any excuse to be with her. I was falling in love with her. What I didn't know, couldn't judge, was whether she cared for me. Or if I was just an available man when she needed a presentable escort, someone with both legs and two arms, who could dance with her. The doctors raised hell, they said the pace I was setting was getting in the way of my recovery. I didn't care. The longer I was in England, the happier I was!"

Denton came in. "I heard voices," he said, looking from Shaw's strained face to Rutledge's. "Thought it might be custom."

"No, it's all right, Uncle Jack."

Denton nodded and left. After a moment, Shaw said, "I'd have married her. But she wasn't interested in living in a wilderness, no matter how beautiful or exotic it might be. She'd grown up in India. 'I don't want to be exiled again,' she said. 'Not if I can help it!' " He managed, somehow, to capture the light tones of a woman's voice. And a subtle hint of selfishness, as if Margaret Tarlton didn't mind how she might have hurt him.

It was the first real glimpse Rutledge had had of the missing woman.

"I asked her—*begged* her—to tell me if there was another man,

121

and she shook her head and kissed me and said I was being silly. But there *was*. I could see his eyes following her. I could see the look on his face when he came into a room and she was there. God, he was a mirror of what I was feeling! And I was stupid enough to confront her with it. The day before I was to sail. She wouldn't see me afterward, wouldn't answer my calls or my letters. It was—that was the last time. When I was sent home again, half my guts cut away, I knew it was finished. How could I go back to her—how could I even tell her I was alive?"

Hamish had stirred, already sure of the answer.

More sure than Rutledge was. "Who was the other man?"

Shaw grimaced, as if the tension of the last ten minutes had brought back the pain in his body. His arms were lightly clasped around his middle, to hold it in. He seemed completely sober now, eyes dark circled and heavy ·with memory, a man with only a past and no future.

"Thomas Napier. If he hadn't had a daughter a year older than she was, I think he'd have married her himself. He wanted her badly enough! It was there, raw and hot, sometimes, when I'd bring her home and we were laughing, clinging to each other as we made our way up the steps, more tipsy with excitement than wine, but how could he know? When I saw her getting out of the Wyatts' motor-car last week, I thought for one horrible instant she'd come looking for *me*! Out of misplaced pity or duty. But Mrs. Prescott soon put an end to that rash hope. She mentioned to Denton that it was the museum that had brought Margaret. Something about coming here as Simon's assistant. Besides, there was no way she could have known I was here. Very few people do!"

"Did you speak to her, before she left Charlbury?"

"God, no! When I can barely stand straight, even now, without all the fires of hell lit in my belly? I've got some pride left, damn it! She wouldn't have me before. What could I say that might have changed her mind now?"

"She wasn't married to Napier, for one thing."

"No." Shaw looked at the dark ceiling, where the beams wore a collection of polished horse buttons. Studying them as if they were more important than anything he was thinking or feeling. A bitter concentration.

"There's the other side of it as well—she was considering moving here, leaving the Napier household for another position."

Shaw laughed, a rough, hollow sound. "She'd have to, wouldn't she, if she was planning to marry him? Margaret has been Elizabeth's secretary for years. Not Napier's social equal, that. But if she were here, under Simon's wing, she'd be safe enough from gossip. People wouldn't be so fast to jump to ugly conclusions. That's the sort of thing Margaret would think of. She must have known very well how to handle him. It was Elizabeth who stood in the way."

His mind occupied on his way out of Charlbury, Rutledge almost missed the woman standing by the road clearly hoping to catch his eye.

She was wearing a faded housedress, the blues nearly gray now, and her hair was pinned back stringently, as if it were being punished for trying to curl in the dampness. Was she one of the women he'd passed on the street? He couldn't be sure. She'd have dressed differently, going to market.

Rutledge pulled over and said, "Were you looking for me?"

"Aye! You're the policeman from London, they say!"

"Inspector Rutledge. Yes." Behind her, in the doorway, he could see three small children peering out with large, sober eyes. Whatever it was their mother wanted, they'd been told to stay out of the way and make no noise. Or the policeman would get them? It was a threat used often enough in some quarters of London, to keep children quiet. "Be'ave now, or I'll fetch the copper on yer!"

The woman nodded, then hesitated, as if reluctant to give her name. But they were just outside her house, with paint peeling around the windows and a look of shabbiness about the roof where it needed rethatching. He could find her again, easily. She said, "Hazel Dixon. I heard tell you was looking for information about that woman guest at the Wyatts'. How she left Charlbury on the fifteenth."

Hamish stirred, and Rutledge tried to keep his own expression bland. "That's right." Let her tell it in her own way, or she might change her mind. . . .

Suddenly there was a hot intensity in the pale blue eyes watching him. "It was her. Mrs. Wyatt. I saw the car. Going on toward noon, it was, two days after that Miss Tarlton came here. I heard the motor and looked out my window, and I saw it passing, in the direction of the crossroads and Singleton Magna."

"Could you see the driver?" he asked. She would have been on the far side of the car, as he was now.

"Well, it was *her*, wasn't it? She's the one drives the car! Mr. Wyatt, he don't care to drive himself, he's used to having people at his beck and call. I've seen her, with a scarf blowing out like some banner announcing her! And the men too, turning to look, wanting in their eyes. It's indecent, lustful! Most of 'em, including my Bill, know what she's like. They was in France and those women had no men of their own, I *know* what went on! My Bill didn't learn to—"

She stopped, this time with a rising flush. She hadn't meant to say such things, she'd allowed herself to be led on by his way of listening.

There were shadows, moving a little, behind the children, and Rutledge realized that other women—at least two? he thought, possibly three—were in the dimly lit front room, moral support for her confession but not intended to hear whatever it was that Bill had—or had not—been taught by any Frenchwomen he'd encountered abroad.

It was a common enough anxiety of wives in wartime. That men far from home, fighting a war against loneliness and fear as well as the enemy, might have found comfort of a sort in the local women. And picked up disease or new tastes. The music halls were filled with jokes and songs about the French.

"It was her!" she repeated fiercely. "I'd swear to it!"

"Was there anyone in the motorcar with her?"

Mrs. Dixon bit her lip. "I saw something rosy—with lavender in it! Must have been that Miss Tarlton. Well, it stands to reason! Who else would have been in that car with Mrs. Wyatt!"

But he thought she might be lying now. Had she seen Margaret Tarlton at the Wyatt gate and known what she was wearing? Or was she so determined to indict Aurore Wyatt that she was piecing together bits of information garnered from the other women listening and invisible inside her house? "What kind of hat was Miss Tarlton wearing?"

Mrs. Dixon stared at him. Then she said, too quickly, "The way that Mrs. Wyatt drives her husband's motorcar, you'd be a fool to wear a hat! It'd be blown off your head before you was out of Charlbury!"

And it was true, as Hamish was busy pointing out, that Aurore herself hadn't been wearing a hat the first time Rutledge had seen her. But he couldn't recall if there had been one in the seat beside her. . . .

"They say that that Miss Tarlton's missing. What do they think's become of her?" Mrs. Dixon asked, unable to stop herself. Curiosity was driving her now. "That man in Singleton Magna, he's already killed his wife—"

"We want to locate Miss Tarlton because she arrived on the same train with Mowbray. She might have seen him, or his family."

"They say he killed his children!" She shuddered, caught up in her own fears, glancing over her shoulder uneasily. "I've kept mine close, I can tell you, since I heard of that."

"I don't believe you have anything to fear from him now. He's in custody."

She turned to go. "I saw that Miss Tarlton the day she came. I was along to my sister's house. If I'd stolen another woman's husband, like *some* I know, I'd not want such a pretty face at *my* breakfast table! Tempting fate all over again, that's what it is. And Mr. Simon already regretting his choice!"

"Regretting? What do you mean?" It was sharper than he'd intended.

But Hazel Dixon wouldn't be drawn into that topic. "I've said enough. I saw the car, and Mrs. Wyatt in it! And that other woman. If that's any good to you, I'm glad!"

Rutledge thought as he let off the brake that Elizabeth Napier's presence in Charlbury was bearing its bitter fruit. In a village already rife with speculation about Simon's wife, rumor had spread from house to house, and Hazel Dixon, encouraged and supported by her friends, was now casting the second stone at Aurore Wyatt.

She wouldn't have spoken out if the village had maintained its wall of silence, an undivided front. Elizabeth Napier, breaking the seal by openly showing her anxiety over Margaret Tarlton's disappearance and allowing the bloody events of the Mowbray murder to find their way—even if topsy-turvy—into the story, had already shadowed Simon's mind with doubt. And as if by osmosis, the Hazel Dixons of Charlbury had picked up the strong scent of distrust and were emboldened to strike out.

He was never sure how such things actually worked in a village. But work they did.

Aurore had been absolutely right. Seeing her in his company, even for so brief a time, had fed the hungry maws of gossip.

Hamish, from his accustomed place deep in Rutledge's mind, asked, "Are you sae certain, then, it's gossip and no' the truth?"

Constable Truit still hadn't returned from the search party he'd been summoned to join. Tired of waiting for him, Rutledge left Charlbury and halfway back to Singleton Magna made up his mind.

It began to rain long before he reached London, and the streets were shining with wet, the trees drooping heavily, when he found the house in Chelsea that he was looking for.

It was small, with a narrow porch, silk drapes crossing the windows and on the steps pots of geraniums in a shade that complemented the brick. Even in the dull light it possessed a decided charm. At the same time it wasn't a house that a young woman on her own could afford. Unless there was money in the family to draw on.

The maid who answered the door was small and dark, with Welsh ancestry in her round face. But her voice was pure London. Rutledge told her who he was. She led him into a small parlor attractively decorated with rosewood furnishings, a French carpet, and pre-Raphaelite prints on the walls. He recognized several of them. Either Margaret Tarlton liked the romantic aura they represented, or she knew its value as a setting. And yet, oddly, he hadn't imagined her as a romantic. Was Thomas Napier? Sometimes men of power and prestige had buried in them a streak of the quixotic when it came to their preferences in women.

The maid offered him a chair and stood before him in her stiff

126

black dress, hands cupped in front of her, feet together, like a child anticipating a reprimand. Worry drew her dark brows together and her face was strained, tired. He asked her name. It was Dorcas Williams. She had been employed as a second parlor maid by the Napiers before coming here to work for Miss Tarlton.

"I don't know what I can say, sir! Scotland Yard has come twice, and still there's no word from my mistress—I've told them all I can think of. There's no news?" she asked diffidently. "Mr. Napier has been here this morning, asking!"

"Not yet. The fact is, I'm more interested in Miss Tarlton herself. Sometimes in searching for someone who's gone missing, it helps to know more about the person. We have a better feeling for where to look."

"Yes, sir." She regarded him expectantly, as if prepared to cooperate in any way. But behind her eagerness, the shadow of fear still lurked.

"Let's begin," Rutledge said as if it had just occurred to him, "with her work for Miss Napier. Did she like what she did—did she get along well with her employers?"

"She liked her work well enough," the girl answered willingly. "She was good at it, at organizing. Seeing to flowers and caterers and invitations being printed—finding the right musicians. Writing thank-you notes. Sometimes she'd say, 'You'll never guess, Dorcas, who's coming to the luncheon on Thursday!' " She smiled. "Oftentimes I'd get it right too!"

"There was nothing she disliked about her work?"

The smiled faded. "I've heard her say she didn't want to spend a lifetime planning parties in the houses of other people."

"Did she get on well with Elizabeth Napier?"

"Yes, sir. Mostly. I think—I think there was some disagreement over her changing jobs. But I didn't understand the rights of that. Miss Tarlton, she didn't want it to be Dorset, and Miss Napier, she said it was just the thing."

"Why was she against going to Dorset? Do you know?"

"No, sir." Her face creased with the effort to remember. "I don't think she ever spoke of that to me."

"This house. Does it belong to Miss Tarlton? Or to her cousins?"

"Oh, it's Miss Tarlton's, right enough, sir. It was two years ago she moved here, and I was engaged along with the cook and an outside man."

Two years ago, Rutledge repeated to himself. About the time Shaw was leaving England. . . .

"Who pays your wages?"

"Miss Tarlton, sir, of course, sir."

"Does she have a private income? Apart from her salary from the Napiers."

"As to that I don't know, sir. She said once her people never did well out of India, unlike some. Her cousins in Gloucestershire are comfortable enough, I suppose, but they don't run to servants, just a daily woman who cleans and prepares the dinner."

He was no closer to seeing Margaret Tarlton as a woman in her own right. Yet he couldn't put his finger on what was missing.

It was Hamish who did. ·

"I'd no' like to think," he said, "that she lived in this house and dressed so fine but had no friends to impress wi' it all!"

"Did she have friends?" Rutledge asked. "Women? Men?"

"She didn't have so many women friends, but there were admirers," Dorcas answered slowly. "Mostly young men, officers home on sick leave. One or two I thought she fancied more than the others. There was a young lord too, took her to the theater a time or two. But 'he's not looking for a wife,' she'd say. 'His mother's a widow, and she'll choose for him, one that suits *her*.' Still, I thought she was fond of him."

Or of his money and position? Hamish asked.

Rutledge said, "What about the young Canadian officer?"

Dorcas grinned. "He called at the Napiers often. I liked him fine," she said, "always a word to make me laugh. Promising to find me an Eskimo when he went home! Fancy that!"

"I understand Miss Tarlton wouldn't see him again before he went back to his regiment. He tried to reach her, and she refused to accept his calls."

Surprised, Dorcas said, "How did you come to know that? I thought for a time—but she'd have no part of Canada. 'Not much better than India,' she'd tell me, 'and not the kind of life I intend to live.' "

"She hasn't heard from Shaw—or seen him—since the war ended?"

"She said he'd gone home. But he hadn't. I heard Mr. Napier, not a month past, tell her he was living in Dorset. 'Is that why you're off to Wyatt's museum?' he wanted to know. 'Because young Shaw's there?' They was having their tea, I was passing the cups, and she nearly spilled hers. So I thought it likely she'd not known whether Captain Shaw was alive or dead. 'Don't be ridiculous!' she told Mr. Napier. But the way she said it—I couldn't tell, somehow, but I thought she might have been wondering if she might just see him. Now—or if she got the position at the museum."

"What was Napier's reaction?"

"He was fiddling with the serviette on his knee. But he was frowning, I could see that. I couldn't help but feel he didn't want her to go to Dorset anyway. And this was just the final straw, to his way of thinking."

"Was Mr. Napier . . . fond . . . of Miss Tarlton?"

"He was very kind to her, she said so often enough. 'But kindness isn't the answer,' she'd say. 'I don't want *kindness*, I want a house and a place in society, and children of my own, and to hold my head up, looking people in the eye, instead of being treated like a *servant*!' That was last May, when she had a bad throat and was in bed for nearly a week. It was the newspaper started it, and I've never seen her in such an ill temper. I said, 'I can't think Mr. Napier and his daughter have ever treated you in such a fashion.' And her answer was 'No, but all their acquaintance do! I thought it would be the best possible way to move into better circles, working for Elizabeth. And it was the gravest mistake I've ever made.' So when Miss Tarlton had finished with it, I looked through the newspaper, to see what it was that upset her." She hesitated. "There was a photograph of Mr. Napier and a lady at a garden party, and speculation that Mr. Napier might be thinking of remarrying. I'd heard her say she disliked the lady intensely. 'Madame Condescension,' she calls her. I don't believe she'd care to work for Miss Napier if Mrs. Clairmont became the second Mrs. Napier."

Afterward, Rutledge walked through the house, still searching for the nature of the missing woman. In the bedroom were a number of photographs: of the Napiers at parties or on horseback; of (according to Dorcas) the cousins in Gloucestershire, wearing country clothes and shy smiles; of a small child in long skirts, seated on a rocking horse or playing with a ball, the cousins hovering protectively in the background.

In the closets hung an array of clothes, all of excellent cut and beautiful fabrics, but without designer labels. Rutledge had the feeling, touching a silk sleeve here and a linen shoulder there, that they had all been sewn by the same seamstress. Miss Tarlton had had the taste to recognize the best but not the money to buy it. It was even possible that she had made most of the clothes herself. The tailoring and needlework showed considerable skill.

There was nothing in the house from India except for a small elephant, trunk uplifted, carved in sandalwood, and a photograph of a man, woman, and two children seated in a tropical garden. She hadn't taken pride in her roots, she had shoved them out of sight. Margaret Tarlton had created a new self for London society, clever, sophisticated, elegant—and reaching for heights she couldn't climb alone.

Rutledge thanked Dorcas and promised to send her word as soon as he could tell her what had become of her mistress.

As the door shut behind him, he found himself wondering if ambition—or accident—had brought Margaret Tarlton to her death.

Rutledge stopped briefly at his sister's house before leaving London.

"You look tired," Frances said, scanning his face on the threshold. "Working too hard, that's what it is! Give up that wretched flat of yours and come back here, where you can be looked after properly."

Here was the London house Frances had lived in since their mother's death. It had been left to brother and sister jointly. Tall, gracious, handsomely furnished, situated in a quiet square of similar houses, it made a proper setting for Frances, whose dark unusual beauty was complemented by a clever brain and a formidable knowledge of people that she kept carefully hidden.

He smiled. "And have you fussing over me morning and night? No, I thank you!" He followed her into the comfortable blue-and-cream drawing room.

"Fiddle! I never fuss and you know it. Well, what brings you here in the rain, my company or Father's whisky?" She crossed to an olivewood cabinet.

"His whisky. I came, as well, for information." He took his accustomed chair, feeling the tiredness she'd already taken note of.

She made a face at him as she poured his neat but listened to what he was saying without interruption. She had always been a good listener, it was a trait their father had cultivated in her. "A woman who pays close attention flatters a man, my dear, and that's the first step in ruling him!"

Even as he spoke, Rutledge found himself thinking that Frances had taken stillness and turned it into an asset, whereas in Aurore it was more than likely a shield against pain. Or a waiting . . . but for what?

"Matilda Clairmont is the widow of James Heddiston Clairmont," she told him when he'd finished, steepling her slender fingers as she dredged her memory. "He was something to do with the Exchequer well before the war. Thoroughly nice man. *She's* the most terrible woman you can imagine, sugary sweet to everyone, just the most helpful and ingratiating way with her I've ever come across. If *she's* likely to be hanged for murder, I can name you fifty women in town who would rejoice! And send the most expensive wreaths they can lay hands on to the funeral afterward!"

He grinned. "What's wrong with being sweet and helpful?"

Frances shook her head. "Darling, you aren't another woman, or you'd know. Females like Matilda are deadly. The kind who can drip venom with such graciousness you'd never scotch the rumors she's set about." Mimicking, her normally very attractive contralto became light and very innocent. " 'My dear, I've been told the most *dreadful* thing about someone, and I can't *bear* to believe it could be true! If you swear not to repeat a *word*, I'll confide in you—I haven't been able to sleep a *wink* since I learned that—' " She returned to her natural voice. "And by the time she's finished, reputations are in ruins."

"Is there any likelihood that Thomas Napier might consider

marrying Mrs. Clairmont? I'm told there was some hint of it in the newspapers in the spring."

Her eyebrows rose in interested speculation. "Now that's a rumor that Matilda herself probably started. I haven't heard it from a reliable source. And if you want my honest opinion, I'd say he's very likely got a mistress tucked away. He doesn't strike me as a man on the loose. One can always tell, you know."

"Could his mistress be his daughter's secretary?"

She considered that. "She might be. But she isn't. I only know Margaret Tarlton to speak to, but she's not one to waste herself in a boudoir. She's ambitious, Ian. There's not a breath of scandal about her, which is the surest proof."

"Who bought the house in Chelsea she lives in?"

"That's an interesting question, isn't it? The money, I'm told, came from a trust fund her father had set up. But somehow I doubt it. He was a very junior civil servant in Delhi, and her mother was a Saddler, from Norfolk. No money there either! Whoever her sponsor is, he's been very careful."

"Could it be Napier?" he asked a second time.

She tilted her head to one side, considering. The lamplight caught her dark blue eyes, and they sparkled like sapphires. "Ian, are you sure about this?"

"No. It's supposition, based on bits of conjecture, not solid fact."

"Thomas Napier is a very fine man. Highly regarded in London, and of course with a political following that makes a false step dangerous. For you—and for him. Why this sudden interest in the Napiers and Margaret?"

"I think she's dead. Murdered, very likely, but whether by the man we have in custody in Dorset or by someone else, I'm not sure."

"But that's horrible! In *Dorset*, you say? I don't understand!"

"It's still only a theory, mind you. But it has to be carefully investigated. She came down to Charlbury to apply for the position of assistant to Simon Wyatt and apparently no one has seen her since then. That's all we have to go on now. Wyatt's opening a museum of artifacts his grandfather brought home from the East."

"Yes, I've heard about that. He's husband to the fascinating Aurore—everyone is dying to meet her! The woman he chucked a promising political career for. Have you seen her? Is she as intriguing as everyone expects?"

"She's—very attractive. An intelligent woman—" He broke off uneasily. The last thing he wanted was Frances on the wrong scent. "Hardly the sensational sort. If that's the only reason for attending the museum's opening, I expect most people will be sadly disappointed. Will they come just for that, do you think?"

But Frances was busy pursuing another thought. "That Chelsea house . . . Richard Wyatt, Simon's father, was absolutely mortified when he discovered Simon was married—it was social suicide, a complete disregard for the proprieties. I remember the uproar at the time—*and* how quickly it ended. But the timing isn't right, is it?" She tapped her fingers lightly on the arm of her chair, musing. "Still, do you suppose Napier went to Wyatt saying Margaret has found a house she wants—it will only be for a year or two, Elizabeth will marry Simon and I'll be free to speak. Then the house will be sold. Lend her the money, to keep Elizabeth from suspecting anything, and I'll see it's repaid in good time. Then—when the news came about Aurore—Wyatt called in his favor, and Napier spread the story that Elizabeth had broken the engagement first. Of course that salvaged her pride but it also seemed to salvage Simon's reputation. Elizabeth is well thought of in London, people felt he'd treated her very shabbily!" She saw her brother's expression and stopped. "What is it? You feel all of that is completely far-fetched?"

"No, but none of it makes any sense. If it came out that either man's name was associated with the Chelsea property, it would ruin Margaret Tarlton too. I don't see Napier taking such a risk." He was playing devil's advocate.

"Well, there are several ways around that. Buying a house for someone leaves traces, I grant you. On the other hand, if that someone buys it for herself, who's to say where the actual pounds came from? Enemies could subject Napier's finances to the closest scutiny and find nothing—they'd never think of looking into Wyatt's bank balance, would they? And here's another small bit of the puzzle. Rumor said that Simon Wyatt's inheritance wasn't as grand as he'd expected. Bad investments during the war, or so the story goes. I've heard that Simon had to sell the Wyatts' London house to pay for that museum of his! Well, that wouldn't be surprising, if Napier wasn't able to keep to his own plans and marry Margaret—after all, Elizabeth is still unwed, so the house couldn't be sold. It might also explain why Margaret got fed up and decided to change jobs."

"It's an interesting possibility. Still, even if you're right that Napier borrowed the money from Wyatt, I can't see any direct connection from that to Margaret Tarlton's murder. How would it benefit anyone?" He stood up, the whisky failing to penetrate the gloom he felt settling around him. "For that matter, so far I haven't found a sound reason for anyone to want to kill her. Except mistaken identity."

"No, but you will." She smiled as she held out her hand for his empty glass. "If there is one."

As she walked with him to the door, Rutledge said, "If you had to dispose of a suitcase that might connect you with a murder, where would you hide it?"

"A suitcase? I'd put it in the one place everyone expects to find luggage—a hotel or a railway station."

"Would you? A hall porter or a stationmaster would come across it in the long run and try to locate the owner."

"Well, then—the one place no one ever goes."

It was a thought that followed him all the way back to Dorset.

14

It was late when Rutledge pulled into the yard of the Swan in Singleton Magna, and he was tired. The rain had kept up most of the afternoon and into the evening, a steady, gray curtain that soaked everything.

He stepped out of the car into a puddle, invisible in the shadowed yard, and swore. His hat, tilted against the rain, dripped unpleasantly down his coat as he turned toward the front of the inn and into the rising wind. He could feel his shirt beginning to stick to his skin across his shoulders.

At the inn door he paused to shake his hat, then squelched across the damp rug put down to stop the influx of water into the lobby proper.

There was a message waiting for him. He opened it and read, "We've looked where we said we would, and had no luck." It was signed "Bowles" in a dainty penmanship that belonged to the smiling woman behind the desk. She nodded as he glanced up. "He said you'd know what was meant."

"Yes. Thank you."

Margaret Tarlton wasn't visiting her cousins in Gloucestershire. Elizabeth Napier had been right.

As he reached the stairs, wondering if it was too late to order a pot of tea and something to eat, the front doors opened again and

Elizabeth Napier herself swept in with a black umbrella cascading rain like a young waterfall. The hem of her skirt was darkly wet as well and her black shoes left tracks on the floor crossing his. Benson took the umbrella from her as soon as she reached the relative dryness indoors and then disappeared. The sound of the car moving off into the night came to Rutledge.

She saw him on the stairs and said, "My God, it's worse than London—the roads turn to muddy ruts and everywhere you put your foot there's a puddle! I looked for you earlier, hoping you might dine with me." She regarded him for a moment and added, "Inspector Hildebrand told me he thought you'd gone to the Wyatt Arms instead."

"No. I had business elsewhere."

Coming up to him, she said, "You look tired! Have you eaten at all?" Taking his silence for no, she turned to the woman at the desk. "Is your cook still here? I'd like a private parlor, if you please, and something hot to eat. Soup will do. With tea." Without waiting for an answer, she said to Rutledge, "I'll take my death of cold, even in August, if I don't change these wet clothes. I'll only need five minutes!" She swept past him in an aura of damp wool that matched his own.

But it was almost fifteen before she came down the stairs again and considered him approvingly. He had changed his shirt and his shoes, and wore a sweater in place of his coat. With his hair still damp and unruly, she thought he looked much younger than he seemed before.

There was soup and fresh bread set out in one of the smaller rooms, with tea on a table by a fire someone had hastily laid. It took a little of the chill and an air of mustiness from the room, giving it a cozy, almost intimate feeling.

Rutledge, curious, wondered what her reasons were for creating this comfortable setting. Whatever they might be, he preferred her company to his own thoughts in the silent room upstairs.

Elizabeth served him and then herself, although from the way she ate he thought it was out of politeness instead of hunger. He felt suddenly ravenous.

The soup was mutton, with barley, carrots, potatoes, and what tasted like turnips. The aroma alone was sustaining. He wondered if Elizabeth had commandeered the staff's first course.

She waited until he'd finished half his soup before launching into her real purpose for waylaying him.

"My father says, if you need more men, he'll ask the Yard to send them."

Wouldn't Bowles be delighted with that request! he thought, but said only "Thank you. But no, they'd only be underfoot. If the searches that Hildebrand's conducting haven't brought us any answers by this time, additional men—and strangers at that—aren't going to." He helped himself to a second bowl of soup and cut more bread. There was butter in a covered dish as well, as he discovered.

She said, "They aren't going to find the children. I know that. You know that. But Hildebrand insists he has to find them. I spoke with the rector here in Singleton Magna this afternoon. Mr. Drewes. I felt I ought to do something about a headstone. My father wanted to remove the body to London. He's taking Margaret's death very hard, I can tell you. Ten years—you grow fond of someone in ten years. It isn't surprising, I was very close to her myself."

He said nothing, letting her carry on in her own fashion.

"Mr. Drewes was rather confused, I must say. He'd been informed of course that the dead woman was Mrs. Mowbray, and I don't think he was too happy at the thought of changing the church records. I told him to blame Inspector Hildebrand for being overhasty." She tilted her head and smiled wryly. "He thinks I'm utterly charming, so I must have put it less bluntly than that. Of course he never said as much to my face, I overheard him talking to that woman at the desk, after he'd very gallantly walked me back to the Swan, holding his umbrella over me and getting himself thoroughly wet. His wife will have had something to say about that!"

He found himself wondering if Mrs. Drewes would even hear the story. Elizabeth Napier had a seductive way of sitting, her back straight, her shoulders slightly at an angle. Her hair, brushed back from her face, was gleaming in the firelight, and he could smell the faint scent of heliotrope.

"My father says if you find yourself in any difficulty with the local people, you have only to tell him. He made it clear to your superintendant this afternoon that he expects you to handle this business about Margaret."

He felt a surge of irritation at her meddling—or was it Napier's?

"I don't believe that will be necessary," he said. "But thank you," he added, knowing it was what she wanted him to say. To satisfy her own sense of self-importance or her father's silent need to be involved in the matter?

"What do you think of Aurore Wyatt?" she went on. She was making conversation as an experienced hostess might at a dinner party, interspersing the salient points as if they were commonplace remarks. Now she was down to what interested her most. She rose to refill his tea cup, indicating she was giving him an opportunity to respond. Out of politeness if nothing else.

"I don't think about her," he said. "My task is to locate the rest of the Mowbray family—if they exist—or find out what part in this business Margaret Tarlton played. Which reminds me. I'd like to know something about her—not as your secretary, but as a woman might see her."

"Which is as adroit a way of changing the subject as any I've seen since my mother's uncle used to make excuses for his forgetfulness!" she said lightly, turning aside his refusal. "I think Aurore has turned your head as easily as she has Simon's. *And* my father's! He likes her, you know. He says if the French army had been made up of soldiers half as brave as Aurore, we'd have won the war three years ago."

Rutledge said, "They lost their best men early on. And the rest lost heart."

"And we paid in British blood for their inadequate weapons and their inadequate generals. Not that we didn't have a few incompetent generals of our own! Frankly I wasn't prepared to like Aurore. But I do. She's got a quality of stillness that I admire—I've never been able to stop my mind or my tongue from working as they pleased. I can quite understand why Simon fell in love with her. And out of love with me!"

"War does strange things to people," he said, falling back on the old cliché and wondering if he could shift the conversation one last time to Margaret.

"It certainly changed Simon," she said, a wistfulness in her voice. "I was frightened by what I saw in him today. A fragility. It wasn't there before! He was a man who had never known personal defeat, never had any doubts, always had his eye well set on the mark. It was what I truly loved in him, you know. His certainty. Not quite arrogance, just an assurance that he knew his way and was confidently following it. It was a guarantee of safety, that assurance. I felt *safe* in his care." Toying with her teaspoon, she stopped, then added, "I asked Aurore if she'd noticed it—after all, she hadn't known Simon before the war, she might not have been aware of any change in him. But she said, 'He's terribly afraid.' " Elizabeth paused thoughtfully. "I can't accept that. I've never known Simon to be afraid of anything. Or any *one*!"

But Rutledge knew what Aurore meant. It wasn't a question of lacking courage. Surviving had frightened Simon. He hadn't expected to live. He couldn't comprehend how he'd deserved to live. And there was a feeling, deep down inside, that God would remember him one day and rectify the error.

"Simon isn't afraid of anyone or anything. That's not what his wife was trying to tell you. He's alive and so many other good men are dead. There's a sense of guilt in that. It breeds fear of a different kind."

She stared at him. "Were you in the war? Do you feel that way?"

Oh, God, he thought, as Hamish echoed the question in the depths of his soul. Guilt was—it was the agony of spirit that made every day bleak. The fear that you might not live up to the cost of your survival—that you might not, somehow, justify the whim of fate that let Death miss you and take so many around you. The drive—and the brake—on all that you did and thought and felt, when the Armistice came and you were alive to see it. The eleventh hour of the eleventh day of the eleventh month. There was a biblical ring to that, straight out of the Old Testament, the sort of resounding phrase that thundered from the pulpit and terrified small boys even when they didn't know what in God's name was being said.

She saw his unwitting reaction and said quickly, "No, don't answer that, I'd no right to ask it of you!"

"Then tell me instead about Margaret Tarlton."

She sighed. "Margaret grew up in India. It made her—I don't

139

know quite how—seem much older than I was. As if all the things she'd seen and done and learned gave her a different sort of maturity from mine. And heaven knows, I'd grown up quickly myself, in a household where political intrigue was mother's milk!"

"Did she come from a family with status? Money?"

"No, although from what I know of her father, he had aspirations, and he used to tell her as a child that England was her hope. If the family could just return to England, they'd be fine. If they could find the money for passage, they'd be fine. I don't know what golden rainbows he saw for her, or why, but he made her hungry for a way of life she wasn't going to have unless she married well. In the end, both her parents died of malaria, and she came without either of them. There was a younger sister too, who died near Suez of a fever several men brought back to the ship after going ashore. Margaret arrived in England alone, with no one to call family but distant cousins she'd never met. She finished her education at the same school I was sent to; there was a family in Gloucester who provided a scholarship. They'd been missionaries or some such, and often did such things in the hope that it might make the recipient think of taking up the same burden. Well, they reckoned wrong with Margaret! She thought the heathen were quite happy with their own ways and would profit very little from being persuaded to try ours. Buddhism, she told me, made life a long series of chances to try to do better and see oneself more clearly. She didn't care for Hinduism as much—she said it was as class-conscious as the Church of England. In my opinion, these beliefs—Hinduism and Buddhism—put far too much emphasis on the fate of the individual rather than on the good of mankind as a whole. It sustained a sort of—I don't know—selfishness. I saw that from time to time in Margaret too, as if she'd been infected by it."

"It seems she'd have made a perfect assistant for Simon. With her deep knowledge of the East."

But Elizabeth Napier evaded that question very neatly. "I'm no judge. It wasn't a subject she usually cared to speak of. Most people had no idea she'd lived anywhere but England."

"She spoke of India to Captain Shaw."

Elizabeth's face went very still. "Captain Shaw heard it first from me," she said. "He couldn't understand why Margaret wasn't in

140

love with him. She wouldn't tell him, and I felt he was owed an answer. I asked him not to bring it up with her, but I think he did anyway. I don't know that Margaret had a capacity for love. If she did, it was buried under such layers of wanting that she'd nearly smothered it. Whatever drove my secretary, it was so fierce she was blind to anything else. I hope her death came quickly; she would have hated dying before she'd gotten what she was after. It was the ultimate failure, you see."

The next morning, before he'd had time to order his breakfast or think about the day, Rutledge came face to face with Hildebrand.

"You ought to come see Mowbray," he said. "He's got something on his conscience, and damned if I can find out what it is. I've sent for Johnston, in the event it's a confession. He might speak to you or his lawyer."

Rutledge left with Hildebrand, crossing the street in time to see Johnston just passing though the station's door.

Inside it was damp and musty from the rain, and this morning, although the clouds were moving northeast, the sun hadn't shown its face.

They moved down the passage to the cell where Mowbray was kept, and Rutledge could feel Hamish growing tense, uneasy.

The heavy key turned in the lock, the door swung back, and the misery inside was almost palpable. The smell of unwashed flesh and hopelessness was enough to make Johnston stop in his tracks. "My God, haven't you allowed him even the decency of soap and water!"

"We've brought him soap and water," Hildebrand said curtly. "We can't dip him into it. My constables are already complaining it's not fit in here for beast or man. That's why you're here. To get to the bottom of this!"

Mowbray sat where Rutledge had last seen him, head in hands, shoulders slumped. The picture of dejection and despair. His hair seemed to have grown longer, wilder than the gray-streaked ten-day-old beard, and his clothes looked worn, shabby, and grimy.

Johnston stepped forward and said, "Mr. Mowbray. It's Marcus Johnston. I represent you. Do you remember me?"

But there was no response, although Johnston gently tried pleading, cajoling, and coaxing for a good ten minutes to break through the man's apathy.

Finally he gave up and moved back out into the passage, breathing as if he'd felt short of air.

Hildebrand turned to Rutledge. "See what you can do, man! I'll take any help I can get!"

Rutledge could feel his own heart pounding, and Hamish was a live presence in his mind. But he forced himself with every shred of will he possessed to step into the cell. The constable on duty was a large, heavy man who seemed to fill the corner he stood in like some ancient pillar rooted there in the dimness. His face was tense, his eyes on Mowbray like a lifeline.

Hildebrand crowded in after Rutledge, and Johnston, seeming to feel his responsibility like a dead weight that couldn't be shoved aside, pushed in after. It was Rutledge's worse nightmare, and he was on the brink of panic when he finally made his voice work.

"Mowbray? Good God, man, what would Mary think of you, filthy and unshaven?" he asked, more harshly than he'd intended. "It's a matter of pride!"

"Mary's dead," Mowbray mumbled at last, as if finally jarred into the present. "She can't see me now, she can't hear you."

"What makes you so certain the dead are deaf and blind?"

"They say I killed her! Is it true?" He looked up, his own personal hell raging in the red-rimmed eyes. Rutledge wondered how much the man could understand, or if this apparent conversation with Mowbray was merely something the sane men in the room believed in.

Catching Johnston's eye, Rutledge answered, "I don't know. A woman's body has been found. You'd been searching for your wife, you'd made public threats against her, whether you remember them or not. The woman seemed to match the photograph of your wife we found in your wallet. What else should we believe?"

"I remember seeing her by the train. *I remember it!* But if she died in London, how could that be? How could she end up in this place? I don't even know where I am." It was as if he'd forgotten that a man was supposed to have been with the woman. He looked vaguely around him, as though his eyes weren't focusing on the cell walls, that they saw things visible only to him.

142

Like Hamish . . .

"What was she wearing when you saw her?"

"I saw her. The wind blew her hair like I remembered, and she had that smile when she looked at the children, that smile. . . ."

"How was she dressed?" Rutledge persisted. "Was she dressed in blue? Green?"

"She wore pink for me. She always did, when she wanted to make me happy. I took a photograph of her once in pink. I have it here—" He fumbled for his wallet and not finding it, gave up.

"And the children? How were they dressed?"

But Mowbray couldn't face thinking about his children, and Rutledge nearly lost him again to the depths of apathy.

"There was a woman along the road. Walking by herself," he went on quickly. Johnston made an abrupt movement, trying to stop Rutledge. Hildebrand opened his mouth to speak and was ignored. "She had on a pink dress, this woman. Pink with lavender and rose. But it wasn't your wife. It was someone else. Did you see her? Did you speak to her?"

But Mowbray's head was back in the cradle of his hands. He was weeping silently.

"God damn it!" Hildebrand exploded. "You'll muddle the waters worse than they are—"

"I didn't agree to this line of questioning!" Johnston began at the same instant.

"Hildebrand. Send the man in the corner there to bring that dress to us. I want to show it to Mowbray."

"No, that's out of order, I won't—"

"I've got to consider the ramifications if he should identify it— we don't know—" Johnston was blustering. "I can't follow your reasoning!"

"I want the dress," Rutledge said. "Send the man for it!"

"It's on your head!" Hildebrand retorted. *Do you hear me?*"

But in the end he relented. And the heavyset constable, relief visible on his face, diffidently strode past them and was gone.

They stood in angry, volatile silence while he was away. Mowbray's weeping had stopped, and he seemed to be asleep where he sat, his breathing very irregular and harsh, as if dreams haunted him. Then suddenly he started into full wakefulness, crying out in anguish, throwing out his hands as if to ward off what had come out of the depths of his mind.

"As ye'll be doing one day!" Hamish reminded Rutledge, chilling his blood.

Mowbray turned and begged, "Where are my children? Have you seen my children? Oh, God, I don't know where to look for them anymore."

The constable returned at that instant, breaking the spell that had held the witnesses in stunned thrall. He carried a carefully wrapped bundle in his hands and looked first to Hildebrand before passing it on to Rutledge.

Rutledge opened it, concentrating on the string and the knot, on the folds that led inward, until he held a garment within the white sheets of tissue paper, dark against their paleness. After a moment, without arranging the dress or the paper, he went to kneel on the cold, hard floor in front of Mowbray.

"Will you look at this?" he asked gently, making no attempt to touch the man, who was staring blindly into nothingness again.

It was some while before he coaxed Mowbray into glancing down at the dress he held out like an offering to some vacant god.

Mowbray frowned as if he couldn't make out what it was, much less recognize it. But Rutledge was very patient. He could feel his feet and knees beginning to ache from the awkward position, but he kept himself steady and quiet, offering no distraction.

After a time Mowbray reached out a work-hardened finger and touched the fabric of the dress as if testing to see if it was real. Lightly, not with interest so much as his inability to decide what it was. Then he saw that it had a shoulder, a sleeve—a collar—and knew.

"I thought the bombs killed her. I wasn't there when it happened. I was in France, Captain Banner was telling me I had to go to London. That something had happened. I think they took me by car to the port. It was raining and dark and I couldn't feel anything—not even in the service in the chapel—"

The dark bloodstains were visible now, black and stiff, a long soaked patch and the splatters, like black dots on the cloth with no attempt to place them becomingly, no sense of artistry, only marks of the intensity of the attack.

"They wouldn't open the casket and let me see her. They said I shouldn't. Was this what she was wearing, then? Is—*oh, God, it must be her blood!*" He recoiled, thrusting his hands deep into his pockets as if to keep them away from the horror. "I wanted to hold her again and they wouldn't let me—*they didn't tell me there was so much blood!*"

"Stop this," Johnston cried, in nearly as much horror as Mowbray. "It's inhumanly cruel, it's—you've got to stop!"

He came forward, pulling at Rutledge's shoulders, forcing him backward. Hildebrand, swearing, was trying to tell the constable to get back into that room, damn it! Their voices echoed in the cramped space, loud and frightened.

Rutledge threw off Johnston's grip, kept his balance by a miracle of muscle and tendon, and protected the dress from the floor. Mowbray, looking in amazement from one to the other, as if startled into brief sanity, said quite clearly, "That's not the pink she liked! Who gave that to her? Was it him? *Was it the man with her?*" He fingered it again, puzzled. "It's the wrong color, I tell you—*I knew when I saw her it was the wrong color!*"

For an instant Rutledge thought Mowbray was going to lunge at his throat and choke him, but it was the dress the hands were reaching for, groping, clutching, then holding it up, peering at it in the dimness, trying to see, and turning toward the door, toward Hildebrand, who'd arrested him.

"It's not hers, it's a trick! She's smaller than this, I know my own wife's clothes! Why did the Hun want to kill her, she was never any harm to anybody, never an unkind word! I'll make him pay, see if I don't! I'll kill every one of the bastards I can put hand to, I'll grind him into the mud—pound until there's no face left, and keep on pounding until you can't tell brains from earth. I swear it to God, I do!"

Hildebrand managed to get the dress out of his grip without ripping it, and Johnston tried to push him back to the cot, while Rutledge stood there and watched the spate of words he'd released.

They hadn't cleared Mowbray of murder. He may not have killed his wife, the dead woman might well be Margaret Tarlton, but he'd just described in passionate, intense detail the way the dead woman had died.

It took time to settle him down again, but when the adrenaline finally subsided and he had some small grip again on his surroundings, he sank back into the same posture they'd found him in, rocking himself with the pain and the uncertainty, as if he had no recollection of the dress, the men around him, or tensions so taut that Hamish was warning Rutledge to go—*go!*

But he stayed, walked back down the passage with Hildebrand and Johnston berating him in vicious terms, spilling out their own shock and horror in a tirade that left them both breathless and stumbling over each other's words without noticing it.

Rutledge stopped at the door to the front room, and turned.

"It may have been unorthodox," he said coldly. "It was most certainly necessary. There's a possibility he saw Margaret Tarlton alive—and killed her thinking she was his wife." *You sacrifice the man for the woman—* "Or even more likely, came across her dead body. Which may explain why he was so quick to believe the charges against him. Because Margaret Tarlton's not in London, not in Gloucestershire, and not in Sherborne. You tell me where she is—and why we can't find her. There's a death certificate for Mrs. Mowbray, but it's Miss Tarlton who's missing! Can't you understand what I'm telling you?"

"You're not going to turn my case into a circus, I'll have you recalled first—"

"How can I build any reasonable defense after what we just heard—"

"That's beside the point," Rutledge said. "I'm not interested in solving your problems, I'm interested in what's at the bottom of this murder. I'm interested in saving that poor devil if he's innocent and convicting him if he's guilty. I want to find answers to the riddle of who's lying in that grave in your churchyard—and why she's there. I believe I'm on the right track. If you won't help me prove I'm right, then for God's sake, show me where I'm wrong."

Johnston said, "You forced my client to all but convict himself out of his own mouth, before witnesses! I don't see how that's supposed to save him!"

"Did you listen at all to what he was saying? That the dress in Hildebrand's hands isn't Mrs. Mowbray's color or size! But Elizabeth Napier swears it's *Margaret Tarlton's* color and size. If we were wrong about his victim, can't you see that we may also be wrong about his part in her death?"

"Are you claiming that it's my investigation that's at fault? By God!"

Rutledge could feel frustration battling his need for air and space. He said, "No. We're all in this muddle together, Hildebrand. Only if we're wrong at the end of it, it will be Mowbray who pays for any blunders we've made, not you or I."

"And what do we do about those wretched children, then? Answer me that—pretend they never existed, and hope to hell we're right?"

The door behind Rutledge opened suddenly, bringing in a sweep of air because the outer door was also standing wide.

A breathless sergeant, red-faced and muddy, said over Rutledge's shoulder, "Inspector Hildebrand, sir? We've found a body, sir. I think—you'd best come and see it!"

15

Rutledge drove. Hildebrand sat in the seat beside him while Sergeant Wilkins occupied the space that Hamish considered his own.

That made Rutledge edgy. If he turned around, would Hamish be there in the shadows beside the sergeant? Or had the sergeant unwittingly exorcized his fellow passenger?

Hildebrand sensed his uneasiness and attacked. "Rather throws your theory into a cocked hat, doesn't it?"

"I won't know until we get there."

Hildebrand laughed. "Yes, that's it, slip off the hook. You've done bloody little else since you got here!" Then, remembering the presence of his sergeant, he added to the man, "Tell me again. Slowly this time!"

The sergeant repeated the story he had spilled out in Hildebrand's office, the words tumbling over each other in frantic haste. His voice was calmer now, as he ordered his thoughts and remembered details. "We'd broadened the search, like you'd said, and it was that young chap, Fenton, who saw the earth seemed different in the one place, sunken like, as if something had been buried and the soil had settled in around it. Well, he began to dig a bit, thinking it might be somebody's old dog or the like, and instead he comes up with a muddy edge of cloth. Appeared to be part of a blanket at first, then we could see the corner, with a bit of lining. A coat, we thought. You could see the color, a dark blue. Then the white of bone. We stopped there and I came for you straightaway. Not wanting to disturb anything before you'd seen it like it was."

"Yes, well done! You're *sure* it's a coat, not a blanket? You'd wrap a dog in an old blanket!"

"It's not made the same as a blanket. And there's no fur, sir. You'd find fur too, if it was an animal. That lasts."

"Yes, yes!" Hildebrand answered testily. "No sense of size— child, fully grown adult?" He was not a man who enjoyed suspense, he wanted his answers now, questions later. Sometimes in police-work there were no answers at all. He'd been afraid this Mowbray investigation was heading in such a direction. But if they'd found either the children or that damned Tarlton woman, all to the good. He felt his spirits suddenly rising. If it was the Tarlton woman, it'd get Rutledge off his back, by God, and leave the Mowbray business out of it altogether!

"No, sir, as I said, we didn't want to disturb the ground more than needful."

A silence fell, and Rutledge found himself thinking, *This is too far for Mowbray to have come.* He'd have had to pass through two villages—someone would have seen him—and bone meant the body had been in the ground for some time. In the trenches, you learned how long it took a man to rot. . . .

He was still tired from the session with Mowbray, feeling the intensity of emotion, the rawness of the man's fears—his own re-action to them.

"I hope to God the body has nothing to do with Mowbray!" he told himself.

"Or with Charlbury . . . ," Hamish added softly, startling him.

By the time they'd reached the makeshift grave, a small crowd had collected, standing just out of sight of the remains. They were mostly from Leigh Minster, according to the sergeant. The news hadn't traveled to Stoke Newton or Charlbury yet.

Rutledge pulled off the road, braked the car, and Hildebrand was out almost before it had stopped moving, wanting to be the first on the scene. The sergeant followed. Rutledge let them go. It was their jurisdiction, after all.

The scrub ground had been pastureland at one time, allowed to go wild and overgrown now with weeds that reached to his knees, a few of them shrubby and tenacious, dragging at the fabric of his trousers like bony fingers. From where he was walking he could see a distant rooftop, a barn, he thought, very likely the last outpost of Leigh Minster. That was to his right, and on the left was a field, already cut. Ahead, a slight rise. He turned to look behind and saw that there was a burned-out chimney marking the ivy-grown foundations of a house across the road. A blackened stump, with rooks perched on the broken edges calling raucously.

If you'd looked for a place to bury a body, this was ideal for the purpose, invisible unless someone came along the road. Which brought to mind the next question: Who had known such a place was *here*? Certainly not Mowbray, a stranger in Dorset!

Rutledge walked through the knot of voyeurs who whispered behind their hands, trying to decide what was behind the sudden influx of policemen and what was attracting their attention just out of sight behind the weeds. The general opinion appeared to be the discovery of the missing children. He heard Mowbray's name several times as he passed. Ahead, around the depression in the earth, stood six or seven men. He recognized the constable from Leigh Minster and nodded to him. Hildebrand and the sergeant were on their knees studying the cloth that emerged like a small sail from the rough hole that had been dug by the sergeant and his men. Blue, and wool, if he, Rutledge was any judge. But cheap wool, thin rather than thick.

It wasn't until he reached the others that he saw what appeared to be a knob, dirty white, with bits of flesh still attached, like a half-chewed bone, and the clinging mud from recent rain.

It was human, not animal—

That was the first question Hildebrand asked, looking up. "Human, then?"

"Yes. I think it is."

Hildebrand nodded. "All right, lads, let's see a bit more, shall we?"

He straightened and moved aside while the sergeant handed the shovel to a thickset constable with sleeves already rolled above his elbows. He set to carefully, as if he'd done this sort of thing before.

Scraping, wielding the shovel as a broom more often than the work it was designed to do, the man made slow progress. Hildebrand, tight-faced, impatience in every line, watched. But he didn't hurry the constable, and after several glances at Hildebrand, the sergeant made no comment either. The clang of the shovel, the grunting of the constable, and the distant rooks broke the stillness. And then the rest of the bone came into view. A shred of stocking clung to the flesh, and at the end, an ankle in a black, heeled shoe.

A woman. The grave was not deep; at a guess no more than a foot of soil covered her body. She appeared to have been wrapped in the coat rather than wearing it.

It had been far too hot for a wool coat the day the woman in the farmer's cornfield had died. This wasn't Margaret Tarlton or Mrs. Mowbray. And it wasn't the missing children.

Hildebrand sighed. Another damned *question* . . .

It took an hour or more to uncover the remains to the point where the men watching and waiting could look at her and form any opinion of age, class, or time in the ground.

The constable from Leigh Minster squatted to peer into the makeshift grave, studying the body. After a time he said, "Don't recognize her! We've no one missing, I'd know if there was. Who is she then? Can anyone say?" He got to his feet, looked around at the men on either side.

It was difficult to judge what she had once looked like. The face was badly decomposed, with signs that it had been damaged before death. The dark hair was tangled and mixed with clots of damp earth. Hildebrand turned to the constable from Stoke Newton. "Anything?"

"No, sir. There was a woman went missing some while back. A maid. But I wouldn't—" He looked more closely and then shook his head. "I don't think this one's been in the ground long enough. It's hard to say, but I'd guess from the coat and shoes she's not a servant girl on her day off. Dressed more like a woman gone to market. Still—early days yet!"

Listening, Rutledge thought, I was right. An able man, that one! Aloud he said, "The face. It hasn't been beaten the way the Mowbray woman was?"

Hildebrand said, "Hard to say." He squatted on his heels as the constable had done. "There's injury here. Nose damaged, and that right cheekbone. But the teeth aren't broken, nor the forehead. We can't be sure a beating's what killed her. Could be there's a stab wound in the body. Or a bullet. Doctor will tell us that." He got to his feet. "All right, lads, send that crowd away, and let's get her back to Singleton Magna." He paused and looked at Rutledge. "Anything you want to add?"

Rutledge shook his head.

"Then it's my business, *Dorset* business, not part of what brought you here." It was a warning. *Stand clear.*

Time enough to challenge that, Rutledge told himself, when and if there was a need to do it. Not now. Not in front of Hildebrand's subordinates.

"So far I've seen nothing to show me that this involves the Yard," he answered neutrally. Because he hadn't. Still, the words were carefully chosen, not signifying capitulation, while reserving the right at any point to change his mind.

Hildebrand chose to regard them as a promise, not as a provisional agreement. More to the point, a promise before witnesses. He was pleased to be magnanimous and added, "Your suggestion that we search a wider area brought her to light. I'm grateful. Look, you'd better drive back to Singleton Magna. I'll stay here until we've got her sorted out, and then I'll send these men on about their search. Could be an hour or so before we bring her in."

Rutledge, politely dismissed, left. But Hamish was already considering the connection between this body and the last one. As Rutledge put up the crank and got into the driver's seat, Hamish said, "It's no' to do with Charlbury. No' the same manner of death. And this woman was put in the ground, not left in a field for anyone to find."

"Yes, that's what interests me. Whoever killed her must have known that she wouldn't be missed. It was safe to hide her body. No search—and there wasn't one, was there?—and no notice taken of her absence from wherever she came from. But in the case of the body outside Singleton Magna, I'm beginning to think she wasn't hidden because there was a scapegoat available—Mowbray—and because Margaret Tarlton *would* be missed. By a number of people, one of them with the power to raise heaven and earth looking for her." He drove sedately through Stoke Newton, where small knots of villagers stood on the street gossiping, as if the news had finally reached them and speculation was rife. Once on the high road again he added, "But I can't believe that was the reason our body's face was battered. I think there was passion behind it, not an attempt to hide her identity. It served that purpose of course—but it wasn't the intention."

"Aye. Which means you're one body short and yon Hildebrand is one body long! Better him than you!"

Rutledge shook his head. "I'd have been happier if that corpse had solved the puzzle of ours. If it meant those children were safe. And that the killer, whoever he or she was, had nothing to do with that poor bedeviled soul in the cell." He couldn't seem to get Mowbray out of his mind.

"You did na' need yon second dead lassie to prove that. You know and I know where the answers are. And I do na' think she'll change what's happened in Charlbury. You've got a murderer to find *there*, and the sooner the better! Unless, like Hildebrand, ye're satisfied to put it on Mowbray's head."

He couldn't. Even Hamish knew that it was impossible.

By the time Rutledge arrived at Charlbury—breakfastless and in a moody frame of mind—the news had flown before him. In the form of a man in the pub of the Wyatt Arms who had enjoyed regaling anyone who would listen with all the gruesome details.

From the sound of them, Rutledge knew, the man had not seen the body.

"Another killing," he was telling a fresh recruit to his gathering audience, "just like the one in Singleton Magna. That man they've got in jail there—might not be the first time he's gone looking for his missing wife. Left a trail of bodies over half of England if you want to know what I think. Sees a woman out on her own, walking along a road, like, or waiting for someone to come fetch her, and the first thing pops in his head is 'There's my wife, by God!' And before Bob's your uncle, he's killed her!"

Rutledge, taking a late breakfast in the corner by the window, tried to shut out the voice. Looking out into the back garden, he realized there was a woman sitting there at one of the empty tables under the trees where the Women's Institute had met. She was turned away from the windows, a glass of something in front of her. The soft green of her dress made her oddly invisible in the leafy shadows.

It was Aurore Wyatt.

He took his tea cup and went out to the garden.

She looked up as he said, "May I join you?"

He indicated the vacant chair at an angle to hers. The wind was softly stirring the leaves, giving a sense of tranquility to the garden compared to the uproar of voices in the bar.

Her eyes looked tired, as if sleep were something she knew very little about. "Is it business? I've heard them talking in there. There's been another body found, I'm told."

"No, not business. I missed my breakfast. Now I've been served bones with my toast. I came out here to escape."

"Then, please, I'd be happy to have company more cheerful than my own thoughts!" She waited until he sat down. "How did you miss your breakfast? Tell me lies, please! Something humorous, and a little silly."

Rutledge grinned, all at once feeling better. "There was a giraffe loose in the kitchen of the Swan in Singleton Magna. The police are still investigating. What are you drinking? I'll fetch another."

She smiled, the light coming back into her eyes. "Lemonade. It's very good. Yes, I'd enjoy another glass."

He brought it to her, along with a fresh pot of tea for himself, and sat down again. Aurore thanked him and said, "Tell me more about the giraffe." She pronounced it "jirr-affe."

"I'm afraid I couldn't stay long enough to find out its history. Sorry."

She turned to study his face, watching the light and shadow of the leaves playing across it. "Then tell me about yourself. But nothing that is sad."

Which put Jean and Hamish and the war and his last two cases off limits. He gave the question some thought. "My father followed the law, and my mother was a very gifted pianist. I grew up in a house full of music and law books. The fanciful and the practical."

"And your parents, did they expect you to follow in their footsteps? Law or music? Or were they pleased you chose to become a policeman?"

"I think my father would have been happy to see me in the law. But it wasn't my calling. In the end I think he realized it."

"You are quite practical, I have seen that. And fanciful?" She tilted her head and he felt the intensity of her scrutiny this time. "You are very sensitive to what people are thinking. It is a gift. And a curse. To be able to put yourself in the minds of others. Is that how you come to find your murderers?"

The light mood had vanished. "Sometimes," he said.

And Hamish stirred, knowing what lay behind his answer.

She said, "Elizabeth came again this morning. She told us she needed work to keep her from worrying too much about Margaret. And so she is helping Simon in the museum today. I couldn't stand it any longer. This was the only place I could think of where it might be quiet. And then there was the affair of the bones, to spoil my escape."

"They don't have anything to do with you," he said gently. "Or with Margaret Tarlton."

"I am very glad to hear it," she told him, but she didn't sound glad.

The sun was warmer now and brighter. He could feel it on his back. It probably would turn out to be a fine day after all. "She won't stay, once this is finished. Once we know what has happened to Margaret, there won't be an excuse to keep her here."

"But will it be finished?" Aurore asked. "I don't think so. I used to believe—as a child, you understand!—that it was very sad when someone died suddenly. That is, without knowledge that it was going to happen until it was there, facing one. I used to think that for such people, it was a severe shock, they were not prepared to die, and so they became ghosts. Intent on coming back to the world to finish whatever it was they had left undone. I'm beginning to believe that Margaret is such a one—the stuff of ghosts."

Rutledge said quietly, "She's dead, Mrs. Wyatt. All that's left is to find out who killed her. And if possible, why."

Aurore sighed. "Yes. I know. But I prefer not to think about any of it. Only, with Elizabeth Napier invading my house and my life, I am not allowed to forget!"

She drained the last of her lemonade and set the glass aside. "I must go to the farm. Cows do not care about ghosts or dead bodies. They are practical creatures, they know when it is time to be milked and time to be let out to pasture, and time to be brought in at the end of the day. The man who took care of them while Simon was away at war is too old now to carry the burden of so much work. I persuade him when I can to sit in the sun and advise me."

She hadn't said anything before about someone else at the farm who might have seen her there, nursing a heifer with colic.

Rutledge asked, "I'd like to speak to him. He might have seen you on the day Margaret left."

Aurore smiled. "I don't think so. He was suffering from a *rheum*—a cold—and avoided me when he could. I think it was actually too much ale, and a sour stomach. In France we say it is the liver rebelling. At his age, any rebellion is a revolution."

"He didn't know you were at the farm? Surely if one of the livestock was ill . . . ?"

"From the barn he doesn't see where I leave my car. Sometimes I go and come without meeting him at all, if he is out in one of the fields."

"But he might have heard the motorcar."

"Well, perhaps. It is kind of you to look for someone who can tell you positively where I was—and was not."

"It isn't kindness, it's necessity," he said, more harshly than he'd meant. "I have witnesses who saw your motorcar in Charlbury that morning and who would swear to that. And to the presence of Margaret Tarlton in it with you."

She shrugged. "I cannot invent witnesses for myself." Despite the shrug, she wasn't indifferent to her predicament. There was an intensity beneath her stillness that he could feel. A very real fear.

The tranquility here under the trees had vanished like smoke on the wind. After a few minutes she excused herself and was gone.

He sat where he was, remembering what Frances had said about the Wyatt finances and wondering if there was enough money in their coffers to pay for a first-class barrister to defend Aurore. Or would Simon abandon her, to preserve his precious museum?

Was that what kept Elizabeth Napier in Charlbury, meddling?

16

Rutledge went to find Constable Truit and finally ran him to earth just outside of Charlbury, where he was supervising a group of men poking through the heavy undergrowth along a small stream.

"Truit? I wish to speak to you," Rutledge called, tramping through a field for the second time that morning.

The man looked up, then walked toward Rutledge.

"Something happened? Sir?" He added it as an afterthought, Rutledge's face warning him that this was not the time for overt insubordination.

Rutledge drew him farther from the curious glances turned their way. Then he said, "You may have heard. There was a body found near Leigh Minster this morning. One of the seach teams came across it."

"Aye, I heard. Nothing to do with *us*." He jerked his head toward the men desultorily digging behind him, half an ear attuned to Truit and Rutledge.

"I understand there was a woman who worked for Mrs. Darley who has been missing for some time. And that she was known in Charlbury as well."

"Betty Cooper, yes, sir. Although she didn't work here, she was known here. But from what I hear, can't be her, she'd have been in the ground longer."

"You're sure?"

"Oh, yes. Of course it's the doctor has to decide, but from what I'd been told, it isn't likely. And she was found over Leigh Minster way—not very likely to be ours, is she? Long way to carry a body, and where she was found isn't a spot strangers would be likely to know was there. Stands to reason."

There was an echo of Hildebrand's voice in the last words.

"Always keep an open mind, Constable!"

"Aye, that I do. Sir."

Rutledge nodded and walked off, unsatisfied. But Hildebrand was right: The second body was none of his business, and he was just as glad to leave it.

He went instead to the Wyatt house, walking into the museum unannounced. Elizabeth Napier turned from the shells she was arranging, a smock over her deep-blue dress and a small feather duster on the floor beside her. "Hello, Inspector!" she said in surprise. "What brings you here?"

"I'd like to speak to Mr. Wyatt. Is he in the museum or at home?"

"Through that door and to your right," she answered, speculation in her eyes. "Has there—has there been any word of Margaret? You aren't asking Simon to break something gently—"

"Nothing, I'm afraid." He kept walking, making his way through the clutter of empty boxes that someone had begun to flatten and set in a pile, preparatory to putting them away. He went through the far door, found a short passage and a small, cluttered room serving as an office, at the end on the right.

Simon was busy with a ledger and what appeared to be a pile of bills. Every surface in the room seemed to be occupied by some half-finished task, waiting to be remembered. He sighed as Rutledge came in, as if the interruption had spoiled his train of thought. Seeing who it was, he leaned back in his chair and began to rub the back of his neck as if it ached. "What is it? Any news?"

"No. I wanted to speak to you. Privately." Rutledge closed the door behind him and pulled out a chair that had been shoved into one corner. After removing the stack of books it held to the floor, he sat down.

"Look, can't this wait?" Simon asked. "I've got to finish this lot, and it's going to take most of the day! I'm not good at this sort of thing, and Aurore knows it. I can't think why she isn't here lending a hand. Thank God Elizabeth can make some sense of those displays. I need every bit of help I can find!"

"No, it can't wait," Rutledge said uncompromisingly. "Take your mind out of that ledger and listen to me!"

Simon reluctantly pushed it to one side, though whether he'd shut the figures out of his mind was another matter. "Very well. What's the problem?"

"I've got a corpse on my hands, I think it must be the woman you were expecting to hire as an assistant, and I have witnesses who tell me that your wife drove Margaret Tarlton back to the railway station. If they're speaking the truth, it means that Aurore Wyatt was probably the last person to see her alive."

He frowned. "I don't see what the problem is. Aurore isn't a murderess!"

Simon Wyatt had also said his wife wasn't a liar. Rutledge found himself wondering if Simon was shallow—or under the stress of his work wasn't able to absorb anything that wasn't connected directly to his museum. "What do you know about your wife—her background, her family?"

"Good God, what do *they* have to do with it!"

"Her parents," Rutledge said patiently, ignoring Hamish's irritated remarks about the constable and now this man.

"They're both dead—mother died some years before the war," he said in some exasperation. "Father killed when the Germans came through—shot, trying to stop the looting of his house and farm. Aurore herself barely escaped—she reached a nunnery just over the Belgian border and was taken in. She was ill for weeks, exhaustion and a fever. Then she tried to make her way south, hoping to stay with a cousin in Provence. I found her, ill again and terrified, in a group of refugees that had come into our sector during the night, and got shot at for their pains. Mercifully nobody was killed, but it was a near thing, scared the very devil out of my men, I can tell you! Word had already been passed that there was movement along the German lines, and then out of the dark! . . . I wouldn't put it past the Hun to think this was a great joke!"

Rutledge understood. You shot at anything that came at you out of the dark without password or provenance.

"What did you do with them?"

"Sent them to the rear, told somebody to take a look at them. That was that. It wasn't until later that I saw Aurore again and hardly recognized her, she'd been so thin, half starved and half out of her mind when she reached us. She had some medical skills, and the doctors must have put her to work."

It was a very superficial account, without emotion, without any sign that the woman he was speaking about was his wife.

"Tell me about your political career," Rutledge asked, trying to find the measure of the man. "I'm told it was very promising."

And Simon changed. There was suddenly a haggardness in his face, a tenseness in the shoulders hunched over the desk. "Why?" Abrupt. Rough. As if Rutledge had turned over a stone and found something unspeakable beneath. Clearly it wasn't a topic he cared to pursue. "It isn't pertinent to murder, is it?"

"Margaret Tarlton was your houseguest for two days. You spoke to her, worked with her. That makes you a suspect, as far as I'm concerned."

For a time Rutledge was sure the man wasn't going to answer at all. Finally Simon said, "Did you know, my father and I sat down and planned my war? Churchill has gotten a good deal of mileage out of *his*! Prisoner of the Boers. Grand escape across a river. People who've been out to South Africa tell me his 'river' was hardly more than a swale, but that's neither here nor there. Good opportunity for a politically minded young man—going to war. I was supposed to write letters home that my father could circulate among his friends and colleagues. Take photographs, keep a journal. Something I could publish privately as soon as the war was finished. We'd even given it a name, that book: *Journey into Oblivion*. And do you know, it turned out to be very apt, that title. I went into oblivion, *and I didn't come back!*"

The pain in the eyes of the man across the desk from Rutledge told him much. It was the same unbearable pain he'd read in Mowbray's. Something so deep, so infinitely dark that it would destroy.

160

Rutledge had seen that look in his own face, bearded and strained, thin and half mad, in a mirror in hospital. *A stranger*, he'd thought, bewildered, *has come back in my place!*

Simon stared at Rutledge, not seeing him, not seeing the reflection of emotion that was there, naked and unguarded, if he'd had the wit to look. He was too busy trying to hold himself together, trying to force the devils back inside the small, crowded box where they'd been locked.

Slamming his fist on the desk, Simon said, "Damn you! *Damn you!*"

His eyes closed, and there was a white grimness about his mouth, as if he felt sick and was fighting hard against the tide of nausea that threatened to overwhelm an iron control.

The silence in the room was so deep that Rutledge could hear a clock striking somewhere in the house, a slow, deep tolling of the hour.

And then, without warning, the door opened and Elizabeth Napier said, *"Dear God!"*

She went protectively to Simon, her hands on his shoulders, the fingers kneading with her anger.

"Leave him alone! Do you hear me!" she cried, lashing out at Rutledge. "I won't have it!"

As if—he thought, his own iron will struggling desperately to reassert control, Hamish pounding in his mind like hammer on anvil—as if small as she was, she could stand in the way of the majesty of the law. "We were discussing the war—" he began in his own defense.

"The war's over," she told him. "It's finished. It killed, it maimed, and it destroyed—and yet none of you will let it go! You carry it around with you like sackcloth and ashes, you live with it in your very bones by day and your dreams by night, and treat it like some Holy Grail you brought back with you! Well, it isn't; it's a legacy of despair and hate and grievous hurt, and I won't let it touch me anymore, do you hear me! I won't let it!"

Rutledge looked at Simon. His eyes were still closed, his breathing ragged and harsh.

But Simon said, "It's all right, Elizabeth. He didn't know—he didn't mean to stir it up. I'm sorry—"

161

But you did! Elizabeth's eyes accused Rutledge. *And it was just as terrible for you as it was for Simon, wasn't it?* "Go away!" she said aloud. "Go away. Before you both find yourselves on the other side of your nightmares!"

And Rutledge got to his feet, knowing he had to leave, that Simon was past questioning and his own frail peace was shattered as well.

"Simon, I'm back—" It was Aurore who had come in, blocking his escape. She looked at her husband, at Elizabeth fiercely protecting him, her hands dug into the white fabric of his shirt, his eyes closed, their bodies touching, her side against his arm, his head resting on her wrist, an intimacy between them that spoke of comfort offered and comfort accepted on a level beyond friendship. She turned to Rutledge, his face grim and his eyes haunted, staring at her as if he too saw her as an outsider.

Without a word she whirled and went out again, with such a deep grief in her movements that Rutledge could feel her pain and his own inability to assuage it.

She was gone, and he still stood where he was, rooted. Until Elizabeth's voice reached him.

"Go to her," she said urgently. "Make her understand! I'll see to Simon."

"No. It's better if you go," Rutledge said. "She won't trust me."

But he found himself walking the three paces between himself and the door, and heard Elizabeth saying, "She needs comfort, and she won't take it from a woman! She's too strong to let me see her cry!"

And he thought that was true.

He found Aurore up by the churchyard, deep into the dark, shadowed clearing under the trees, her hand lifted to one drooping branch, her head against her upper arm.

Not wanting to startle her, he said quietly, "Is there anything I can do?"

She said huskily, "Go away. No."

He moved closer, still some six yards from her, but near enough that his voice wouldn't carry to anyone else.

"I brought back the war, that's all it was. Simon had built a very high wall, but not high enough. It was—Elizabeth came to see what

162

was wrong, she must have heard us—and she thought I'd badgered him. Blame me for what happened."

Aurore turned to face him. There were streaks of tears on her face. He felt a surge of self-disgust, as if he himself had been the one to make her cry. "You brought back the war. Yes, I think that was true. But it was Elizabeth who used it for her own ends. He won't turn to me for comfort anymore. Did you know? He shuts me out, as if he doesn't want me to see what he believes is weakness in him! He thinks—if this museum is a success, I'll admire him, look at him with love and pride for what he's accomplished. He thinks—he thinks that it will wipe out the past. I saw him break, you see. A man can forgive a woman anything but that. If I'd slept with half the British army, he could forgive me. If I had betrayed his soldiers and got them killed, he'd find a way to forgive me. But not *this*!"

He understood her better than she realized. He found himself wondering if perhaps Jean had been clever enough to know that he might come to hate her in the end, if she'd married him after seeing him in hospital, broken and in despair. Then he knew it wasn't an excuse he could make for her—Jean had been half embarrassed, half horrified by what she couldn't understand. She'd been so tightly wrapped in her own dread she hadn't seen the urgent need to reach out and comfort him.

He said, "There were men who came home damaged. Physically, most of them. Emotionally, a good many of them."

Aurore replied with a heaviness that spoke of long sleepless nights waiting for a man to show he cared. "I don't think most of the English soldiers who went to France were prepared for what this war was going to do to them. Battles, yes, they expected battles. Great glorious charges, like Waterloo, where there's no time to think or feel, just the intensity of trying to survive. Instead they sat in filthy trenches. How do they explain this at home? Simon's father wrote over and over, 'Where are the letters you promised? Why are they not coming through? Is it a problem with the censors? And the photographs, where are they? Is the camera working? Do you have film? For God's sake, why are you letting this opportunity slip through your fingers? *Where is the next Churchill?*' And Simon couldn't tell him what was wrong. That he was faced with mortality, and what he'd been born and bred to do no longer seemed to matter. I think he realized for the first time that he hadn't chosen his political future, it had been thrust at him. But in its place, what did he want? What else was he fit for? How do you decide such things on a battlefield? He was the walking dead. Waiting for death to remember he was still there and come for him. There *was* no future. And yet he desperately wanted one."

For an instant she put her hands to her eyes, as if pressing them might stop the aching in her head. Or the aching in her heart. She took a deep shuddering breath, to steady herself.

"Do you even know what I'm saying? I gave him hope. I gave him something to hold in his heart until death came. My body and my love brought him a little peace before the end. Only—he lived. And he wasn't prepared for that. Or for a marriage that might last after all. Or for his father dead and Thomas Napier furious with him for jilting Elizabeth, who was desperately trying to be brave and noble about it. He came home to change—and an accounting. And I was the living symbol of how far he'd fallen from grace in the eyes of those whose good opinion was important to him."

She turned to look up at the church tower, truncated and heavy. Like a wasted promise . . . When she went on, there was no self-pity in her words.

"It was very difficult for both of us. But divorce is hard to come by, you know, it leaves a stigma. And I am Catholic, there is nothing for me afterward. I believed I'd be happier trying to make my marriage work than standing at the quayside and waving good-bye, admitting that I'd failed Simon. And myself as well. I was braced to fight. But I can't fight them all. I don't know how. It would be much better for me to be hanged, guilty or not, sparing Simon the embarrassment of publicly acknowledging that his marriage was a mistake."

She stopped, her body suddenly rigid. "No, I didn't mean that! He would never harm me. He still cares. . . ."

But she had just given Rutledge a motive for her husband to kill.

He said carefully, after a time, "I told you before that I didn't believe Elizabeth would stay. After this is finished. There's nothing to keep her here, except blatant self-interest. And somehow I don't see her confessing to that."

"If I am convicted of murder, she will have Simon without the messy aftermath of divorce. And if I am not, she will have shown him that she still cares. It is something from the past, you see. Something he had thought he'd given up. I don't know—"

He could see the tears glistening in her lashes. "He'd be a fool to choose Elizabeth Napier over you!"

She gave him a watery smile and said for the second time that day, "You are very kind. But you know and I know that this murder has brought to the fore more than just one woman's death. It is something I must face. I don't know how I shall do that. I don't know where it will end, but I shall find the strength I need."

He stood there, helpless, unable to touch her, unable to offer any comfort that didn't sound like *kindness*.

"Mrs. Wyatt—Aurore—"

She shook her head. "No. You must not say anything. Tell me again about the giraffe in the kitchen of the Swan. Forget you're a policeman and I am a suspect, and tell me instead how the giraffe came to wander so very far from home." She gasped as she realized that what she'd said was a reflection of her own dilemma.

Hamish was vigorously protesting that Aurore was trying to distract him.

Rutledge ignored him. He said, "It wasn't so very far from home. Or lost. Only misplaced for a little while. I shouldn't worry for its sake."

"Animals have no complexity in their lives, do they?" she agreed. "How very fortunate they are!"

She walked away, leaving him there in the trees, her back straight, her head held high. Not toward the house but to the church. She was telling him that she wanted privacy and a little time alone.

But he thought perhaps she hadn't stopped crying.

When Rutledge came back for his car, which was parked by the inn, he saw Mrs. Prescott, Constable Truit's neighbor, with a market basket over her arm and a sense of mission in her stride.

She saw him and crossed the street hastily to waylay him.

"What's to do with Mrs. Wyatt? She seemed that upset when she came hurrying out of her gate! Walked right past me without so much as a how-do-you-do, Mrs. Prescott! And you on her heels, like the wrath of God!"

"She's well enough," Rutledge answered. "There was something about a giraffe, I think, worrying her."

Mystified for a moment, Mrs. Prescott then gave him a lopsided smile. "Which is another way of saying I ought to mind my own business. Well, you wouldn't be the first to tell me that. But gossip's like making a quilt. Sorting where the patches belong and where they don't. Weighing size and color and shape. That takes skill, of a kind. I like to gossip, anybody in Charlbury will tell you that!"

"What's Charlbury saying about this body found outside Leigh Minster?"

"I could tell you how many teeth she had in her head, and whether her stockings was cotton or silk!"

"Can you put a name to the teeth?"

"Not yet. She's too long in the ground, they say, to be Miss Tarlton, and too fresh to be that Betty Cooper. Another stranger, d'you think? We're getting fair swamped with strange corpses! I'm told it's none of your business, anyhow. Except that it keeps Inspector Hildebrand busy on two fronts and out of your way." She paused, then said tentatively, "If you don't mind my asking, do you think a man or a woman's behind Miss Tarlton's killing?"

"I don't know. I don't think anyone does at this point."

"What killed her then?"

"We don't have a murder weapon."

"If that's what's worrying you, I'll give you a free word of advice," Mrs. Prescott said. "A man, now, he'd pick up any tool and feel comfortable with that. A woman will be more likely to reach for something familiar, something she's used to. If I was angry enough to kill, I'd pick up that iron doorstop of mine. The one shaped like an owl—"

She could see the change in his face. The thought awakening in his mind. Curiosity was lively in her eyes. She started to speak, then thought better of it.

He thanked her and was already hurrying toward his motorcar.

It was stupid of him! he told himself. A rank beginner would have thought about it a long time ago. But then a rank beginner might not have been dazzled by Aurore Wyatt's unusual attraction.

He hadn't gone out to the Wyatt farm. Where Aurore claimed she'd spent the morning Margaret Tarlton was scheduled to leave. Where the car had been driven that same morning, instead of being available at the house to take a guest to the station . . .

The farm . . .

He could hear Frances's voice: "*Where would I hide a suitcase? Where no one ever goes. . . .*"

In the back of his mind Hamish was saying, "I've tried to tell you—"

17

The road that ran west through the village climbed a low knoll on its outskirts, twisted down again, and within a hundred feet passed a pair of stone gates that stood at the head of a narrow lane. An ornate *W* was engraved on a worn tablet on one of the posts. The farm itself was nearly invisible behind a stand of trees. He turned in through the gates, swearing as his wheels bumped heavily along ancient ruts made by carts and drays. The lane was arrow straight, leading through a double row of trees, shaded and quiet except for a blackbird singing somewhere in the thick branches. It ended in a muddy yard, where a small stone house was backed by a great barn, a long open shed for farm equipment, and a number of smaller, shabby outbuildings. The property was not run down, as he'd expected, but the signs of neglect were there to be seen: in the old thatch on the house that should have been renewed five years ago; the shingles missing from the barn's high roof and the pointing badly needed in some of the courses of stone; the weathered wood of the sheds; the rank grass that grew up in corners and under rusting bits of gear scattered about the barn's yard behind the house.

Chickens could be heard, clucking and squabbling, and a horse neighed from the dim, cool recesses of the barn. The hay rick, not fresh and new, was half gone, the new hay left in the sun to dry.

The house seemed empty—sometimes, Rutledge thought, you could tell by the feel of it. He walked to the door and peered in the nearest window. The room he could see was clean and tidy, but the furniture was castoffs from the past, the carpet threadbare, and there were no curtains at any of the windows. He could just see a staircase that rose to the next floor from the entrance hall. When he tried the door, the knob turned under his hand, but he didn't go inside.

He moved on to the barn, stepping inside the great open door. Dust motes floated in heavy air smelling of manure and hay and moldering leather. An old side saddle was propped over a wooden bench. In the far dimness, a pair of horses turned their heads to stare with interest at him. A cat, stretched out along the top of a shelf, yawned and stared at him as well, through narrow, yellow eyes. Doves cooed desultorily from the rafters of the loft.

And where was the caretaker? Out in the fields? Or in one of the scattered outbuildings?

He went back to his motorcar and blew the horn. Once, then twice. In the silence that followed he thought he heard the lowing of cows, softened by distance. He blew the horn again. After a time a man in ragged coveralls peered out of one of the smaller sheds. He was tall, wiry, his white hair cut short, his face weather-lined. It was hard to judge his age. Fifty? Older, Rutledge thought.

As he came warily toward Rutledge his stiff gait said closer to seventy.

"Lost, are ye? Well, that's the difference between one of them newfangled motorcars and a horse. A horse has sense when you don't!"

He smelled strongly of ale and a mixture of manure and dried earth.

Rutledge said easily, "My name is Rutledge, I'm helping the local police look into the disappearance of a young woman who was found murdered a few miles from here—"

"You're not a local man," the farmer said, shading his eyes from the sun to stare at Rutledge's face. His fingernails were crusted with dirt from working in the vegetable gardens, and his chin was poorly shaved, as if he couldn't see to use his razor.

"No. I'm from Scotland Yard."

"Ha! London, is it?" He spat. "That Truit needs all the help you can give. Whoring son of a bitch, can't keep his eyes or his hands to himself. *Or* hold his liquor!" There was disdain and disgust in the loud voice. "*Constable*, my left hind foot!" He considered Rutledge for a moment. "I thought they'd caught the man who'd done the killing."

"We don't know if we have or not, Mr.—" He left the sentence unfinished.

After a moment the caretaker said, "Jimson. Ted Jimson." He was still watching Rutledge closely.

"How long have you worked here?"

"Worked here? Nigh all my life! What's that to do with a murder?"

Rutledge said idly, as if it was more a matter of curiosity than anything else, "I understand that Mrs. Wyatt was here on fifteen August, from around eleven o'clock until well into the afternoon, working with a sick animal."

Jimson thought for a time. "The fifteenth, you say? Aye, as I recollect, she was. That colicky heifer had to be fed from a bottle and cosseted. Damn near lost it, and we'd paid high enough for the bull! Stayed till nigh on four, I'd guess, getting it back on its legs. I'll say one thing, French or not, she has a way with cattle!" He gave the impression that he was of two minds about his mistress.

"And where were you?"

"Loitering in my bed, waiting for the servants to bring me my breakfast! Where the hell do you think I might be? Working, that's what! Besides the milking, there was rotting boards in the loft that had to be shored up and potatoes to be dug, and the fence in the chicken yard had rusted, some of the little 'uns was running loose." Yet Aurore had said he had had a cold . . . or a hangover.

"Could you see Mrs. Wyatt from where you worked?"

"You don't keep a heifer in the loft, nor with the chickens!"

"Could she see you?"

"I doubt she could, but she wouldn't miss the hammering in the loft. What's this in aid of, then? You think *I* had something to do with this killing?"

Rutledge felt a sense of tension in the man, as if he had told the truth but skirted the edges of lying. How far would he go for Aurore—or for Simon Wyatt?

"We need to be sure where everyone was that afternoon. Often people aren't aware that they are witnesses. Was Mrs. Wyatt driving that day, or did she walk here?"

"Aye, driving. I saw her when she came up the lane in the Wyatt car. She waved to me when she got out. But it didn't appear to me she wanted to talk."

"Did the car leave during the time you thought she was here?"

"Not that I could say. But I didn't set and watch it either."

"And so Mrs. Wyatt stayed with the sick heifer, missing her luncheon?"

"How should I know? When I'd finished with the chickens and wanted my own meal, I didn't look for her to ask permission!"

"You didn't offer her lunch?"

"Lord, no! What I cook ain't fit for a lady's taste!" he said, horrified. "Bacon and cheese, it was, with *onions*!"

A countryman's meal. But the French took the same simple ingredients, added eggs and herbs, producing an omelet. It was all, Rutledge thought, in what you were used to.

"You are sure neither Mrs. Wyatt nor the car went away, from the time she arrived to the time she left. From eleven, let's say, until four."

The watery gray eyes flickered. "I didn't see her leave," Jimson answered. "But she'd come in to wash up, her boots was out by the kitchen door."

"You mean she didn't leave between eleven and four, or you didn't see her go home at four?" He couldn't seem to get a straight answer from Jimson.

"I didn't see her go at four. When I came back from mending a fence down by the water, closer to five it was, the car was gone. I know, because I went around the house to fetch the milk cans from the road, and the lane was empty."

Rutledge turned and looked back the way he had come. The trees were old, heavy with late summer leaves, the shadows under them dark and cool. Once this had been a thriving farm, children had been born and patriarchs had died in the house behind him, smoke had risen from the chimneys, washing had hung on the lines, the smell of fresh bread and baked pies had wafted from open windows. Dogs had run in the yard and flowers had bloomed in the weed-grown beds. Until the first Wyatt discovered the power and authority of Westminster, and the family had bettered itself.

"Do you live in the farmhouse?" he asked Jimson.

The man didn't answer. Rutledge turned around and repeated the question, his mind still probing the past. If Simon Wyatt hadn't gone to war, Aurore his wife would never have come to England and this place. Was it very like the home she'd left? Was this farm her sanctuary, however run down it was, because it reminded her of her parents and peace and a life very different from the one she lived in Charlbury?

Jimson said testily, "I've a room at the back. That and the kitchen, it's all I want—or need."

"Does anyone else use the other rooms?"

"Aye, we've got the King in one and the Queen in t'other! Are ye daft?"

"It's a large house for one man."

"The Wyatts always had a tenant and his family living here. I come over daily from Charlbury then. Mr. Oliphant, he went to New Zealand in 1913, and that was the end to that. The other dairymen went off to fight the Hun. Mrs. Wyatt says there's no money to hire 'em back now, *nor* to fix the barn roof! I moved to the house after my wife died, just to keep an eye on the place. Mrs. Wyatt, she keeps some things in one of the upstairs rooms. Towels and coveralls."

Rutledge had run out of questions. And yet he had a strong feeling that because he'd been partly distracted, he had overlooked something. What?

Jimson watched him, waiting.

The man wasn't lying, Rutledge was fairly certain of that. Jimson was telling the truth as he saw it. But police work had taught Rutledge that a witness could reply to questions exactly, even honestly—and still manage to avoid the whole truth.

And suddenly the answer was there, in the man's very watchfulness.

Jimson hadn't heard the sound of Rutledge's engine—and he

wouldn't have heard the Wyatt car leave—or return. Speak to him directly, while he stared at your face, and he could follow a conversation well enough to give reasonable answers. It took concentration and to some extent a painfully learned ability to read lips. This most certainly explained the tension in him.

The man wasn't lying. He was going deaf. He had told Rutledge what his eyes had seen, but there was no way for him to know what sounds he might or might not have missed. Anyone could have come—or gone—from here. And at any time. Jimson could only say with any certainty when Aurore had come.

As an alibi for Aurore Wyatt, he was useless.

Yet she must have known . . . so why had she left her own safety to hang on such a fragile thread?

Rutledge asked if he might look through the house or the barn, but Jimson shook his head. "Not without permission," he said staunchly. "I don't have authority to let you go poking about in Mr. Wyatt's property. He might not like it, policeman or no."

The last thing Rutledge wanted to do was ask Aurore for permission.

Neither Hildebrand nor Bowles would authorize a search warrant. Both of them would be far more likely to read him a lecture on the exact nature of his responsibility in this inquiry.

If the suitcase was here—the hat—even the murder weapon—they would have to remain here until he had enough evidence to show cause to search.

And yet as he stood in the drive, he had a feeling that this farm had played a role in Margaret Tarlton's death. How or why, he wasn't sure. Alibi—or evidence? For—or against Aurore Wyatt?

Instinct, light as the breeze that ruffled the leaves of the trees and toyed with the grass at his feet, made him say to Jimson, "No matter. It was purely curiosity, not police business. This was quite a prosperous dairy in its day."

"Aye, it was," Jimson said, sadness in his voice as he looked around him. "The best dairy in the county, to my way of thinking. Now we've not got thirty cows in milk, and I see to all of them, with Mrs. Wyatt's help. I was that proud to work here, man and boy. That's the trouble with living too long. In my time I've seen

173

more change than I liked. Mrs. Wyatt, now, she says change is good, but I don't know. I'll be dead and in the ground before this place turns around. There's no money, and no hope here. If I was her, I'd go back to France tomorrow and leave it to rot, instead of watching it fall slowly to pieces."

"She has a husband. She can't leave."

"Simon Wyatt's not the man his father was. I never saw such a difference in all my life as when he came home from the war. What's he want that museum for? Dead, heathenish things!" He shook his head. "Mrs. Daulton, now, she says it might be better for him than standing for Parliament. Choices are a good thing, she says. There weren't no choices when I was a lad, you did what your pa did, you counted yourself lucky to find a good woman to marry, and you raised your children to be decent, God-fearing Englishmen. And the dead didn't wander about in the night, talking to fence posts and trees, looking for their soul!"

Startled, Rutledge said, "Who wanders about in the night?" The first name that came to mind was Henry Daulton. He wasn't sure why, except that Henry must find his mother's steadfast belief in his full recovery overwhelming at times.

"Ghosts!" Jimson said direly, gesturing around him, and turned to walk back to the barn. Rutledge called to him and then swore, remembering that the caretaker was deaf.

But no amount of persuasion could pry another word out of the old man.

18

The police spent all day trying to find a connection between the corpse that had been discovered in the field near Leigh Minster and any of the communities ringing the location—Leigh Minster itself, Stoke Newton, Singleton Magna, or Charlbury.

But just as the constables had reported, there were no missing women. And no newly hired domestics who had failed to appear at the time set for them to begin work. No cousins, daughters, wives, sisters-in-law, or other female relatives unaccounted for. She was clearly a stranger, then. Except that there were seldom any sound reasons for killing strangers.

Hildebrand marked her down as an unsolved murder and went back to looking for the Mowbray children. He drove the teams of searchers with a determination that was both praiseworthy and single-minded.

Dr. Fairfield, a small man of few words, established the time of death at approximately three to four months earlier.

"She couldn't have been in the ground longer," he told Rutledge later, stripping off his white coat and hanging it on a hook behind the door of the bare room where he kept the dead. "And her clothing supports the timing. This is August. I daresay she died in late April, early May. Cool enough weather to have her coat with her. Cause of death? I'd say she was choked but not killed by strangulation. It was the beating about the head that finished the job. I found a fracture just above the temple, small but sufficient. I don't think she was sexually molested. There's no indication of it, from what I can see now, and her clothing is oddly tidy, as if whoever buried her had laid her out carefully on the coat."

"Was it the same person, do you think, who killed the Mowbray woman? Or Margaret Tarlton, as she may be?"

The doctor frowned, rubbing his chin. "That's harder to say. This one's skin is gone, you don't see the damage as readily. But yes, it might have been the same killer. *Might*, mind you! I'm not an authority on murder. Still, both women appear to have been attacked by someone who clearly intended to kill them but, in the end, didn't know how to finish the job quickly or properly. When it's anger that runs amok to the point of destructive force, there's generally more damage—to the head, the throat, the shoulders. Then the blows land randomly, you see, driven by rage and intended to inflict as much hurt—and therefore as much satisfaction—as possible. Here the blows were confined to the head, mainly the face, as if to conceal identity as well as to kill." He looked up at the taller man before him. "Does that seem odd to you? What I'm saying?"

"Not to a policeman. No."

The doctor sighed. "Of course murder is seldom premeditated, is it? That is, with planning and preparation. And the fact is, the human being isn't easy to murder, without the proper tools. A knife. A firearm. A garrote. Even a hammer will do. Whoever killed these two women—whether it was the same person or two different people—it was emotion that drove him or her in the beginning. And then necessity took over. He had to silence the victim, you see. And he had a quite nasty job there. If I were you, having to search for the right person, I'd find someone who"—he paused, seeking the right words—"who was determined to go on, however gruesome the task, until the woman's pulse stopped."

"That can run either direction—a secret to be kept, or merely the realization that a live victim can point a finger at his attacker," Rutledge responded, thinking about it.

"Hmmm. Secrets take many forms, don't they? From the sins of the flesh to the sins of the soul." The doctor smiled, but without humor or lightness. "This one is terrible enough that the killer was willing to suffer horror himself—herself—in order to keep it safe. Until you've battered someone to death, Inspector, you can't conceive of how much blood and flesh and bone are spattered about. Only a madman can relish that, or someone so deranged by emotion that the flecks are not even registered, until it's over. Or someone grimly carrying on to the bitter end." He turned out the light in the hall and led the way to the side door of his surgery. "Does what I've told you help at all?"

"Yes," Rutledge said tiredly. "Unfortunately, I think it does."

"Well, I'm glad to hear it," the doctor said, taking up his own coat and putting it on. "I'm late at a dinner party, and my wife won't be happy about that. Hildebrand didn't find my information useful. He's a good man, Inspector, but he makes up his mind to suit the facts. If I took the same approach in medicine, I'd have filled the churchyard with my mistakes!"

Rutledge walked back to the Swan, thinking about what the doctor had said. Hamish, in the back of his mind, was reminding him that blindness could be worse than deafness. Rutledge ignored him as long as he could and then said, "It isn't blindness. Human nature enters into it. I can't see Aurore Wyatt beating anyone to death. You said as much yourself once."

"Women," Hamish said, "will kill to protect their bairns—and their man. Margaret Tarlton was Simon Wyatt's past, returned to haunt him. *She* did na' want that. And the woman wasn't going away, she was staying."

"Jealousy? No, I don't see Aurore Wyatt being jealous of Margaret or anyone else." Yet she was afraid of Elizabeth Napier.

"Who's spoken of jealousy?" Hamish demanded.

Rutledge stopped, watching a carriage coming up the hill toward the inn. The streets were deserted, it was just the dinner hour. He stood still and could hear laughter coming from the house on his left, and people's voices. The carriage rattled past and disappeared among the trees at the top of the hill. A cat stepped out of the inn's yard, ears twitching, catching the distant sound of a dog's raucous bark. Something fluttered overhead—a bat, he thought.

But deeper was another thought. Why had Simon Wyatt turned away from his future in Parliament? What was the *real* reason?

A foreign wife might not be an asset—but with the proper backing, even that might be overcome. If Elizabeth Napier's father had turned against Wyatt for rejecting his daughter and putting in her place a French nobody, he was—by all accounts—an astute enough politician to know that you didn't have to *like* the men you backed, you only needed to be sure of their support in the future. The Wyatt name had been magic in this part of Dorset for more than one generation. A safe seat for this constituency.

Simon and Aurore blamed his decision on the war. But what if there was something more than war weariness—or a devotion to his other grandfather—that made a very able and personable man choose seclusion over a brilliant career? A small museum without the resources to grow, hidden away in the Dorset countryside where visitors were few, where the exhibits would surely have a very narrow appeal, however interesting they were in their own right . . . It didn't quite add up.

"It's no' what I was saying—" Hamish began.

But Rutledge cut him short. His eyes moved across to the police station where Mowbray still sat in his gloomy cell, watched day and night. "It's a beginning, isn't it?" he responded. "That's all that matters!"

The station door opened and Hildebrand came out, then paused as he saw Rutledge looking toward him. An instant's hesitation, and he walked on, as if the man on the other side of the street didn't exist.

"You've spoiled his investigation," Hamish pointed out. "He will na' thank you for it."

"Mowbray might," Rutledge said. "Nobody else seems to care about him."

After eating his dinner without being aware of what was on his plate or his fork, Rutledge went out to his car and turned it toward Charlbury.

It was late in the evening to be calling on police business, but often the unexpected worked more successfully than the routine.

The road was dark, nearly empty, except for a dog that trotted into the undergrowth as the car's headlamps flicked over the crest of the rise. But Charlbury was brighter, and the Wyatt house looked as if it was expecting the King. There were lamps lit in most of the rooms, and in the museum wing. He left his car up by the church and walked back, making his way to the wing on foot. He thought: Curious . . . so much light and no sounds of voices, of people shouting or talking or laughing.

The museum was empty. The masks leered at him in the brightness, mouths agape or dark slashes, eyes black with speculation or alarm, and the weapons, doubled with their own shadows, gave the rooms an air of tension. He walked through the three main areas, into the small, empty office, and then into the room across from it, hardly more than a large broom closet. He had never been there before. It held a bed with only a blanket, military in its folds, a chair, and a wooden table of indeterminate age, rescued from the attics or a jumble sale. A cupboard held a pair of shoes and some underwear, a clean shirt and a folded, freshly pressed pair of trousers.

Rutledge stood there in silence, not needing Hamish's comments to tell him that this was where Simon Wyatt spent most of his nights.

A gasp from the doorway made him spin around.

Aurore was there, grasping the frame with fingers that were white. "For a moment I thought—" She stopped. "Were you looking for Simon?" Her voice had steadied, sounded nearly normal. "Couldn't you have come to the door and knocked, as everyone else does?"

"—that I was Simon?" he asked, finishing her first, unguarded reaction. "I didn't come to the door because I saw the lights here and thought he was in this wing. I preferred not to disturb the household, calling so late."

"Simon . . . is out," she said.

But her eyes were showing the strain of worry, and he said, "What's wrong?" His words crossing hers.

She let the door frame go, then shrugged, that French expression of *I wash my hands*. . . . "He doesn't sleep well. At night. He hasn't since the war. He rests here sometimes, when he doesn't want to disturb me, moving about the house in the dark. Or if he's very tired, sometimes in the afternoon. That's why the bed is here. It doesn't signify."

It was an apology for her husband. Perhaps for the state of her marriage. And an attempt to distract him. But the tension in her was palpable.

He read her eyes, not her words. "What's wrong?" he repeated.

"You misunderstand, there is nothing to worry you." She looked away.

He stood there, watching her. In the end, she turned her face back to him and said, "It isn't a police matter! Simon has gone somewhere. I was worried when he didn't come to dinner. I waited, and finally I went to find him. But he isn't in the house. Or in the grounds. I've looked. Elizabeth Napier took it upon herself to walk up to the church and to the Wyatt Arms. He won't be there, but it gave her something to do."

And took her out of my way. . . . The thought if not the words hovered between them.

"How long has he been gone? Did he take the car or one of the carriages?"

"Since teatime. I think. The motorcar is still here, and the carriage."

"Then he must be in the village—at the Arms or at the rectory, perhaps."

After a moment she said, "It—this isn't the first time he has gone without telling me. But not this long, before. That's the only reason I worry."

She stared at him, her eyes begging but saying nothing. Refusing to betray her husband.

The dead didn't wander about in the night, talking to fence posts and trees, looking for their soul. Jimson's words echoed darkly in his mind.

"Can I help? Mrs. Wyatt?"

Hamish was telling him that it was not his affair, it was not police business. But Rutledge had an intense feeling that it might be. Men like Simon Wyatt didn't walk out their door at teatime and disappear.

"You can help by returning to Singleton Magna and calling again in the morning. Everything will be well in the morning, I promise you!"

"Will it? Let me help you find him. Discreetly. People are used to a policeman prowling about. God knows, we've searched for days in every conceivable place for those children! Where shall I begin?"

"He hasn't—" She stopped, then after a moment said, "Before this, he was always in the house or the gardens." Yet her voice seemed hollow, even to her own ears. "Always."

Again he read her eyes, ignoring her words. "But you aren't sure of that, are you? If he often slept here, in this bed, or worked long hours in this wing, how could you be sure? Where he went—or when—or for how long! During the day or in the night."

Aurore bit her lip. "The house—with Elizabeth Napier here, moving between the house and the museum, he must feel—I don't know. *Caught*."

"But he was proposing to hire an assistant. She would have been in the house and the museum day after day."

She said angrily, "I don't know! Explain it however you will!"

"Do you want to come with me?"

Aurore shook her head. "No. I'll stay. In the event . . ." She let the sentence run into silence again. *In the event he returns of his own accord . . . and needs me.*

He walked past her, near enough to smell the fragrance of her hair and perfume. Lily of the valley . . . But she didn't turn, she didn't say anything more.

At first he quartered Charlbury, down toward the inn, up toward the church. He saw Elizabeth Napier speaking to someone by the church door and thought it might be Joanna Daulton. Nothing.

He went on to the motorcar and began to drive toward the farm, thinking that it was a logical place for Wyatt to escape to if he wanted peace from the two women who drew him first this way and then that.

Jimson had seen him in the night—it has happened before. Rutledge didn't need Hamish to tell him. He had already gotten there on his own.

For some reason the old man must have thought the ghosts of

the Wyatts were walking their farmland again, unable to rest in peace. Peering out a window in the night, seeing the shadowy figure crossing the moonlit yard, he wouldn't have questioned it, he would have accepted its right to be there.

The farmhouse was dark, save for a single light—a lamp—in a back room that must mark Jimson's bedchamber. The barn too was empty save for the animals that belonged there. No one challenged Rutledge as he moved about. And the only sounds were those that belonged to the night, not to restless spirits.

Turning the other way, back toward Charlbury, he drove through the town and slowed, peering beyond his lights into the fields, trying to pin any tall, manlike shadow against the sky. He'd been good at that, in the war, as Hamish reminded him. Spotting scouts or the first wave of a silent attack coming across no-man's-land. Swift vision sometimes made the difference in surprise. . . .

He was close to where he'd seen the dog earlier when he realized that a tree in the middle distance had what appeared to be a double trunk. Rutledge pulled off the road and left the car, crossing the fields with swift, long strides. The figure didn't move. It wasn't leaning against a tree, it was simply standing beside it, as if in conversation with it. *Talking to trees . . .*

"He's mad, no better than you are," Hamish was saying tensely.

Rutledge ignored the voice. As he slowed his pace and moved silently nearer, the figure didn't look up or show any sign of awareness. It simply stood, a black line against the horizon, as if put there by a sculptor's hand.

Rutledge was now within five yards. He said, "Wyatt?"

Nothing. No response at all.

He came within reach, he could have put out a hand and touched the still, straight shoulder. It was uncanny. The silence went on, unbroken except for the sound of their breathing.

Unnerving. He'd spent too many nights on the Front, listening to the sound of breathing as men waited. But what was this one waiting for?

"Wyatt?" He spoke gently, firmly, trying not to startle the other man.

Nothing. Except Hamish, growling a warning.

Undecided, he stood there, observing, peering into the darkness at the expressionless face, the rigidity of the body. Simon Wyatt was oblivious to his surroundings. Wherever he was in spirit, he neither heard nor saw anything.

After a time Rutledge touched the man's arm, lightly, undemandingly, no more than one man would touch another in the way of acknowledgment, comfort.

Simon stirred.

Rutledge said quietly, without fuss, "It's Inspector Rutledge. From Singleton Magna. Can I give you a lift to Charlbury? I've got my car. Over there."

The sentences were short, the tone of voice neutral.

Simon turned to look at him, but even in the starlight Rutledge was sure the blank eyes were not actually seeing him. Wherever Simon was, it was a very long distance from here.

Then he said, unexpectedly, the strain intense in his voice, as if his throat were tight with fear or some inner conflict. "Major? They aren't firing tonight."

Rutledge felt a jolt of shock but kept his voice level. "No. It's over for tonight. It's time to go back."

Simon said only, "Yes." And when Rutledge turned tentatively, to walk back the way he'd come, Simon silently fell into step behind him.

When they reached the car, Simon spoke again, this time in a perfectly natural, if rather tired, voice. "Nice of you to give me a lift back, Rutledge." As though he'd gone walking after his dinner and nothing else had happened.

"My pleasure," Rutledge answered, and turned the crank.

They were halfway to Charlbury when Simon added, "I wonder what time it is." When Rutledge told him, he said, surprised, "That late? I must have walked farther than I realized. Aurore will be worried."

"Walk often in the evening, do you?" Rutledge said, as if making conversation and not caring whether the question was answered or not.

"No. There's so much to do, readying the museum. No time for country pleasures. As it is I'm behind schedule. The invitations have already gone out, I can't change the date now. Elizabeth and Aurore between them are already handling the arrangements for the catering."

It was as if Simon Wyatt had no memory of where he'd been—or why.

19

$\mathscr{A}$urore, watching for them from the windows of the museum, came out to greet them on the front walk. Her manner was interesting. She neither touched her husband nor asked him, as a worried, frightened wife might do, what he'd been thinking of, where he'd been. Only her eyes mirrored her distress.

She said, "You must be tired."

"I am, rather. I think I'll turn in, if you don't mind." He nodded to Rutledge.

She shot a warning glance at Rutledge and said, "Yes, do that." Then stood silently beside the man from London as her husband walked toward the house and went inside alone. Rutledge could hear her unsteady breathing.

"Where did you find him?" she asked in a low voice. "You've been gone for nearly an hour!"

"I went to the farm but I don't think he'd been there. There were no lights in the house, except in the room the caretaker uses. And the barn was empty as well. I decided I should go in the other direction, out the Singleton Magna road. I found him in a field beyond the town. Standing there like a pillar of salt. He neither saw nor heard me coming, and he didn't know who I was, until we started back to Charlbury." He stopped, not wanting to tell her about their brief exchange in the field. And Simon hadn't been

185

talking to a tree—he had simply been standing, as far as Rutledge could see, in its shelter.

She nodded. "That's how it happens. He seems completely lost to his surroundings. It isn't wine, it isn't a drug. By this time surely I'd know if it was those things!"

Rutledge said only, "No. He hadn't been drinking, and his eyes were blank, but the pupils were normal. As far as I could tell he wasn't sleepwalking either." He paused, then added, "Mrs. Wyatt. That man is under intense stress. Do you see that? Have you spoken to a physician?"

She smiled wryly. "What can I say to a man of medicine? How could I persuade Simon to believe he needed to see such a one? If I say he suddenly loses awareness of where he is and what is happening around him, they will say oh, he is in excellent health, I assure you. Perhaps with so much on his mind, he is forgetful—"

She broke off as Elizabeth Napier came out of the house, walking toward them with swift, intent strides. "He's home, he's perfectly fine, Aurore! Whatever was all this alarm about? Oh, good evening, Inspector. Did she summon you as well, in her distress? How silly! All for naught."

Aurore said nothing, as if Elizabeth's words had put a seal on what she had just been telling him. Rutledge said, "I was driving down the Charlbury road and happened to see Mr. Wyatt there. I gave him a lift."

"Ah! His father often took walks after his dinner. He said it cleared his head wonderfully. It's not surprising Simon feels the same way just now, with the opening so near." It was meant to be reassuring but managed to point out at the same time that Aurore wasn't a part of the Wyatt legend, couldn't be expected to know such things, wouldn't remember—as Elizabeth did—what ran in the family. "Well, it's late. I must go to the inn and to bed myself. Did Inspector Hildebrand tell you? I'm staying in Charlbury for the next week. Will you see me safely to my door, Inspector?"

"With pleasure." He turned to Aurore. "I'd like to speak to you—"

But she shook her head. "As Miss Napier says, it is late and I am

186

tired. Whatever you wish to tell me or to ask me, please, tomorrow will be soon enough."

Upstairs a light went out. Seeing it, Rutledge wondered if Simon Wyatt was sleeping in his own bed—or making his way down to that cramped room in the back of the museum. Elizabeth Napier took his arm and said good night to Aurore, then let Rutledge lead her to the gate, closing it after them.

Aurore stood where she was, on the front walk. Light from the house windows framed her hair like an aureole but shadowed her face. He wondered what she was thinking and found himself distracted by Elizabeth Napier's comments.

"I shouldn't have said what I did! It's just that I've known Simon for so long I feel exasperated sometimes when Aurore fails to understand him. And that's my own failure, really, not hers. I'd worry about my husband too, in her place; the strain of this museum opening is telling on both of them!"

He wondered suddenly if she was rattling on because she knew more than she wanted him to see. Then he decided it was merely a matter of covering her tracks. They walked down the quiet street, nodding to several men passing by but to all intents and purposes they were quite alone.

"Do you think so?"

"Yes, there's a distance between them, you can feel it. I think— I'm afraid she feels that this museum may come between them. But it won't," Elizabeth said positively, taking his arm as they crossed the dark street. "No, he's doing this because he felt he owed something to the maternal side of his family. It's an obligation he strongly believes in. I think the war made him realize that. Once it's done, once he's finished organizing it, someone else will be given the day-by-day responsibility of running this museum, and I see Simon returning to the world he was bred to."

"London. And politics," Rutledge offered. Wondering if Margaret Tarlton had been sent here to take over the museum once its purpose had been served, allowing Simon Wyatt his freedom. And keeping Margaret out of London and Thomas Napier's eye.

"Of course. I don't believe Aurore appreciates how strongly the tradition is in this family. To serve, to lead. To set an example for others. I know Simon far better than she does. I should do, I've known him most of his life!"

"Have you told Aurore—Mrs. Wyatt—what you believe his future may hold?"

"Good heavens, no! That's for Simon to do when the time comes."

"What do you think happened tonight?" They had nearly reached the Wyatt Arms.

"Nothing. A lover's quarrel, most likely, and Simon went out to walk it off. And it upset Aurore when he didn't come back. She must be a very possessive woman. Well, politics will soon teach her that *that* isn't wise!"

"It wasn't a misunderstanding with you—over his future—that Wyatt wanted to think about? Away from the house."

Elizabeth Napier pulled her hand from his arm and turned to stare up at him. "Whatever gave you that idea! Don't tell me Aurore felt—or was it something Simon said, as you brought him home?"

"This has nothing to do with Aurore Wyatt," he said, opening the inn door and holding it for her. From the bar he could hear voices, Denton's rising to answer someone, and then laughter, the chink of glasses and the smell of beer and smoke and sausages. "Nor with anything Wyatt said to me. I'm asking you for your observations of his mood. Since you know him so well."

She cocked her head to one side, her eyes on the sign swinging blackly against the stars above them. "Do you really want to hear what I believe? Or does Aurore have you so completely under her spell that you can't view any of this objectively?"

"She doesn't—" he began, irritated, but Elizabeth cut him short.

"Don't be silly," she said for a second time. "Aurore Wyatt is a very attractive—and very lonely—woman. Men find that an irresistible combination. It isn't surprising. All right, I think she wants to keep him here, bucolic and safe. She may even have been the one who first put the museum idea into his head. I don't know and I don't actually care. The fact remains, you don't understand what pressures *she* brings to bear in that household. You take her at face value, this lovely, foreign, exotic woman. You don't sit across from her at the breakfast table, nor do you have to live with her every day. Simon does. Ask yourself what she's truly like, and you may have some glimmer of what Simon's life is like. Don't misunderstand me, I'm not speaking as the jilted woman here, I'm telling you what my observations are—today—now. If I wanted to compete with Aurore Wyatt for her husband, I'd hardly be likely to drive him to wander about the countryside in the dark, to escape me. Would I? There are a thousand more subtle ways of destroying his marriage and bringing him back to me. The question is, then, do I really need to scheme for him if his own wife has already estranged herself from him? Good night, Inspector!"

And with that she turned, walked into the inn, and, without looking back, went up the stairs with that regal manner that had so impressed everyone at the Swan in Singleton Magna.

As his eyes followed her, Rutledge became aware of movement at the corner table under the stairs. A very sober Shaw was looking at him with a grin on his face.

"Yes, I heard all that. Women are bitches," he said softly, "however well bred they may be and however blue their bloodlines are. Come in, and have a drink with me, before my uncle calls time. You look as if you could use one!"

Rutledge took up his invitation and sat down. The rings on the table had either been wiped away—or they hadn't accumulated this night. Shaw was nursing one pint that appeared to have gone flat long since. He called to his uncle, who brought another pint for Rutledge.

"The lovely Aurore isn't Simon Wyatt's problem," Shaw was saying. "It probably isn't the lovely Miss Napier either. What's bothering him is a guilty conscience."

Interested, Rutledge said, "Guilt over what? Putting this museum before his father's expectations of him?"

"The war. What he learned about himself out there in France. Because you do. You soon know if you're a coward or not. Most of us are, only we find ways to hide it, at least from other people."

It was something all of them had faced. The question of bravery. Of courage—and these two were not the same. Of mortality. Of what life was. And what death meant. *He himself had brought Hamish home....*

Losing for an instant the thread of the conversation, Rutledge said, "You're saying that he failed himself?"

"No, I'm saying he didn't like the man he turned out to be. I don't suppose his father expected the war to last, and I don't suppose Simon did either. Well, none of us did! Quick in and quick out was the idea. Only it wasn't that way, and in the end, those of us who survived knew what kind of men we were. Some of us even learned to live with it, however little we liked what we saw. But Simon, told all his life that he was Jesus Christ, son of God, fell far below his own estimation and never recovered."

"That's a very . . . sober . . . assessment," Rutledge answered. He had nearly used the word *cruel*, and changed it at the very last.

"I *am* sober. The pain isn't so bad tonight. I saw Wyatt leave his house."

Without particular emphasis, Rutledge said, "Did you indeed? When?"

"Tonight, damn you! I said good evening as we passed in the street. He never answered. He walked past me as if he hadn't seen me. And I could have touched him, I was that close. Gave me the willies, I can tell you. His face was empty. As if his body was moving of its own volition."

"Sleepwalking?"

"God, no. His eyes were open, he didn't stumble or weave, he moved like a man with a destination. Only he was deaf and dumb."

"Your imagination," Rutledge said. "He may just have been pre-occupied."

"It wasn't shell shock either," Shaw said, ignoring him. "I recognize that when I see it, we had four or five men in our unit who were shambling wrecks before we got them out of the front lines. Pathetic, shaking, barely human."

Rutledge felt the sudden, unstoppable jolt run through him, jerking the glass in his hand until it spilled. He swore and looked down at his cuff, to conceal his face and Hamish's swift response: *Barely human . . .*

"So it has to be something else," Shaw went on, oblivious, buried in his own feelings. "Something inside the man that he himself doesn't see. Until it manifests itself in sudden blackouts. Which tells

190

me it's some sort of deeply buried guilt, and he can't face it. What other reason is there?"

"It might be more recent than the war. It might be Miss Tarlton's death."

Shaw laughed without any hint of humor. "Are you trying to say that he lapses into these states and commits murder? Or the other way around, commits murder and then lapses out of guilt? You must really be at a loss to find answers for all these bodies you've turned up!"

Rutledge studied him. "You've been thinking about this, haven't you? Ever since you met Wyatt in the street? Or even before that."

"Oh, yes," Shaw said bitterly. "That's all I have left to me. An interest in my fellow human beings. We all walk with shadows. You've got your own, haven't you, it's there in your face and your eyes. I wonder what they are. And if *they* came out of the war, or from your work." His eyes scanned Rutledge.

Forcing himself to ignore the challenge, Rutledge waited.

After draining his glass in one long swallow, Shaw said, "I wish I could have gotten drunk tonight—" After a time he picked up the thread of the conversation again. "I watch them all. Daulton, because he spoke to her just before she left Charlbury. Wyatt, her host and therefore responsible for her. Aurore, who should have gotten her to that train safely, and didn't. And let's not forget Elizabeth Napier, so busily using Margaret's death to throw herself at Simon again. *Or* her famous father, who is conspicuous by his absence. If Margaret hadn't meant anything to him, he'd have come storming into Hildebrand's office long before this, making political mileage out of his righteous anger. No, they're all on my list, and I'm just waiting for a single mistake that might tell me which one is guilty."

"You've left Mowbray out of your accounting."

"No, I haven't. He's my last resort, if I'm wrong about the others."

"Have you reached any conclusions yet?"

"No," Shaw said, wincing as he moved too suddenly in his chair. "Except that Margaret's death doesn't seem to have left even the briefest mark on anybody's life except mine. And possibly Thomas Napier's, who knows?" He sighed heavily, shaking his head. "I don't know whether I loved her or hated her, in the end. I might have killed her myself, if she'd hurt me again. Someone else did, and now I want to find him—or her."

"For vengeance? It doesn't work out the way you think it might."

"Doesn't it?" Shaw said wryly. "If I discovered her killer to-night, I don't know what I'd do about it. Turn him over to you. Or batter the life out of him myself. It doesn't matter, I'm dead anyway. Still—it frightens me, not knowing how I'll feel. When I loved her so much. That's why I'm sober, Rutledge. I'm suddenly afraid to drink. . . ."

20

It was the next morning when Rutledge finally ran Simon Wyatt to earth in the museum, shut the doors to the room he was working in, and said curtly, "Sit down."

"I've got too much to do—"

Rutledge cut him short. "The museum can wait. The opening can wait. I want to talk to you."

Something in Rutledge's voice broke through his wall of isolation. Simon reached for a chair that was filled with boxes, shoved them off the seat, pulled it to him, and sat down. "All right. Five minutes."

"There's a very good chance that the murder of Margaret Tarlton can be laid at your wife's door."

"Aurore? Don't be stupid, man, she's no more guilty of murder than I am! If this is what you want to say to me, I've got more important things to attend to!"

Rutledge reached out and pressed Simon back into his chair. "You'll listen to me until I've finished, damn it. And I'll decide when that is!"

He had spent a long sleepless night going over many things in his mind, but there was no one except Hamish he could have said them to.

"The plan was, as I understand it, for Mrs. Wyatt to drive Margaret Tarlton to the train station at Singleton Magna. She tells me that she didn't, that she was at the farm working with a sick heifer. All right, that means that Margaret Tarlton is still in this house, looking for a way to the station. Mrs. Daulton sees her at your front gate, waiting—wearing the clothes she had changed into. The dress, in fact, she was wearing when the body was found. Elizabeth Napier has told me that she's quite sure the dress belonged to Margaret. I'm sure Edith could identify it as well. Or Mrs. Daulton."

"I haven't heard about this—" Simon began, incensed. "Why hasn't anyone told me?"

"Because you've got your head buried in this museum and don't hear what's being said to you," Rutledge told him in exasperation. "To go on. Your maid Edith, concerned that Miss Tarlton might miss her train, hurries down to the inn to ask Denton if his nephew Shaw can drive Miss Tarlton. But while she's gone Miss Tarlton, for reasons of her own, walks down to the rectory and asks Henry Daulton if he or his mother can take her to Singleton Magna. He leaves Miss Tarlton on the steps while he goes to the garden to speak to his mother, but as he turns away she says, 'There's Mrs. Wyatt,' and leaves, angry that she's already running late. A woman who lives on the other side of the inn tells me that she saw the car leaving town soon afterward, that your wife was driving, and that she believes Margaret Tarlton was a passenger."

Simon started to speak but Rutledge cut him short. "Whether her evidence is reliable or not doesn't matter; this places your wife in the car with Margaret Tarlton, heading toward Singleton Magna in time to make the train. Miss Tarlton's on her way to Sherborne, where she's to spend several days with Miss Napier."

There was a look of surprise on Simon's face, but he said nothing.

"According to the stationmaster, she isn't one of the passengers on the train going north and certainly not on the train going south. She doesn't arrive in Sherborne on fifteen August, nor on the following day, because Miss Napier and her chauffeur Benson have gone to meet her, Miss Napier herself on the fifteenth and Benson on the sixteenth. Meanwhile in London, her maid Dorcas Williams hasn't seen or heard from her, nor have her cousins in Gloucestershire. Miss Tarlton, it appears, has vanished from the face of the earth. But we do have a body in Singleton Magna who is wearing what appear to be her garments. It would seem, then, that Miss Tarlton died on the road outside Singleton Magna sometime in the afternoon. And if your wife took her out of Charlbury in your motorcar, then your wife was most likely the last person to see Miss Tarlton alive. Do you follow me?"

Simon Wyatt, frowning, said, "Yes, of course I do! I just don't accept your reasoning. My wife is not a murderess, she'd never met Margaret Tarlton before the thirteenth, when she went to collect her at the station, and I can't imagine any possible reason why Aurore would want to kill a comparative stranger!"

"Miss Tarlton was very likely going to accept your offer of a position here."

"And what's that got to do with murder! No, your theory is full of holes, man! Aurore may have taken Margaret as far as Singleton Magna, but it doesn't tell me what Margaret Tarlton did once she got there! If Aurore set her down in the town, someone else could have as easily met her there. Have you thought of that? Have you made any effort to find out?"

He hadn't, as Hamish was busily pointing out.

Shaw. Elizabeth Napier. Thomas Napier. Who else?

"Does Miss Tarlton know anyone in Singleton Magna—or for that matter in Charlbury?"

"God, no! She's been here once or twice with the Napiers, but she's not the kind of woman who likes the country very much. London is her métier, she's at home in parlors and salons and theaters."

"All the same, she was willing to work here. To leave London."

Simon made a deprecating gesture. "She came to help me make a success of the opening, and then I hoped to attract a student of the East to come in and see to preservation of specimens, the proper cases, some sort of cataloging, all the trimmings of a proper museum. I don't have the money for that, not at the moment, but the quality of exhibits is quite high. I've already shown some of the better examples to Dr. Anderson in Oxford." Simon grinned. "I expect he hoped I might contribute them to his own private collection. My grandfather was a skilled draftsman and has drawn birds in New Guinea and Sulawesi that created quite a fuss when Anderson showed them to specialists. Many of them hadn't been described before." As he spoke, his eyes flashed with more life and enthusiasm than Rutledge had ever seen him show.

"And you told her this was short-term employment?"

"Margaret herself said she wouldn't stay—six months, a year at best. She spoke of other plans after that. I thought it might be marriage. The way she tilted her head when she said it, with a sort of pride."

"Any idea who the man might have been?"

"No. But then I've been away for four years. Someone she met in the war, at a guess. I don't see Margaret Tarlton winding up a spinster."

"Someone she met in the war? Not Thomas Napier?"

Simon stared at Rutledge. "Elizabeth's father? Good God, what put that idea into your head! I thought I was the only one who knew about that!"

"Someone had helped Miss Tarlton purchase a small house in Chelsea. I thought it might have been her employer."

A cold look turned Simon's face hard. "No. It wasn't Thomas Napier. It was my father. She bought it through a trust fund he set up for her."

Surprised in his turn, Rutledge said, "Why? That's an expensive gift."

"He didn't see fit to tell me. And they weren't lovers, if that's the conclusion you're jumping to! He said it was a business arrangement, that he'd done it because he'd known her father. Poppycock! Tarlton never came here, and my father was never in India. I'd wager Thomas Napier's behind it!"

"Are you saying Napier was in love with Miss Tarlton? If he'd wanted her to have a house of her own, why didn't he buy it for her?" It was the first independent corroboration of that he'd had.

"Politics, mainly. And because he wouldn't want Elizabeth to know. She'd be angry and hurt, if he'd conducted an affair under his own roof. I expect that's why he hasn't come down to Singleton Magna and given Hildebrand hell for dragging his feet in this business. He's being discreet. For his sake, and for Elizabeth's. And for Margaret's, if it turns out all of you are wrong."

"If there had been another man in her life, what would Napier have done?"

"For a man of his clever, controlled nature, he was besotted with Margaret Tarlton. If you're asking me if he would have killed her, no, but I'd hate like hell to be in the shoes of the other man!"

"And your father wasn't in love with her—or receiving favors from her?"

"If it was blackmail, it wasn't sexual. He may have owed Napier a political favor, or some debt. My father left a letter explaining about the house. I worked out the rest of it myself. Mainly because my godfather had been so cooperative when I asked him to speak to Elizabeth for me. I'd expected him to turn on me."

"What happens to the house now, if Margaret Tarlton is dead?"

Simon's fair brows twitched together. "I'm not sure. It was some sort of trust, arranged through lawyers. I was told there's a clause protecting my father's claim to the house, based on the fact he'd had some connection with Margaret's family. If she married or died without children, the trust reverted to him."

"Your father is dead. Does this mean the house comes to you now?"

Simon answered slowly, "I expect it does. But it's early days yet to cross that bridge. No one knows for certain, if you're telling me the truth, whether Margaret is dead—or has simply disappeared for reasons of her own. If there's one thing I've learned about women, Inspector, it's that they have a logic all their own! She might well turn up alive and surprise all of us."

Before turning to go, Rutledge asked, "Will you go back to politics, if the museum is a success and you've satisfied your duty to your grandfather?"

"Why does that matter so much to everyone?" Sudden anger sent a flush into Simon's face and he looked directly at Rutledge. "What was your excuse for leaving Scotland Yard to fight in France? Or are you the only one who's allowed to dig into another man's soul?"

Rutledge owed Wyatt honesty for honesty. He said slowly, "I believed it was a sense of duty. Of responsibility to King and Country. Not patriotism, you understand, it wasn't the parades and speeches and flag waving. I remember thinking I have an obligation here. If these men can walk away from their families and their careers, and serve, so must I."

And Jean had said only, "You know, you look very handsome in uniform!" As if he were dressed for a masquerade . . . dear God.

"Why did you go back to the Yard? Afterward?"

"Because it was what I did best."

"Duty, again. I'm no longer sure I know what that means. Even the women in my family were politically astute and politically ambitious. It never occurred to any of them that I might not be cut out of the same bolt of cloth. It never occurred to me. I went away to war to be a hero. I came home a failure in the eyes of most people. No medals, no appetite for politics, no fashionable marriage."

"Is that why you have taken the trouble to build this museum?" Rutledge gestured to the shelves around them, the mysteries of another world, another culture. So foreign in this English house in an English county. And with a French wife . . . but that was something he couldn't say aloud.

It was as if Simon hadn't heard him. "I wasn't a bad soldier, I fought hard, I served as well as any man. I don't know why I survived. I don't see how any of us did. It was a bloody lottery. I win, you lose."

Rutledge felt the coldness of memory. The times he'd been terrified that he might die—and the long months when he was terrified that he wouldn't.

"It wasn't a pretty war," Simon finished. "And I discovered that I was no Churchill. In the shambles of the trenches I couldn't make a pretense of being dashing and flamboyant. It would have been obscene."

Rutledge, feeling a flatness that pervaded his spirit and gave him a sense of loss, walked slowly back to the inn, where he'd left his car. Had he finally reached the bedrock of Simon Wyatt? In those last words, he thought perhaps he had. *"I discovered that I was no Churchill."* Was that the torment that sent him out into the night alone, reliving something that was past?

"Nae mair than you do!" Hamish said with savage honesty.

All right then. Why did he himself persist in this business of policing? Why had he ever taken it up after the war?

198

"Because it was all you are fit for," Hamish reminded him.

It was, after all, what he had told Wyatt.

"Then why do I sometimes get it so bloody *wrong!*"

He started the car and climbed in, shutting the door and letting in the clutch with half his attention on his thoughts. All at once he realized that Shaw was coming out of the inn and hailing him, bent almost double with the effort it took to hurry and shout at the same time.

Rutledge stopped the car so suddenly he killed the engine. A sense of cold foreboding swept through him.

Shaw reached the passenger side and said breathlessly, "Bloody hell, Rutledge, didn't you hear me?"

"I'm sorry—" Rutledge began, but Shaw shook his head.

"You're needed in Singleton Magna straightaway. As soon as you can get there. Hildebrand had someone telephone to the Wyatt house, but you'd already left. Aurore passed the message on to my uncle."

Rutledge thought, They've found the children. . . . But all he said was, "Very well, I'm on my way."

His mind was in turmoil. He swore silently as he cranked the car again and, with a wave to the still-flushed man in front of the inn, drove down the road at speed, startling a horse being taken to the smithy for shoeing. It reared and shook its head, wild-eyed, while the farmer holding the reins shouted at Rutledge to mind what he was about.

Driving hard and fast, he kept his mind on the road, not allowing his thoughts to break through his concentration. He reached Singleton Magna, left the car in the yard behind the Swan, and with his heart thundering against his ribs walked back toward the police station. *If they'd found the children, it meant he'd been wrong from the start.*

There was a small knot of people standing outside the inn—he hadn't seen them as he came up the street, but he noticed them now. It confirmed his fears. A ripple of excitement swept them as he passed by, but no one called to him or tried to approach. Crossing the busy road between two young girls on horseback and a dray carrying milk cans, he ran lightly up to the door of the station and opened it.

There was nothing else he could do.

Inside the air was thick with ominous tension. Constable Jeffries saw him over the heads of the men jamming the small room and spoke. "We've found the children," he said grimly. "Inspector Hildebrand is waiting for you. In his office."

Rutledge felt the coldness settle into his very bones. He'd seen dead children before. Somehow he wasn't prepared to see these. He nodded to the constable and went down the dark passage to Hildebrand's door, knocking before turning the knob to enter.

"You sent for—" Rutledge began on the threshold, and stopped as if he'd been shot.

In the small room, Hildebrand, stiff with strain, stood behind his desk. He glared at Rutledge.

"You took your time getting here," he said. "Never mind. It seems that I've done your job for you."

21

The other chair in the room, across the desk from Hildebrand, was occupied by a man holding a small boy on his knees, one arm protectively around the little girl some two years older, who was leaning anxiously against the side of the chair. Both children stared at Rutledge, eyes round and frightened. The boy began to suck his thumb. The man, looking up, was dark haired, of medium height and weight, his pleasant face wearing a distinctly uncertain expression.

Rutledge, with Hamish hammering at the back of his mind, took a deep breath, like a drowning man coming up out of the sea into life-giving air.

"The Mowbray children?" he asked into the lengthening silence.

Hildebrand, rocking on his toes, anger apparent in every line of his body, held Rutledge's glance as it swung back to his grim face. "No. But close enough. At least it seems that way. You're the expert from Scotland Yard. That's why you were sent here. You make the decision."

Anger of his own surged through Rutledge, but he turned to the man in the chair, holding out his hand. "My name's Rutledge," he said, "Inspector Rutledge."

"Robert Andrews," the man said, taking it awkwardly over the boy's head.

"And these are Albert Mowbray's children?" He paused. "Tricia and Bertie?" He smiled at them, first the girl and then the boy.

The children stared back at him, unmoved by familiar names.

Andrews looked quickly at Hildebrand. "Well, no, they're mine, actually. This is Rosie and young Robert." The little girl shyly smiled as her father spoke her name, her head pressed against his shoulder. They were pretty children, both of them—*and of the ages Bert Mowbray's son and daughter had been on the day they died in London.*

"Then how are you connected with this—er—investigation?"

"Hasn't he told you?" Andrews asked, looking again at Hildebrand. "I thought—Well, never mind what I thought!" He cleared his throat. "I was on the train that passed through Singleton Magna on thirteen August. My wife was expecting our third child in two weeks, and I'd promised to take Rosie and her brother to Susan's mother—she has a house down along the coast—close to the time. And I did. Rosie was tired and wishing the long trip over, weren't you, love?" He touched her hair briefly with his free hand. "And she tried to leave the train, only she fell on the platform and scraped her knee. That was when the woman came over and bound a handkerchief around the cut, telling her what a brave little girl she was. . . ."

He looked at Rutledge, not sure how to go on.

"Why didn't you come forward sooner?" Rutledge asked. "We've had sheets printed, police asking questions, going from house to house." He tried to keep the anger and the shock out of his voice, for the children's sake and his own. "It was in the papers repeatedly, both a photograph and a request for help."

"Well, I went straight back to London, didn't I? And a damned—and a good thing I did, because Susan suddenly went into labor that same night, and everything else went out the window, didn't it? It wasn't until I went back to fetch the children that my mother-in-law told me about the—er—what happened to the woman and said I was lucky it wasn't my wife and my two that was missing. She said she'd had nightmares for days about the poor little dears. Mind you, I'd have never gone to the police if she hadn't talked on and on about the horror of it all. Which set me to thinking." He shook his head. "She has a morbid taste for tragedies, that woman does!"

"What happened?"

"The police saw fit to arrest me on the spot, that's what happened, and if the rector in the church who'd married us and christened these two hadn't come forward, I'd probably still be there!" He frowned indignantly, still unsettled by the injustice of it all. "That was last night."

"I'm sorry," Rutledge said soothingly. "They were trying to do their job."

"I fail to see how arresting an innocent man is part of any policeman's job," Andrews replied, with the first show of spirit.

"Do you remember what the woman was wearing? The one who helped the children?"

"God, no, I don't know anything about women's clothes—" he began.

"Was it pink? Or perhaps yellow?" Rutledge waited. All this time, Hildebrand had been standing at his back, across the desk, silent and watchful and hoping—believing!—that Rutledge might still fail.

Andrews shrugged. "I tell you, I don't know."

Rutledge turned to the little girl, squatting on his heels before her. "Can you remember the woman who helped you at the train, when you fell?" he asked gently, smiling at her. "Was she pretty? As pretty as your mother?"

Rosie looked down, playing with the sash of her own dress. "Yes," she said so softly it was just a whisper.

"Tell me."

"She was pretty," Rosie repeated.

Over her head Rutledge asked, "Do you still have the handkerchief?" Andrews silently mouthed *no*.

"I liked her hat," Rosie said into the exchange. "I want one."

"Do you? What color was it?"

He waited, patient, silent. After a moment she pointed to a carafe of water on the desk, a crystal jug with an upturned glass for its lid. A band of silver at the neck caught the reflected light of the courtyard, shining and clear. "Like that," she said, and smiled shyly.

"Like light on water, silvery," the Wyatt maid Edith had said.

Rutledge slowly straightened and turned to Hildebrand.

The inspector said abruptly, "If you'd excuse us for a moment, Mr. Andrews?" Without waiting for an answer, he went around the desk and looked at Rutledge.

The two men went out into the dark, cramped passage, carefully closing the door behind them and moving away, out of earshot. At the far end of the passage, the other door that locked Mowbray away was deep in shadow. Rutledge found himself thinking about the man inside.

"He didn't kill them," he said, more to himself than to Hildebrand.

"We don't know that," Hildebrand said.

"That child just identified the color of the hat Miss Tarlton was wearing. If it was Miss Tarlton at the station, if it *was* Miss Tarlton that Mowbray saw and came looking for, it means his wife must surely have died in 1916, with the two children. And it was only his imagination—" He stopped. Knowing—who better?—how imagination tricked the mind. How what you believed was shadowed and shaped by what you had done. Mowbray hadn't been in London to save his wife or his children, he'd been away in France. He'd come home to bury them. He'd missed them every day since. To the point that in a desperate time of his life, he had seen what he wanted most in the world to see . . . a return to what had been.

"We don't know that!" Hildebrand repeated stubbornly. "A child that age in a courtroom? It would be a farce, the questioning could tangle her into knots. Are you willing to put that family through such a nightmare?"

"What are you going to do instead? Will you continue this search, widen it, go on looking until there's nowhere else to try?"

"I fail to see that it's any of your business! If we *have* found those children, you may return to London and leave the rest to the local police."

"Then allow me one final test. Let Mowbray see them—"

"Have you run stark mad—"

"No, listen to me!" As their voices clashed, the constable on duty at the desk opened the door at the head of the passage and stared down it. He quickly shut it again at a gesture from Hildebrand. "What I want to do is this."

An hour later it was arranged. Not without complaints from Robert Andrews and from Hildebrand and from Marcus Johnston, Mowbray's attorney.

A call put in to Bowles in London by an irate Hildebrand caught the man in a fierce mood, not a receptive one. Even when the receiver was turned over to Rutledge, Bowles's voice rang down the line in deafening vowels.

"I've had Thomas Napier calling in from his office to see what progress we've made toward finding Miss Tarlton," he said shortly. "I don't like to have politicians breathing down my neck. It's your *fault*, Rutledge, for dragging the Napiers into the issue in the first place!"

"If the dead woman is Miss Tarlton, Mr. Napier will do more than breathe down our necks," Rutledge said. "He'll be camping in your office! From all reports he was as fond of her as he was of his own daughter." Fonder, very likely. . . .

"Then find out, once and for all, if these children are Mowbray's or not. Do you hear me? Put Hildebrand on again, I'll set him straight."

And so it was arranged.

When they went to fetch Mowbray, sunk in the darkness of his terrors, he came shuffling and blinking into the light in Hildebrand's room, his face gaunt, unshaven, his hair lank and dull. He said nothing as Johnston, his own face stiff, greeted his client. A silence fell.

Mowbray seemed not to know or care who they were, what they wanted. He had been brought here. He suffered that with the same awful patience he gave to everything he did now, from eating his food to lying on his cot through the night. Nothing touched him. In the courtyard outside Hildebrand's windows, a ball came bouncing across the debris of leaves and dust.

Johnston was talking when the first child appeared. It was the same age as Robert Andrews, and nearly the same coloring, a little boy chasing exuberantly after the red ball.

Mowbray started up, crying, "No—don't torment me—"

Rutledge said quietly, "Is that your Bertie, Mr. Mowbray?"

"No, God, no. I killed my Bertie, you told me so yourself!"

Another small boy came running into the yard, fiercely demanding his turn with the ball, and the first turned away with it, leading to a screaming match between the two. A third boy appeared, a little older now, closer to the age the Mowbray boy would have reached if he'd lived.

Watching Mowbray carefully, Rutledge said, "You must look at them, Mr. Mowbray. You must help us know if one of these boys is your son."

Mowbray, his eyes wet with frantic tears, turned toward Johnston for help. Johnston, shaking, said, *"Inspector!"* in warning.

The fourth child came reluctantly into the courtyard. Mowbray suddenly started, half rising from his chair. Johnston reached out to stop him, and Rutledge reminded him softly, "Remember! There is no way he can reach them!"

Before Johnston or Hildebrand could move, Mowbray had come across the room to the window, sinking to his knees before it, his face contorted with tears. "Bertie?" he cried, his hands raking the glass. "Bertie? *Is it you, lad?*"

Robert Andrews the younger turned toward the man at the window, looking at him in alarm. Then he turned back to the ball players and scooped up the ball they had dropped in their struggle. Racing away up the walk toward the street shouting, "Mine! Mine!" he vanished.

Mowbray cried, "No—no—come back! *Bertie!*"

And at the same time he caught sight of Rosie, being led by the hand into the courtyard by a slightly older child. On such short notice, they'd had difficulty finding girls of the right age. . . . He stared at her, drinking in the sight of her, a strange look of wonder on his face. Rosie, her hand confidingly in that of the other girl, looked straight at the window and then away again. That same shy smile lit her face.

"Tricia, love?" Mowbray asked, his body trembling as if he had a fever. "They said I'd killed you and left you in the dark for the foxes—"

He broke down then, his eyes turning to Rutledge for one brief

206

moment, in their depths something shining. It was the brief, terrible spark of hope.

Johnston was openly moved, his face wet with tears. Hildebrand swore under his breath, the same words over and over and over again.

Rutledge, ignoring the savagery of Hamish's anger, looked at Mowbray and told himself that it had had to be done—for Margaret's sake—for Mowbray's sake, above all else. He went to the prisoner and touched his shoulder. "They are the children you saw," he said gently. "The children at the train station. Is that what you're telling me? The little boy who picked up the ball, and that smaller girl. Are you quite sure?"

"Yes, yes, they're my children, they're *alive*—" His shoulders moved with the sobs racking his lungs, his words turmbling out incoherently. He pressed his face against the glass as the two girls turned and went back the way they'd come, eyes straining for a last glimpse of them. He repeated the words, more clearly this time, as if finding them easier to believe with each breath.

"No," Rutledge said. "No, I'm afraid they aren't Bertie and Patricia. Their name is Andrews. Think, Mowbray! Your Bertie would be four now, nearly five. Like the older boy you saw. And the little girl, Patricia, would be seven by now. These two children—the ones who remind you so much of your own two—are younger, the ages Bertie and Patricia were when they died in London."

"Their mother?" Mowbray asked huskily, suddenly remembering. "Is she out there too?" Raw need gleamed like fire in his eyes.

"No." His voice was very low, with infinite compassion in its timbre. "The mother of these two children who remind you so much of your own is in London, recovering from the birth of her third child. She's auburn haired, and—er—plump." He pulled from his pocket the photograph that Robert Andrews had let him borrow. "Do you see that?"

After a moment the words seemed to register. Mowbray looked at it, frowning with the effort. The woman captured by the camera had dark hair, far darker than that in the photograph Mowbray himself had carried, and she weighed at least two stone more.

"That's not Mary!" he said in surprise. "She doesn't look anything like Mary!" His eyes swiveled to Johnston and Hildebrand. "Where's Mary?" he demanded accusingly, as if she might still be conjured up with the children.

Hildebrand opened his mouth but Rutledge got there before him. "Look at this photograph," he said, passing the one he'd borrowed from Elizabeth Napier. "Do you see your wife among these women, Mr. Mowbray? Look carefully at all of them, and tell me."

He studied it, distraught and weeping. "She's not there," he said, hope dying again. "She's not there." He looked up at Rutledge and said with such pathos that it brought silence to the three watchers, "Did I kill my Mary, then?"

Rutledge stood there, looking down at the frightened, ravaged face. Against the judgment of the policeman he'd trained to become, he said quietly, "No. You didn't kill her. The German bombs did, a long time ago. She can't suffer anymore. And she can't come back to you. Neither can the children."

But he made no mention of Margaret Tarlton.

After the angry doctor had taken Mowbray back to his cell and given him a sedative to swallow, Johnston walked out of the police station saying only, "I don't know what you've accomplished. I just don't know what to believe!"

The constable was busily sorting out the children by the front door, thanking the parents from whom he'd borrowed them, and watching Andrews crossing to the hotel with a very sleepy little boy on his shoulder and a little girl dragging her feet in the dust, head down and yawning.

"What happened?" the constable asked Hildebrand, and then quickly went back into the station, minding his own business with industry.

Hildebrand said, "Johnston is right. What've you accomplished? If those are the children we've been searching for—and for the sake of argument, I'll accept it for now—there's still the dead woman. If she happens to be this Miss Tarlton, Mowbray killed her mistaking her for his wife! That's the long and short of it. Stands to reason. We've still got one victim, and we've got her killer."

"Have we? He didn't recognize Margaret Tarlton, did he? How did he meet her? And where is her suitcase? Where is her hat? We're back to the same quandary we've faced all along. If Mowbray killed that woman and then went to sleep under a tree, ripe picking for the police when the body was found, why did he bother to clean the blood off himself, get rid of the weapon, and hide her suitcase? *To what end?* Why not leave them there, beside her?"

"Who knows what goes on in the mind of a madman!"

"Even the mad have their own logic!"

"No, don't come the Londoner with me, Rutledge! Madness means there's no logic left in the mind."

"I submit, then, that whoever killed Margaret Tarlton took away the suitcase, the hat she was wearing, and the weapon."

"Oh, yes? Walking down the road with them in his hand, was he?"

"No. He—the killer—was taking Margaret Tarlton by car to the station in Singleton Magna. And it was into the car that he shoved the hat and the weapon and the missing suitcase, until he could dispose of them later!"

"Oh, yes?" Hildebrand repeated. "But came through his front door spattered with blood and said, 'Don't mind this lot, I'll just have a quick bath before tea!'"

"Yes, it's the blood that's the problem," Rutledge admitted. "We don't know where either Mowbray or anyone else might have washed off the blood."

But there was only one place, and he'd already felt the words burning in the back of his mind like red-hot brands.

At the farmhouse, Aurore Wyatt could easily have walked inside after tending a sick heifer and bathed her face and hands and thrown away a stained shirtwaist, or burned it in the kitchen fire. Except for the deaf old man who worked there, who would have seen or paid any heed to what she did? By the time she got back to her own house, she'd have been clean. . . .

Rutledge, standing there in the late-afternoon sunlight while a saw droned on and on somewhere in the distance, suddenly knew how Judas had felt. A traitor—a betrayer of someone who trusted him . . .

Or who trusted in her spell over him?

22

When it was finished, when Hildebrand had walked back into his office and the waiting knot of people—starved of news—had wandered away, Rutledge drew a long shuddering breath and went back to the Swan. He felt dazed with weariness, the emotional trial in Hildebrand's office still searing his conscience.

What choice had he been given?

At what price had Mowbray won some respite from his own horrors? Or had they only been scored more deeply into the man's tormented mind? And was he a killer at all, but only the victim as much as the dead woman in the pauper's grave by the church?

Hamish, who disapproved of much that Rutledge did, holding him to the high standards of a man who was Calvinist in heart and soul, said, "When ye're done feeling sorry for yoursel', there's the ither woman with nae name and nae face. What aboot her, then?"

"What about her?" Rutledge said. "Mowbray couldn't have killed her, he couldn't have made a practice of riding trains and murdering any woman with a passing resemblance to his dead wife! And she was dark-haired, not fair!" He suddenly lost patience with Hamish. "What has she to do with Margaret Tarlton, for God's sake?"

"Aye, that's the question. But look, if she has a part in this matter, she deserves justice even if there's nae MP calling for answers!"

Tired to the bone, Rutledge said, "If we've cleared Mowbray of killing his children, and if we've shown that the dead woman is very likely Margaret Tarlton—if Miss Napier has told the truth about recognizing that dress—then we're back to the people who knew her best. The Napiers. Shaw. The Wyatts."

"Aye. Find that hat, forebye, and you'll ha' the answer."

"You said that about the children," Rutledge said wearily. "And it wasn't enough."

He had reached his room, but without any memory of walking into the inn or up the stairs or down the passage. Closing the door behind him, he took off his coat and threw himself face down across the bed.

Two minutes later, Hamish's complaints notwithstanding, Rutledge was deeply asleep, where not even dreams could reach him. The dark head on the pillow stirred once as the church bell struck the hour, one arm moving to crook protectively around it and the other hand uncurling from the tight fist of tension.

You don't, Rutledge told himself over a late dinner, lose your objectivity if you want to be a good policeman. You learn to shut out the pain of others, you learn to ask the questions that can break up a marriage, set brother against brother, or turn father against son. Willy-nilly, to get at the truth.

But what *was* truth? It had as many sides as there were people involved and was as changeable as human nature.

Take Margaret Tarlton, for one. If you believed the stories told, she was Elizabeth Napier's friend and confidante, Thomas Napier's lover, Daniel Shaw's heartbreak, and a reminder of Simon Wyatt's glorious past, when he was still destined for greatness. A reminder to Aurore Wyatt that her husband was vulnerable to the blandishments of the Napiers. *Most murderers know their victims.* It could be one of those closest to her—or it could be someone who had followed her from London.

It could be that by purest chance Mowbray had come upon her and killed her, just as they'd believed all along.

Or take the working-class woman who had died and been buried in a fallow field. On the surface of it, she'd nothing to do with Mowbray, and very likely little to do with Margaret Tarlton. Was

211

she, then, a red herring? Or was she the first victim of the same killer? And how did you find the name and direction of a working-class woman who hadn't been reported missing and who apparently had no connection with anyone in Charlbury? She could have come from London—Portsmouth—Liverpool. She could have come from the moon.

But he thought there might be one person who could tell him.

The next morning, while Hildebrand was busy interviewing Elizabeth Napier—tiptoeing on eggshells, as one of the constables put it—Rutledge drove back to Charlbury.

In every village, the one person who could be counted on to know every facet of the lives and failures of each parishioner was most often the rector's wife. Whereas in a town of any size, it was usually the constable who could provide the smallest details about anyone on his patch.

Rutledge called on Mrs. Daulton. Henry answered the door and said, "She's in the back. And rather too mucky, I think, to come inside. I'm not much of a gardener myself," he added, and as if in explanation, "I always pull up the wrong things."

"I'll find her. Thank you, Mr. Daulton."

She was in her garden, a shabby smock over her shirtwaist and skirt, a kerchief around her head, and what appeared to be her husband's old boots on her feet. From the look of the boots she'd been wading in mud at some point. She was currently pruning the canes of a climbing rose that had grown too exuberantly that year. Her hair was pulled from its tidy bun by the thorns, and there were scratches on her face. She seemed to be thoroughly happy.

"Inspector," she said, when she looked up to find him striding down the path from the side of the house. "How thoughtful of you to come to me. As you see, we are our own gardeners here at the rectory." Straightening her back as if it hurt, she added, "Mind you, I recollect the day when there were two gardeners and a lad to keep these grounds! Not that I stayed out of them even then." She took off her gloves and extended her hand. "What can I do to help you?"

Rutledge smiled as he took her hand and said, "I need your knowledge. Of people, and of one person in particular."

212

She looked at him straightly. "I will not help you put Simon Wyatt in prison for a crime he's innocent of."

"I shan't ask it of you," Rutledge promised. "No, my interest is in a maid who vanished some time ago."

"The body in the field." She nodded. "I doubt it's Betty Cooper, but then you never know, do you?" She set the gloves beside the trowel and the pruning shears in the barrow at her side. "Come along, then, we can sit over there."

Over there was a small rustic bench in the shade of a great, ancient apple tree, its branches bowed down with green fruit. Before them the beds and borders of the rectory garden spread out like a fan toward the house. It was a pretty scene, peaceful and quiet. Rutledge followed her and sat down beside her. She sighed, as if tearing her thoughts from the rosebush and bringing them to bear on what he wanted to hear.

"I can't tell you much about the girl. But enough, perhaps, for your purposes. Betty came to Dorset during the war. From a poor family near Plymouth. Many girls went into war work of some sort, omnibus conductors and the like. Mrs. Darley ran a large dairy farm and needed help. Betty was sent to her because the girl had some experience with animals and the work was to her liking, or so I was told. At any rate, she pulled her weight until the end of the war and afterward asked Mrs. Darley to give her some training as a parlor maid. As I heard it, Betty didn't want to be a clerk in an office or a shopgirl, she wanted to be the person who opened doors to guests and served tea. That's a rather silly view, maids do more than that, but Betty had aspirations, you see, and they included learning how to dress and how to speak properly. And she was quite pretty; it was only a matter of time before the lure of better prospects took her away. Mrs. Darley," she ended dryly, "entertains less than stellar company. She's a farmer's wife, not a society hostess."

Rutledge was suddenly reminded of the farmer's wife and daughter he'd interviewed only days before, who had been on the same train as Mowbray. No, housemaid to a farm wife wouldn't appeal to an ambitious young woman out to make her fortune.

"I suggested to Simon that he take her on, when he came back from France and brought Aurore to Charlbury. He interviewed Betty, but there wasn't any money for a second girl. And Edith had been with Simon's father. She's the cook's niece, you see, and wanted to stay on."

"That refusal was the turning point for Betty?"

"Yes, it was. Not a month later she was gone in the night, slipping away with her belongings and not leaving so much as a note. Mrs. Darley would gladly have given her a reference."

"Was there a man in the picture?" he asked.

"No," Mrs. Daulton said, considering the possibility. "I think not. Betty had . . . ambitions. She might flirt with every man she met, including our own Constable Truit, but it was harmless, she was hoping to do better than a farmer's son. At any rate, as far as anyone knows, that's the last news of Betty Cooper." She smiled wryly. "I consider Betty one of my failures. You and I know very well what happens to most of the hopeful young women who go to London without references or prospects. It's a dreary end to ambitions, isn't it?"

"There's no possibility of finding her, there are too many like her in London. If that's where she went."

"There's no family in Plymouth that I'm aware of. No reason to go back there." She smoothed the dirt from one palm. "The war gave girls so many new opportunities. Still, I don't know that it's a good thing to offer a glimpse of a new way of thinking and then snatch it back the minute the men come marching home from war. What will they do? These girls with a taste for independence?"

"Betty had no other training?"

"To hear Mrs. Darley tell it, she was a cross between Mata Hari and the Whore of Babylon! But no, she had no skills. She was pretty enough for Dorset, but I doubt she'd attract all that much notice in London. Still, who can say? She might have settled somewhere and found happiness by now!"

"Describe her, if you would, please."

Mrs. Daulton considered for a moment. "Very dark hair, very white skin—which made a striking combination, as you can imagine. I don't recall what color her eyes were. Blue, at a guess. Slim, but only of medium height. I had a feeling she might run to plumpness in middle age."

The description came very close to the body they'd found. But Betty had left Dorset months before the physical evidence pointed to a time of death.

"She never came back? You're quite sure of that?"

She smiled. "If Betty had come home like a beaten dog, Mrs. Darley would have shouted it to the world. As vindication for dire predictions."

He said slowly, "I shall have to ask Mrs. Darley to look at the body."

The smile vanished. "No. I know how she feels about Betty, she'd like to think the girl got her just deserts. It wouldn't be an objective identification. She's not vindictive, but she was badly hurt by what she perceives as the girl's callousness. Well, it was a personal rejection of a sort, wasn't it? Mrs. Darley offered Betty the best she had, and it wasn't good enough for the girl. At least that was the way Mrs. Darley felt her friends must see it."

"Someone has to tell us if the dead woman is Betty Cooper. Or not."

She took a deep breath and stood up. "I'll do it. Just give me a moment to change into something cleaner."

"You must think about it carefully," he warned her. "It won't be a very—pleasant—experience for you either. She was bea—"

"No!" she said sharply, cutting across his words. "Don't tell me. I can stand it better if I don't know how she suffered." She turned to look at him. "Are you reaching for straws, Inspector? I have heard—various accounts, I assure you, and none of them kind—about what was done yesterday. I'm very glad those children were found alive. But I think the methods used to be certain were rather cruel."

"It would have been far more cruel to have hanged an innocent man."

She said, "It is no excuse, all the same."

They arrived at the doctor's surgery half an hour later. Rutledge had telephoned the police in Singleton Magna, asking Hildebrand to make the necessary arrangements. There was a message waiting for him at the surgery. "I'm pursuing my own line of inquiry. Handle this yourself."

Dr. Fairfield was distinctly cool, but did as he was asked.

Henry Daulton had insisted that he come as well. "My mother will need me afterward," he said simply. "I saw dead people in the war. She won't like it."

All the same, they made him wait outside.

In the spare, scrubbed room, Mrs. Daulton was shown the articles of clothing first. She looked at them, then shook her head. She was very white, her lips drawn tightly together. After a moment she said with some constraint in her voice, "No. I don't recollect Betty wearing anything like this while she worked for the Darleys. But then I wouldn't know her personal wardrobe. Or what she may have bought later. I'm sorry. That's not much help, is it?"

The musty smell of earth and death filled the air as the clothes were refolded and put away.

"Would you like a cup of tea?" the doctor asked solicitously. "Before we go on? My wife will be glad to have you step across to the house, Mrs. Daulton."

Her eyes strayed to the white screen in one corner of the room. "I'd rather—" She cleared her throat with an effort. "I'd rather finish as quickly as possible," she said. "If you don't mind?"

As he led her forward and withdrew the screen, she looked at Rutledge with anxious eyes. "I tell myself this is no worse than comforting the dying. Or helping to lay out the dead."

The body had been made as presentable as possible, which wasn't saying much. Even the sheet covering it seemed stark and horribly suggestive.

When it was drawn back, Joanna Daulton gasped and seemed for an instant to cringe into herself. Then she recovered, from what inner wells of strength, Rutledge couldn't tell, but he felt only admiration. She looked down at the battered face, tatters of rotting flesh and yellowed bone, the broken nose. Her eyes were wide, observing. Careful.

Then she shut her eyes, reached out a hand, and turned away. Rutledge took the trembling fingers and held them in his. They were icy cold.

"I—that might be Betty," she said shakily. "There's—a resemblance—of a kind. Still— Could I have some air, please?"

Rutledge transferred his grip to her arm and led her out into the main surgery, while the doctor quietly drew the sheet back over the dead woman's face. Mrs. Daulton took the chair Rutledge drew away from the desk for her and sat down with a suddenness that told him she was close to fainting.

He thrust a waiting glass of cold water into her hand and said bracingly, as he would have done to a raw recruit shaking with reaction after his first battle. "That was well done. You were very brave, and it's over now."

"No, I wasn't," Mrs. Daulton said quietly after she had drunk the water and rested for a moment. "I shall see that face in my nightmares for a very long time to come. The sad thing is, I appear to have been no help at all to you. I'm sorry."

And to his astonishment, she buried her face in her hands and began to cry.

Rutledge delivered a subdued Mrs. Daulton and her son to the rectory in Charlbury and then, after two other stops, went back to Singleton Magna for his lunch. He was sick of death and bodies and questions.

But there was no respite. Halfway through his meal, there was a telephone call from London.

He expected it to be Bowles, complaining and demanding. Instead it was Sergeant Gibson.

"Inspector Rutledge, sir? I've been doing some digging in Gloucestershire, looking for that Tarlton woman. No luck, I'm afraid, but I've come across a small bit of information that you might want to hear. The cousins who live there are middle-aged, I'd say closer to forty than thirty. They've got a little boy of three or thereabouts. Proud as punch of him, they are. But one old gossip down the street tells me Mrs. Tarlton—that's the cousin—couldn't have children, it was the sorrow of her life, and this is a miracle baby."

Rutledge felt a ripple of excitement. "Have you spoken to Mrs. Tarlton's physician?"

"Aye, I did that, and he said—mind you, he didn't like it one bit!—that Mrs. Tarlton had seen fit to go to Yorkshire to have the lad. He hadn't even known she was pregnant. Returned with her baby, looking like the cat that ate the cream, very pleased with herself indeed. He didn't have the direction of the doctor who'd delivered the boy, didn't know, if you ask me! So I took it upon myself to look up the boy's birth certificate. Very interesting reading, that. Sarah Ralston Tarlton, mother, father listed as Frederick C. Tarlton. Which is as it should be, if the boy's truly theirs. I went next to the attending physician in York, and he says Mrs. Tarlton stayed in a rented house with her sister-in-law, an older woman. Her husband came several times to visit."

He waited.

Rutledge said, "Any description of him?"

"Vague. Fits Freddy, right enough. The doctor said they were there only a few months, until Mrs. Tarlton and of course the baby were fit to travel. They were emigrating to Canada, he thought. But I'll be willing to wager that it was all a farce, and our Miss Tarlton had a baby which she handed over to the cousins. She wouldn't be the first young woman in London to slip up with some soldier."

But was it "some soldier"? Or was the child Thomas Napier's? If the arrangements had been so carefully made from the start, that link would be buried deepest. Napier had enemies; they would like nothing better than to catch even the faintest whiff of scandal.

"Well done, Sergeant! You're vastly underrated. Has anyone told you that? I owe you a drink when I get back to London."

"As to that, sir, rumor here says you've taken root in Dorset." There was a deep chuckle at the end of the line as Gibson hung up.

"Interesting information or no'," Hamish was saying, "what's it got tae do wi' this business?"

"Everything—or nothing," Rutledge said, replacing the receiver. "It could give Elizabeth Napier a damned fine motive for murder."

"Or yon Daniel Shaw. If he was to learn what happened."

Or even Thomas Napier, if he was tired of moral blackmail. . . .

None of which accounted for the second body.

Rutledge found himself restless, unable to settle to any one thought or direction. Every time he'd made any progress in this investigation, he seemed to slip back into a morass of questions without answers. He walked as far as the churchyard, then turned down a shaded lane that led past the back gardens of half a dozen houses before winding its way to the main road again.

The source of his restlessness was easy to identify. The problem of Betty Cooper. He'd stopped at the Darley farm on the way back to Singleton Magna, to question Mrs. Darley. She had been bitter, as Joanna Daulton had foretold.

"I did my best by that girl! I gave her a home, I taught her to be a good maid, and I would have helped her find a place when she was ready. Instead, she walked away in the night, without a thank-you or a good-bye. Whatever trouble she got into afterward is none of my concern." She was a woman with thinning white hair and a harassed expression, worn by years of hard work. "I'm sorry if she's got herself killed, I wouldn't have wished that on her. But a green girl goes to a place like London and she's likely to find trouble, isn't she?"

"Would she have been likely to come back to you for help? If she'd needed it?" he'd asked. "If she'd found herself in trouble?"

The room was full of sunlight, but there was a darkness in Mrs. Darley's face. "She'd have been sent away with a flea in her ear, if she had! I have no patience with these modern girls who don't know their place or their duty."

"Was there anyone she was close to in the neighborhood? A man or a woman? A maid at someone else's home?"

"Women didn't much care for her, she put on airs. Above herself, she was. As for men, they'd come around, as men will, but she wouldn't give them the time of day either. Saving herself for better things, she was. Well, that's all right in its way, but she had notions she shouldn't of. When Henry Daulton came back from the war, she said if he hadn't been wounded so bad, she'd have had a fancy for him. Then she met Simon Wyatt, and she was all for finding herself a gentleman. Mr. Wyatt had interviewed her only as a favor to Mrs. Daulton, but she couldn't see that, could she? Took it personal, just because he'd seen her himself, rather than leaving her to his French wife."

"She told you this?" Rutledge asked, surprised.

"Lord save us, no! I overheard her talking to one of the cowmen. He was teasing her, like, and she said a gentleman didn't have dirt under his nails nor smell of sweat, nor drink himself into a stupor of a Saturday night, and knew how to treat a lady. Much taken with Mr. Wyatt she was. She said he'd gone and got himself a French wife, but it wouldn't last. He was home now, and not in France.

That's when I came around the corner from looking at the cream pans and told her I'd not have talk like that under my roof. My late husband didn't stand for that kind of sauciness, and neither do I! It wasn't more than ten days later, if that long, before she was gone. And I haven't seen her, nor wanted to, since. I don't wish her harm, no, but some learn the hard way, don't they?"

Rutledge also tracked down Constable Truit, who had—according to Joanna Daulton—tried to court the dead woman.

He shook his head when Rutledge began his questions. "Inspector Hildebrand asked me to have a look at the body when it was first brought in. I couldn't see any likeness to Betty. Miss Cooper. Sleek as a cat, she was, sunning itself in the window. Not like this one, thin, cheap clothes and shoes. Not Betty's style." His confidence was solid, convincing.

Rutledge wondered if Truit saw what he wanted to see or if this was a considered opinion. All the same, the answer contradicted Mrs. Daulton's tentative identification.

A dead end. And yet . . . if the dead woman was Betty Cooper, she'd come back to Dorset. Someone had killed her, when she did, to silence her.

Just as someone had killed Margaret Tarlton, when she came back to Charlbury for the first time since 1914.

"That's wild supposition," Hamish said.

But was it?

What did these two women have in common? Or—to put it another way, what threat had these two women posed, that cost them their lives?

The common thread, if there was one, seemed to be Simon Wyatt. And a savage beating that was the cause of death in both cases. But it was as tenuous as gossamer, that thread. One tug, to see where it might lead, would snap it. . . .

If Elizabeth Napier had killed her secretary because Margaret had borne an illegitimate child to Thomas Napier, it made no sense for her to have killed a serving girl months before.

If Daniel Shaw had killed Margaret out of jealousy, he had no motive to kill anyone else.

If the connection was Simon Wyatt, then he, Rutledge, was back to Aurore.

"Or Simon himsel'," Hamish pointed out. "For yon bonny house and the money it will bring in."

Thanking Truit, he found himself thinking with cold clarity that there was one way that Simon Wyatt might win on two fronts: retrieve the money he needed so badly from Margaret's Chelsea house and rid himself of his French wife. Leave her to hang for murder. . . .

Coming out of Truit's house, he was waylaid by Mrs. Prescott.

"I don't see why you haven't moved into the Arms," she told him. "You're in Charlbury more often than the doctor or the priest."

"By accident," he said, smiling.

She looked up at him. "Pshaw! It's a pretty face bringing you back."

He could feel a flush rising. "Margaret Tarlton's face wasn't pretty when her killer had finished. That's what brings me back here. Did you have something to tell me?"

Mrs. Prescott nodded. "My brother, now, he's a good listener. Says his voice dried up the day after his wedding and hasn't been heard since. But he's a great one for the gossip over a pint at the Arms. You'd think he knew more about wood than any man alive."

"Wood?" His mind was only partly on what she was saying.

"He's a carpenter. Like the Lord, only not liable to wind up on some of his own handiwork! Makes chests and bed frames over to Stoke Newton. And he's the one told me about the body they'd found by Leigh Minster."

"And you're here to tell me the identity of it?"

"No, it's not anyone I know. Not that Miss Tarlton, if this one's already rotting. Nor yet anyone around Charlbury, that I can think of. But it makes you wonder, don't it, if a woman's safe these days, out on the roads. When I was a girl, you could walk to Lyme Regis, if you'd cared to, and not a thing to fear any part of the way. I ask you again, do you believe that man Mowbray's to blame?"

"What do you think?"

She tilted her head to look up at him against the sun. "I don't see this part of Dorset is a likely place for murderers to congregate by the half dozen, waiting their chances! They'd be more like to die of boredom!"

He said, keeping his face grave, "Are you saying the killer is a local man—or woman?"

"I have a thought or two I'm working on," she told him, an undercurrent of seriousness changing her voice. "Mind, I'm not saying it's the most likely way things happened! Only that I suppose it could have."

Surprised, he thought she was telling the truth, rather than trying to tweak his interest.

"I'd be careful who I told," he warned her. "If it's not Mowbray, safely locked away, your thought or two might well make a killer very uncomfortable."

Mrs. Prescott gave him a straight look. "I'm no fool," she told him bluntly. "You're Scotland Yard, and safe enough. Constable Truit," she added, glancing over her shoulder at his house, "*is* a fool. I hear the talk around this part of Dorset. Only it doesn't go in one ear and out the other. Like that quilt I was telling you about—bits and pieces, bits and pieces—they add up."

"Have you got enough to baste together a whole story? If you do, I'd like to hear it."

She shook her head. "Not yet. No, early days yet! I just wanted you to know that I was working at it." She smiled crookedly. "I've a fond spot for Simon Wyatt. And I detest that Hazel Dixon. I'd just as soon see her nose put out of joint! She's one to cause trouble out of spite. Pure spite!"

He said again, "I'd refrain from meddling, if I were you."

"I won't meddle," she told him. "I'll just listen, that's all."

23

Rutledge realized that his unguided steps had led him to the small surgery of Dr. Fairfield. The doctor was in and prepared to give him five minutes. The coolness was still there, but Fairfield knew his duty and did it precisely.

"There's only one question, it won't take more than five minutes. It's about the body found here in Singleton Magna—Mrs. Mowbray or Miss Tarlton. I'd like to know if that woman had borne children?"

"That was one of the first questions Hildebrand asked me. And yes, she had. At the time, my answer provided additional evidence that she must be the Mowbray woman. Whether it applies as well to Margaret Tarlton, I can't say."

"It may be that Miss Tarlton also had a child. Out of wedlock."

Fairfield said, "I'm afraid medical science can't tell us whether the mother was wearing a wedding band or none at the time of birth."

"And the body at Leigh Minster?"

"I'd say she hadn't. It is harder to be sure, given her time in the ground. That's two questions." He pulled out his watch and glanced at it.

Rutledge took the hint as it was intended, and left.

He found himself wishing he could interview Thomas Napier, to test the theory of his involvement with Margaret. But Rutledge knew what Bowles would have to say to that request. And Napier himself might well refuse—he had made a point of staying in the background, except for what might be judged as reasonable concern for a young woman in his employ and still under his protection. Even his visits to Bowles's office could be construed as a man acting in the place of a father. Bowles would most certainly interpret it that way. It made his own life simpler and easier.

The next best choice was Thomas Napier's daughter.

It was time to ask Elizabeth Napier a few blunt questions.

She was in the museum, a pinafore over a pretty summer dress in blues and greens, busily dusting the new shelves that had replaced the fallen ones.

Rutledge greeted her and asked her to come for a walk with him, out of the house and away from other ears. Somewhere he could hear the maid Edith beating a carpet and Aurore's voice speaking to Simon.

Surprised, Elizabeth removed her pinafore and said, "I don't see the need for such secrecy, I've nothing to hide. But if you insist— very well."

They walked down toward the common and the pond. A dog slept peacefully by the water's edge and ducks swam smoothly in small flotillas, conducting loud conversations as they went. Rooks called in the trees, and he could hear the blacksmith's hammer. There was a bustle in Charlbury's streets, the shops doing a brisk business, but here it was quiet enough except for Hamish, mutter-ing in the back of his mind.

"You promised Bowles you'd no' tread on toes!" he was re-minding Rutledge with vigor. "Do you want to end your career on a political blunder?"

Someone had set a bench under a tree some ten feet from the pond, and Rutledge led Elizabeth to it. She inspected it, then sat down, leaving space for him to join her. A light wind lifted the curls at the sides of her face, giving her a vulnerable, almost childlike quality as she turned expectantly toward him.

"I want to ask you about Margaret Tarlton. I find it helps if I understand the background of the victim. Not just where she came from, but how she must have felt about those around her, how she lived her life, how she arrived at a time and place where someone believed she had to die. It often brings me closer to finding the murderer."

"I thought the police in Singleton Magna were satisfied that Mowbray had killed her. Inspector Hildebrand is not a man who changes his mind lightly."

"Mowbray is a strong possibility. We can't overlook him. The problem is, so many pieces of this puzzle don't fit together properly. And that tells me that I've yet to fill the empty spaces between them. It seemed to me that you'd rather not have the Wyatt household hear what I'm about to ask you." He was choosing his words carefully, aware that she might leave when he finally got to the point.

"I've nothing to hide from Simon!"

"No, but your father might. I've heard—from a number of sources—that your father was more than fond of Margaret. He was very likely in love with her."

She turned to face him, her eyes bright, her face shocked. "Who on earth has told you such lies?"

"Are they lies?" he asked gently, apparently watching the ducks.

"My father is very fond of Margaret. You've known that from the start! As for *love*, I don't believe he's paid more than polite attention to any woman since my mother's death."

"Sometimes a daughter is the last to know a father's feelings."

"No, you don't quite see what I'm telling you. My mother was very important to him, and I've done what I could to fill her place. But superficially. I sit at the head of his table, I entertain his guests, I attend public functions with him, and I spend hours with very dull women who must be handled with the greatest care because either their husbands' opinions or their money carries weight. My father is a man who keeps his emotions tightly locked inside. He hasn't spoken my mother's name since the day he buried her. I'm well aware that men have physical needs, but for all I know my father buried those with my mother too."

"For all you know," he repeated, no inflecton in his voice.

"Since her death I've never seen him show affection, even to me, in public. He doesn't touch people if he can avoid it, he doesn't care to be touched. Whatever natural human contacts there are, he accepts but doesn't encourage. To Margaret he was kind, considerate, and protective, as he was of me. He told me once that she had no family to speak of, and he felt responsible for her as long as she resided under our roof. He saw to it when she was required to spend time on his affairs that she was properly escorted home afterward. I daresay any man of breeding would have done the same!"

She stopped. In the silence that followed he thought about what she had said. If she was lying, she was practiced at it. He considered mentioning the child and decided against it. It was a tenuous charge and, right or wrong, could hurt a goodly number of innocent people. But if Sergeant Gibson's information was correct, Thomas Napier now had a son to put in his daughter's place.

"Very well. You believe that your father has no more than a natural fondness for Margaret. Let's turn the coin over. Was she fond of him?"

"Of course she was. He's a man who engenders loyalty. And that's not a daughter's blind assessment, you can ask anyone who knows him well."

"Miss Napier, Margaret lived with you for five or six years—"

"No! If Margaret was in love with my father, she successfully kept it from me. And very likely from him as well. She was ambitious, I grant you, but she also understood that scandal of any kind was political fodder. Margaret was very like my father, you know, not a woman who wore her heart on her sleeve. The pair of them would make very dull lovers!"

And yet Shaw had said he saw passion, hot and raw, in Napier's eyes.

"Why had Miss Tarlton chosen to leave your employ? I've been given several reasons for her decision, but I'd very much like to hear the truth."

Elizabeth shrugged. "She wanted a change. The museum reminded her of India, possibly. Or she was tired of London."

"She carefully concealed her Indian background, Miss Napier. I don't believe she would elect to come here to Charlbury and open that door again. Nor was Dorset likely to foster an ambitious young woman's prospects. I think you persuaded her to come, to give yourself an excuse to call on Simon Wyatt from time to time. I'm sure that's why you felt some sense of guilt when you were told Margaret was dead—"

"I wouldn't—"

"But you would. You've come now yourself and you're staying. A foot in the door. Still, your motives aren't important. What matters is why Margaret agreed to your scheme. Was she happy for an excuse to break her ties with you, to leave London and to put some distance between herself and your father? Or, if she wanted to marry him, she must have realized that he wouldn't ask her as long as she was a nobody, your secretary, vulnerable to cruelties from women who took pleasure in reminding her of her place. Even moving to another house hadn't changed that. She was, as she put it herself, still a servant." He smiled, to take some of the sting from his words. "She wouldn't be the first woman to feel that leaving him might make up a man's mind for him. He was already jealous, he knew that Captain Shaw was living here. He must have told her he was afraid she'd rekindle that old romance, that Shaw might persuade her that a ring on her finger was better than the shadowy life of a mistress—"

"Nonsense!" Elizabeth's face was flushed with anger. "You've twisted the truth to fit your own muddled evidence! She was never my father's mistress!"

Rutledge turned to her. "I don't intend to embarrass you or your father, Miss Napier. I simply want the truth so that I can sort out the rest of this tangle and find Miss Tarlton's killer. And I think I *have* found the truth, finally."

Elizabeth got up, her skirts brushing against him as she turned to go. "I'd like very much to know who gave you this information. You said 'a number' of sources. Was that true? Or simply a euphemism?"

"Yes. It was true. I've heard it from enough sources that I have no choice but to believe it."

She frowned, mentally running down a list of possible names. He could see her mind at work. Then she smiled. "Well. It doesn't matter. My father is safe, isn't he? Either way. If Margaret is dead. And it wasn't I, was it, who drove Margaret to the station that last morning. Good day, Inspector!"

He watched her walk on toward the inn, her stride graceful, her bearing giving her that aura of royal dignity that made up for inches. But he thought, his eyes on her straight back, that she was upset, as if he'd touched a rawness in her that bled inside.

Rutledge considered the possibility that whatever the station-master might have said, Margaret Tarlton reached Singleton Magna, and Elizabeth Napier met her there, offering to drive her on to Sherborne. And killed her along the road, to put an end to any connection between Margaret and Thomas Napier.

But that brought him around again to the question of who drove Margaret to Singleton Magna.

He was beginning to believe he knew . . . if it hadn't been Aurore in the Wyatt motorcar, it might have been Simon. In spite of Mrs. Dixon's certainty that Aurore was driving, it was the vehicle and not the occupants she'd seen. He was persuaded of that by his own instincts and the woman's vehemence.

But why would Simon kill Margaret Tarlton or anyone else? Why would Aurore be terrified that he might have?

It was on the way back to his car that he halted by the smithy and stood thinking intently for several minutes as he watched the activity around him. People going about their own business moved past him with curiosity in their eyes, nodding but not pausing to speak to him. He was the bringer of misfortune, in a sense. They wouldn't ignore him completely, but there was no warmth in their faces as they went on. The sooner he left, the sooner life in Charlbury could return to normal.

As, in a way, it already had. In spite of police activity in the neighborhood, in spite of the discovery of another body some distance away, no one had been murdered in Charlbury itself, and no one had been arrested in the village. The initial shock had begun to wear off and, with it, some of the tension. That explained the activity on the street. He found that very interesting.

If Aurore was guilty, then the village had not lost one of its own. . . . The stranger could be taken away, grief would disrupt Simon Wyatt's life for a time, but the familiar face of Elizabeth Napier was assurance perhaps that he wouldn't grieve for long. All would be as it had been.

Hamish, wary, noticed her first.

Rutledge became aware that someone was speaking his name and turned to see a woman standing beside him, casting a look over her shoulder as if afraid that she might be seen with him. She was a plump woman, attractive in a way, but with the small mouth and narrow eyes of a spiteful nature. Her dark hair was pinned up with an effort at style, and she was wearing a very becoming summer dress. He thought, if she smiled, she might even be pretty.

"Yes, what can I do for you?" he asked, giving her his full attention.

"My name is Marian Forsby. I only wanted to tell you that I haven't seen anything that might help you with your inquiries, but I thought perhaps—" She paused, casting another look around her.

He said, "This is a very public place, Mrs. Forsby. May I offer you a cup of tea at the Wyatt Arms?" He smiled, some of the forbidding harshness of his thoughts vanishing with it.

Gratefully she accepted, and in a very few minutes they were ensconced under the trees where he had talked with Aurore, a pot of tea in front of them. Mrs. Forsby poured it delicately and served him with a practiced air of gentility. But her work-roughened hands told him otherwise. Would the women of Charlbury have been any kinder to Margaret Tarlton than they had been to Aurore? Or perhaps Margaret had expected to be here for a very short time.

There was no one else in the back garden, yet Mrs. Forsby still had an air of looking over her shoulder, even without turning her head, as if every nerve ending were attuned to movement around them.

"I am married to Harold Forsby, who owns the ironmonger's shop. We have a house just up the way from there," she said, busying herself with her cup so that she didn't have to meet his eyes. "I've been concerned for some time—you see, I'm often occupied with the children—they're four and eight, very active, they are. Which has made for some difficulties between myself and my husband." Her cheeks flushed, but she went on resolutely into his interested silence. He wasn't sure where this was leading, but a policeman quickly learned that patience was a valuable tool.

"I don't quite know how to say this, Inspector. But Hazel Dixon mentioned that you were interested in Mrs. Wyatt's activities. I

229

thought it best to speak to you myself, since I was in a position to tell you some things others might not have thought it necessary to pass on. Mrs. Wyatt is—well, to put it bluntly, she is a woman who attracts the eye of a man, and she knows it. Very French, she is, and that does seem to add to her appeal. That slight accent, and the way she dresses. Well, I can only imagine what her relationship is with her husband, but a woman who is promiscuous often has a very—er—jealous nature. She doesn't like competition! I'm sure that's why she persuaded him to give up standing for Parliament and take on this silly museum of his! Such a waste, wouldn't you say? We've had Wyatts representing us for ever so many years, he's so suitable for the task!"

"Promiscuous?" he asked, moving directly to the key word.

"Oh, yes, I can't imagine that any decently behaved woman would attract so much attention to herself if she was not—well, of that nature. She can't be ignorant of the looks cast her way! A married woman neither invites nor encourages such bold notice. It's neither proper nor genteel. And with Mr. Wyatt so busy with this museum of his, he hasn't taken steps to put a stop to it!"

Her mouth tightened until the lips were a thin, short line.

The third stone was being cast at Aurore. . . .

"What has this to do with my investigation, Mrs. Forsby?" He tried to keep the anger out of his voice, picking up his cup and burning himself with the scalding tea. He realized that there was no sugar, no cream in his. Setting it down, he remedied that, courteously waiting for Mrs. Forsby to answer.

"If I were a woman like that," she said after a moment, "and another very pretty woman came into my household, I shouldn't like it! I suppose it's a natural jealousy in someone who prefers to be the center of attention at home as well as in the neighborhood. The talk was, they'd find a male assistant for Mr. Wyatt, someone from one of the colleges. Mrs. Wyatt would have preferred *that*, I'm quite sure, another besotted male in the house. It might have kept her from straying farther afield, at least for a time. But it didn't turn out that way, did it?"

"Are you telling me that Aurore Wyatt has taken lovers in Charlbury?"

She put down her own cup and said, "I don't know about lovers,

Inspector, I can't speak for Mrs. Wyatt. I think—at the moment—that it's probably her deep need for male attention. But you know where that leads in the long run! I've seen the way Harold looks when she comes into the shop, and I've seen Denton at the Arms and Bill Dixon, and even Constable Truit hanging on every word she utters, their faces wreathed in silly smiles, their eyes avid, and God alone knows what's going through their minds! It may not be true adultery yet, but it's only a matter of time. She'll tire of their admiration and want more. No, I don't think Mrs. Wyatt would have liked to see competition under her roof, and I'm sure if you don't act soon, something will very likely happen to Miss Napier as well. I'm not suggesting that it will, but one must do one's duty before something terrible happens, and not in hindsight. Well, there you have it!"

It was a tangle of jealousy and envy, with no reason behind it but a woman's need to retaliate, to strike out at the interloper.

"Are you saying that I should arrest Mrs. Wyatt for murder? On what evidence? And the murder of whom?"

She lifted an impatient hand. "Miss Tarlton, of course. Mrs. Dixon swears she saw Mrs. Wyatt in the car driving Miss Tarlton to Singleton Magna. I'm sure she's not the only one to notice the car, if the truth be told. And I've just explained to you why I believe Mrs. Wyatt could have done such a terrible thing. I don't speak up lightly, Inspector! I came to you after considerable thought and prayer. But if a person breaks one of the commandments, it isn't such a great step from breaking others, is it?"

"But you've no proof that Mrs. Wyatt has betrayed her husband?"

She smiled tightly, then drank her tea. "What proof do you need? If that woman they found just the other day is Betty Cooper, then you ought to consider that Mr. Wyatt was thinking of taking her on as a second maid. Edith is rather plain, but Betty had a way with her. Mrs. Wyatt wouldn't have liked her about the house, flaunting herself! It was not long afterward that Betty disappeared. No one remarked it at the time, but it's very likely she met the same fate."

"The woman found at Stoke Minster has been dead for only three months or so. Betty Cooper left Dorset long before that."

"Did she? She left Mrs. Darley, right enough! She may even have gone to London for a time. But in the end she came back, didn't she? And wanted that job Mr. Wyatt had promised her. If she came to the Wyatt door on Edith's day off, and Mrs. Wyatt answered, what do you think could have happened?"

It was an interesting theory.

"Let me get this straight," he said. "If Mrs. Wyatt has, as you say, an eye for the men in Charlbury, why should she object if her husband took a fancy to Margaret Tarlton or Betty Cooper? I should think that would provide Mrs. Wyatt with more opportunity to indulge in her own affairs."

"But I just told you!" Mrs. Forsby said. "She wants to hoard them all, Mr. Wyatt, my Harold, any man with eyes in his head to see her—even you. I've watched her with her hand on your arm, smiling up at you like Miss Innocence herself! Even a London inspector from Scotland Yard is fair game for that one!" She finished her tea, her face pink with a sense of righteous triumph. "Mrs. Wyatt got her hands on Mr. Wyatt in the war, even when he was engaged to Miss Napier. It's not right, it's not proper. And if she had no respect for a man already promised to someone else, then she won't let marriage vows stop her."

It was Hamish who put the thought into his head. That Aurore Wyatt had escaped a war-ravaged country by marrying Simon.

"Did you or anyone else see Betty Cooper after she disappeared six months ago? Did anyone see her come back to Charlbury? Hearsay won't do, we need hard evidence. The body wasn't found in this village, after all. It could be unrelated to Margaret Tarlton's death. It may not have anything to do with Aurore Wyatt."

She touched her lips with the serviette in her lap and folded it neatly before laying it beside her empty cup. "Nobody said she was a fool. And she'd have to be, to leave bodies lying about on her own doorstep! What I ask myself is, who else had any call to harm Betty Cooper? Or this Miss Tarlton. Can you tell me that? No, I didn't think so! And where's it all to stop? I ask you."

Rutledge walked with her to the door of the Wyatt Arms. Denton nodded to him as he passed, but Daniel Shaw was nowhere to be seen. Mrs. Forsby was still talking about how difficult it had been to come forward, as if she wanted his reassurance that she'd done the right thing. But the air of triumph was still there.

232

He thanked her and watched her walk back the way she'd come, with a neck stiff with righteousness beneath her summery hat.

But Hamish was pointing out, with some force, that Aurore had tried her charms on him, and it had worked.

"You canna' fault a woman like yon, for wanting her own back on the foreigner who takes her husband's eye, when she has a husband of her own."

He was angry all the same. Defensive, for Aurore's sake. Surely Wyatt had some inkling of the feelings that were rampant in Charlbury! Or was the man so blinded by his own pain that he couldn't see what was happening?

"You're no' her champion," Hamish reminded him. "You're a lonely man who's lost the one woman he thought cared for him. You see the loneliness in her, and it turns your head. But it's no' the same—your Jean walked away and is marrying anither man in your place. Yon woman already has a husband!"

"I'm not in love with her!"

"No," Hamish said thoughtfully, "I'd no' say you were. But she can pull the strings, and you dance like a puppet at the end of them! Because she's hurting as much as you are. And like calls to like. It's no' love, but it can light fires all the same in a man!"

Rutledge swore, and told Hamish he was a fool.

But he knew that Aurore cast spells. Except over her husband. Whatever he'd felt for his wife in France when he'd married her, it was quite different now. And for all he, Rutledge, knew of it, Aurore herself had changed as much as Simon had. That was the centerpiece of their marriage—change—and it might not have been all on one side.

If Aurore's marriage was empty, she might well be frightened of other women catching Simon's eye. If Simon neglected her, she might well be driven to having an affair, to point out to him that others wanted very badly what he chose to cast off.

Which might explain why the husbands of Charlbury were besotted and the wives were prepared to see Aurore Wyatt hang, if it took her away from there.

24

Rutledge was halfway to his car when he saw Hildebrand coming out of the Wyatt house. The Singleton Magna inspector saw him as well and signaled Rutledge to wait. When he reached the car, there was a nasty gleam in Hildebrand's eyes. For a moment he studied Rutledge, and then said, "Well, you can pack your bags tonight and leave for London in the morning. I've got the Tarlton murder solved. Without the help of the Yard, I might add. You've been precious little help from the start, come to that."

"Solved? That means an arrest, then."

"Of course it does. Keep my ear to the ground, that's what I do. Truit tells me what he doesn't tell you—well, no reason why he should, is there? You were here to find the children. And they've been found, haven't they?"

He was gloating, his face gleaming with it, his manner offensive but just short of insulting. He paused to let Rutledge respond.

"That's good news," he answered.

Hildebrand still waited and, when Rutledge had nothing more to add, went on with malicious pleasure. "I'm having a search warrant brought. We'll find the murder weapon and that suitcase you were so fond of throwing in my face. And when we do, I'll have my murderer. Ever seen a woman hang? Delicate necks, over swiftly."

Rutledge felt cold, not sure whether Hildebrand was telling him the truth or trying to rouse him to anger. "Stop beating about the bush, Hildebrand!"

He held up a square hand, the back of it toward Rutledge, and began to tick off the points, bending down each finger as he went. "Witnesses saw Mrs. Wyatt driving the victim to Singleton Magna, even though she denies it. Mrs. Wyatt wasn't happy about the Tarlton woman coming here. Jealousy, I'm told. Mrs. Wyatt could wash up after the murder at that farm of the Wyatts', and nobody was the wiser. Handyman didn't see her leave and didn't hear her return. That's where she tucked the murder weapon and probably the suitcase as well, out of sight into the hay or under one of the sheds. Who'd notice a worn spanner or an old hammer in that yard full of rusting junk?"

"Why did you change your mind?" Rutledge forced himself to ask. "I thought you were convinced that Mowbray had killed Margaret Tarlton, mistaking her for his wife."

"I was fairly sure of that, given the evidence. But we found something else interesting today. I sent one of my men to Gloucestershire, where the Tarlton woman's relatives live. They were that upset, to hear she was dead, not just missing. They asked my sergeant if she'd left a will, and he was smart enough to go to London to find out. Lawyer wouldn't let him see it, but Miss Tarlton had left everything to her young godson, the cousin's child, we got that much out of the old fool. And her house to Simon Wyatt. There's the motive right there! Miss Napier may've thought she was engaged to Wyatt, but she wasn't the only string to his bow. Must have put both their noses out of joint, when he came home with that French wife! And must have put his wife's nose out of joint when she discovered his mistress was coming to live with them!"

"I don't think—" Rutledge began through the clamor Hamish was raising in his head.

"You aren't paid to think," Hildebrand said, unconsciously quoting Old Bowels. "You're paid to find murderers. Stay out of my way until this is finished, I'm warning you!" He strode off, marching purposefully toward the car waiting for him at Truit's house. Watching him go, Rutledge swore.

Hildebrand had hardly passed from view, on his way back to Singleton Magna, when the Napier car came down the same road, making for the inn. Rutledge assumed it was Benson, going to fetch Elizabeth Napier, then realized that there was a man seated beside him.

The car pulled up in front of the inn and Rutledge saw Benson pointing in his direction. Benson's passenger nodded and got down, walking toward Rutledge. The distinguished face, the trim beard, the broad shoulders told him at once that this was Thomas Napier.

Napier said, as soon as he was within hearing, "Inspector Rutledge?"

"That's right." Rutledge had been in his car on the point of leaving, but killed the engine and got down to take the hand Napier held out to him.

"Thomas Napier, from London. Is there any place where we can speak privately?" he asked, looking around. "That bench over there by the pond, I think?" he went on, unconsciously choosing the place where Rutledge had questioned his daughter. The ducks had gone, leaving the surface of the pond like a mirror, reflecting the sky.

They walked in silence in that direction, and Rutledge let the older man choose his own time, his own words. But curiosity was rampant, and the tension in the other man had stirred Hamish into questing life.

"I don't trust that fool Hildebrand," Napier began. "Miss Tarlton's solicitor called me today. He said that one of Hildebrand's people had come to ask about Margaret's will. There's a clause in it that could cause a good deal of trouble for a good many innocent people. Margaret's memory as well. I've spoken to Superintendant Bowles, and I'm not overly impressed by him either."

They had reached the bench, and Napier sat down, scanning Rutledge from head to foot. "You look like the sensible sort. In the war, were you?"

"Yes," Rutledge answered, obeying Napier's gesture and taking the other end of the bench. "I was." The words were more curt than he'd meant.

"Hmm. Then I daresay you'll understand when I tell you that Simon Wyatt is a man living on the edge, as it were. He's my god-

son, I care deeply about him. The war came damned close to breaking his spirit, and he hasn't been able to recover the balance of his
mind. I've not encouraged him to stand for office, I've felt that he
was probably better off working on this museum of his, finding his
feet again in his own good time. Dorset is quiet, a healing place, as
I know myself." The tone of voice was fatherly, concerned. It was
as if the rupture caused by Simon's marriage to Aurore had never
occurred.

"I understand, but I don't see that this is important enough to
bring you from London to tell me."

"Simon may not know some of the terms of Margaret's will.
They may need explanation. But they have nothing to do with this
murder, and they have nothing to do with Margaret's affairs.
Simon's father was kind enough to arrange a loan for her when she
needed it, and that was that. He wasn't involved with her in any
way, he simply felt that she deserved a measure of independence,
and helped provide it. You never knew Margaret, but she was a
very able young woman, very charming, very attract—"

His voice broke, and for several seconds he fought for control.
"She was all that a man might want in his daughter," he ended
lamely. "I would have done the same for her, if she'd asked me,
but she no doubt felt it was improper, since she lived in my house.
It was the sort of arrangement that could have political repercus-
sions, and she was astute, politically—"

"Unsafe for you—but safe enough for Simon's father?"

Napier turned to look at him. "Don't be purposely obtuse!"

"No," Rutledge answered. "All right, then, you don't want Wyatt to know why the house is left to him. But that's out of my
hands. Hildebrand is going for a search warrant for Wyatt's farm.
He apparently believes Aurore Wyatt killed Miss Tarlton because
she was under the impression that Miss Tarlton and Wyatt had had
an affair. That Simon Wyatt bought the Chelsea house. And that
Simon Wyatt might well be the father of the child Miss Tarlton
bore. She could hardly want his mistress moving in with them." It
was a mixture of fact and fiction, but Rutledge was interested to
see how well this balloon flew. And what reaction it provoked. He
might have only this one opportunity to confront Napier. . . .

The expression on Napier's face was a mixture of shock and

horror. "How do you know all this? About the child? And why should Aurore Wyatt know of it? It wasn't Simon's, he was away at war—"

"Was it his father's?"

"God, *no*! Whatever you think about Margaret Tarlton, I assure you she—"

"Then who was its father? Daniel Shaw? You? I'm not interested in Miss Tarlton's child. I'm only interested in what bearing it might have on her murder."

"The child is dead—it was born dead! It has no bearing on anything!" There was an undercurrent of wild grief behind the defensive words. A wrenching pain.

"Mr. Napier, if Hildebrand learns of it, it could send a woman to the gallows. It gives her a clear motive, don't you see that, to kill a suspected rival."

"No. I've met Aurore Wyatt several times. She isn't my concern; she can take care of herself, she's clever and resourceful and strong. Simon is very vulnerable. Whatever this fool Hildebrand is trying to do, he's wrong. I think Margaret was the unwitting victim of that poor sod they've got in the jail at Singleton Magna. There's no more nor less to it than that. What I want from you is the assurance that my daughter—and Simon Wyatt—won't be dragged through the newspapers on the whim of an incompetent policeman!"

"Mr. Napier, I don't believe Bert Mowbray killed Miss Tarlton. I think that her murder was no accident, it was a deliberate attack on her personally. And I suspect that there has been another murder of a young woman, some months ago. How they're related I can't say at the moment—"

"Do you believe Simon is guilty of either of them?"

"No, why should I—"

"But one of them might be set at the door of his wife? Possibly both?"

"As to that, I can't tell you—"

"Then find the answers, damn you! I came to warn you that I don't want my daughter's name dragged into this. I'm taking her back to Sherborne at once. And I don't want to read about Simon in the papers either, nor about that house in Chelsea, nor about any child that might or might not have been born."

Rutledge said, "Margaret Tarlton's murderer has covered his tracks quite cleverly. Still, there's an answer somewhere. Ferreting it out may open the Wyatts to speculation and some scandal. I'll avoid that if I can, I've always tried to shield the innocent. But in the end there may be nothing either of us can do to protect them. The other woman who may have died by the same hand—"

"I'm not concerned with another woman! I want you to stop this fool Hildebrand from walking in heavy boots through the life of a man who is very easily destroyed. Personally, professionally. Do you hear me? If any of this touches Simon Wyatt, I'll hold you personally responsible. I'll see to it that you suffer the consequences. I want this business cleared up without damaging Simon or Margaret, I want Margaret's killer hanged, and I don't want any foulness from this affair touching my daughter in any way. You would do well to believe me, Inspector! I am a man who never makes idle threats."

Napier got to his feet and stood looking down at Rutledge. Whatever he read in the other man's face, he changed his tactics abruptly.

"There's that fellow, Shaw," he said roughly. "He was in love with her in the war, and he's still in love with her for all I know. If Mowbray didn't kill her, then Shaw probably did. Find out, and make an end to it."

Rutledge felt himself welling with anger as Napier walked away. Napier had protected his own, he hadn't cared about anyone else. He had willingly sacrificed Mowbray, he had callously abandoned Aurore to the mercy of the police. Even Daniel Shaw was expendable. Politicians made difficult decisions; Napier was used to sacrificing one good for another. But this was ruthlessness.

Walking away from the pond, Rutledge toyed for a moment with the possibility that Napier had killed Margaret himself, out of jealousy or anger at her refusal to carry on with an affair that she may have considered, in the end, was taking her nowhere. But Napier was too well known in Dorset—even whispers of his involvement would ruin him. This was, possibly, what drove him harder than his concern for Simon Wyatt. If he'd wanted Margaret dead, surely he'd have killed her anywhere but here.

By the same token, to be fair, Napier had been unable to show his grief, his love, his loss, in public. He had had to stand aside and let strangers bury Margaret, turning whatever it was he felt inward, to fester and rankle. He may have made his threats out of love for her rather than any fear for Simon.

They were still threats, and Rutledge took them very seriously.

"It's no' in your hands," Hamish reminded him. "Whatever Napier has said. But either way, ye're sacrificed as well."

"Not if I can help it," Rutledge said as he turned the crank and brought the car to sputtering life. He got in and drove to the Wyatt farm, his mind full of Hamish:

"If you no' can finish this business, you'll be back in yon hospital, crouched in a dark corner of your soul. It's got to be finished, look you, and not for the woman's sake, for your own!"

Jimson was working in the yard, mending the wheel on a barrow, his gnarled hands deftly shifting the shaft to bring the worn place within reach. He didn't look up until Rutledge's shadow fell across his shoulder and onto the dirt-stained wood of the long handles.

"Lord, you know how to startle a man!" Jimson said, straightening up and dropping the shaft. "Now look what you've done," he went on in an aggrieved voice, his face twisting to see Rutledge against the brightness of the sun.

"I need your help," Rutledge said. "I can't go to your master or your mistress, the police from Singleton Magna are coming soon with a search warrant. But I want to go through the house and the barn. Now. Before they get here. Will you walk with me?"

"What're you looking for, then? What's the police after?"

"A suitcase belonging to a dead woman. A pretty hat. A murder weapon."

"Pshaw! There's no pretty hat here. Nor suitcases I don't know about. If it's a murder weapon you want, take your pick." He gestured to the array of tools lying in the dust at his feet. "Any one of those will kill a man."

Hammer, a spanner, a pair of clamps, all of them—he was right—potential weapons.

But Rutledge shook his head. "No. Not these."

"Then what?" Jimson demanded. "That stone? A length of wood?"

"I don't know. All right, we'll forget the weapon for the time being. The suitcase. We'll search first for that."

"What does it look like, then? Mrs. Wyatt, she has suitcases in the attic."

"I don't know, I tell you! If I did, I wouldn't be here. Look, this is useless, Jimson! I need to walk through that house, I need to see for myself what's in the barn. Hildebrand and Truit will be here in the morning—"

"Truit, is it?" Jimson demanded, incensed. "We'll see about that. All right, then, the front door's open, and I can see it from here. Touch anything that don't need touching, and I'll know it."

Rutledge thanked him and walked around to the door. It was unlocked, as it had been before. Thinking about that, Rutledge opened it wider and stepped into the hall, where the stairs rose to the first floor. To his left and right were a pair of rooms, opening into the broad hallway. He gave them a cursory glance, certain that they would hold no secrets. The floors creaked as he moved about, but Jimson wouldn't hear that. The old man's bedroom was in the back to one side of the kitchen and appeared to have been a maid's room at one time, for there were roses on the wallpaper and the iron bed had a floral design at its head. The lamp was serviceable, as were the chair, the stool, and a table. The washstand was oak and had seen better times, the mirror cloudy with age. A jug of water stood on a second table by the bed, and there was a pipe rack next to it, with a tin of tobacco beside it. From the look of the pipes, none of them had been smoked for years, but the aroma of Turkish tobacco lingered and stirred when Rutledge moved one or two.

Upstairs were several bedrooms and a pair of bathrooms. One of the rooms had a rocking chair beside a marble-topped washstand with fresh towels on the racks on either side, a pitcher of water in the bowl. Clothes hung in the closet, mostly coveralls and worn men's shirts that must have been Simon's at one time but carried Aurore's scent now. A pair of straw hats stood on the closet shelf, one of them with a hole in the brim, the other with a sweat-stained band.

The room had an intimate feel to it, as if she'd just left. The candlestick on the bedside table was burned down to half. He wondered if sometimes she'd spent the night here. The bedsheets were soft with age but freshly washed.

The other rooms bore the signs of neglect, a fine sheen of dust on the furniture, a cobweb hanging down above a bedpost, but clean enough for all that. No one had been in these rooms, he thought, for months.

The attic was filled with bits and pieces of old furniture, leather luggage green with age, chairs without seats, broken lamps, a child's crib and a nursing rocker. He looked into corners, behind the head-boards of beds, beyond the empty trunks, into the empty cases, and there was nothing to be seen.

In the end he gave up and went to the barn, quartering it while a cat followed him about, rubbing against his trouser legs when he stopped to look at a box of gear or a stack of tiles or old boots crammed into a bin.

But the barn yielded nothing, and he stood there in the loft, looking at the thick piles of hay, wondering if it was worth his while to dig through the lot. Hamish, tired and irritable, said, "You'll no' solve the riddle here. . . ."

And it was true, but he made the effort to look into the out-buildings and into overturned carts, startling a hen with a clutch of eggs under one. She squawked sharply at him, dashing off with wings flapping.

When he came back to where Jimson was finishing his work on the barrow, the old man said, "Well, you wanted to do it, didn't you? And for what? You haven't found what you was looking for."

"No." He turned to look at the sky. The sun was sinking toward the west, casting long shadows and golden stripes across the lawn and the fields behind the barn. It would be dark quite soon. Seven or eight heavily uddered cows were staring at him from the gate near the milking shed, and he could hear the lowing of others making their slow way home. Jimson wheeled the barrow toward the barn. Rutledge called his thanks but remembered that the man couldn't hear his voice. Couldn't hear a car or footsteps in the house at night . . .

He found himself wondering if Aurore might have entertained lovers there.

Feeling depressed, he got back into the car and drove to Charlbury.

"At least," Hamish offered, "you did na' find anything."

"I was one man. Hildebrand will bring half a dozen. More."

Henry Daulton was standing by the churchyard, his eyes on the
rooks wheeling above the truncated tower, settling uneasily for the
night. He waved as Rutledge passed. Then Mrs. Prescott was hailing
him, and he stopped the car.

"I hear that there's to be an arrest tomorrow. That Inspector
Hildebrand is coming to do it himself. I thought you were in
charge! The man from London."

"No. It's his investigation. I came to coordinate the search for
the children. That's finished." He felt tired, his eyes gritty from the
dusty barn and the staleness of the farm's attics.

"But what about Mr. Simon? What's to happen to him?"

"I don't know. Nothing. He isn't the person Hildebrand is
after."

"Why would anyone want to kill Betty Cooper," she demanded,
"much less a friend of the Wyatts! It makes no sense. That's what
you ought to be saying to the police in Singleton Magna, why
would the Wyatts want to harm her? If you want to save Mrs.
Wyatt from the gallows and her husband from a death of grief,
that's the question you ought to be asking!"

Rutledge shook his head. "I've asked that question and found no
answer. If you have any, I'm willing to hear them. Besides, no one
can be sure that the other body *is* Betty Cooper's. The timing isn't
there, Mrs. Prescott, whatever you want to believe. Betty left six
months ago, not three."

She was vehement, her face ablaze with purpose. "I told you
once, if you want to hide the recent dead, do it in a fresh grave.
Betty Cooper wanted to work in a gentleman's house. Mr. Simon
couldn't hire her, he already had Edith. I can't see that he'd have
sent her away empty-handed! Not Mr. Simon. He'd have done
what he could for the girl, for Mrs. Daulton's sake. Have you even
asked him? What they talked about, those two?"

Rutledge stared at her, and she grinned self-consciously. "No,"
he said slowly. "I don't think anyone has."

"Well, I'd not let it linger on the tongue too long, or that Inspector Hildebrand will be back tomorrow with his warrants!"

He saluted her and backed up the car until he was in front of the Wyatt gate. He met Elizabeth at the front door, her face anguished. She caught his arm and dragged him into the parlor, shutting the door. "For God's sake, what's happening? No one will tell me. Aurore is in her room, I think she's crying. Simon has shut himself up in the museum and won't let me in. And my father was here in Charlbury, I saw him speaking to you, but he wouldn't come to the house, he just sent Benson with a note telling me to leave straightaway. That madman Hildebrand's to blame, isn't he, it all went wrong when *he* came! For God's sake, what's it all about?"

"I don't know. Hildebrand has finally convinced himself that Mowbray didn't kill Margaret Tarlton—we were all fairly certain of that, it isn't news. But if Mowbray didn't kill her, then it has to be someone from Charlbury, you see. And it was Aurore Wyatt who was set to take Margaret Tarlton to meet the train."

"Aurore." She said the name unconsciously, as if tasting it on her tongue. "You're saying that it was Aurore? But *why*?"

"I don't know. There are several theories making the rounds. It seems she's become the popular candidate, now that Mowbray's out of the running."

"But Simon will feel responsible! It was Simon who wanted Margaret to come here as his assistant!"

"No," Rutledge answered bluntly. "It was your scheming that brought her here to interview for the position of assistant."

"But what about that man Shaw?" she demanded frantically. "He was wild with Margaret for not seeing him. He taunts me every time I go into the Wyatt Arms. I can't imagine Aurore battering anyone to death, but Shaw could do it! He's been a soldier, he knows how to kill!"

"Knowing how to kill doesn't make you a murderer," he told her. But he had killed his share of men, in the war. Was that so very different? He could feel Hamish asking that same question in the depths of his mind. "Simon was also a serving officer. If Daniel Shaw is suspect because of his war record, we mustn't forget Simon Wyatt."

"Stop it, do you hear me? Simon hasn't killed anyone! I'd believe Aurore did it before I'd believe Simon could have! I've never understood her, I can't think why he ever married her! Can't you do anything? Can't you find out what it is Hildebrand wants?"

There was a pounding at the door that cut short his response. Elizabeth said something under her breath and went to answer it.

From where he was standing, he could see the heavy door swing open at the same instant a slurred, angry voice cried, "I want to know, damn you! I want to know who killed her!"

It was Shaw standing there, his face white, his body tense with pain.

"You're drunk, disgusting! Go away!" Elizabeth said curtly, preparing to close the door in his face. Behind him the night was black, clouds having moved in with the sunset and now obscuring the stars. Somewhere in the garden a toad sang its mating call, and a moth swept through the bright square of light cast across the lawns. Shaw struck the door with his arm, forcing it open again, and stepped inside. Rutledge, moving swiftly from the parlor, was there to meet him, at Elizabeth's back.

He said, "Go home, Shaw. I told you I'd give you a name, once it was certain. But it isn't certain. Hildebrand has jumped the gun."

"Truit's in the Arms, bragging. They're prepared to make an arrest, damn you!" He stared over Elizabeth's head at Rutledge's face, pain in his eyes that wasn't all from the pain in his body. "I'm not drunk. I want the truth!"

"Wait by my car, and I'll tell you what I know," Rutledge said. "If you don't go, I'll have you arrested for disorderly conduct."

Shaw bit his lip against the pain and said, "I'll wait here on the step. I don't think I could walk that far!" He stepped backward, nearly lost his balance, and sat heavily on the step, crouched protectively over his wound.

Elizabeth said, "You *are* drunk!"

Rutledge caught her arm and pulled her from the door as he shut it.

She turned on him, saying, "The wolves are gathering!"

"Listen to me! This can matter more than your wolves. Does the name Betty Cooper mean anything to you?"

Something stirred in her eyes. Curiosity? Calculation? He couldn't be sure in the dim light that reached the hall from the parlor.

"She was a serving girl, if that's the one you mean. Simon suggested we might consider finding her a place in London. We'd lost two of the younger maids to other positions, he must have known."

"And so he sent her to you from here?"

"Well, we expected her to come to us on a trial basis, but she never arrived. I don't see what this has to do with anything! There isn't time!"

"When was that?"

"Nearly six months ago. Just after Simon came back from France and opened the house here in Charlbury. That's not important, I tell you—"

"Yes, it is," he answered her. "If Betty Cooper didn't arrive at your door, where did she go?" And why hadn't she taken up Simon's proposal that she work for the Napiers? It was a position beyond the dreams of a country girl who wanted to make her way in London. Nor did it explain why the body was only three months dead. Mrs. Prescott was wrong; his questions led him nowhere.

"How should I know? Girls go to London every day, I can't be responsible for the fate of any of them!"

But what if Betty had gone to London after all, avoided the Napiers for whatever reasons, spent three months there in the city, found it not to her liking, and come back to Dorset?

That was possible—but was it likely that in coming *back*, she'd meet her death here before anyone had seen her?

Unless her return threatened someone? But that wouldn't take into account the fate of Margaret Tarlton. . . . The two women had nothing in common.

There was a connection somewhere. There had to be. Or else they were all wrong, Mowbray had killed Margaret and Betty Cooper was a separate crime altogether. There was only the doctor's suggestion that the murders were similar.

He was aware of Elizabeth expostulating, telling him she wanted him to help Simon, to do something before Hildebrand made a grave mistake.

He put his hands on her shoulders to silence her and said, "Look,

246

I've got to go. But I'll be back before Hildebrand comes tomorrow. Is that fair enough?"

"Fair—" she began, but he was already out the door, speaking to Shaw, giving him the same promise.

Shaw, getting stiffly to his feet, stared balefully at Elizabeth and turned to move awkwardly down the walk to the gate. Over his shoulder he said to Rutledge, "I can't fight you now, but if you don't come to the inn by midnight, I'm taking matters into my own hands. Do you hear me?"

"I hear you," Rutledge said, and then: "Can you make it on your own?"

"Damn you, I don't want your pity! I want answers!"

Rutledge watched him go and waited until Elizabeth, unsatisfied, finally closed the front door. Upstairs at one of the windows overlooking the walk, he could sense Aurore's eyes on him.

He walked to the museum wing and knocked on the door. When no one answered, in the end Rutledge opened it and walked inside.

He looked carefully through all the rooms. But it was to no purpose.

Simon Wyatt was in none of them, though the door from that wing into the main house was locked.

25

Rutledge stood in the middle of the front room of the museum, mocked by the shadowed masks on the wall and the dancing shades of small gods with their strange faces and contorted bodies.

Hamish too was mocking him, reminding him that Hildebrand was ahead of him, that he'd been dragging his feet, that the arrest made tomorrow was one he could—should—have made before this. Only he hadn't been able to bring himself to it. "You're faltering, you're no' the man you think you are!"

He couldn't think, he couldn't bring all the pieces together. Like the gods on the shelves, he was twisting and turning—going nowhere.

But what was the connection—damn it, where was it? What had he missed?

He walked out of the museum and closed the door behind him. And where was Simon Wyatt?

He went out of the gate and stood looking around him, making sure that Shaw wasn't loitering in the shadows, waiting for another chance to confront the Wyatts. Which was why he saw the movement among the trees by the church.

He walked that way, taking his time, certain that it was Simon, blacked out again by whatever stress it was that drove him to wander in the night.

His wife's guilt? Was that what had taken Simon back to the war, where death was imminent and wiped out pain, memory, thought—

He reached the trees, where the shadows were deeper, where only the pale reflection of clothing showed that someone waited. Rutledge hesitated, unwilling to startle Simon, unwilling to give away his own presence if it was someone else.

He walked on, softly, battle trained, but the voice that came to him out of the darkness was not Simon's, nor was it Shaw's.

Aurore said, "I hoped you would come. I couldn't say this in the house, not with Elizabeth there. I couldn't do that to Simon. I won't shame him again!"

He could see her now, the light-colored sweater she'd thrown over her dark dress was a luminous mantle about her shoulders. Her face was even paler, a white oval with dark hollows for eyes. As he came nearer, he could sketch in the details of eyebrows, lips, the curve of her hair, the line of her cheekbone. He could smell her scent, faint and warm, like her breathing.

"Where is your husband? Do you know?"

"He's in the museum. He has locked me out. He's taking it very hard, the things Hildebrand has said to him. He thinks he will see me arrested tomorrow."

"Yes. I know. But Hildebrand hasn't told anyone else."

"The story is everywhere, Constable Truit has seen to that. I sent Edith to stay with Mrs. Darley. I didn't want her to be dragged into our scandal."

He was on the point of telling her that Simon was missing again, but before he could speak, she had moved closer to him, her hands outstretched, and for an instant he thought she was going to touch him, take his hands in hers or rest her fingers on his forearms. Instead something hard, uneven, brushed against the cloth of his coat. Instinctively he reached out to take it, and his fingers closed over smooth, woven straw. Confused, he ran his left hand over it and realized with cold shock what it was.

A hat. A woman's straw hat. He could see it more clearly now, the shape and texture, the upswept brim. Ribbons from the crown tangled around his fingers as he turned the hat first this way and then that.

249

"This is proof that I killed Margaret. It is the hat she was wearing when she left Charlbury. I have kept it, in case of need. The rest of her belongings I burned at the farm, with feathers from a plucked hen we'd eaten for our dinner. Edith will tell you that it is the same hat that Margaret was wearing when she left, and no doubt Margaret's maid will confirm that it is hers." She was silent for a time, and he found himself unable to trust his voice to question her.

"You may arrest me, as you promised, and take me at once to London. I don't want to see my husband shamed by Hildebrand walking in with all the people in Charlbury goggling, then taking me away with fanfare."

"I don't know that this is Margaret's hat—" he began, and reached into his pocket for the small lighter that he'd carried in the war. With one smooth action he slipped the cap and the flint. The small flame seemed to flare like a blaze of orange light between them. He could see her eyes, large with surprise, the pupils dilated and then sharpening.

He tore his glance from her face and examined the hat. It was just as Edith had described it. If it wasn't Margaret Tarlton's hat, it was too damned near it for comfort. He could feel the ache in his throat as he examined it.

"I have a small case there, under the trees. I am ready to leave," she said, her voice steady. But her eyes were wells of uncertainty.

He capped the lighter again and slipped it into his pocket, Hamish clamoring in his ears. Over the deafening sound he said, "Aurore—"

"No! Don't say anything more. We must go before Elizabeth or Simon comes out to find me. Please! It was our bargain, you can't tell me you don't remember! You, of all people!"

"Aurore. Why did you kill Margaret Tarlton?"

"I shall tell you on our way to London. *Please!*"

"I can't do this. I don't believe you. Whatever you are confessing to, it isn't murder." He turned the hat again in his hands, striving to ignore Hamish, striving to sound patient, untroubled, the policeman doing his duty.

But not to protect the innocent, only to find the guilty—

"You promised!" she said again, her voice husky with hurt.

250

He said, "Listen to me! I want to know where you found this hat and why you think it was Simon who killed Margaret."

She gasped, and this time her fingers did grip his arm in the darkness. "It was I who killed Margaret. I hit her and hit her and hit her, until my shoulder was tired and I couldn't lift the rock any more. I drove back to the farm and bathed the blood away, and I left my things in the room there, along with her things—I knew Jimson would never open my door! It was safe, no one comes there!"

Her words and her grip were tight, convincing, and he could feel her desperation, the need to make him believe.

Rutledge said, closing his mind to Hamish and to her pain, "All right. I believe you. But tell me, why did you have to kill Betty Cooper? What had that poor girl done to make you batter her into unconsciousness and then death?"

She moved convulsively, her hand on his arm showing him as clearly as if she stood in full daylight, what emotions were passing through her body.

"Ah, yes. I thought we might come to that as well. Betty was very pretty," she said. "But that wasn't the reason. Simon was sending her to London, to Elizabeth. I thought—I thought she would be used by Elizabeth to drive a wedge. As Margaret would have been, later. An excuse to call Simon and say 'About Betty . . . I should like to know what you think about her wages—her behavior—her future.' It was such a small excuse. *But it was an excuse!*"

When he said nothing, she went on in a low, trembling voice. "I am not the woman you think I am, Ian Rutledge. I cannot be endowed with virtues I never possessed. I'm French, I think differently, I feel differently. I am a murderess, and I have lied to you from the start."

He couldn't see her face, he couldn't watch her eyes, and the telltale hand had been withdrawn. But he knew beyond doubt that he had to accept her confession now.

He had no choice but to arrest her for two murders and let the courts decide for him whether she was guilty or not. The hat in his hand was proof enough, and if the suitcase had been burned, it didn't matter. Confession, evidence . . .

251

"What did you do with the murder weapon?"

"It was a smooth stone from the car. I kept it there to put under a tire on a hill. I saw a lorry in France roll down a hill into a crowded wagon, full of refugees. It killed so many of them. I carry the stone to prevent such a thing from happening again. It is still in the car. If you look, you will find it below the rear seat. I daresay it still has Margaret Tarlton's blood on it."

He stood there, listening, hearing the ring of truth, hearing too the deep grief behind it. Hearing the ragged breathing.

Aurore knew too many of the details. She had brought him the hat, she had given him the murder weapon, she had given him what—to many women—would seem a reasonable motive for two deaths.

And yet—and yet his instinct told him she was a consummate liar, not a murdereress. He knew now who she was shielding—though not yet why. What was it she knew that drove her to this confession? What had given Simon away, in her eyes? The hat, perhaps lying forgotten in the back of the car? Coming out of the barn that afternoon to find the car was not there, where she'd left it? Simon's insistence that she had taken Margaret to the train, when he knew she had not? How long had it taken her to put the facts together? A bit at a time? Or one terrible blow she hadn't expected?

Yet Rutledge found himself thinking that Simon had been too obsessed with his museum to plot so clever a murder, so clever a way of convicting his wife. Or had that been another lie? Diabolical and cruel . . .

There was another possibility—that someone else had seen to it that the finger of guilt pointed at Aurore, and Simon was unwittingly suffering the same agonies of doubt and fear as she was. Had the first attempt to be rid of Aurore—killing Betty Cooper—misfired when the girl's body was not discovered? And Margaret Tarlton, the next sacrifice, had nearly backfired too, when Mowbray took the blame for her death. Until Elizabeth Napier came to Charlbury and set Hildebrand straight . . . but could any of that be proved?

Rutledge said, "Very well. I'm arresting you, Aurore Wyatt, for the death by murder of Margaret Tarlton and Betty Cooper." It was, after all, what she wanted. And it would forestall Hildebrand.

He could feel the tension drain out of her, a smothered sob of relief.

"I'm so very glad it's over," she said quietly. "You don't know how hard it has been to live a lie."

But he did—he lived one every day, he told himself as he took her arm and started for the car. His lie was that he was a competent policeman, an experienced and capable officer of Scotland Yard.

Hamish was reminding him of it with vitriolic pleasure.

26

They had gotten no farther than the edge of the trees when a cry, cut short, rang through the night. Aurore stopped still, listening, her head turned toward the church. "I think it came from there!" she said anxiously.

"Wait here!" Rutledge ordered, already moving.

"No! I'm coming with you!" She was at his heels as he ran toward the front of the church. There were lights coming on in the nearer houses and a light moving down the path from the rectory.

But when they reached the church porch, all they found was Elizabeth Napier in a crumpled heap by the steps, her head buried in her arms. In the blackness of the night she seemed terribly small and vulnerable.

Aurore went quickly to her, touched her shoulder, said, "Help is here, what has happened?"

Elizabeth looked up, the whites of her eyes like half-moons in her pale face. She said roughly, her voice breaking on the words, "I was attacked—"

The lantern bobbing up the walk from the rectory reached them, and Joanna Daulton said with brisk calm, "What's wrong? Can I help?"

Her lamplight fell on Elizabeth, on the dark hair spilling down in waves over her shoulders and the torn collar of her dress. There were red marks like bruises on her throat. Elizabeth put up her hand against the invasion of the light and said, "Oh, God, I was so frightened!"

Rutledge said, "Who was it? Did you see?"

Elizabeth shook her head a little. "No—one minute he was there, startling me, his hands on me, and when I screamed, he reached for my throat, and I could feel his breath on my face—" She shuddered, her body beginning to shake with reaction. Aurore, after the slightest hesitation, knelt to put her arms around Elizabeth, cradling her head against her breast.

"It's all right, you're safe now, don't think about it," she was saying over and over in a low, soothing voice that seemed to touch all of them.

Rutledge said, "I'll have a look around—"

"No!" Elizabeth cried. "No, don't leave me!"

"Mrs. Daulton and Mrs. Wyatt will stay with you. I must go after him now. There may still be time to—"

"No, please, take me back. I—I don't want to be alone," she pleaded.

He thought it was more than that and remembered suddenly that Simon hadn't been in the museum. That very likely Simon hadn't been in the house.

He left the thought there and helped Elizabeth to her feet. As he did, he realized that neither he nor Aurore had Margaret's hat. He swore under his breath. An attack—or a diversion? If it was a diversion, it had been successful.

Rutledge gave Elizabeth his arm and they moved silently down the church walk and across the road. As they reached the Wyatt gates, Mrs. Daulton said something about reassuring the neighbors, and he saw her go on to intercept the men hurrying in their direction. Aurore opened the house door for them.

Rutledge deposited Elizabeth on a sofa in the parlor, getting his first real look at her. Her pale face was drawn with fear and shock, but her mind was working clearly. She said huskily as she made an awkward attempt to bind up her hair again, "I don't want to wake Simon, please don't bother him with this! It will only add to his distress."

Aurore's eyes met Rutledge's over Elizabeth's head. She said only, "No, we won't disturb Simon. It's best."

Rutledge, using the excuse of fetching water, went down the hall and began a swift, methodical search of the house.

The connecting door to the museum was still latched, and he walked next into the garden. But it was dark, given over to the sounds of the night.

Instinct told him—instinct honed by night marches and night attacks—that the gardens were empty. Even Hamish felt nothing there.

Wherever Simon was, it wasn't in the house or on the grounds.

Had he been walking again, had he been at the church? Had he seen the hat in Aurore's hands, there among the trees?

Or was Elizabeth trying to play her own games?

There was always the chance that Daniel Shaw had attacked her, wanting answers he hadn't gotten at the Wyatt door earlier. At least, Rutledge told himself, this couldn't be laid at Aurore's door; she'd been with him.

But something about the first glimpse he'd had of Elizabeth in the light of Mrs. Daulton's lamp had set off alarm bells. In one odd, inexplicable, fleeting instant she had reminded him of Betty Cooper lying in her tidy grave. And yet it was something people had said, he thought, not what he'd seen. He could hear the echo of it, but not the words. Not yet . . .

He turned and went back into the house, filling a glass with water and carrying it to the parlor. Simon Wyatt's grandfather was staring down at them from his frame above the hearth, as if the difficult silence between the two women met with his disapproval.

Elizabeth had succeeded in putting up her hair and was lying with her head against the back of the sofa, her eyes closed. Aurore, sitting stiffly in a chair, her face still, looked up as he came in. He shook his head but made no other explanation for the time it had taken to fill one glass with water. He thought she must have guessed that Simon was nowhere to be found.

He gave the glass to Elizabeth, who drank it slowly with her eyes closed. The red, bruised marks on her throat were very clear now. They looked very real as well. Studying them, he couldn't see how she could have made them herself.

She said, returning the glass to him, "Thank you." She coughed and swallowed again, as if her throat were painful. "I have never been so terrified! I thought—for an instant I thought I was going to die!"

"It was a man?" Rutledge asked.

"Oh, yes. He was tall, strong. It was horrible!" The distaste in her face was real as well. "I thought I was going to die!" she said again, unable to stop herself from thinking it. "It was Shaw, it must have been! The man is mad, he ought to be put in jail. I won't go back to the Wyatt Arms tonight, I won't!"

"I'll look for him," Rutledge said. And added to Aurore, "Please lock the door when I leave. You'll be safe enough."

"You'll come back?" she asked.

"Yes." He knew why she was asking. Come back to arrest her.

"That's all I need to know." She went with him to the door, and as he stepped out onto the walk, she said, "Please—Simon—"

"Aurore. I must find the hat. That's why I'm going."

She seemed startled, remembered it, and said, "Yes, of course!" as she shut the door firmly.

The townspeople had gone back to their beds, reassured by Mrs. Daulton. He could see her lantern bobbing up to the rectory again. It occurred to him that she was a very courageous woman. But then she was no longer young or pretty. As Margaret Tarlton and Betty Cooper were said to have been. As Elizabeth Napier was. Perhaps that was why she had felt safe. Or perhaps it was in her nature to take risks for the sake of others. Some women did. He had seen them nursing the worst influenza cases, working with septic wounds, braving weather that would have given a strong man pause.

As he walked toward the church, his mind was busy. What was it Mrs. Prescott had said about Margaret Tarlton, and Truit had told him about Betty Cooper? "She had such lovely hair." Mrs. Prescott's voice came back to him, admiring, envious. And Truit had said "—sleek as a cat sunning itself in a window," or words to that effect.

They weren't merely pretty women. They were both quite sure of their attractions . . . not flaunting them, just *sure* of them. . . . Tantalizing. Tempting.

But that still left Shaw out of the equation. He'd been in love with Margaret. At least he'd claimed he was.

If it had started with Betty Cooper—and Rutledge was now almost certain it had—then love had a great deal to do with the murders. But there wasn't time to go into that now.

With Hamish alive in his mind, Rutledge was already scanning the shadows, looking for Wyatt, looking for Shaw. The hat was nowhere to be found, although he searched carefully. The small case that Aurore had left leaning against the trunk of a tree was still there. He walked up to the church, on guard, wary.

But there was nothing there. The stand of trees, the graveyard beyond, the shadows by the heavy walls, were empty of life. He went around the church itself twice, moving cautiously, slowly, taking care to be sure. Then he tried the door on the porch.

It opened under his hand, swinging with a deep groan across the stone paving. In an island of darkness, there were candles ahead, burning on the stone altar, casting strange, flickering shadows across the aisles, the Norman pillars, the high arched roof. There was a golden warmth to the light, and the man sitting in one of the chairs in the nave turned to look at him, his own face golden in its reflection.

It was Henry Daulton. "I've looked everywhere. There's no sign of anyone. I stepped in here instead of going back to the house. It's quiet here. I thought Simon might come back. I don't like to hear a woman scream, it tears at my nerves."

"Yes. It's very quiet," Rutledge answered, his voice echoing and his footsteps rebounding from the stone paving as he walked down the aisle toward Henry. "Did you see what happened?"

"I was out looking for Simon Wyatt. He was walking again, Shaw told me. He'd seen him and then lost him. A few minutes later Elizabeth asked me to help her find him. She was worried about him. I told her it was all right, that he'd come home on his own, but she insisted."

"You knew he walked?"

"I don't sleep well sometimes. Once or twice I've seen him go out on the lawn and stand like a statue for a quarter of an hour or more. Another time I met him coming down the shortcut from the farm—it ends over by the churchyard. My mother's concerned about him, she says he's on the edge of collapse. But he isn't. He's worried about money and Aurore and the museum. He doesn't see how it's going to work out, and that's what makes him black out. To stop thinking."

Which was an oddly penetrating observation.

"About tonight—" Rutledge reminded him.

"He was in the church earlier. Standing there in front of the altar, lighting candles. Praying, I thought at first. Then he took one of them and started in the direction of the crypt. I don't think he was walking then."

"What would interest him in the crypt?" He remembered something Henry had confided to him when he first came to Charlbury. "There are hiding places in the church, aren't there? Does Simon know about them?"

"I don't know. He probably does. I didn't stay very long. But later he came out with a suitcase. I'd seen it before, someone had left it under that stone altar down in the crypt. The old altar, from the Saxon church. Nobody ever uses it, but there's an altar cloth on it. My mother ironed it every week when my father was alive and kept fresh flowers on it. My father always said it was useless work, but she took pride in it. It's keeping to tradition, she'd say. I'd hide under its skirts whenever I didn't want to be found. I think I told Simon about that, but I can't be sure. I don't always remember things now."

"Henry. He knew the suitcase was there—or looked and found it there?"

"Well, he came out carrying it. And don't ask me where he went with it, I can't tell you because I don't know. But I don't think he wanted to be seen. And almost in the next instant Elizabeth Napier was coming up the church walk again. And you were there under the trees talking quietly to Mrs. Wyatt. I thought it best to go home then."

If Simon had collected the suitcase, where would he have taken it?

Rutledge thought he knew. The farm— And the police were going to search there in the morning. Damning evidence against Aurore, if it was found there!

He said to Henry, "I've got work to do still. Will you be at the

259

rectory or here?" He hadn't finished with Henry, but there wasn't time to ask him any more now. It could wait. Simon couldn't.

"Here, probably. When I can't sleep, I come here to think. My father had always hoped I'd be rector, just as Simon's father had expected him to stand for Parliament. But the war put paid to such hopes, didn't it? I suppose that's why I can't sleep. Guilt that I'm not the man I might have been."

It was a poignant remark, but Henry seemed to accept his circumstances stoically, whether his mother did or not. As if he knew, and shielded her as best he could from the truth. Her insistence that he was making steady, observable improvement must have hurt him many times. The scar was very deep. It had healed. But not the brain behind it.

Rutledge nodded and left, his footsteps echoing again in the stillness. From the nave, Henry called, "If Simon is wandering, don't startle him. Let him finish whatever it is he wants to do first. Will you be careful about that?"

"Yes. I'll remember." But he didn't believe Simon was anything but very much himself, well aware of what he was doing.

He went out to his car, started the motor, and drove with haste to the farm. It was dark, dark as the night. He left the car by the gate and walked swiftly up the murky blackness that was the rutted lane, swearing as he missed his footing several times in the deeper patches. A man could break an ankle here with ease, he thought. And who would know? Jimson wouldn't hear any calls for help!

When he reached the house, he walked carefully around it, staying in the shadows as much as possible. But he couldn't see any lights, he couldn't pick out any sign of Simon Wyatt's presence. Inside the house or out. Hamish was alert in his mind, wary, watchful.

Rutledge moved on, into the barn, and saw at once that the horses had been taken out. Even the barn cat wasn't anywhere to be seen. He strode swiftly, silently, down the empty, dusty passage to the back doors and discovered that the cows, usually penned for the night behind the barn, had been loosed in the fields. He could just see them, ghostly white patches against the darkness of the pasture. As he came back, he realized that the door of the chicken coop stood open and that the chickens had scattered, roosting on the tops of overturned wagons or the roofs of sheds.

He had nearly reached the front of the barn, his mind occupied with myriad possibilities—Hamish was already warning him about the most likely of them.

And then, among the loose piles of hay in the loft, a yellow ball of fire, bright as the sun, began to blossom into roaring life with frightening intensity.

Simon had set the barn alight!

Rutledge ran, his steps muffled by the packed earth, echoed by the paving stones, his eyes sweeping the stalls, the tack room, the loft. Searching every corner, even as time ran out. He began to cough from the heavy, swirling smoke, and then he felt the heat on his back as the flames took hold behind him. He found himself stumbling for the nearest door, and then turned around as something caught his eye at the foot of one of the great oak beams that supported the loft and the roof. It was in the shadow of the beam, nearly invisible, black against black, but the fire was dancing on the silver catches that locked the suitcase. It had been left where the fire would burn the hottest, around that beam, consuming it fully— melting even the metal in the end.

Whatever Hildebrand might suspect tomorrow, there would be no *proof*. And suspicion would still fall heavily on Aurore. Had Simon intended to save his wife—or damn her?

Although Hamish was calling to him to leave it, Rutledge dashed back into the smoke, palling and black, and reached down to grip the handle, his other arm raised to shield his eyes. Was the hat here too? He groped for it, along the floor, and in an instant lost his bearing. He was blinded, disoriented, unable to tell in the thickening air which way he had come from. There was a curtain closing in on him, choking and smothering, cutting him off. Suffocating him in a claustrophobic cloak, sucking at his will. Hamish was a roar in his mind, louder than the roar of the fire, hammering at him to *go!*

"Simon?" Rutledge shouted, realizing all at once that a fire could destroy a man as well as a barn and a suitcase, and felt the rawness in his throat. *"Simon!"*

But there was no answer and time was down to seconds before he himself was trapped. He could hear Hamish screaming at him now. Sparks were setting every wisp of straw to burning. He ran again, this time blindly, his face seared by flames as he passed within their sphere. And then he was through them, blundering first into a wall, feeling the draft of air that was feeding the blaze, and stumbling finally out the door. Still coughing hard, he ran on, to pound heavily on the back door of the farmhouse. Once the blaze was at its height, there would be no saving the house either.

He came through the door shouting for Jimson, checking the dark, empty ground-floor rooms already reflecting the dawnlike brightness from the barn, and ran up the stairs, searching there as well. The old glass of the windows on the back of the house mirrored the flames against the wall in shimmering images, lighting his way. In the front it was stygian darkness still, and he quartered each room carefully, making absolutely sure. But Jimson was not here. Nor was Simon. Wherever they were, they weren't in danger of burning to death.

He came out into the night again, his lungs burning from the smoke. It was rolling now, billows of it, as it fed on old wood, dust, and hay. The grass by one of the sheds was already flickering with fiery dewdrops. He searched the sheds and found them empty, bales of hay waiting in them for the match to come.

The air was thick, heavy. He could hear horses in the distance, neighing shrilly in alarm. Hamish was telling him to go, to hurry.

The sound of the flames was greedy now, soaring into the night on a pillar of black smoke and sparks.

Rutledge hesitated, yet he knew he could do nothing for the barn. There was nothing one man—or an army of men—might do as the flames fed hungrily on the hay and then jumped to the dry, old wood of stalls and pillars and walls. He stood staring at it in despair, knowing what its destruction would mean to Aurore.

Finally retrieving the suitcase from the porch where he'd left it, he turned and hurried back down the drive to his car.

Wherever Simon was, he had to find him. He had the strongest feeling that it was already too late. But he had to try. To live with himself, he had to try.

But there was no sign of Wyatt on the road, and Rutledge thought as he coughed raggedly, I couldn't have missed him coming here—the fire wasn't that far along when I arrived. He must have taken a shortcut from here to Charlbury—he must have come out somewhere near the church where no one would see him. He's ahead of me!

Driving very fast now, his headlamps probing the darkness, he made the trip to Charlbury in a matter of minutes.

The Wyatt house was alight, not with fire but with lamps. He braked hard, skidding to a halt, and was out of the car almost as soon as the engine stopped.

Aurore was in the front garden, her face wild with fear.

"Simon isn't in the house," she said. "I can't find him, I've looked everywhere. Oh, God—can you see those flames? We must do something—Jimson—"

"Jimson's safe. Simon was at the farm—he set the barn to burn, Aurore. It will be gone in a short time. But he wasn't there, nor was Jimson. And the cattle, the horses are safe. There's nothing that can be done."

But the fire bell by the common was ringing loudly, and men, stuffing nightshirts into trousers, were gathering by the inn and piling into carts, wagons, whatever they could find, throwing buckets among the packed bodies. Rutledge caught sight of Jimson among them, yelling fiercely.

"He burned—but *why!*" Aurore ignored the chaos, her mind only on Simon.

Rutledge said, "The suitcase. He wanted to destroy it and anything else that might have been left there, any evidence that could still be found. It was the only thing he could think of doing before Hildebrand came tomorrow. Aurore, you must tell me now, where did you find that straw hat?"

"The suitcase—Margaret's?" She was very still. "I don't understand."

"It was hidden in the church, Aurore. Henry knew about the hiding place there, and Simon. Simon went to fetch it tonight. You hadn't destroyed it, had you? If you lied about that, you lied about the hat—"

Elizabeth Napier had come to the door. "I heard voices—is that you, Simon?" She peered out into the garden, seeing only the tall man beside Aurore.

"No, it's Rutledge."

"I smell smoke!" she exclaimed as she stepped out the door. Her voice was still rough. She turned in the direction that men and wagons were moving up the road and saw the distant flames leaping into the night sky. *"My God!"*

"It's the farm, there's nothing we can do. I don't know where Simon is. Elizabeth, did he know of hiding places in the church? Behind the old altar, for one, under the altar cloth? The one that Henry used as a boy? Who else did?"

"We were never allowed to play there—I've never heard of a hiding place. Has Simon already gone to try to save the farm buildings? We ought to be there, helping him! Be quick, Aurore, we need the car!" She started down the walk.

"There's a suitcase in the back of my car. Will you look at it and tell me if you recognize it?" The hurrying men had disappeared, but there were clots of women near the Wyatt Arms, some staring toward the fire, some of them packing another wagon with picks, shovels, buckets, a barrel of ale.

Aurore began to move, but he gripped her arm, holding it firmly.

Elizabeth said, "I'm not *interested* in suitcases! Why isn't Benson here when I need him? Will you take me, Aurore, or not—"

"Please do as I ask." There was an inflection in his voice that stopped the flow of words as if they'd been cut off. She stared at him, surprised by his intensity.

Then she moved through the gate and turned to look at Rutledge again with an expression that was hard to read—anger he thought, because her primary concern was still Simon. *But it was his as well.* She went on to the car.

After a moment she called in surprise, "I know that case! That's Margaret's! Where on earth did you find it? I thought the killer had taken it?"

"You're absolutely sure of that? It belonged to her?"

"Of course I am! My father gave her this case for her birthday two years ago. It's part of a set." She turned and said, with sudden understanding, "It means you know who killed her, doesn't it?"

"I think, Miss Napier, that you'd better go back into the house and telephone Inspector Hildebrand in Singleton Magna. Tell him, please, that he's wanted here. That there's an emergency. Meanwhile, Aurore, you must help me find Simon!"

Elizabeth stepped away from the car and looked at him with fierce passion. "What's happened? Why won't you tell me! Aurore, *make him tell me!"*

Aurore opened her mouth to say something just as the silence was shattered by the sound of a gunshot coming from the direction of the museum.

"Oh, God—" She was already running, fleet as a wraith, her skirts lifted, her body tense with fear and terror.

Elizabeth screamed, one long heart-tearing sound, a name, and was after her in a flash of skirts and flying heels.

But Rutledge, swifter, was there ahead of them, at the door of the museum, opening it, rushing into the empty room, and then the next and the next, until he'd reached the small office that Simon had used.

At the door he came to such an abrupt halt that Aurore cannoned into him, and Elizabeth was a poor third, pressing at their backs, calling Simon's name.

"Don't come any closer!" he said, putting out an arm to stop Aurore.

"No, I must go to him, I've had training, I can—oh, God, let me go!"

Elizabeth, pushing her way past both of them, reached the threshold, and for an instant Rutledge thought she was about to faint. She swayed on her feet, grasped the door's edge, and began to whimper with soft, short breaths.

Aurore broke away and went into the room.

Rutledge knew what it held. He had seen. In that one brief, anguished glance, he had seen it all in the lamplight. Simon Wyatt, seated at the desk, a sheet of paper on the top in front of him, a pen beside it, and his blood blown across it by the impact of the bullet to his temple. The pistol on the floor beside his chair was German, a war souvenir.

The Germans, Rutledge thought helplessly, had got him after all.

And Hamish, aware of the grief and the pain and the horror of what had happened, said, "Look well. See yoursel'. If it's no' the Germans waiting, it will be me."

Rutledge stood there for an instant, frozen, seeing in his mind's eye his own shattered face lying on one arm outflung across the bare wood.

27

$\mathcal{R}$utledge made himself walk into the room and look at the sheet of paper under Simon's arm, although he had guessed what was written on it. It was addressed to Hildebrand. It said only, "You were wrong. I blacked out and killed them both. She didn't know. It is better this way." And the signature read, with a flourish, *Simon Wyatt*.

Rutledge softly swore, the waste of a man's life shocking him.

Aurore was kneeling beside her husband, her arm across his shoulder, saying "He's still warm, there must be a pulse, if I can stop the bleeding—"

Elizabeth was clinging to the door frame, sobbing heavily, her eyes unable to look away.

Rutledge bent to Aurore, touched her shining hair briefly, gently, then forced her to let Simon go, lifting her to her feet, turning her to face him. "He's dead, Aurore. He's dead, there's nothing you can do."

She buried her face against him then, and he thought she was going to cry, like Elizabeth. But she was only searching for strength, her body at the point of breaking, her mind already broken.

She said, "I was so afraid. I was so afraid that one day— And now I'll never need to be afraid again."

She let him lead her out of the room but seemed unaware of the chair he seated her on or the handkerchief he thrust into her hands.

Elizabeth refused to go, clinging to the door, her eyes unable to leave the crumpled shoulders, the untidy fair hair, the great black stain of blood.

Rutledge finally got her to move back into the museum, and that was when she straightened, seeming to tower in her anger, and loosed the storm of it at Aurore.

"It's your fault, you *killed him*! You took him away from all he knew and all he wanted, and made him into what *you* believed he ought to be, and in the end, it killed him. He needn't have died but for you and your damned, selfish *blindness*! I hope you're satisfied, I hope his spirit haunts you every day of life and breath left to you and that you never, never, know what happiness is, ever again!"

Rutledge went to her and shook her hard, until she broke into tears again and sank in the chair he quickly shoved toward her. Burying her head in her hands, she began to moan Simon's name, over and over, like a litany.

Aurore, white and strained, still hadn't cried. She looked up at Rutledge, her eyes filled with ineffable pain, and said only, "He didn't do it."

"You thought he had. He thought you had. He killed himself because he couldn't face losing you, he couldn't face the scandal, he couldn't face another change in his life. He was trying to protect you."

"Hildebrand came to him today—"

"I don't know how Simon knew of the suitcase. Whether he put it there—or found it there. If it's any comfort to you—"

He broke off as the door opened and Joanna Daulton came through the outer rooms toward them. Her hair still pinned up, the white streak like a blazon, but she was wearing a robe over her nightdress. She looked from Aurore to Elizabeth, saying something about the fire, and then seemed to shrink into herself as she took in what their faces told her as they lifted to hers. "Simon?" she asked Rutledge. "Gentle God! Where!"

He nodded toward the back room, then said, "Don't go."

She walked past him without a word and into the small office, staying only for a moment. He thought he heard her saying words of prayer from the service for the dead. Then she turned, her face chalk white, and said, "What can I do?"

"Will you call Hildebrand for me? Ask him to come directly. And then if you would, you might find some help for Miss Napier and Mrs. Wyatt. I think both have been through enough for one night. They need tea, warmth—comfort."

"I'll see to it," she said, but some of her usual efficient crispness was gone. "I loved him," she added simply, "I watched him grow from childhood. I thought, if I had another son, that's what I'd want him to be. Someone like Simon." She shook her head, as if to clear it. "I hope he's at rest—I hope he's at peace!" Her voice broke, and she went out the door, leaving him with the two women while she made the necessary arrangements.

Aurore said, "This has changed nothing in our bargain. I will not have this put at Simon's door. Do you hear me?" It was as if she hadn't taken in what he'd been saying earlier.

"Aurore—"

"No. He will not be remembered as a murderer. If there is a paper saying so in that room, please, for the love of God, destroy it. Don't let it destroy him!"

"I can't destroy evidence!"

"Then I will."

She got to her feet and was nearly to the door of the smaller room before he caught her, his hands on her arms.

"Aurore. Listen to me. It isn't over yet. Give me time! If you destroy that letter, you will probably hang. And he died to prevent that. Can you understand me?"

"He died because he couldn't endure any more pressure from anyone."

He made a swift and measured decision. "Come with me. Back to the house. I must lock this wing until Hildebrand arrives." He took Elizabeth's arm, supporting her, while Aurore—Aurore the widow—walked unaided by his side, one foot placed precisely in front of the other, as if she were half alive. It was always the Elizabeths of this world, he thought in a distant corner of his mind, around whom people gathered in a crisis, offering sympathy and comfort and human warmth. They seemed so vulnerable and helpless. And yet the Elizabeths were often tougher than all the rest, more deeply centered on how the crisis deprived them than moved by unbearable grief. How did you comfort Aurore, when you knew that even touching her was anathema? That beneath the incredible strength lay stark despair.

He locked the museum door with the key he found there and escorted both women across the front gardens. The side of his face was beginning to hurt, where the flames had seared it.

By the time they reached the house, Elizabeth was near to collapse. That spoke volumes to Rutledge—he understood clearly what she had done—and how it would affect the remainder of her life. And so did she. Simon's death lay at her door as much as at Hildebrand's. If she hadn't meddled—if she hadn't tried to bring him back to her somehow—anyhow—again and again . . .

When Elizabeth had been settled on the sofa in the quiet parlor, a pillow under her head and the light shielded with a shawl, he turned toward the door.

Aurore said, "Where are you going? I want to know. I want to go with you."

"I'm not going to London. Only as far as the church. I want to see this hiding place. Aurore, tell me the truth. You found the hat, didn't you? Where?"

She shook her head, stubbornly adhering to the story she'd given him.

And she stubbornly followed Rutledge to the church, as if afraid he'd leave her, breaking their bargain. Or afraid that left alone, she couldn't hide from grief any longer?

Inside, the candles still burned and the odor of incense was very strong. It took him some time to find the stairs to the crypt, hidden in a corner of a side aisle. As Simon had done before, he took a candle to light his way down the narrow, crumbling steps and into the cool stone chamber that had once been a small church, its heavy pillars squat, its arches broad and ugly rather than graceful. Sturdy, strong enough to support the building that had been put up over it, windowless and bare, almost spiritually bleak, the crypt now served to house the dead. Wyatts for the most part, but there were others as well, he could see eight or ten tombs spaced unevenly around two walls, leaving the center of the stone-paved floor empty.

Along the other walls were stored a broken pew, bits of stone from rebuilding, boxes of hymnals, shovels and picks for digging graves, containers for flowers, lengths of canvas, buckets—all the oddments of death and burial. You could see, he thought, that nothing could be hidden among or behind them.

Neither he nor Aurore had spoken.

At one end of the crypt was a stone altar with no grace. A monolithic slab with a vine pattern running around it set upon three square, heavy stones. An altar cloth, thin from damp and age, draped the stones, covering them to the floor. In the center of the top was a squat stone cross, powerful in its roughness. A bronze vase, empty, stood to one side, as if waiting for flowers. And under the altar cloth, as it hung like a tent, was a narrow three-sided rectangle, the back open.

He went there and knelt on one knee to look more closely at it. It yawned, empty.

The dark space was large enough for a suitcase like Margaret Tarlton's, or for a small boy gleefully escaping from adult supervision. But who had put the suitcase in there?

He thought he had part of the answer now. He felt heavy with sadness.

Aurore was just behind him, staying close in the pale light of her own candle, her breath uneven, as if the place disturbed her. He thought she might be sorry she had come now. But she stooped to look at the small space too and then gasped as another voice spoke. It seemed to rise from the ground under their feet, although that was a trick of the echo.

It was Henry, on the stairs, saying, "My mother told me about Simon. I'm sorry. She's very upset, she feels responsible." He didn't have a candle.

Yes, she would, Rutledge thought. The final tragedy in her life.

Rutledge straightened up and came across the uneven floor toward Henry. "Was this your hiding place? Was this the place from which Simon Wyatt took the suitcase tonight?"

Henry said, "I'd rather not tell you. Let the dead lie in peace."

"It will help Simon. He isn't guilty; neither is Aurore."

Henry frowned, a move that emphasized the deep scar. "But it will harm someone else, won't it? It will hurt me."

"That very much depends on why it was put here, as well as by whom."

Henry came down the last of the steps and moved across the crypt, the candle flames dancing with his passage. "It would have been safer over here," he said, coming to a stop in front of one of the tombs there. "The suitcase."

The low rectangular stone vault was small, plain. The top was engraved with a name, date, and a few lines of scripture. But no figures at the sides supported it, and no designs ran like filigree either across the top or down the corners. It seemed to squat on the floor, out of place among its more ornate brethren, as if unfinished.

"The end stone here isn't sealed. The tomb's actually empty, did you know? It belonged to the wife of another Simon Wyatt, some three hundred years ago. The next wife didn't want her to lie here in Charlbury and had the body sent to Essex. It's one of the family skeletons, in a manner of speaking."

He stooped by the tomb and pushed one side of the stone that marked the foot. It scraped across the floor but moved with fair ease. "You wouldn't have needed much of a space, to slip a suitcase in there. But most people can't tell it's free. I knew. Even my father didn't."

Rutledge said quietly, "You couldn't have moved that as boys. It was too heavy. Would it be too heavy for a woman?" He was thinking of Aurore.

"Probably not. If she knew about it. The old sexton showed it to me when I was six or seven. He had a ghoulish nature; he said I'd wind up here if I misbehaved in church. Rather a cruel thing to tell a child, wasn't it?"

"Yes. It was." To one side of Rutledge Aurore stood with that stillness of hers that he so admired.

Henry frowned, thinking. "I must have told Simon about these hiding places. That's how he could find the suitcase, when he came looking tonight. I asked him what he was searching for, and he said it was a suitcase no one else wanted. He said Aurore had put it here, but she hadn't."

Aurore, turning to Rutledge, opened her mouth to speak and stopped.

"No, I don't believe she had put it here either." Rutledge said, his voice attuned to Henry's mood. "Who did? Do you know?"

Henry shook his head. "It was in the attic for a time."

"Whose attic? Simon's?"

"No, of course not. It came from my mother's."

"How did she come to have it? It didn't belong to her. Did you give it to her?"

"She brought it home one day. I asked her where it came from, and she said it was better if I didn't worry about it. There was another one too, but she put that one on a train from Kingston Lacey to Norfolk. I expect she wanted to put this one on a train too but hadn't had time."

Where do you hide a suitcase? Where there are other suitcases. . . .

Aurore was staring at Henry. She said, "How did Simon know that the suitcase was here?"

"I don't believe he did. He'd searched the farmhouse. And the barn. After the inspector here had gone this afternoon. Then he came here, to search the church. I don't think he was very pleased to find it."

"No," Rutledge said. "I shouldn't have thought he was at all pleased. It proved something he didn't want to believe. I think—Henry, it's time we found your mother."

"Why?"

"Mrs. Wyatt needs her."

Henry said, "I like Mrs. Wyatt. She doesn't know it, but I've watched her often. I like pretty hair. Hers is very pretty."

Rutledge, standing very still, said softly, "Auore, will you trust me? Let your hair down. Slowly. Give me the candle."

After an instant's hesitation, she handed it to him and slowly began to unpin her hair, collecting the pins in her teeth. The knot at the back of her neck loosened and unwound. As she took the pins in her left hand her hair spilled in long gleaming waves, falling over her shoulders nearly to her waist. She looked at Rutledge, frowning but unafraid. Her hair was not pretty—it was beautiful.

Henry, mesmerized, sucked in his breath and walked toward her, his eyes shining in the light. His hand moved, reaching, then drew back. "You won't scream if I touch it?" he said to Aurore. And to

Rutledge he said, "I like to touch it. But it always makes them scream, and I hate that part."

"No," Rutledge said firmly, "you can't touch it tonight." Henry stopped where he was, uncertain. Rutledge passed one of his candles to Aurore, her face white and stark now, and stepped into Henry's path. "Mrs. Wyatt, would you mind fetching Mrs. Daulton for me? You should find her at your house, with Elizabeth. Ask her to come here, but don't come back with her, do you understand?"

"Ian—" she began, moving toward the stairs.

"There's no need, I'm here," Joanna Daulton said, coming down the crypt steps. Dressed now, composed, she stood there, blocking the only exit from the low-ceilinged, cold stone undercroft of the old church, another candle in her hand, and Rutledge felt himself succumbing to the numbing fear of being shut in, cut off from the outside air. Hamish was urgently telling him to pay heed—

In Mrs. Daulton's left hand, half hidden by her skirts and the shadows, was the straw hat that had belonged to Margaret Tarlton.

Aurore was moving closer to Rutledge, one hand fumbling at her hair, gathering it together. But Joanna Daulton said, "You needn't be afraid, my dear. Henry never hurts anyone. He just has a fascination about seeing a woman's hair flowing down her back. I don't think he even understands why this compulsion is there. The physical implications. Nor does he understand that respectable women don't care for such attentions. He only wants to touch, and to him that's not—wrong. Like a child wanting to touch something very pretty, he sometimes can't stop himself." The last words seemed to be wrenched from her.

"He tries to choke them when they scream," Rutledge said.

"Yes, it frightens him, he tries to shut them up. If they stood still, he'd stop at once. But that's as far as it ever goes. He never does any harm."

"He tried, tonight, to choke Elizabeth Napier."

"Yes." She turned tiredly toward Aurore. "I wouldn't have had Simon die for anything in the world," she said, her voice heavy with sorrow. "I mean that, Aurore. I never intended for any such thing to happen."

"I shall have to take Henry in for questioning," Rutledge said. "Will he understand what I'm doing and why?"

"Of course he will," Joanna said sharply. "He's not a fool. But it won't be necessary. He didn't kill those women. I did."

He looked at her, infinite pity in his eyes. To protect her son . . .

"How many have there been?"

"It started in London. I'd taken rooms near the hospital while Henry was there recovering, and they'd let him out of hospital, in my care, with a nurse to come three days a week. He tried once to unpin her hair, and she screamed, and he choked her. She was very angry, she threatened to tell the doctors, to have Henry put away. I gave her a great deal of money and bought her passage on a ship leaving for New Zealand. And that was that. Afterward, I watched him very carefully. But when Betty came to the house, to tell me that Simon was giving her an introduction to the Napiers, Henry was alone with her in the parlor. I was finishing the washing up. I didn't know, I thought he was out. I didn't know until I heard her scream. I offered her what money I had and told her she'd be better off going to London with a small fortune in her pocket than settling for being a maid to the Napiers. And she went. But the money didn't last. She came back, demanding more."

Joanna Daulton shuddered. "I couldn't give her any more. I didn't have any more to give. But she was a greedy little bitch, she threatened to have Henry put away, and in the end I had no choice but to kill her. It was horrible. I hated myself, I hated her, I hated having to connive and lie and live with such a thing on my conscience. I told myself, in future I shall never let him out of my sight again, I'll watch even more closely. It won't happen again, I could see he was showing great improvement—"

"But he wasn't, was he?" Rutledge asked gently. "He has never fully recovered. He never will."

"No." The word seemed stark and anguished, matching her eyes. "And I shan't be there to care for him. He will have to go back to hospital now whether I want him to or not."

"The next woman he was alone with was Margaret Tarlton, looking for someone to drive her to the train."

She sighed. "I hate to say this about the dead, but Margaret Tarl-

275

ton was worse than Betty. I knew, from something Richard Wyatt told me once, when he and Margaret had a stormy affair in 1913, that she had a way of getting whatever she wanted. I think she'd have married Richard, if he'd had enough money to satisfy her. And now she had the power of the Napiers behind her. She was hard, and very angry, very unforgiving. I didn't have any money to offer her. She said she didn't care what happened to Henry. She said it was what he deserved." Joanna Daulton turned to Aurore. "I told her, You aren't a mother, or you'd understand. But she said it doesn't matter, he belongs behind bars, he isn't stable. We argued again outside Singleton Magna. I was driving your car, Aurore, there wasn't enough petrol in mine. I'd walked over to the farm and borrowed it, and all the way to the train Margaret Tarlton was insisting on going to the authorities in Singleton Magna. I couldn't persuade, I couldn't bribe—she made me stop the car and put her out. That's when, God help me, I took that stone you keep in the back of your car and I killed her! And that poor man Mowbray took the blame, because to save him, I'd have had to destroy my own *son*!" Her voice twisted in anguish.

Aurore said, "Don't—for God's sake, don't!"

Mrs. Daulton said, "I'm glad it's over. I thought when I heard Elizabeth scream tonight, it will go on and on and on, until one day I can't bear it anymore. But I love him, you see. I really wanted him to be whole again. I told myself that Simon was recovering—Henry could recover too. I told myself a hundred lies. I told myself that I could make Henry well myself, if I had time enough and peace enough. It was all so terrible. But I couldn't harm *Elizabeth*. I've known her almost all her life. It was hard enough with people I barely knew. With Elizabeth—" She shook her head. "I couldn't kill her, Aurore. I couldn't do it. But I killed Simon, didn't I? Inadvertently. I'd have liked to kill myself, but I haven't that kind of courage. I suppose women generally don't." She smiled across the room at her son. "Henry, darling, I don't think you've understood a word of what I've been saying, and just as well. Come along, let me put you to bed. And then I must go with the inspector for a while. It will be all right, you'll see. You liked hospital, didn't you . . . ?"

Her voice trailed off as she held out her hand, dropping Margaret Tarlton's hat on the steps. Henry came to take her cold fingers in his, and Rutledge watched, letting it happen. Henry looked across at Rutledge, and there was a strained smile on his face. He understood far more than his mother wanted to believe.

Mrs. Daulton turned and led her son up the steps. Aurore said quickly to Rutledge, "I don't think she should go alone!"

"It's all right. She won't harm him. She won't harm herself. I'll take you home and then go to the rectory. By the time Henry is settled, Hildebrand will be here."

"You believed her?" She followed him across the crypt, her candle flame shaking because her hand was shaking badly.

"Yes. I've been half certain, since that damned hat went missing tonight." They had all made a connection between Henry and the dead women, and dismissed it. Shaw had more anger in him than Henry had ever shown. But Shaw had had no reason to kill Betty Cooper . . . while Simon or Aurore might have. Or Elizabeth Napier—

At the stairs, as he bent to retrieve the hat, Rutledge said, "I saw Henry once with a small bird in his hands. It was oddly childlike. He may have tried to stop these women from screaming and frightened them badly. Himself as well. But he wouldn't have beaten them, on and on until they were dead. As his mother had had to do, to silence them. He's not mad. It's just that much of his mind is gone. Whatever abilities and skills he once had, he's lost them."

He took her arm to help her up the steep, crumbling steps. Her scent was strong in the cool air, a sign of her distress. He said, "Will you tell me now where you found this hat?"

"I took the shortcut to the farm the day after Margaret left. It was in the bushes there; Joanna must have dropped it. But I thought Simon had. And someone had started the car while I was in the barn—I heard it leave and come back. I was sure Simon had taken Margaret to Singleton Magna." Her breath seemed to catch in her throat. "He was desperate for money. I thought—I had so little faith left in him! I had seen his father's letter. About the house in Chelsea. And he had insisted on hiring Margaret . . ."

There was no comfort he could offer.

She said as they reached the aisle and he blew out their candles, "If only Simon had waited for the morning!" There was infinite sorrow in her voice.

"I know," Rutledge said quietly, but the stone took his words and gave them a haunting echo. "He was a good man, Aurore. He just lost his way. A lot of us did, in the war. And we weren't all wearing visible wounds. That was the worst part of it. No one could look at us and say, 'See what the war has done. . . .' "

"I loved him so much," she said, tears coming at last. "I thought he didn't love me."

After a moment he said, "What will you do?"

She said, into the echo of his words, "I shall open the museum, if I can. And make it work. And after that, I shall go far away from here. We have all died, in a way—myself, and Simon, Henry and his mother, Mowbray, those poor women. I can't bear to think about it."

They had reached the door of the church. He handed her the key to the museum. She turned to him and said, "I shall go from here alone. Do you understand?"

"Yes."

"Whoever she is, this woman you have loved, she is not worth your grief, do you know that? Find a love of your own, and don't lose it as I did!"

And she was gone, hurrying down the path toward her house, where he could hear cars arriving and voices raised in alarm. In the bright sky behind him, the barn and the house still burned out of control, flames leaping high, garishly, into the night.

He felt very tired, and very much alone.

Hamish said, "You're a better policeman than you think you are."

"Am I? I'd have saved him if I could. . . ."

"Aye. But he'd no' have thanked you. He died for her; it gave his death a meaning. It was what he was after, and it was far better than dying a coward."

Rutledge walked out of the shadows of the trees. He could see Aurore standing in the doorway of the museum, unlocking it. He braced himself and called to Hildebrand, stopping that surge of people toward the house long enough for Aurore to remove the note from Simon's dead hand. There was no reason to cause pain where it wasn't needful.

She paused as the museum door swung open and looked blindly back toward the church. But Rutledge was already standing among the policemen from Singleton Magna, handing the hat to Hildebrand, swiftly and clearly telling the staring faces what had happened. As he finished, a number of them went on to the museum; the others, led by Hildebrand, went toward the rectory.

Shaw, by the gate, stood waiting until they'd gone. He looked at Rutledge and said, "Is it true? What you just told that lot? Or a pack of lies? About Mrs. Daulton?"

"It's true."

Shaw rubbed his face, drawn and exhausted. "I wanted someone I could kill. I wanted it to be Napier. Or Simon. Or even Henry. I can't touch that poor woman, even for Margaret's sake. Hanging will be a blessing for her!"

"It will be an end, but not a blessing."

Rutledge turned the crank, got into his car, and said, "Can I give you a lift as far as the inn?"

Shaw shook his head. "I need to walk awhile."

Rutledge drew away and in the night watched his two headlamps plow gaudy furrows down the dark road. He felt empty, drained. But Mowbray was still in his cell. The man deserved compassion, and help. Rutledge would see to it.

Hamish said, "You could na' let Mowbray hang for murder. He never touched a soul. She'll fare well enough. You must na' fret." It wasn't clear whether he was speaking of Aurore or Joanna Daulton.

Rutledge said, "No." But he knew he would remember Aurore's face and her stillness, and the French way she had of shrugging, whenever he thought of Jean. They were inextricably linked, because he and Simon were linked. He could still see the pistol beside the chair, he could smell the powder and the blood.

There but for the grace of God go I. . . .

But Hamish said into the roar of the engine and the sound of the wind whispering through the open car, "Not now. Not yet."